DUPLICITY

JAMES LALONDE AMATEUR SLEUTH MYSTERY
BOOK 2

A. D. HAY

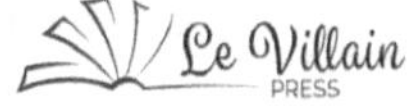

This is a work of fiction. Names, characters, places, and incidents either are the products of the author's imagination or are used fictitiously. Any resemblance to actual persons, living or dead, businesses, companies, events, or locales is entirely coincidental.

Duplicity. A James Lalonde Novel, Book 2
Copyright © A. D. Hay (2022). All rights reserved.

www.authoradhay.com

ISBN-13: 978-1-9163483-8-7 (paperback)

Book cover design by Le Villain Book Covers at levillainbookcovers.com

Le Villain
PRESS

FRENCH IN DUPLICITY

À bientôt: *adv.* See you soon

Entrée: *noun.* The small course that precedes the main course in a three-course meal.

Euh: The French equivalent of "um."

Maman: *noun.* Mother, mum, mom

Mamie: *noun.* Grandmother

Merde: *noun.* A mild, humorous substitute for "shit."

Oh, la vache: An expression of surprise similar to "damn" or "oh my god."

Oui: *adv.* Yes

Santé: *noun.* To your health—used as a toast, similar to cheers.

Vert: *adj.* Green

PROLOGUE
GLASTONBURY ABBEY, 1184 AD

THE LIGHT, intoxicating aroma of the oil lamp filled the scriptorium of Glastonbury Abbey. Illuminator Brother Guiscard dipped his brush into the round wooden bowl next to his easel. A spring evening chill blew through the room. Hunched over, he continued to paint the tiny dragon on the initiums in the *Commentary on Daniel* by Jerome of Stridon.

He paused, leaned back on his stool, tilted his head, and gazed at the leather-bound manuscript. His bright-green eyes floated across the immaculate handwritten black ink. It was a stunning piece of literature. Pity it would end up in a private collection. The midnight hours were the only time he could dedicate to the secret commission. Peter de Marcy, the newly appointed abbott, would never have approved such a project. Brother Guiscard crossed his fingers and hoped he wouldn't get caught.

He sighed.

Reaching across the book, he dipped the brush into the wooden vessel. After surveying the empty scriptorium, Brother Guiscard leaned forward and continued to paint the initium.

A *creak, putter, putter* broke the midnight silence. Hairs on the back of his neck stood on end. With his hand on his chest, Brother Guiscard rested the brush in the small wooden dish as he sensed another monk creep up behind him. He was caught red-handed. *Please don't be the abbott.* He turned his upper body. In the flicker of light created by the oil lamp was Brother Piers of Damerham. *Praise God.*

'Piers, you scared me.' Brother Guiscard rubbed his trembling hands along his brown tunic then stared at the manuscript.

Brother Piers shuffled up behind Guiscard. He leaned over, stared at the masterpiece on the easel, and chuckled. 'The abbot will not appreciate the symbolism in the initium.'

With a pinched expression, Guiscard sighed and turned to Brother Piers.

'The initium is appropriate to the context and the theme of the *Commentary.*'

'Guiscard, I'm not criticising you. I'm just preparing you for the inevitable argument coming your way.'

Brother Guiscard shook his head as he glanced at the manuscript. 'The *Commentary* is a commissioned piece. He doesn't have a say.'

Brother Piers raised his eyebrows. 'I know nothing.' The monk lifted his hands in the air as he gazed over Guiscard's shoulder at the initiums.

The two Benedictine monks stood and gazed at the manuscript.

'The initium is beautiful.' Brother Piers patted him on the shoulder, breaking the awkward silence.

At that instant, a whiff of acrid smoke wafted into the scriptorium. Brother Guiscard gasped as he whirled around on his stool. 'Do you smell that?'

Brother Piers ambled towards the dark-stained timber library door on the opposite side of the room. 'The stench is stronger here.'

After sprinting across the room, Brother Guiscard halted. Smoke streamed out from under the door.

Grabbing Brother Piers's arm, Guiscard pulled him to the centre of the scriptorium. 'You must wake the librarian. Only he has the keys.'

Brother Piers peered at Guiscard with a grim expression. 'I fear it's much too late to save the books. I will sound the warning bell. Save what you can.' Brother Piers scurried towards the entryway and disappeared into the abbey.

The smoke formed a light fog in the scriptorium. Paralysed with fear, Brother Guiscard surveyed the room. His entire life was about to go up in flames. Was the fire deliberate?

The smoky atmosphere thickened, jolting him into action. Guiscard coughed and grabbed the *Commentary on Daniel*, the only manuscript within reach. Then the flames tore through the library door.

———

THE HEAT BURNED his skin as the crackling, roaring blaze filled his ears. Brother Guiscard sprinted through the abbey's pews. He was moments away from freedom, but Guiscard couldn't find Brother Piers. He had disappeared five minutes ago and hadn't returned. *Maybe Piers had left.*

The blaze swept through the abbey, engulfing everything in its path. Brother Guiscard wept as he ran towards the exit, the flames nipping at his heels.

Clutching the manuscript, he sprinted out of the abbey doors, across the lawn, and towards the forest. Brother Guiscard shuddered at the terrified voices of his fellow monks trapped in the monastery. Everything within him wanted to run back into the abbey, but he couldn't save them. That moment would haunt his dreams forever.

He needed to get help from the nearby village. Brother Guiscard dragged his weary body through the woods. It was all up to him. He tore through the woodlands, and up ahead, a simple brown tunic and hood came into view—Piers.

ONE

WEDNESDAY: 10:01 A.M.

JAMES LALONDE UNZIPPED his navy-blue bomber jacket, revealing a pristine white T-shirt as he walked along the High Street in Oxford, smartphone in hand. Just ahead, two large bay windows with a familiar brown trimming came into view. As he reached the first bay window, he hesitated. For a split second, his reflection stared back at him. How he had aged since he'd last graced the establishment. He was only twenty-nine, and his first wrinkles were showing. "Laughter lines," his grandmother, Valerie, had told him. But he suspected she was telling a small white lie to spare his feelings. Or perhaps that was what she told herself when she looked in the mirror and saw lines on her face.

Leaning forward, he peered into the window. The Queen's Lane Coffee House was deserted. So that was the place where the man wanted to have brunch? James had read the email a dozen times that morning, and he was running late, a habit James had sworn to correct but at which he had failed spectacularly. That day was no exception. With two quick clicks, James stared at the email on his screen. He wasn't hallucinating—he was in the right place. James glanced up from his device and surveyed the tourist-laden streets, looking for the infamous black Bentley. The man always drove a Bentley, not that *he* drove. He was always driven.

A loud tap on the glass behind him caused James to jump. He whirled around. Hovering in the large bay window was a man with a head of thick dark-blond curls. Alexander Harper Thompson had closed the coffeehouse for their brunch. How embarrassing. The door of the Queen's Lane Coffee House opened, and James stepped inside.

Before him lay a sea of small, dark-stained round tables, each with two or three matching chairs. A familiar, comforting menu was etched with precision on chalkboards suspended above the bar and counters. To his left, an array of pastries, cakes, and sandwiches sat in the refrigerated display case. The place was a small slice of heaven, and it hadn't changed. Like magic, it transported him back in time to when things were less complicated and all he had to do was read and study. He was officially old.

Alexander gestured at a table for two in the centre of the room. 'I trust you read the report on your late mother's estate. Nothing much has changed. That's not a bad thing, considering the current economic climate.'

James sat. At a table against the back wall of the coffeehouse, a tall greying man dressed in black was sipping a cup of tea. The man was old, possibly in his seventies judging by the depth of the grey. He had an eerie atmosphere about him. There wasn't a particular quality that gave James this uncanny impression but an overall vibe. Upon first impression, the man seemed to go about his business, drinking tea and reading the paper. But after a few seconds, James sensed that he was being watched. And the man seemed familiar.

A couple of months ago, a black car with tinted windows had followed James around Northampton as he went about his mundane existence. The driver was old. *No, I'm being paranoid.* His estate manager had hired a bodyguard. That was all.

Alexander cleared his throat.

James returned his attention to Alexander. 'Yes, everything seems great, just as it has always been.' James nodded. 'I haven't examined her assets. They don't feel like mine. It feels disrespectful, almost.'

Alexander sighed. 'Your mother left these to you in her will so you could enjoy them, not tuck the financial records in a drawer.' He shook his head. 'Lucky you have me to tend to them.'

James chuckled. 'You're not a gardener.'

'Actually, I am, in a way.' Alexander pulled the napkin off the table and shook it into his lap. A man wearing a black T-shirt and a freshly pressed white apron tied around his waist walked up to the table. He placed a cappuccino and an espresso in front of them.

'The food will be out in a moment,' he said as he dashed to the kitchen door.

Alexander pointed at the coffee bar. 'I remember that after your graduation, where we first met, we went through your new assets in this same tiny coffeehouse. Almost seven years ago.'

'You get less time for manslaughter.'

'Still sarcastic.' Alexander sipped his cappuccino.

James grimaced as he picked up his espresso.

'Your mother took a disliking to my love of cappuccinos. When I used to meet up with her in Paris, she pressured me to drink espresso. It was the Parisian way, apparently.' Alexander's eyes glazed over. 'Emmanuelle thought a cappuccino was more of a dessert than a coffee.'

James smiled. 'The milk content, most likely.'

'Sorry. I didn't mean to put a dampener on our brunch,' Alexander said as the attendant burst out of the kitchen, slamming the door against the wall.

The pristine white apron tied around his waist had bright-red and light-brown smudges. He sprinted across the coffeehouse, holding a full English breakfast in one hand and a croissant in the other.

'I ordered your usual,' Alexander said, ignoring the staff member hovering around them.

'That's perfect.'

'You're so French.' Alexander shook his head. 'Have you ever tried a full English breakfast?'

James rolled his eyes. 'It's too much food first thing in the morning.'

———

TWENTY MINUTES LATER, the two men finished eating brunch. James sat opposite Alexander and peered over his shoulder at the mysterious greying man still reading the newspaper as before, tucked away in the corner of the café. Deciding not to ask about the man, James glanced at Alexander and wondered if he should ask him more questions about his mother—the same dilemma as always. But he knew that prying those secrets out of Alexander's vault would be fruitless. He had to wait for anecdotes to slip out.

'Something on your mind?' Alexander picked up his second cappuccino then took a sip.

His chest tightened. 'No,' James lied.

Alexander narrowed his eyes. 'I guess you're wondering why I moved this quarterly meeting up to August instead of the usual September brunch.'

James nodded. 'I'm a little curious about why you're in town. You rarely leave New York.'

'That's not true. But of late, I've been preoccupied with my companies.' Alexander placed his cup back on its saucer. 'I'm considering adding to my mediaeval sword collection. It's for my private exhibit.'

James's eyes widened. 'You have a private exhibit?'

The crinkling of paper in the background broke his train of thought. A pair of green eyes glared at him over an edition of the *Daily Voice*. *Wrong question?*

'Yes, I have a private collection. It's minuscule. Usually, I purchase items and loan them to museums for further study. But my collection is a bit lacking of late.' Alexander stared off into the distance.

'Anything legendary or infamous?' James kept one eye on his elderly stalker.

The elderly MI6 wannabe hadn't tackled him to the ground yet. *Interesting. So Alexander has the man on a leash.*

Alexander laughed. 'Isn't that the dream? But tragically, that's just for the cinema. Real life is a lot more disappointing.' He returned his gaze to James. 'I'm interested in a piece from the late Middle Ages. It's at Christie's in London. Oxford wasn't too far away.'

James nodded. 'It's a little over an hour away by train.'

Alexander raised his eyebrows.

Too posh for the train. Noted.

'Have you given any thought to what you want to do now that you're a free man and have resigned from the *Northampton Tribune*?'

James smiled. 'I want to travel around Europe. I grew up in France with my grandparents, but I'm embarrassed to say I haven't seen enough of Europe.'

'Travelling is great. You should add New York to that list.'

James grimaced. 'I want to focus on Europe for now. Maybe some other time.'

A distant expression formed in Alexander's eyes as he took another sip of his cappuccino. 'Your mother dreamed of living in New York. It's all she would talk about.'

'Really?'

'I don't know why because she lived in Paris. And I

thought living in Paris was every model's dream. But not your mother. She was different.'

The two men sat opposite each other, engaging in further small talk. As the minutes ticked by, James's hope of hearing more stories about his mother faded. With a heavy feeling in his chest, James said goodbye to Alexander and wandered out of the Queen's Lane Coffee House and onto the High Street.

With almost eight hours until his reunion dinner with Liam and their friends, James had some time to kill, but the tourist attractions of his former home didn't appeal to him. All he could think about was going back into the coffeehouse and asking more questions about his mother. Would Alexander understand his need to ask? Was he being selfish by asking? Often, there was great sadness in Alexander's eyes after talking about her. For that reason, asking felt wrong.

TWO

WEDNESDAY: 6:58 P.M.

JAMES PRESSED THE DOORBELL, stepped back from the porch, glanced at the redbrick Victorian maisonette, and listened to the chiming as it echoed through the house. The sweet, pungent aroma of the overgrown gardenias in the front garden made his eyes water. The place hadn't changed since he was last there. In fact, Oxford felt as if it existed in a time loop.

He listened to the chatter within the house. As James recognised the voices, he smiled. His friends had all graduated in 2008. A few went off to find employment, while others stayed to complete a master's degree. Liam, his best friend, worked for All Saints College. And Liam's girlfriend, Kate, worked for the Radcliffe Camera library. James didn't understand why people wanted to stay in the same place for a long time. It wasn't his thing. When they'd all graduated with their undergraduate degrees, the friends had promised to keep in touch. It was easier said than done, but seven years later, they organised a reunion dinner followed by drinks. Maybe next time, he would take the initiative and do the organising.

The door slowly opened. A short ginger-haired man stood opposite him and chuckled.

James lifted a baguette and bottle of red wine into the air. 'What?'

'No cheese?' Liam stood aside, leaving room for James to enter.

He rolled his eyes. *Not that again. Every time.* The joke was never going to get old.

'I hate cheese.' James sighed then shook his head.

Liam chuckled. 'It's just so weird and not to mention not very French.'

James pursed his lips. 'Like an Englishman wearing sunscreen on holidays.'

'Look at me.' Liam's hazel eyes widened. 'My skin is practically translucent, and I have freckles. I'm ginger. I have to wear sunscreen.'

'Not everything I do has to be French.'

Liam stifled a laugh. 'Next time, say that sans baguette and bottle of Bordeaux.'

James strolled into the maisonette, paused by the stairs, and turned around. 'This is a polite gesture. Besides, you need excellent bread and wine for this meal.'

'Wait.' Liam closed the door and slid the chain along its tracks. After a quick peek through the spyhole, Liam asked, 'How do you know that wine will go with the meal I'm cooking?'

'I texted Kate,' James said nonchalantly.

Liam yawned. 'So Kate's still enabling you.'

'I know bread and wine, and this will go well with the meal.' James handed over the baguette and the bottle of red.

'I'll take these and start preparing them.' Liam dashed through the sitting room towards the closed white door. Without slowing, he raced to the kitchen, and the door burst open.

Standing by the stairs, James yelled as the door slammed shut. 'Don't refrigerate the wine or the baguette!'

Propped up against the mantelpiece, Manesh listened to

the chatter in the room with a smile. An aroma of garlic, thyme, and onions floated into the sitting room, masking the faint smell of the burnt-out orange blossom candle on the mantel. To the right was a buffet table with cocktail sausage rolls and smoked-salmon-and-cream-cheese blinis. It seemed like only yesterday that Liam had been in the kitchen, burning milk in a tiny saucepan. But Liam had been domesticated. Perhaps Owen would find a use for that old whip-sound-effect app once again.

As James strolled towards the fireplace, he waved at Tom and Georgiana, who sat in the cove of the bay window. Tom's usual short black hair was long, scruffy, and desperate for a cut. Tom caressed Georgiana's lips as he snuggled into her. It was out of character for his reserved friend, but Tom was in a new relationship with a woman who, until that moment, James had been quite certain wasn't real. The stories—more like bragging opportunities—had seemed too good to be true.

Upon arriving at his destination, James patted Manesh on the shoulder. On the mantel above the fireplace, next to the candle, was a half-drunk glass of gin and a smartphone lying faceup.

'Easy, Frenchy. He knows what to do.' Manesh glanced over James's shoulder in the direction of the bay window.

'No, he doesn't.' James kept one eye on the door.

Manesh grinned. 'Are you trying to tell me you drink wine, eat bread at every meal, and are still shaped like a beanpole?'

'You don't have to drink the entire bottle. Besides, I prefer boxed wine because the tap prevents air from getting in the box, unlike, say, a bottle. A little wine every day is the key to happiness.'

A snort followed by a series of chuckles came from the room's far corner. Glancing over Manesh's shoulder, Owen held a hand over his mouth and hid a mischievous grin. But his hazel eyes gave him away. That infamous twinkle was still there seven years later. *Some people never leave college.*

'Not this again.' James tilted his head towards the mirror and stared at Owen, who leaned against the bookcase opposite Ben. 'My *h* wasn't aspirated that time. I said it right.' James stared into the mirror as he braced himself for the chaos that was about to ensue. 'I didn't say *app-iness.*' James shook his index finger at Manesh, who had doubled over laughing.

'It's still too funny,' Manesh said as the room erupted with laughter.

James pointed at Manesh. 'You were supposed to be my assistant professor, and you laughed at me that day, in front of a packed lecture hall, during freshers' week. Everyone thinks this is funny now. Even at graduation, people were still saying *app-iness* to me.'

Manesh placed his hands on his hips then looked at his feet as he clearly attempted to rein in his laughter.

'In my next life, I'm choosing better friends. You guys are a bunch of pricks,' James said as Liam burst through the door with a small glass of plum-red wine and raised his eyebrows at James.

As James stepped aside, he grabbed the glass from Liam's hand. Waltzing around James, Liam nestled against the small ledge above the fireplace. Liam picked up his glass of gin, turned it in his hand, and stared at the churning liquid. Clearly stifling a laugh, Liam stared over Manesh's shoulder into the distance.

Things must be tense in the lab.

James sipped from the frosty wineglass. The astringent dark-cherry liquid swirled around in his mouth, its flavour intensifying with each swirl. As the bitter wine slipped down his throat, James became more curious about the tension between his two friends. Was it just a bad day or something else? The more he contemplated Liam's usual defensive strategy, avoiding all logical discussion and making no eye contact, the more he couldn't resist giving the situation a gentle poke. Maybe James needed a story. He hadn't chased an interesting story since that fateful day in May when he'd turned up at Elizabeth's flat and found a crime scene. *What's the worst that could happen?*

'So, how's work? I heard you're doing a second PhD.' James nodded in Manesh's direction.

Manesh dived into what sounded like a rehearsed monologue, saved for such occasions, as he peered over his shoulder at the bay window.

Is he keeping an eye on Tom? Or is my imagination running wild again?

Sitting in the cove of the bay window, Tom avoided Manesh's gaze. As the monologue continued, Liam stiffened. Regret building within him, James surveyed the room.

With the Bordeaux in one hand, James sauntered to the buffet table and picked up a smoked salmon blini. He grimaced at the taste of the tangy cream cheese. A delicious appetiser, ruined. Desperate to escape from the brewing argument, James gazed over his shoulder as the chatter in the corner of the room subsided. It was unusual for Owen not to talk. It meant only one thing—trouble was in the making. That was just what the reunion needed: more drama than an episode of *Coronation Street*.

In the background, Manesh continued his monologue, seeming unaware of the commotion around him and utterly oblivious to all the bored faces and the fact that James had slipped away. James wondered whether he himself was like that when he talked about a story. Truth be told, he didn't want to hear the answer to that question. A part of him already knew.

Over his shoulder, James watched as Owen crept across the room, nudged the door, and slipped inside. A look of amusement twinkled in Ben's bright-green eyes as he glanced in the direction that Owen had disappeared. *So you're up to no good, both of you.* What were they planning? It was out of character for Ben to mix in with the drama—he preferred to stay out of things. Perhaps he had changed. Ben's gaze wandered around the room then settled on his watch. A few seconds later, Ben faced the bookshelves and took a sip from the tall glass of beer in his hand.

Liam slammed his empty gin glass on the mantel. Startled, James jumped then turned his attention from Ben and observed the heated discussion in front of him.

'The *Commentary on Daniel* isn't from the fifteenth century. The initiums are clearly twelfth-century style.' Liam's face turned a slight crimson. 'Its pages are vellum, widely used before the mid-twelfth century. By the time the fifteenth century came around, they had imported paper from China.'

Manesh smirked. 'Vellum was still around in the fifteenth century, and poorer monasteries would have used it. But of course, you can't know for sure without resorting to carbon dating.'

Liam took a deep breath. 'Come off the grass. The monasteries weren't poor. They were practically supporting the poorer people in the towns surrounding them. They would have used the latest paper. The *Commentary* was created extravagantly, so they would have used the best resources.' Liam's jaw clenched.

As the two men continued their verbal smackdown, James hung his head and crept away, clutching his glass of wine. He joined Owen and Ben, who were silently smiling. Ben nodded to James then trekked to the door as Liam stormed across the room and followed him into the kitchen.

'I see you're up to your old tricks.' James made a stirring gesture with his wineglass.

Owen smirked. 'I don't know what you mean.'

Of course he doesn't. That's the point of reunions—to attend and see who hasn't changed after all these years. At least he doesn't disappoint.

Owen shook his head. 'Fine. I swapped a few place tags around on the table. Let's just say Ben is now sitting next to Manesh.'

Merde.

James rolled his eyes. 'Does Ben know?'

'Maybe I led him to believe I put Manesh next to Liam.' Owen shrugged.

James shook his head. 'Still have that whip-sound-effect app?'

'Lalonde, you surprise me.' Owen narrowed his eyes. 'I thought about it after realising that Liam had prepared all of this.'

The doorbell chimed, and the kitchen door slammed against the stairs, shaking the trays of food on the buffet table. Liam shot through the sitting room and to the entryway. After peering through the spyhole, he unlocked the dead bolt, slid the chain off its tracks, and flung open the Victorian-style door. Before him stood a tall, thin woman with curly brown hair—Amber Cooper.

She smiled. 'Sorry to interrupt. I need to deliver this to Manesh.'

Liam guided Amber into the house. She blushed as her eyes fixed on Manesh, leaning against the fireplace and scrolling through his phone. Ambling across the polished wooden floor, she held a red-and-black USB drive in her palm.

She hasn't aged.

Owen nudged him. 'She's barking up the wrong tree if you know what I mean.

James rolled his eyes. 'She's just shy.'

'And too old,' Owen whispered.

James leaned away from Owen. 'She's twenty-six.'

'And too smart for him.' Owen chuckled.

James placed his empty wineglass on the dark-stained bookshelves and listened to the conversation.

'I insist you join us. There's room for one more,' Liam said as Manesh groaned while twirling the USB drive between his thumb and index finger.

Owen whispered into James's ear, 'Where's he disappearing to?' Owen angled his head towards the steps.

After a quick glance over his shoulder, Tom continued to glide up the staircase. Soon after he left, Manesh snuck away from Liam and Amber. He sat next to the voluptuous dark-haired woman Tom had kept to himself since the evening began. Leaning in, Manesh caressed her cheek. Georgiana blushed as she pulled away.

As Manesh made his obvious but passive-aggressive point, his smartphone lit up. Two messages had come through. Sure, it was poor form to view someone's phone, but James couldn't help himself. The first message, James recognised. It was from his favourite member of the All Saints faculty, Professor Xavier Watson. Underneath the first notification was a second text, sent two hours ago, from Stanley Whittaker, bearing the simple message:

> We need to talk.

James wondered why that name sounded familiar.

THREE

AFTER TEN MINUTES of listening to Owen's sarcastic remarks and the odd chuckle from Ben, James meandered into the kitchen. The sweet aroma of beef bourguignon and potato mash brought a smile to his face. Hunched over a sage-green cast-iron casserole pot, Liam lifted the lid, stirred the contents, then placed the large spoon on the countertop. *Is that Le Creuset? My grandmother would lose her mind if she saw that pot.* Everything in her kitchen was pale-pink Le Creuset. It was that pink colour reserved for ballet costumes and little girls' bedrooms.

Behind Liam, high in the sink, were saucepans, frying pans, and other dishes. Liam was actually cooking. No cheating and buying a Gastropub meal from the refrigerated section in Marks and Spencer but instead cooking from scratch. *What's next? A veggie patch in the garden? Should I check?* That man burnt milk and porridge but now cooked a complex and often needy meal that required monitoring and stirring. It wasn't a typical stew that could be left to simmer. James was impressed.

Liam lunged and grabbed a purple bottle of eco-friendly surface spray off the windowsill. James sauntered through the kitchen and propped himself against the breakfast bar as Liam tugged at the paper towel holder. With a torn paper towel in his hand, Liam sprayed the sheet. After placing the surface spray on the countertop, he dashed to the stovetop and mopped up the splattering of sauce off the dark-green-porcelain splashback tiles.

James slid his empty wineglass across the dark-granite kitchen counter. 'Smells great.'

'Thank God. I've been obsessing over this for the last two days between meal prep, planning, and now cooking.' Liam glanced up then shrugged.

James smiled.

'Things are tense out there.' James pointed across the room towards the closed door.

Liam closed his eyes and shook his head. 'Frenchy, I'm not sure if we're all going to meet like this again. Everyone is on bad terms with someone else.'

'Maybe I can try to smooth things out between people while I'm here.' James hung his head and slipped his hands into his pockets. 'Or we could deliberately not invite Manesh or whoever seems to cause the most trouble.'

Liam sighed. 'If we don't invite Manesh and Owen, then that's half the group gone. And it feels mean. I don't want to be that guy.'

The simplest solution was often the best. James nodded as he stared at the simmering casserole pot. 'When did you learn to cook?'

'Don't you dare start.'

James held his hands up in mock surrender. 'I was just curious because you're quite good.'

Liam sighed. 'I got Kate some lessons because I thought she would enjoy the experience. She took offence at the gift, so I took the lessons to prove a point.' Liam placed the scrunched-up dirty paper towel on the bench next to the stovetop. 'And I was right. It was fun. Not that she'll admit it, but she was a little jealous of the fun I was having.'

James shook his head. 'Kate has turned you into her own personal chef. You realise that, right?'

'I enjoy cooking. And I'm not her chef.' Liam furrowed his brow. 'Kate cooks too.'

Sure, she does.

GLANCING up through the kitchen skylight above the table where he sat, James snorted at the faded ketchup stain from 2006, for which he was entirely responsible. It was summer. Liam and Kate had introduced James to the typical British summer barbecue, and the ketchup was stuck at the bottom of the glass bottle. Like an idiot, he shook the bottle with the lid off. He would never forget the sight of the bright-red trail of sauce on the ceiling and down the light-green walls of the breakfast room. Thankfully, Liam and Kate had thought it hilarious.

Liam jumped up as a robotic *quack* screamed out through the tiny speaker of his smartphone. 'Dinner is ready.'

He sped into the kitchen and prepared the main meal. It had been twenty minutes since Liam served the summer salad entrée, and the light beefy fragrance made James's mouth water.

A warm, petite hand brushed his forearm, causing him to jerk back in his chair.

'Sorry to startle you, but I've just noticed that Tom and the other fellow are missing,' Georgiana said with an awkward smile.

James leaned back in his chair and looked out the French doors into the partially lit back garden. No one was outside, and he wondered where they had gotten to. He didn't recall seeing them slip away after the entrée. While waiting for the main meal to finish cooking, Owen had made use of his whip-sound-effect app after noticing Liam jumping up and checking on the beef bourguignon every five minutes. James blamed himself for that app.

Ben groaned then glanced at his watch. 'They disappeared the second the entrée dishes were taken away. Maybe twenty minutes ago.'

'I'll find Tom and Manesh and tell them dinner is ready.' James stood then sauntered around the narrow space surrounding the table, through the kitchen, and into the empty sitting room.

———

A FEW MOMENTS LATER, James dashed through the sitting room and ascended the internal staircase. Clutching the newel post of the bannister, he caught his breath. As his heart rate slowly subsided, he surveyed the short hall. Only one light beamed from under the four closed doors—it was coming from the bathroom.

Inching forward, knowing that a loose floorboard was only millimetres away, James listened. Muffled voices came from within the bathroom. *What are they up to?* Careful to leave room for a quick escape, James crept closer and kept his eyes on the carpeted floor, hoping not to set off the infamous creak. Again, he listened to the conversation.

'I need you to pay back the money you owe me.'

A second voice groaned. 'How many times do I need to say this? I need more time.'

'What about a part payment?'

'What part of "I need more time" tells you I can make a payment? You're ridiculous. I don't have the money.'

Without warning, the door flew open. James's heart raced. He needed to get to the kitchen.

JAMES SPRINTED down the stairs and through the sitting room, pushed the kitchen door open, and raced across the beige tiles. He slipped into his chair next to Georgiana. Gasping for air, James placed his hand on his chest and felt the rhythm of his racing heart.

Tom dragged his wooden chair across the tiles. 'What's wrong with you?'

James gazed down as Liam slipped a plate of beef bourguignon under his nose. 'Asthma.'

'Sounds bad. Do you take medication?'

James exhaled. 'Honestly, I'm fine.'

James picked up a slice of the baguette then pulled apart the hard crust and dipped it into the stew, listening to the chatter surrounding him.

Hovering around the table, Liam poured James a small glass of red wine then moved on to Georgiana, who was already holding her glass out for him.

'Do you have time off from work over the summer?' Manesh asked as he stabbed his fork into a small piece of beef.

Ben's eyes widened at the sound of Manesh's voice. He stared at his plate for a few moments then peered across the table at Tom. 'Are you still working for the British Library?'

Manesh glanced across at Tom for the third time that evening. Tom scooped two pieces of beef and a lump of mashed potatoes into his mouth. Holding up a finger to Ben, he chewed.

'So, Manesh...' Owen wore a sly smile. 'Are you still in contact with Bianca? How is she doing?'

Cough, cough. Manesh drew his napkin to his mouth as he recovered from his choking fit. Ben glared at the two men sitting next to him. For a moment, rage filled Ben's eyes then disappeared. James shifted in his seat as the tension in the room intensified.

Manesh regained his breath. 'She's still a freelancing photographer.'

Ben stabbed another piece of beef with his fork as he stared straight ahead. He thrust the food into his mouth and scraped his teeth against the fork tines. A slight smile formed on his lips.

Tilting his head, Ben stared across the table at Tom. 'Actually, she's training to be a primary school teacher.'

'I didn't know she liked the little rug rats.' Owen leaned forward and gazed down the length of the table.

Amber, who hadn't uttered a single word since the meal began, sat at the end of the table between Tom and Ben, eating and avoiding eye contact with her neighbours.

Poor Amber. Someone should have told her she was eating with a pack of crazed hyenas.

'While we're on the topic, I've been getting into a bit of freelance photography,' Ben said as Manesh shifted in his seat and stared at his plate. 'Tom, do you remember how we used to do our own photography at night-walking events?'

'Yeah, we made quite a bit of money for a two-hour stint,' Tom reminisced as he moved the beef around his plate with a fork.

'Really? Was this recent?' Amber asked, a hint of curiosity in her voice.

'No, we marketed the walks to tourists. It helped me pay for my extracurricular activities, as the baron would say.' Tom smirked.

Ben bit his lip as if attempting to stifle a laugh. He peered at his watch.

'Do you not enjoy working for the British Library?' Amber asked.

'Work is fine. I just miss the creativity and chatting with people.' Tom studied the leftover scrap of beef swimming in the Burgundy sauce.

Georgiana screwed up her face.

FOUR

———

WEDNESDAY: 9:58 P.M.

GLUG, *glug* was the background accompaniment to James's fifth attempt at ordering five beers. The handle of the beer tab sprang back as the bartender released his grip, slammed the pint onto the oak bar top, and leaned in towards James. Despite his many years of study in the small university town and his years of learning English, people still struggled to understand his thick French accent.

James glanced around the small thirteenth-century pub, the Turf Tavern. It was almost ten on a Wednesday evening, and the little pub was teeming with locals and tourists. People gathered outside in small groups, drinking and enjoying the summer night, while others gathered next to the bar. The pub had no standing room, and the bar owners encouraged people to enjoy their beers outside in the garden. The small tavern's back entrance was along a quaint cobblestone lane near Hertford Bridge. The pub had a modern British menu with the perfect price for student budgets. And it hadn't changed one bit since James had studied nearby at All Saints.

James stared at his best friend, Liam, waving his hand in the air, holding up five fingers. Perhaps Georgiana had decided she wanted a beer.

It had been twenty-four hours since he'd packed up his desk at the *Northampton Tribune* and said goodbye to his position as editor, off to travel around Europe, Asia, and perhaps America. But he wasn't sticking to a strict schedule. Instead, he planned on taking each day as it came. James craved freedom and a break from the wonderful world of journalism and editing, at least for the next few months, plus a Belgian beer. He couldn't wait to get out of Oxford and start travelling.

James ran his fingers through his thick dark-blond hair and leaned over the bar. 'Five Affligems!' he yelled as he rolled his eyes.

What bartender doesn't understand what an Affligem is?

Dave, the bartender, leaned over the counter, cupping his ear with his hand. 'What?' he asked for the sixth time.

'It's a Belgian beer.' James shrugged at Liam, who was still standing in the archway leading to the next room of the pub.

Liam frantically pointed into the room behind him, so at least they had a table.

'Sorry, I don't understand your accent.' Dave gazed across at the next customer, pointing at the third bar tap.

'I want five bottles of Affligem Blonds.' James pointed at the beers inside the small bar fridge.

Moments later, James grabbed the beers from the bartender and walked towards his small group of friends in the next room, rolling his blue-green eyes. They were all sitting at a brown wooden table, a rare find.

'Cheers,' the four friends said as they took the beers from his hands, waiting for James to respond.

'*Santé.*' He lifted his beer with a slight smile as they all groaned.

'Frenchy, you're so stubborn.' Liam nudged James.

James rolled his eyes, hating the nickname given him by his short, ginger-haired friend. James had first met Liam at freshers' week on his first day at All Saints College. His grandparents had taken the trip from Poitiers, France, to Oxford, England, to say goodbye to their beloved grandson. They acted like he was never coming back. Liam was on his own, walking around campus with a giant map, trying to figure out the quickest way to his lectures when James bumped into him by accident. James had called Liam a nerd out of jest. Liam immediately laughed at his pronunciation. That was how his nickname started. And it was there to stay forever. There was no changing it.

'Just say cheers. Just this once.' Owen gulped his beer.

'No,' James replied.

From the corner of his eye, James watched Owen undo the buttons of his thick black hooded coat as he sipped his beer. 'What's with the coat?' He pointed at Owen.

'What?' Owen gripped the lapels of his coat.

'It's summer.'

Owen glared at James. 'It's chilly outside.'

'Chilly? It's not that cold. It's sixteen degrees, a beautiful summer evening.' Georgiana brushed Owen's arm and felt the thick, furry texture of the coat.

'So, where's Manesh? What's his excuse for not being here?' Owen asked, changing the subject as Tom visibly recoiled then fixed his attention on his smartphone. 'Has he traded us in for his usual twenty-year-old?'

'Probably.' Liam stared vacantly across the table. 'I was hoping he would be here. I wanted to show you this new mediaeval manuscript we received in the lab.'

Tom looked up from his smartphone. 'Not this again.'

'I'm not going to your lab. It's supposed to be a fun night out.' Owen wiggled his finger at Liam.

'Manesh thinks he knows the most about the *Commentary*.' Liam turned his attention to Georgiana.

'Why are you so obsessed with this manuscript?' James asked.

'It's a *Commentary on Daniel* by St. Jerome. It was rescued from Glastonbury Abbey before it burned down in 1184 if the stories are to be believed. It's one of a kind and has these beautiful initiums.'

'Sounds like a yawn.' Tom slipped his phone into his pocket. 'I need to make a call.'

Tom headed for the pub's front door, leaving his girlfriend with his friends. He pushed through the crowd and disappeared into the breezy summer night.

'What's with the phone addiction?' Liam pointed in the direction that Tom had gone.

'Maybe it's porn.' Owen said as he and Liam laughed.

Georgiana turned a slight pink as the two men laughed. That night was the first time Tom had brought his girlfriend to one of their occasional get-togethers. There she was, stranded in a small pub in Oxford with her boyfriend's friends. It was strange. At that stage of the relationship, he should have been keen to impress her and show her a good time. Something was up.

James shoved Owen before gesturing to Georgiana.

Owen gently tapped her hand. 'Oh, sorry. I'm sure it's not porn.'

'Perhaps he's addicted to his job,' Liam suggested.

'Yes, Tom works long hours.' Georgiana leaned over the table. She twirled the beer bottle and stared off into the distance.

'He's not cheating on you if that's what you think,' James said.

Georgiana studied James. 'How do you know?'

'If he were cheating, he would be more secretive,' James explained. 'And he doesn't appear to be texting or typing. So he could be addicted to a game.'

'Liam's addicted to *Farmville 2*. I always see your game updates on FriendSpace,' Owen said. 'But I suspect Tom's addicted to something way cooler than that.'

'Hey, that's not true.' Liam thumped the table in protest.

Owen smiled. 'It's all over your FriendSpace profile.'

'Where's Kate?' James elbowed Liam. 'She should be here keeping Georgiana company.'

Liam gazed off into the distance as if in a trance. 'She's busy. Something about working in London.'

James grimaced. 'Doesn't she work in the Radcliffe library?'

'Supposedly, it's a team-building thing. Kate posted an update from a bar in Soho.' Liam stared into his half-empty beer bottle.

James tapped his fingers on the tabletop. 'So a bunch of librarians are hitting a few bars in Soho?'

'I got an invitation to the wrong event,' Owen said as he scanned the bar. 'And where's Ben?'

'Who's Ben?' Georgiana asked.

'He's the tall guy with green eyes. He's about six feet tall and sat next to Manesh at the dinner,' James explained.

Georgiana blushed. 'Is Manesh the charismatic guy from India?'

'Yes, Ben was sitting next to him.' James watched her turn crimson.

'What was with the constant watch checking?' Liam asked before he took a sip of his beer.

'Every time I glanced in Ben's direction, he was checking his watch,' Owen said as he surveyed the tavern.

'And he disappeared early,' James said. 'I remember when you were all fun.'

James peered at his empty beer bottle.

Liam smirked. 'You're not that much fun, either.'

'I'm fun.' James placed his hand on his chest and stared at Liam.

Throughout the rest of the evening, James and his friends sat around the table, taking turns buying rounds at the bar. As the clock on the wall approached eleven thirty p.m., James realised he was drunker than expected.

After getting up, James made his way through the sea of people and ordered a bottle of water at the bar. As he waited for his order, James searched the bar for Tom. He wasn't inside. James grabbed the bottle, ambled over to the door, and peered outside. Tom was gone.

The drinks and the reunion dinner hadn't gone as James had hoped, but Tom's leaving without any warning was rude. His group of friends had changed. As James had spoken with Liam about the idea for the reunion, he was excited to see his friends again and perhaps had built it up in his mind. Was his disappointment the result of unrealistic expectations? Perhaps everyone had changed. If he were honest, he would admit to being more cynical and a tad jaded. Perhaps life was similar for his friends too. Maybe cynicism was an added bonus collected along the way to becoming an adult.

FIVE

WEDNESDAY: 11:48 P.M.

WHITE, metal, and glass stretched as far as the eye could see. Surrounding James, nestled in glass cabinets, were eleven mediaeval manuscripts. The beautiful leather-bound covers were open, revealing the middle pages. James's nose wrinkled as he breathed in the chemical fragrance of the research lab. He grimaced.

Curiosity had dragged James from the Turf Tavern to the research lab at All Saints— that and the excitement in Liam's eyes as he babbled incessantly about the *Commentary on Daniel*. It sounded unique and expensive, "one of a kind" as Liam had advertised in a comically hushed tone. And James was drunk. While drunk, he could be talked into almost anything. Knowing that, Liam had dragged him there almost two hours later.

Naturally, he was told not to touch a thing. James discovered, after careful examination and a few moans of disapproval, that all the other cabinets were locked and the treasures stored away from prying hands, as Liam had so eloquently explained.

'It's airtight,' Liam said over his shoulder as he jiggled the keys into the lock.

'Sorry?' James walked around to the opposite side of the bench, his hand trailing.

'The lab has its own oxygen supply and multiple backup generators. We're trying to provide a more suitable environment for the books.' Liam gazed down the glass cabinets, each housing a text from a bygone era.

James nodded as he surveyed the room.

The cool-to-the-touch silver laboratory bench under his fingers sent shivers through his body. Liam slid the glass cabinet open, exposing the *Commentary on Daniel* to the room's elements. Its vibrant-coloured vellum pages and leather-bound cover glimmered in the bright lights. Liam walked to the table and put on a pair of crisp white gloves that were laid out on the counter. With his hands stretched out, he sauntered back to the row of glass cabinets. His gloved index finger floated down the faded red edges of the manuscript before gripping its cover. Clearly mindful of every step, Liam carried the mediaeval text to the countertop.

'You need to wear the gloves.' Liam placed the book on the metal table and glanced at the second pair of white cotton mittens next to James. 'I can't risk the oils from your fingers spoiling the fragile pages.'

James pulled on the white gloves and watched with immense fascination as Liam continued examining the pages. 'You know, this isn't my first time on earth.'

With a pinched, tension-filled expression, Liam ran his index finger down the margin of the vellum. 'Always the smart-arse,' Liam muttered to himself.

What a grump.

James smirked. 'So, you think it's from the twelfth century?'

'The official line is we're not sure. Mainly because Manesh hasn't caved yet. We're trying to date it,' Liam replied. 'It's consistent with other religious texts from the late twelfth century, but we don't know for certain. Manesh thinks he knows the most. He spends a lot of time in this lab, inspecting the pages.'

And is just a tad obsessed.

Liam narrowed his eyes at James then leaned in. 'Amber has been helping him a lot, and she didn't make the team, but she doesn't seem to care. Smart woman. She dodged a massive grenade.'

As James turned the left page, a flicker of bright ink caught his eye. 'There's something in the margins,' he said with a hint of excitement as he inspected the invisible ink.

The two men moved closer to the text and stared at the edge of the vellum. A rustling sound disturbed the stillness of the room as James carefully turned the page. Glistening in the bright lights was a short poetic verse.

Silence filled the room as James's blue-green eyes widened.

James gawked at the dazed expression on Liam's face. 'It's written in modern English.'

'It's strange because the Commentary is written in ecclesiastical Latin. It was the only language the Catholic Church used for printed materials in the Middle Ages,' Liam explained. 'Someone else must have added this several years later. Who would do something like that?' Liam stared at James.

'Hold the page like this while I try to take a photo,' James said as Liam supported the fragile vellum with his thumbs and forefingers.

Click, click. With his eyes glued to the phone, James slid his thumb and index finger across the screen to get a closer look at the images. 'I've got it,' James mumbled as Liam peeked over his shoulder.

'Obviously, Manesh knew about this.' Liam peered over the manuscript and held the edge of the vellum. 'Why didn't he share this with me? I could've helped him figure out its meaning.'

James stifled a laugh. 'Someone has dreams of treasure hunting.'

Liam nudged James. 'My eighty-eight-year-old grandfather is less cynical than you.'

'Come on. Where is this crazy riddle going to take you?' James pointed at the text in Liam's hand. 'To a lost treasure map where X marks the spot?' James peered at his phone and struck the home button. The words "No signal" glared back at him from the top left-hand corner of the screen.

He rolled his eyes and slipped his smartphone into the back pocket of his dark-rinsed jeans.

Bang.

'What was that?' Liam dropped the page and walked over to the door of the lab.

'It was probably a car backfiring.' James slid his hand underneath the vellum and tilted it.

'At this time of night?' Liam strolled to the bench and turned the page in James's hand. 'Do you think there are more hidden messages?'

The vibrant colours flipped by as Liam benevolently turned pages of the manuscript.

James rested his hand on the delicate vellum. 'Wait. Go back. I think there was a symbol in the corner.'

Liam flicked through the book and held each margin towards the light. As the light from the lab shone through the page, a symbol lit up in the corner.

James reached into his back pocket, pulled out his phone, and snapped another picture. 'The symbol appears to be a flame,' he said as he showed Liam the picture.

Liam fixated on the image as James ran his finger down the margin next to the blue initium. 'There's a dragon in the initial. I didn't notice it before. Do you think it's a coincidence?'

'No, it's a commentary on the book of Daniel. It's considered apocalyptic literature by biblical scholars. The dragons fit in with the theme of Daniel.' Liam grimaced as he studied the image on the screen.

Buzz, crack. The lab fell into near darkness except for the dim glow from the light of the exit sign above the door. The familiar hum of the air-conditioning unit ground to a halt.

Liam gazed at the ceiling as James grabbed the smartphone out of his hands.

'The power should come on again soon,' Liam said. 'It happens all the time. We have several backup generators.'

A feeling of uneasiness swept through James's body as he surveyed the lab. He gestured towards the door. 'Shouldn't we leave?'

'No, we won't be able to leave until the backup generator starts up,' Liam said matter-of-factly.

James glared at Liam, who was hunched over with his face millimetres away from the page as if he had no place to be and no care in the world. How was he even seeing anything on the page? Had Liam developed superpowers since they last spoke? In the meantime, they were running out of oxygen. *Typical Brit, phlegmatic to the end.*

'Are you saying we're sealed in here?' James started to panic.

'You've got to calm down.' Liam peered up from the Commentary. 'Sure, the lab is airtight and runs on its own oxygen system, but the generator will turn on in a few moments.' Liam shrugged off James's paranoia.

'Really?' James looked at Liam.

'No one has ever run out of oxygen.'

Up till now.

Liam wrinkled his brow as he stared at the ceiling then smiled at James. 'You resigned from your position as editor at the *Northampton Tribune*. What's next?'

'Maybe a holiday. I want to see more of Europe. I lived there for so long, and I'm sad to admit that I've seen very little,' James replied as his heart continued to race.

'Have you heard from Valentine since your breakup?' Liam gave James a sympathetic smile.

James closed his eyes and took a deep breath. The topic was bound to come up at some point. James's eyes opened then glazed over. 'No, she erected an ice wall and froze me out.'

The two men stood in silence.

'What about you?' James attempted to steer the conversation away from his nonexistent love life.

'I don't know.' Liam looked at the floor. 'I think my relationship with Kate might be over. It's feeling a little forced of late. We're both strangers. I don't know what to do.'

'Sorry, I'm a disaster with relationships.' James patted Liam on the shoulder. 'I've never been good at fixing things when they go south. So I end up creating more trouble.'

Liam groaned.

'Maybe I'm better off alone.' James sighed as he noticed a blinking green light coming from the panel near the door. 'Ah, Liam.' James pointed at the panel. 'We still have power. I think the problem is with the lights.'

Liam walked to the door, leaned towards the panel, and squinted. 'Perhaps the door is running on a different source of electricity? Manesh should be here any second now. He still lives in the same maisonette.'

James pulled out his smartphone and tapped the flashlight app, illuminating a small area in front of him. He turned the pages in search of the verse he had found earlier, taking his attention off the drama unfolding in the lab.

'The riddle could be connected to the page it's on or even the symbol.' James continued to fix his eyes on the pages in front of him.

'Like a cryptic message.' Liam walked to the metal table, stood next to James, and leaned forward to see the *Commentary on Daniel*.

'The message makes little sense. It reads like a poem. And this is apocalyptic literature,' James said as he faced Liam.

'I wonder if Manesh is close to deciphering its meaning?' Liam mumbled as he stared at the page.

'Do you think he hopes the message will lead him to an archaeological discovery?' James asked. 'That could explain his secrecy.'

So, Manesh discovered a riddle in the margins of the *Commentary on Daniel* and didn't tell anyone about it. *Interesting.* There was going to be some kind of fallout over this, and James was going to be caught up in the middle of it. The perfect end to a reunion with friends.

SIX

———

THE LEAVES of the giant oak tree whispered overhead in the breeze. Assistant Professor Manesh Warren hunched over and wrapped his arms around his torso, bracing himself against the cool summer evening as he strolled under the tree's ever-expanding branches. The wind tousled his curly dark-brown hair as he scurried up the path towards the entrance hall.

Crack.

Manesh froze. He took a deep breath and listened to the quietness of the college grounds. Recently, every late-night sound had put him on edge. He was becoming paranoid, as he had reassured himself over the last few evenings. Then a gentle flapping noise caused his heart to race. Manesh turned around, but there was nothing behind him. He was losing it.

As Manesh resumed his stroll, the edge of a black coat disappeared from behind the empty bike racks only a few metres away. He paused. He had no time to give in to his paranoia.

All he'd wanted to do before drifting off to sleep was read a book—the perfect end to a long day—when he'd gotten a text from Liam. Guilt had dragged Manesh out of bed, not the message asking him to discuss the college's latest acquisition, a *Commentary on Daniel* by St Jerome.

Manesh was in his fifth year as a research fellow at All Saints College and had contemplated starting a second PhD in mediaeval literature nine years after finishing his first. But that was not the source of the pain shooting through his head. That pain resulted from dehydration and excessive alcohol consumption, a perfectly acceptable consequence of a reunion dinner with friends. He and Liam were friends, in a way. Although, if Manesh was honest, he would admit he was a lousy friend.

He'd first met Liam the year the class of 2008 began their undergraduate degrees. Manesh was in the final year of his first PhD in mediaeval and modern languages.

Liam and his friends took Manesh's Introduction to English Language and Literature class and befriended him. They all kept in contact after they graduated. Liam and Kate stayed on to study in the master's and PhD programmes at All Saints. The invitation to their reunion flattered him. But a phone call at twelve minutes to midnight to discuss a manuscript was pushing the boundaries of friendship. Although it was late, he walked to the entrance archway.

As he passed through the archway and towards the rear buildings, Manesh glanced over his shoulder. He again had that feeling of being watched. A lone figure in black lurked in the shadows under the archway. *Am I dreaming? This can't be real.*

Manesh darted across Whittaker Quadrangle and through the second archway. He picked up his pace and sprinted across the Garden Quadrangle and towards the bright-blue door of the back building. Sweat trickled down his brow and glistened against his caramel skin in the moonlight. The tall figure in black passed through the second archway.

After some panicked fumbling, Manesh located his keys. He surveyed the square as he slid the key into the lock and turned the handle while his stalker inched closer. A creak called out, disturbing the eerie silence of the grounds. He opened the antique door and sprinted up the stairs, leaving the figure in black in the chilly summer evening.

———

INSIDE THE SAFETY of the building, Manesh walked down the dark corridor lined with doors. Ahead of him was the entrance to his lab. Access was permitted via an iris-scanning machine mounted on the wall. He wondered whether he would be safe in the lab.

The front door to the building slammed shut, disturbing the tranquillity of the offices. Manesh rushed to the end of the long hallway. He didn't know why the man was chasing him or what he wanted.

He had made a terrible mistake by entering that building. But it wasn't the only mistake he had made of late. He had taken advantage of people and not just anyone but friends— good people. Karma was catching up with him. Maybe he could outrun it that day, but eventually, it would catch up with him.

Gasping for air, he reached the security door and the iris scanner, which led into the airtight laboratory. Getting past the layers of security would take time, and time was running out. Even though gaining admittance would take less than thirty seconds, it wasn't worth the risk of getting caught. Manesh turned the corner and kept running. He gazed over his shoulder. The figure in black was getting closer. He directed his attention to the path in front of him.

In the distance loomed a grey door bearing the word "Janitor."

'You can't outrun me,' the figure in black called out from over his shoulder.

Manesh turned his trembling body to face the figure in black.

Towering over him at six feet tall and with broad shoulders, the figure in black stood in the shadows with a large hood and a gold Venetian mask concealing his face.

'Where is it?' the figure asked as a hand with five chipped, painted fingernails protruded from the sleeve of his thick winter coat, clutching a gun.

Manesh's heart quickened as he stared down the barrel of the pistol. *Does the figure in black know about the riddles in the margins?* Manesh swore he hadn't told a soul about the existence of the riddles except for Professor Xavier Watson. Or maybe Stanley Whittaker knew more about the *Commentary* than he'd let on. It made little sense. A sliver of moonlight shone through a nearby window and scattered across the metal barrel.

'I don't know what you're talking about,' Manesh replied with a shaky voice, knowing lying wouldn't help him.

He needed time to figure out how to get away, or hopefully, Liam and James would come out of the lab—if they'd heard the commotion.

'You're lying,' the figure in black replied. 'You know I want the manuscript.'

The stalker stepped into the light, but all Manesh could see was a pair of bright-green eyes, hypnotising and familiar. It was as if he had stared into them before now.

A click from the revolver broke the silence. 'Perhaps this will jog your memory.'

'It's in the lab over there.' Manesh glanced over his shoulder. 'There are many layers of security. You'll never get in without authorisation.'

'Then open it.'

'No, the bio-security won't work when I'm in a panicked state.'

'Open it.'

'No.'

A loud bang echoed around the corridor. The bullet sped towards Manesh and buried itself in his chest. An overwhelming wave of pain rushed through Manesh's body as the bullet's momentum flung him backwards. As he fell to the ground, Manesh remembered he had seen the figure in black before. They were friends.

'Wait, I know you—' Manesh clutched his chest and gasped for air. Blood poured out of his chest and drenched his white-collared shirt.

SEVEN

—

THURSDAY: 12:18 A.M.

SPLAT, *drip, beep.* I pressed the swollen eyeball, still attached to its optic nerve, up against the iris scanner of the research lab in All Saints College. Blood drained away from the eye, down the optic nerve that trailed into the palm of my hand. A sharp pain shot down my little finger and into my wrist. Sweat dripped down my face, a not-so-great side effect from wearing my gold Venetian theatre mask. As seconds ticked by, the pain grew more intense. But worst of all, it spread down my arm and into my shoulder joint. I had less than thirty seconds to go. After that, all I had to do was not move. Simple.

Suffering in silence and careful not to move, I waited for the scanner to identify Manesh's eyeball. Pushing through the ever-increasing waves of pain, I focused on my task. The mission was simple. Retrieve, deliver, and leave as little evidence as possible behind. So far, everything had gone to plan. The murdered professor had never been a part of the plan, but he'd complicated the assignment. There were consequences for not fulfilling the mission. As a result, I became a whatever-it-takes kind of person.

'Manesh Warren, access granted,' the security system's robotic voice announced after what felt like an eternity.

Finally, I dropped my arm and felt immediate relief. Standing at military-style attention, I waited for the security door to slide open, clutching the eyeball. Blood from the optic nerves dangled to the floors, staining the white tiles.

Then a high-pitched beep rang across the quiet, empty corridor. Finally, the doors opened, and I stepped into the short hallway.

As the main door closed, I fixed my eyes on the second layer of security. A thicker, more reinforced metal door awaited at the end of the short corridor. Discarding the eyeball on the floor and ignoring the blood trail, I strolled towards the steel door. The muffled voices within the lab made my task even more difficult. Ideally, there would be no witnesses, which meant no casualties and bodily fluids on the *Commentary*.

Weighing the options, I listened to the voices in the laboratory. From the outer perimeter, the lab was soundproof. Now that I was inside the second layer, my awareness of the comings and goings in the lab was building. But was it both ways?

My safest course of action was to take as few risks as possible. Every move had to be made with discretion if I wanted to keep the element of surprise. Even though the laboratory was in complete darkness, I expected the other four senses of whoever lay within the lab to heighten.

With an ear on the conversation, I reached inside my hooded coat, pulled out the bloodied knife, and clenched it. I could hear only two young male voices from within the lab, and from the conversation, they were research fellows. One voice, I recognised because I had heard it every day over the last few weeks. And it drove me crazy. The other voice was new but familiar.

I wiped the excess blood off the blade and onto my coat. Even though it was two against one, I loved the sound of those odds. I crept forward one step at a time, aware that my next step could trigger the swift opening of the door. Clenching the knife, I stood tall and took one more step forward.

Whoosh, pop. The reinforced metal door slid open, silencing the conversation within the lab. *They're making this too easy for me.* To my right, the *Commentary* lay open on the steel bench.

EIGHT

––––––

THURSDAY: 12:24 A.M.

THUD, *thud.* I cringed as my boots hit the tiles. *Talk about amateur hour. Why don't I just email them and tell them I'm about to steal the artefact and kill them if they don't oblige me?* I paused to allow my eyes to adjust to the darkness of the lab.

As the room came into view, the silhouettes of two men became clearer, thanks to the light from the exit sign above me. It couldn't have been more perfect if I had staged it. Liam Kennedy stood before me, squinting in the dark. He was practically blind, and he was vain and never wore his glasses. The other one, James Lalonde, All Saints' own Don Juan, was useless.

'Manesh?' Liam stepped back into the shadows of the lab.

Yes, Kennedy, Manesh regularly cuts off the lights and walks into the research lab cloaked under cover of darkness. Idiot. Not wanting to make the first move, I stood and waited. I shuddered inside as Lalonde slammed the manuscript shut, potentially crinkling the pages. At least he'd had the sense to wear the white gloves. Lalonde cradled the leather-bound red text in his arms and backed away from the steel bench. He had seen the knife.

Lalonde continued to step back. Then, as I predicted, he

46

found himself pinned against the wall of glass cabinets. The panicked expression on his face was priceless. I took a few steps forward, closing the gap between me and the text. It would soon be in my grasp.

A cold burst of air swept over my fingers as I clutched the blade's handle. I didn't flinch. Over the last few weeks, I'd visited the lab several times a day, accompanied as a guest.

'Hand it over, and you won't get hurt,' I warned him.

Lalonde inched towards the adjoining wall of glass cabinets, possibly planning to make a run for the door behind me.

I sensed that he realised the futility of his plan to make a break for it. My six-foot frame blocked the exit. As I crept closer, he froze and stared at the ground. And that was when he tried to make a run for it.

In a mad moment of panic, a frazzled Lalonde sprinted for the exit as I lunged, knife in hand, trapping him in the back corner of the lab. A warm liquid oozed over my hand.

I had stabbed him. I could have sworn the knife missed.

The *Commentary on Daniel* hit the white tiles and bounced around before finding its resting place, the very thing I'd wanted to avoid.

I pulled out the knife. Lalonde's face turned pale, and his blue-green eyes rolled to the back of his head. His body fell onto the white floor. Lalonde's head struck the ground as a small pool of blood formed underneath him.

The sound of metal grinding against metal filled the lab. *Kennedy, I know where you are.* I considered picking up the artefact and making a run for it. But I had a loose end to tie up. Those things were never pleasant, but I'd come all that way, and I wasn't going soft in the final hour.

A smaller figure shuffled across the side of the lab. I charged him, confident of my surroundings. As I got closer, Kennedy was cornered between a refrigeration unit and a wall.

He glanced up at me as I put the knife inside the left

pocket of my coat and pulled out the gun. It was jammed, but Kennedy didn't know that. And besides, there was more than one way to use a handgun. The thing with Kennedy was that he might come in handy. His brain might prove helpful later. So death wasn't ideal. I inched forward.

'You can take the manuscript. I know that's what you're here for.' Kennedy cowered near the floor. 'It's too dark. I can't identify you.'

'True, but I don't like to take chances.' I crept closer.

Kennedy looked up. A moment later, he shot up and sprinted to the exit, leaving his best friend and the manuscript he had worked so hard on over the last few weeks. He frantically slapped the wall, searching for the round green exit button that wasn't lit up when the lights were out. Most likely, that had been an afterthought during the design phase of the building.

I crept up behind Kennedy and hit him on the crown of his skull with the revolver's handle. As his body fell, he smacked his head against the metal door.

After I turned Kennedy over onto his back, his eyelashes fluttered. I wanted to check his pulse but refrained. I'd already left too much DNA behind.

I walked to the back of the lab. Lalonde lay in a pool of blood that was inching towards the manuscript. Just in time, I picked up the text. With care, I turned it over in my hand, stroked the cover, and sighed—new dents. Maybe the buyers wouldn't notice. I headed for the exit, and pressed the green button.

Whoosh. The door opened. I stepped into the short hallway and pushed the second button to unlock the first security entrance. A loud grinding filled the empty upper-floor office block as the electricity supply clicked over to the backup generator. The lights flicked on in the lab, revealing a trail of bloody footprints across the floor.

But I had the manuscript, and that was all that mattered.

By the time Lalonde and Kennedy awoke and were released from police custody, the *Commentary* and I would be long gone.

I strolled along the hall, down the stairs, and out of the building, leaving in the direction I came, with the *Commentary* tucked under my arm. As I reached the gate, I slipped the *Commentary* inside my coat and walked down the street outside All Saints, careful not to show my face on any CCTV that might be in the area.

NINE

THURSDAY: 1:08 A.M.

THE CHILLY EVENING breeze blew through my coat as I hunched over and waited at the first bend in New College Lane, exactly forty-four metres from Oxford's Bridge of Sighs. A bit too cliché for a drop-off point, I thought. For some time, the second streetlight in New College Lane had been out. I guess that gave the location its appeal. With the *Commentary* nestled inside my coat, I slid my hand into my left pocket and gripped the revolver as I waited in the darkness. The freshly cleaned gun was the perfect insurance policy if something went wrong. It was better to expect the best but prepare for the worst. That mindset had gotten me far in life, and there was no reason for it to fail.

There was something about the man I had met all those weeks ago. He was sitting by himself at the bar in the Turf Tavern. The tailored suit should have been a red flag. No one dressed like that anymore. He had an alluring smile, an American accent, and a presence full of promise. I could tell he thought it was a killer combination. He was smug, almost like a politician. I felt like a moth flying headfirst into a bright light, but it wasn't a sexual thing. My first instinct was to be wary. Instead, I had been lured in by his persuasive spiel.

And then there was the most peculiar thing of all, the mystery of how a wealthy American man knew about a mediaeval manuscript purchased by All Saints College. The only reply I received was "I'm an avid collector of things." And the more I thought about the situation, the more questions I had and the less inclined I was to seek answers. Perhaps I was being a bit hasty about releasing the *Commentary*. But it was too late. Eventually, the bodies would be discovered, and the police would hunt for the book and the killer. Possession of the manuscript would be enough to convict, so keeping it was out of the question. I had gone too far.

A black car turned the corner and slowly rolled down the narrow laneway. It stopped a few metres ahead, under the shelter of the footbridge. *Typical American.* The back passenger-side car door opened, and the American man stepped out. Then the driver's-side car door opened, and a tall older gentleman stepped out, stood in the background, and watched.

Interesting. So the old man isn't a personal assistant. Wouldn't a personal assistant open the car door? Something about the older gentleman scared me. He was always watching in the background, just out of sight. Only someone paying attention would notice him. And he was at least eighty, but he moved like he was twenty years younger.

'You're early,' the American man said as he approached me. 'I'm a huge lover of efficiency,' he added as he looked down the laneway in the direction I had arrived. 'I trust there are no loose ends.' He reached out as if expecting to receive the Commentary.

I nodded. Perhaps there was going to be no trouble. I needed to keep my paranoia under control. I released my grip on the gun, reached into my coat, and pulled out the book.

The American picked up the manuscript, caressed the leather cover, then glanced up at me. 'They don't make books like this anymore.' He opened the Commentary and carefully turned the pages, looking at the imagery and handwritten Latin text. 'It's beautiful,' he marvelled. 'And do you understand its secrets?' He peered at me.

'I'm almost done cracking the riddle.'

'I like you,' the American said. 'You say little, work hard, and don't leave loose ends.' He bowed his head in obvious gratitude.

'And the payment?' I asked in a confident voice, just as I'd rehearsed several times.

'Yes, I prefer to deal with cash. Keep things off the books,' the American said. 'I think it's the best solution for both of us. I will deliver your payment in a black suitcase. First thing tomorrow morning.'

It was interesting how all the measures the American took were for his own benefit and to keep himself out of the theft if anything should go wrong. But I had bigger and more important things to worry about, and one of them was cracking the crazy riddle in the manuscript's margins. It made no sense, but I needed to deliver on my promise. I needed to keep myself useful and valuable to him. Maybe Manesh had left notes. Hopefully, they were legible.

'As agreed,' the American said, 'we will meet again at the second location in twenty-four hours. I will provide you with your second payment and a one-way flight to New York with a visa so you can work on this at my company.' The man gestured towards the manuscript. 'It's been lovely doing business with you. I will keep in touch.' Then he turned and walked to his car.

Thank God he didn't notice the new dents in the book.

The American opened the car door and threw the Commentary onto the back seat. I bit my tongue and tried not to think of how the academics working on the manuscript would have a heart attack if they saw it being thrown into a car in that way, even if it was a Bentley.

I watched the American and his creepy companion reverse down the narrow laneway. The Bentley turned in to Catte Street before disappearing. After a few moments, I surveyed the area to check if anyone was watching. Then I walked up the laneway in the opposite direction.

TEN

———

THURSDAY: 1:18 A.M.

AMBER COOPER, a slender PhD student with thick, curly dark-brown hair, ascended the stairs of the research building, hunched over by the weight of the heavy books cradled in her arms. It was 1:18 a.m., and she had been up all night conducting research for her thesis on mediaeval and modern languages. Her thesis was due to be defended in two years, and she had the opportunity to study an original manuscript. Preparation was everything.

She had developed a reputation as a student who was prepared to spend hours studying to achieve top grades. Amber had always felt she needed to prove herself as an undergraduate because she was on a scholarship. She wanted to show that the university's money wasn't wasted on her. Because of her conscientious study habits, she found herself alone with very few friends, but she always found her associates in mediaeval literature friendly and obliging.

A few hours earlier, Amber had sent Manesh an email asking further questions about the thesis he had loaned her that morning. Manesh mentioned that he was meeting Liam in the Mediaeval Literature Research Laboratory and said she was welcome to join them. But time had slipped away, and there she was, ninety minutes later, trudging towards the research building of All Saints College.

As she reached the door and opened it, she noticed the entire office, including the internal staircase and the second level, was dark. A strange smell greeted her as she stepped into the building. The aroma was a nasty concoction of raw meat, urine, and stale beer.

She walked up the stairs then turned right and walked along the corridor in the dark, the smell increasing in potency. She glanced down the hall to her left and wondered whether someone was hiding in the shadows. The strange smell intensified as she inched towards the lab.

Her ballet flats shot out from underneath her. She landed on the cold floor, and her thick curls cushioned her head. Then something unexpected softened the impact on her legs. Her pile of thick textbooks flew into the air, over her head, and crashed against the wall.

Amber shuddered at the sound, fearing the spines and covers were damaged in the fall. A pungent, ironlike aroma overpowered her as she sat in a cold pool of liquid, shivers running down her spine. She had to look. She reached inside her tailored tweed jacket, pulled out a smartphone, and lit up the area with her flashlight app.

Amber sat up and surveyed the room. The smartphone trembled in her hands as she hyperventilated. She was sitting in a pool of blood, and Manesh's lifeless body had broken her fall. Amber moved the tiny spotlight towards the window. Rocks formed in the pit of her stomach as she stared at the man on the floor. He had been shot and lost an eye, and her hands were covered in his blood. Amber needed to clean up. She had an overwhelming desire to scrub her skin. She needed to go home and take her medication. Then she remembered the lab. She wasn't alone.

Amber shot up and dashed to the entrance of the lab and pounded her fist against the door.

'Liam!' Amber yelled as she thumped on the cold, thick metal.

A dull pain built up in her knuckles. The thick stench from the upper level made her want to gag. Then Amber felt something rise from the pit of her stomach and up towards her oesophagus.

She turned and sprinted along the corridor, down the stairs, and out of the building. Vomit projected out of her mouth, all over the path, and onto the Garden Quadrangle.

There was no going back inside and revisiting the carnage. With tears streaming down her face, Amber turned off the flashlight and dialled 999.

ELEVEN

DETECTIVE ALICE O'DONNELL sipped her coffee as she walked along the path towards the blue iron gate that closed off the garden square. She needed to keep her eyes open. She had been coordinating the crime scene at the university since she'd arrived at 1:28 a.m. Two questions gnawed at her. Why steal just one manuscript when there was a treasure trove within arm's reach? And what was so special about it? Crime scene tape stretched around the perimeter of the building. Two tall police officers stood outside the tape and guarded the entrance to the building.

'Detective Alice O'Donnell,' she said to the first police constable, who clutched a clipboard.

He checked his watch and recorded her name and the time she entered the scene. She walked over to the police vehicle, which was parked at an angle near the tape. Alice put a protective layer over her uniform and a net over her auburn hair. Kneeling down, she put on white plastic covers over her shoes. Then she pulled a fresh pair of latex gloves out of the box and put one on then tucked the other into a small plastic bag and slipped it into her pocket. She picked up her coffee and walked to the barrier.

The second police officer lifted the tape. She passed underneath and walked through the rusted blue gate, down the path to the open door. Alice took a deep breath and shook her head as she walked around the vomit spread across the pavement then entered the building for a second time that morning. Ascending the stairs, she was greeted by the first attending officer, PC Ellie Trotter, and the fresh chemical fragrance of the upper level.

Ellie trailed Alice as she walked around the obstacle course of evidence, marked by a series of numbered plastic yellow markers, and towards the lab and the victim.

'The pathologist, Dr Zach Dalgleish, arrived a few seconds after you left for your coffee. He's doing a preliminary exam before he takes the victim back to his lab.'

Alice nodded.

'As you can see by the smear, the caller, Amber Cooper, slipped on a pool of blood, which resulted in the body sliding over to the right by fifteen millimetres. A few hairs are mixed in with the blood from when she slipped. So there could be traces of her DNA on the victim. I guess I don't have to tell you how irritating that is going to be,' Ellie said as Alice hesitated, assessing the scene. 'Now, you're going to find this interesting.' Ellie walked down the corridor to the janitor's closet, where a pair of bright studio lights revealed a large smudge leading to the victim. 'We found gunshot residue on the ledge here. So the victim was shot and then dragged towards the lab access point, and then the eyeball was removed. All of this has been touched by the witness.'

Alice grimaced. 'Have you got contact details for the caller, Amber Cooper, and an address?'

'Yes,' Ellie said. 'I called Amber, and she mentioned she was at home. Apparently, she left because she had Manesh Warren's blood all over her and was scared that his killer could be nearby.'

'So she knows the victim.' Alice frowned and nodded at Ellie.

'Yes, he's an assistant professor and teaches undergraduate English literature classes,' Ellie explained. 'I almost forgot to mention this. According to Amber, no one told her to stay at the crime scene.'

'Nice. So Ms Cooper left a trail of evidence between here and her home.' Alice handed Ellie her empty cup.

'Most likely,' Ellie said as Alice pulled the clear bag out of her pocket, removed the second glove, and put it on.

'I want a copy of the emergency call.' Alice handed Ellie the bag.

'And Dr Dalgleish just pointed out to me that there are three sets of footprints. The interesting thing is that two of the sets appear to be the same size. Upon closer inspection, one footprint appears to be from a heavy military-style boot and is half a size larger. The other appears to be a thin ballet-flat-style shoe. His sister wears a lot of those shoes, which is why he recognised its pattern.' Ellie smirked.

'And the third?'

'It belongs to the victim,' Ellie said. 'And the mud appears to be from the same place. There's a patch of mud on the lawn beyond the gate. Both the victim and the perp must have walked through it.'

Alice surveyed the footprints. 'So they could have followed the victim?'

'Yes, that's what the evidence suggests,' Ellie said over Alice's shoulder. 'Zach would like to share a few observations with you.'

Alice looked behind her, and the pathologist had already placed plastic bags on the victim's shoes, hands, and head. In only fifteen minutes, the man had already completed the initial evidence processing.

'I'm Dr Zach Dalgleish.' He pulled a pair of headphones out of his ears then held out his hand.

Alice stared at him. Great, a newbie.

'I've already arranged for crime scene photographs of the victim, and I've recovered a few fibres from the hair.' Zach pulled the plastic bag from the victim's head. 'As you can see, the victim was shot here.' Zach pointed at Manesh's torso. 'I believe the victim was shot first, then the eye was gouged out using a knife, as you can see here by the sloppy work.' Zach pointed at the eye socket.

Alice leaned towards the gruesome discovery. *Is he critiquing the perp's knife skills?*

'A professional did not do this,' Zach continued. 'The victim was killed for access to the lab. We know this because the perp dropped the eyeball once they had access to the lab.'

'Hmm.' Alice walked to the eyeball and bent down to look closer. 'What about the time of death?'

'Not sure. I need to take the victim to the lab to get an accurate time of death.'

Zach pulled the bag back over the victim's head and followed the detective to the lab.

'The two men have been removed because they were still alive but unconscious, not dead.' Zach turned around and glared at Ellie.

Alice nodded. 'Okay. So James Lalonde and Liam Kennedy are alive and are now witnesses that need a follow up.'

Ellie blushed. 'I have the details of the hospital where they're being treated.'

'As you can see, the eyeball has been damaged upon impact with the floor, but the optic nerves are still intact. That's not a simple thing to achieve with a knife,' Zach said. 'The perp is someone prepared to take their time and do things right, with heavy attention to detail. But they're not a medical professional,' he added as Alice stood and surveyed the scene.

'What about those books?' Alice pointed at the textbooks near the wall.

'They belong to the caller because the placement of the books isn't consistent with the evidence of the murder,' Zach said as he studied the body.

'Is there any evidence of a struggle?' Alice walked over to the victim.

'There's no sign of a struggle. Also, the victim was facing the perp when he died,' Zach said over his shoulder.

Ellie called out from behind Alice. 'Here's Amber's address.' She handed Alice a piece of paper.

'How did she sound on the phone?' Alice crouched next to the victim and peered at the strands of thick, curly hair in the blood pool.

'A little freaked out,' Ellie replied.

'Do we know how tall the perp might be?' Alice faced Zach.

'It's hard to say, but somewhere between five foot eleven and six foot three inches.' Zach shrugged.

'That's a wide range.' Alice narrowed her eyes.

'It's just an estimation. I'll have more accurate results when I return to the lab.' Zach walked around and squatted on the other side of the victim.

'Don't disturb the evidence as you leave with the body,' Alice ordered as she walked the corridor towards the exit. 'I'll interview the caller. She sounds like a flight risk.' Then she yelled, 'Ellie, I need you back at the station!' as she strolled down the stairs.

TWELVE

UNDER COVER OF DARKNESS, a man in black crept through the hallways of All Saints College. A patter of feet and hushed chatter from the upper level disrupted the silence of the lower-level hallway—he wasn't alone. *The police must be searching the entire upper level.* He halted in the doorframe, clutching the metallic yellow handle, and his ear pointed towards the ceiling. *Shit. I'm going to get caught.*

The dull shuffling from above moved back in the direction from which it had come. He ambled down the three steps and into the research section of the building before closing the door behind him. The blue wooden door audibly protested as he sealed off the passageway between the adjoining buildings. Shuddering at the sound, he strolled through the sea of closed office doors, all bearing brass plaques engraved with names.

As he drew deeper into the building, the voices from the upper level became clearer. He hesitated, turned his head, and again positioned his ear towards the ceiling. Based on the chatter from above, police officers were tagging the crime scene and figuring out Manesh Warren's last moments. *Fingers crossed they don't sweep the building.*

After taking a deep breath to calm his racing heart, he

inched along the passage and stopped outside the third door. It bore a brass plate with the name "Manesh Warren" etched on it. Leaning in, he pressed his ear against the wood, hoping to discern the whereabouts of any surprise guests. *It has to be in here.*

With a trembling gloved hand, he turned the handle and pushed the door open. Stiffening, he braced himself for the worst-case scenario. He sighed as he listened to the stillness of the ground floor and the chatter from the upper level. Slipping inside Manesh's office, the man navigated the familiar surroundings, careful not to touch anything. *What a pigsty.*

He hovered over the wooden desk in the middle of the room. It was piled high with papers. He slid his gloved hand under the blanket of paper, feeling around. Finally, his fingers brushed the edge of a thick rectangular piece of metal. *Bingo.*

A faint rustle broke the silence as loose pages slipped off the top of the pile and fell onto the floor. He paused, listened to the room's noises, then continued to feel around the piece of metal. *Click.* The man released the MagSafe lock from the computer and pulled it out from under the sea of paperwork. After sliding the laptop under his arm, he walked out of Manesh's office and down the corridor and disappeared into the night.

THIRTEEN

ALICE STOOD opposite a grey-painted door in a three-story block of flats almost fifteen minutes from the crime scene. She had called Amber a few minutes before to confirm that she was at home. No sound came from within the flat, not even footsteps. Alice had noticed the witness was calm on the phone—suspiciously calm. She knocked on the door and waited.

'Amber, this is the Thames Valley Police,' Alice called out in a stern voice as she waited.

The light footsteps became louder as they approached the door. Then there was silence.

'Amber, I'm Detective Alice O'Donnell from the St Aldates Police Station. We spoke on the phone only a few minutes ago.' She listened for movement from within the flat.

Then Alice heard a chain sliding across a small track and the turning of a dead bolt. The door opened.

'Hello.' A pale female face peeked past the door.

'I need to ask you a few questions about what you saw when you discovered the scene. Just a few routine questions. May I come in?' Alice peered through the gap between the door and the frame.

'Yes, sorry.' Amber stepped back and opened the door. Her curly wet hair was in a bun on her head. She wore white floral flannel pyjamas with fluffy pink socks. *Great. She's washed away the evidence.*

<hr>

AS ALICE STROLLED across the wooden floor, her footsteps echoed throughout the apartment. She stood in the middle of the living room next to a flat-packed coffee table. A set of books sat in the middle, stacked according to weight and size.

Amber closed the door, locked the dead bolt, then slid the chain across its tracks.

Once she'd pulled out a notebook and pen, Alice made a few notes. A tingling sensation built up within her. She glanced up to find Amber standing close, watching with a hint of curiosity in her eyes. Most people kept their distance during interviews and at social gatherings. Regretful, curious citizens always took a step back after she shared her profession. People worried that she would jump out and arrest them. She preferred things that way. She loved being alone.

'Amber, why did you leave the crime scene after you called it in? The call centre operator asked you to stay behind for questioning,' Alice said. 'And I can see you've washed your hair.'

'Yes.' Amber patted her wet bun. 'I couldn't help it. I was freaking out.' She gazed at the floor.

'In what way couldn't you help it?' Alice's pen was poised over the page.

Amber ran a finger through her hair. 'I have OCD. I was concerned I might contract a disease from the blood. Something incurable.'

Alice scribbled a few notes on her pad, flicked the page

over, then focused on Amber. 'What made you think you would contract a disease?'

'Two years ago, I was diagnosed with obsessive-compulsive disorder. I guess most people would call me a germaphobe.' Amber took a few steps back.

'Really?' Alice asked with a hint of suspicion.

Amber rubbed the back of her neck. 'I'm seeing a psychiatrist for my illness. And I'm taking medication to stop my OCD from taking over my life.'

Oh, great. I'm being an insensitive prick.

Alice smiled. 'Amber, I'm just collecting your statement.' She pointed at her pad. 'At this stage, I'm trying to piece together Manesh's last moments. That's all.'

The tall, thin brunette in front of her sighed and released her hand from her neck. 'I know.'

'You seem stressed. Maybe we could sit down and have a cup of tea.' Alice gestured to the grey modular sofa.

'I'll make some chamomile.' Amber sprinted across the open-plan living area, past the white round table and chairs and into the small kitchen. Soon, the kettle hummed in the background.

Alice watched Amber busy herself in the kitchen then jumped back into the questions. 'How bad does it get for you? If you don't mind me asking.'

'It's hard to function and do everyday things,' Amber said over her shoulder. 'My medication has been a lifesaver. I ended up taking a two-year break between my master's and the start of my PhD.'

'You haven't mentioned why you left the crime scene.' Alice leaned over the arm of the couch and watched Amber stiffen her slender frame.

'I went outside to throw up because I didn't want to contaminate the scene. And I felt an overwhelming need to wash my hair. I couldn't help it. My hair was covered in blood.' Amber turned around. 'I ended up washing my hair and body at least three times. To be honest, I lost count.' Amber rubbed the reddened skin on her neck.

'And you're taking your medication?' Alice scribbled more notes and flipped over another page.

'Yes, I take an SSRI. It's an antidepressant. I had an emergency session with my therapist when I got home because I was struggling,' Amber explained. 'Thanks to the therapy and medication, I'm much better than I used to be. Now, I only wash my hands ten times a day.'

She keeps track of her hand washing.

Alice raised her eyebrows. 'Can I get your therapist's number? I want to ask a few more questions about your condition.'

Amber's eyes widened as she swallowed a lump in her throat. 'Okay.'

With trembling hands, Amber walked to the kitchen bench. She picked up the phone off the bench and scrolled through her contacts list.

'Here.' Amber headed to the couch and handed Alice her phone.

Alice glanced up from her notepad and grinned inside as she considered the potential answers to her next question. 'What did you do with your clothes?'

'Oh, I have them here. I put on gloves then put the clothes in a bag just in case the police wanted them for evidence.'

'Okay.' Alice continued to write notes. *The forensics team won't like this.*

'I'll get them for you,' Amber said as she disappeared down the hall towards the back room.

The wooden floors of Amber's apartment had that just-washed shine. Everything in the home appeared to be in place and organised. Alice's years on the police force had made her sceptical. Everyone was a suspect or at least a potential suspect. But the woman standing before her was different. *There's no way she could have done this.*

As Amber reappeared from the short hallway, Alice wrestled with her thoughts. Finally, Amber smiled and handed over the large transparent plastic bag. Upon grabbing the bag, Alice placed it at her feet.

'How did you discover the body?'

'I was walking down the corridor to the lab to speak with Manesh Warren,' Amber explained. 'He mentioned in an email that he would be there and said we could have a quick chat.'

'Okay.'

'When I arrived at the building, I noticed an awful smell. So I followed it down the corridor. The odour reminded me of the smell of a homeless person. I suspected someone had taken shelter in the building.' Amber walked into the kitchen and tapped the side of the kettle.

'Has that happened before?'

Amber opened the cupboard above her and pulled out two identical white mugs. 'During winter, people take shelter in the corridors. Sometimes, people forget to lock buildings.'

'What happened after that?' Alice's eyes were glued to her pad.

Amber walked to the coffee table and set down two coasters then returned to the kitchen. 'I saw something lying on the ground in the corridor as the building turned to the left. It was dark as I stepped closer. I slipped in what I now know to be Manesh's blood.'

'What made you think the blood belonged to Manesh?'

Amber picked up the mugs off the countertop and walked to the coffee table. 'I assumed it after I saw his body.'

Amber placed the mugs in the centre of the coasters.

'What happened after you slipped?' Alice gazed at her notebook.

'Something broke my fall. I looked over, and it was Manesh. His eye was gouged out.' A tear trickled down Amber's cheek. 'Someone must have wanted something from the lab. I'm not sure why because the items in the lab are specialised.'

Alice glanced up from her notebook. 'At what time did you make this discovery?'

'I think it was around one a.m.,' Amber said. 'Yes, I arrived at my office, checked my email, read the reply from Manesh, and made my way to the research building. That was at twelve fifty-five a.m. So I must have arrived around one a.m.'

'According to our records, you placed the call at one twenty-two a.m.'

'Yes, that's right. I ran outside to throw up, and then I calmed myself down. After that, I called the police.' Amber stared at the ground.

'Why were you at the university? Isn't it late to be studying?'

'This is the second year of my PhD. I'm hoping to complete the research in three. I like to be prepared and not leave everything to the last minute,' Amber said. 'My thesis is in mediaeval languages.'

'Okay, that sounds fascinating. Were you working on this when you went over to the lab?' Alice wanted to keep the conversation on track.

'I was studying at home but needed a few books from my office. About a month ago, Manesh lent me his thesis, and I had a few questions about it. He completed the same course a few years back.'

'And that's when you emailed Manesh?' Alice picked up the mug of tea and took a sip.

'No, I emailed Manesh before I left to go to my office at the university,' Amber said. 'I noticed the reply when I checked my email at my office. That's when I went to the lab.'

'Was Manesh the type of person to work until the early morning hours?'

Amber paused for what seemed like the longest minute.

'Not really. He's not an all-nighter kind of person. He's a morning person. Often, he's at work first.'

Alice nodded. 'Did he tell you why he was going to the lab?'

'Yes.' Amber nodded. 'According to the email he sent me, Liam had summoned Manesh to the lab. He didn't sound too impressed, but Manesh said it was okay for me to come and join them and we could talk about his thesis then.'

'Can anyone confirm you were present at these locations?'

'There's CCTV in the hall near my office,' Amber said. 'If they turned it on.'

'You seem calm considering your illness and the recent events.' Alice wrote a few more notes.

'I'm on medication. I can't function without it.' Amber walked down the hall. She soon returned, clutching a small orange pill bottle, and handed it to Alice.

'What happens if that doesn't work?' Alice peered up at Amber, who was hovering above her.

'I need to call my therapist and go to the closest hospital.'

After going through Amber's account of events, Alice slipped her notebook into her pocket and said goodbye with a promise to keep in touch to clarify things as they arose. As Alice left the apartment, she pulled out her phone and sent a text to PC Joseph Abaagihab.

FOURTEEN

AS HE AWOKE, a bright light from the ceiling shone directly on his face. It was menacing, like something out of an interrogation scene in a police procedural television show. Instead, he was in an operating room. He closed his eyes. A sharp pain pierced his wrist, and he flinched. James opened his eyes again to see a nurse in her late thirties with tight black curls. Her ID tag read Martine Bianchi. With a warm smile, she inserted an intravenous drip into his arm. Was she enjoying that? He closed his eyes as a sharp pain shot through his left side. The events from the lab flipped through his mind as the pain intensified.

'All done.'

James opened his eyes and squinted at the white lights. Martine darted to the door and disappeared.

A tall, thin man with caramel skin and thick dark-brown hair burst through the door. He wore a knee-length white coat and a hospital ID tag bearing the name "Dr Kumar Shah" and a photo most likely taken a few years prior.

'Do you know where you are?' the middle-aged doctor asked with a smile.

'Accident and emergency?' James narrowed his eyes as he attempted to read the small print of Shah's ID tag.

'Yes, you're at the John Radcliffe Hospital accident and emergency department,' Shah said. 'And what year is it?'

'Euh, 2015.' James lay back on the pillow.

'And what's your name?'

'James Lalonde,' he replied as Shah pulled out a small torch and shone it into his right eye then his left.

'No signs of concussion,' Shah told Martine, who stood beside him.

James peered over the doctor's shoulder at the short, petite Italian woman wearing dark-blue scrubs.

'There's something about you, Mr Lalonde. Perhaps I've met you before,' Shah said.

'Ah.' James stared at the man hovering over him. 'Not that I recall.'

'Thanks, Martine,' Shah said as she passed him a syringe.

'This will only hurt for a second.' Shah injected a clear fluid into the second vacant tube in his intravenous drip.

'What is that?' James asked as Shah pulled the needle out of the tube.

'It's a local.' Shah spoke without looking at James. 'I'm waiting a few minutes for the anaesthesia to set in before I stitch up your wound.' He pulled at his gloves. Martine reappeared, pushing a small trolley with an array of surgical tools wrapped in plastic and paper packaging.

'You remind me of someone I used to know almost twenty-two years ago,' Shah said as he opened the surgical tools on the metal tray. 'Her name was Emmanuelle Lalonde. She was a French model, tall and blond. Unfortunately, she passed away. She died from cancer.' Shah prodded the skin around James's wound with the surgical knife.

James flinched.

'The last time I saw her was during my first trip to New York. A few days later, her death was announced in the *Daily*

Voice. I guess I'm sharing this because your last name jogged my memory.' Shah smiled at James. 'Is it a popular surname in France?'

'Emmanuelle Lalonde is my mother's name.' James stared at Shah in amazement. 'And you saw her in New York?'

'Yes. I was in the New York Library, and she was in one of the reading rooms. The south, I think.'

'Where's my stuff?' James asked as he tried to sit up. The room spun.

'Here.' From the metal bedside table, Martine pulled out a plastic bag containing his clothing, phone, wallet, and keys. James opened the bag and removed his wallet. He opened the wallet, pulled out a photo of a tall blond woman holding a small child with curly thick blond hair, and handed it to Shah.

'Yes, that's her.' Shah stared at the photo. 'I didn't realise she had a son. But she was a private person.' He shrugged. The man seemed shocked to see the picture. Did he have a thing for her? 'And she loved fashion and modelling but hated the spotlight.' Shah handed the photo back to James.

'While we wait, you could tell me how this happened.' Shah pointed at the stab wound. 'The ambulance mentioned the police were involved and something about a crime scene.'

'I was in All Saints College's research lab with my friend,' James said. 'What happened to Liam? Did they bring in another guy with me? Is he alive?' James again tried to sit up.

Shah attempted to lay him back on the bed.

'I'll check for you,' Martine said as she left the room.

'The manuscript.'

'What manuscript?' Shah asked.

'I was in the research lab with my friend, Liam, and he was showing me a rare copy of a *Commentary on Daniel* by St Jerome. We discovered a few symbols and messages written on the margins of the pages. The inscriptions are only visible under the right lighting conditions.'

'Sounds fascinating.' Shah glanced at the clock on the wall.

'It turns out that we weren't the only ones interested in the manuscript,' James said. 'Someone cut the electricity to the lab, and a few minutes later, someone dressed in black entered the room.'

'Could you see the person's face?' Shah sat at James's bedside.

'No, the man in black was wearing a gold Venetian mask. My friend hid when we realised it wasn't Manesh. The hooded man stabbed me with a blade as I grabbed the text and tried to make a run for the other side of the lab. But we were trapped. There was only one exit, and the hooded man was blocking it.'

'James, you're lucky. While you were unconscious, I cleaned and assessed your wound and noticed the knife missed major organs and arteries. It cut into your layer of subcutaneous fat and, in your case, muscle.' Shah pointed at James's abdominals. 'Your toned abs saved you.'

Martine walked through the door and stood next to Shah. 'I'm sorry, but your friend isn't in this section.' She gave him a sympathetic smile.

James closed his eyes and tried to hold back the tears. *Was Liam murdered by the mysterious intruder? Who would want the manuscript? What's the significance of the riddle? Perhaps the intruder understood it.*

'We're ready to get started. You should feel a pulling sensation, nothing more.' Shah reached over to the metal tray beside him.

FIFTEEN

ALICE GRIMACED at the overwhelming smell of antiseptic as she sat in a polished timber chair and stared at the images on her screen. Her shoes squeaked against the grey linoleum as she shifted in her seat. If a person needed urgent medical attention, four o'clock on a Thursday morning was the best time. Not that accidents were planned. That was going by the next-to-no traffic within the accident and emergency waiting room of the John Radcliffe Hospital over the last ninety minutes.

Over her shoulder, a pair of brown eyes watched in silence. Heavy breathing disturbed the calm ambience of the waiting room. Glancing over at PC Joseph Abaagihab, she smirked. A bead of sweat trickled down his flawless dark-brown skin. He seemed nervous. Joseph tapped his fingers on his knees and gazed across the room.

Returning to her phone, Alice stared at the series of images Ellie had found on Instagram.

A loud snore broke her concentration. It wasn't Joseph. That much, she knew. In the far corner of the room, a middle-aged man leaned against the wall with a Red Sox cap over his face, shielding his eyes from the bright lights overhead. His long, lean legs were stretched out in front of him. She hadn't even noticed he was there until then. Maybe he was asleep.

Leaning back in her chair, Alice watched the lanky Red Sox fan.

Joseph nudged her then shook his head. 'Always suspicious.'

Waving Joseph off, Alice stared at the clock at the top of the screen.

'They'll let us in when the patient is conscious, not before,' Joseph said in a relaxed tone.

'He was awake when I found him in the room.'

'Alice, you barged into the emergency room and searched for James. What were you expecting to happen when you got caught?' Joseph held back a smile. 'And he was in shock and disorientated. Not in a fit state to be interviewed.'

'Know-it-all,' she whispered.

Joseph smiled. 'You missed me.'

Alice placed her index finger on her lips as she looked at him.

'No one will believe me.' Joseph peered at the smartphone in Alice's hand. 'I see you've already pulled up all the victim's social media images.'

She bit the inside of her cheek and took a deep breath through her nose. Glancing up at Joseph, she pointed at the second partially identifiable silhouette. 'He's a suspect.'

Joseph narrowed his eyes. 'He was stabbed during the murder-robbery. So that makes him a victim, for now at least.'

Alice showed Joseph her screen. 'You don't know who this man is, do you? He's an avid art collector. If we were in a comic book, he would be an eccentric billionaire who has money to burn. Which he does. But he also has a thing for the mediaeval period—swords, books, armour.'

Joseph shook his head.

'So what you're saying is, it's a complete coincidence that

this man has flown to England and was in Oxford and had morning tea with James Lalonde.'

Alice stiffened.

'Then later that evening, a mediaeval manuscript goes missing. Did I mention that it's one of a kind?'

Joseph pursed his lips as he looked over at the snoring Red Sox guy in the corner of the room. 'You think James Lalonde met up with this man to discuss the acquisition of a manuscript then was stabbed during a murder-robbery he staged?'

'You're deliberately making it sound ludicrous.' Alice shook her head. 'Obviously, they hired a third man, and James was present to ensure nothing went wrong. He coerced his friend Liam to lure Manesh Warren to the lab so the third man could get access and steal the manuscript, thus keeping James's allegiance with this man and the intruder a secret. It would be difficult for James to steal the manuscript from his friend while in the lab.'

Joseph sighed. 'You've heard of Occam's razor?'

Alice smirked. 'Nice to see your philosophy degree isn't totally wasted.'

Joseph stared at her with his dark-brown eyes. 'The explanation that requires the least number of assumptions is usually correct.'

'It's our job to consider all the possibilities and create theories.'

Joseph stood. 'I'm going to see if James Lalonde is awake and enquire about Liam's whereabouts.'

Alice peered over her shoulder as he sauntered to the white reception desk. He waved at the nurse through the panelled glass wall behind the desk. The nurse rose from her table and dashed through the open door. Concerned she would be left out of the conversation, Alice walked to the desk and hovered in the background behind Joseph.

The nurse's eyes widened. 'You're enquiring about the stab victim, aren't you?'

A rock formed in the pit of Alice's stomach.

'Yes.' Joseph smiled. 'Is he awake yet? We need to ask him a few questions.'

The nurse stepped back from the desk. 'Sorry, I didn't realise you were still here.' She peeped over Joseph's shoulder at Alice. 'He's gone.'

'What?' Alice grimaced as she observed fear flooding the nurse's eyes. *Now that's suspicious behaviour.*

Joseph glanced over his shoulder and smiled. 'I know it's not your fault. We'll catch up with him in his hotel room.'

A look of relief swept across the nurse's face as a loud siren raged in the background. Then she sprinted to the emergency room's double doors and disappeared. With a sigh, Joseph faced Alice.

'He's evading my questions. That's suspicious.'

'Perhaps.'

Alice narrowed her eyes at Joseph. He had been away from the job too long. Joseph was usually quicker at spotting police-evading behaviour. Sure, he was ultraconservative and liked to have all the facts, but Joseph seemed a little rusty. Before his shooting, he was razor-sharp, quick to connect the dots. She wondered whether Joseph had been pressured to return to fieldwork too soon. After all, it had been only nine months since the shooting. Poor Joseph. What was she going to do? She needed to question James alone. Biting her cheek to suppress a smile, Alice silently took a deep breath.

'If my theory is correct'—Alice bit her lip—'then he could tip off the other two individuals in the photo and the unknown third person, and they could leave the country. Interpol will not get involved with this. It's not high-profile enough.'

Joseph nodded. 'Maybe. It's strange that he's discharged himself so quickly.'

'I need you to organise twenty-four-hour surveillance on James. I want to know his every move. That way, if he is involved, we'll catch him.'

SIXTEEN

THURSDAY: 5:08 A.M.

JAMES GOT off his bed and placed his hand over the white dressing covering his stab wound. An hour after they stitched his injury, he discharged himself from the hospital. Dr Shah was furious with James's decision, but the doctor had to let James leave. James's release was, however, conditional—he had to rest. After an hour of being confined to his hotel room on bed rest, James was bored, and sleep wasn't possible. He shuffled across the room to the small desk to the left of the TV. Each step was more painful than the last. He opened his black messenger bag and pulled out a laptop. His hip twinged as he trekked to the bed.

James couldn't stop thinking about the news he had received from Dr Shah. *Did my mother die in New York? Are my grandparents lying to me? And why lie about the death of my mother?* If they'd lied, there must be something significant about her death. Maybe New York held the answers to those questions. Despite being born there, he had never been back.

When he was six, his grandparents had told him—after his constant questioning—that his mother had met his father in Paris, where he was born. But a few months later, James had discovered his birth certificate on his grandfather's messy table.

It listed his place of birth as New York. His grandfather was a stubborn old man and stuck to the story about his parents' meeting in Paris. His grandfather, Francois, told James the discovery was a shock to him. The intriguing thing about the details of his birth was that his father's name was "unknown." Even at six, he was sceptical. That day, someone deeply regretted teaching their grandson to read at age four.

James flipped open his computer and searched for flights to New York. Something was gnawing at him. Could he really trust the doctor's recollection of events?

A sharp knock at the door of his hotel room put an abrupt end to his search for the truth.

'It's the police. Open up,' a stern voice demanded through the door.

Rolling his eyes, James got up off the bed, wearing nothing but navy-and-bottle-green-checked pyjama pants and a white dressing on his lower left side. On the way to the door, James placed his open laptop on the desk.

James peeped through the spyhole and noticed a short police officer waiting on the other side. He opened the door and smiled. The police officers in France didn't look like that.

Her auburn hair was in a high ponytail. A pair of sharp green eyes and long eyelashes stared at James with a hint of scepticism. The black uniform outlined her petite but curvy figure. Maybe it was the uniform or the painkillers at work, but she was attractive. She can arrest me anytime.

'I'm Detective Alice O'Donnell.'

James gazed at the woman. She smiled, revealing a perfect set of teeth.

'May I come in? I need to ask you a few questions about the events that unfolded in the lab early this morning,' Alice said with a smile like the cat that ate the canary.

'Ah, yeah.' James stepped aside and watched her walk into his hotel room. He shut the door and followed her closely.

Alice pulled out a notebook and pen. After flipping over

several pages of notes, she stared at James, clearly ignoring his chiselled bare chest and stab wound.

'I went to the hospital and waited for hours before I was told you discharged yourself. You have a serious injury.' Alice raised her eyebrows.

'I've heard the same speech from my grandmother,' James replied. 'The wound is superficial.'

'Dr Shah didn't share your point of view. Could you please tell me what happened leading up to your stabbing?' Alice positioned her notepad and pen.

'My friend Liam was keen to show me this manuscript dated back to the twelfth century. He took it out of the glass case and showed me the pages. That was when we noticed a riddle written in the margins. I took a few photos. Would you like me to send them to you?' James gestured towards the desk.

'Hmm.' Alice grunted as she scribbled notes.

'Your number?' James asked with a hint of amusement.

She narrowed her eyes at him. 'Why?'

James shook his head. 'Aren't you supposed to be collecting evidence?'

Alice pursed her lips and hesitated. 'If I think the images are evidence, I'll just collect your phone.'

'You can't take my phone.' James threw his hands up in disgust. 'The images are on my French phone. I need it to contact my grandparents.'

'Does that mean you have two phones?' Alice squinted and wrinkled her brow.

'Yes. If my grandparents call me on my French phone, they get charged local rates.' James ran his fingers through his hair. 'They're old and find technology challenging. So it's best for them to call me on my French number.'

James clenched his jaw and took a few deep breaths through his nose. How was the existence of two phones suspicious? That was the problem with people who never left their hometown. The simple things in his everyday life were deemed strange. The existence of his second phone always meant he was hiding something. Every small-town cop he had ever met, with the exception of Anwar, had an issue with his two phones. And this woman was no exception.

Tilting her head, Alice grimaced. It was as if she was making the decision of a lifetime, like a contestant on that *Who Wants to Be a Millionaire* quiz show his grandmother watched religiously.

'I ought to stick to the correct procedure,' Alice said as her eyes lingered on the phone in his hand.

James sighed.

'It's for professional purposes.' Alice reached into the top pocket of her stab-proof vest, pulled out a Thames Valley Police business card, and shoved it into his hand.

James smiled as he strolled over to the desk, picked up his phone, and typed. He could feel her watchful gaze as he typed the pass code and pulled up the images.

'Are you planning on leaving?' Alice pulled his laptop closer and looked at James. 'You're not allowed to leave until this investigation is over. So I'm putting a hold on your passport.'

James rubbed the back of his neck. 'You can't do that.'

'If you try to leave, you'll be arrested for disrupting the course of justice,' she warned as she searched his bag.

'Detective, do you have a warrant?' James's hands were on his hips as she pulled out his passport and wrote the number in her notebook.

She didn't reply. Alice flicked through the pages of his passport.

'I was stabbed, and it was too dark. I saw nothing.' James hovered over her as she continued to scribble notes.

'James isn't a French name,' Alice said a few seconds later. She glanced at him as if expecting a reply.

'Congratulations, Detective. If you bothered to notice, I

was born in New York. However, my mother is French, and I spent most of my life living in Poitiers, France, with my grandparents. Perhaps that explains my English first name.'

'So, what happened after you discovered the hidden messages?'

'The electricity went out. Liam said it always happens and the backup generator would switch on,' James explained. 'I turned on the flashlight on my phone, and we continued to examine the book. That's when I realised the control panel for the door still had electricity.'

'What happened after that?' Alice glanced around the room as if looking for clues.

'The second security door to the lab opened. It was dark, and I couldn't see who it was. He was dressed all in black with a hood.' James peered at the carpeted floor, trying to recall the events as they'd happened.

'Did you see the perpetrator's face?'

'No, it was dark. The man was wearing a gold joker mask,' James said. 'Of the Venetian theatre variety.'

Alice raised her eyebrows. 'Was the perpetrator male or female?'

'What is this? Guess who?' James asked with a hint of frustration.

'Answer the question, Mr Lalonde.' Alice glared at him.

'I guess the person was over six feet tall, slim build. He was definitely taller than me,' James said. 'And he wore large, heavy boots, military style. Most likely male.' James threw his hand in the air.

'I thought you said it was dark?' Alice jerked her head up and studied his expression.

'Yes, but I could still hear.' James ran his fingers through his hair. 'The footsteps sounded heavy. And I could make out the shape of the person. I wasn't blind. My eyes had adjusted to the blacked-out lab.'

'What happened after that?' She fixed her eyes on her notepad and continued to scribble notes.

'I grabbed the manuscript and moved to the back of the lab, then he charged at me. This was when I noticed the knife.' James sat at the desk. 'I then tried to run to the other side of the lab.'

'What happened after that?'

'Are you serious?' James pointed at the white dressing over his stab wound. *Worst detective ever.*

'What happened after that?' Alice asked again, rolling her eyes.

'The guy grabbed me, and then I felt a stabbing pain as the knife left my body. It all happened quickly.'

'What about the manuscript?'

'Sherlock, was the manuscript at the crime scene? I think not because you didn't seem to know about it before I mentioned it,' James snapped.

'How do you know that?' she asked, looking up at him with a hint of suspicion in her voice.

'I'm an investigative journalist. It's my job to notice stuff like that.' James got up off the chair, glowered at Alice, and crossed his arms.

'What was Liam doing while all of this was going on?'

'I don't know. I was a little preoccupied with being stabbed,' James huffed.

Alice shook her head as she slipped her pen into her pocket, stepped closer to James, and stared at him. 'Remember, I'm watching you.' She tapped the centre of James's chest with her notebook.

'You do that, Detective.'

SEVENTEEN

AFTER LYING through his teeth to bypass the security guards at the giant blue gates along Broad Street, James walked along the path to the entrance archway, just as he had almost every week during the last year of his undergraduate degree. This time was different. Instead of visiting an assistant professor whom he admired, he was investigating the death of a dear friend. Since the riveting news about the block on his passport, the investigation was his only option for using his journalism skills.

The gentle morning breeze sent a chill through his body as James strolled under the archway. As he wandered across the Whittaker Quadrangle, he contemplated whether his time as the chief editor at the *Northampton Tribune* had made his journalistic skills grow stale. What had drawn him to journalism was his innate curiosity, his desire to uncover the truth. His need to expose the truth was born out of the darkness surrounding his past and the questions left unanswered.

James hesitated in the middle of the square as a realisation dawned. He hadn't thought things through. How would he enter the research building without a key or an appointment?

James sighed. He would figure it out.

He dashed across the quadrangle and through the second archway. In the Garden Quadrangle, a group of workers from a local self-storage company were loading archive boxes into a small truck. *Bingo.*

Hunched over, James ambled to the open blue door and slipped behind the second self-storage worker as she exited the research building. The passageway to his left was lined with ivory doors, all bearing engraved brass plates except for one lone door. White-and-blue police tape bearing the words "Police line, do not cross" was stretched across the door.

James stopped and listened to the chatter outside. Inside, the building was silent. After much deliberation, he sauntered down the hall. Upon reaching his destination, he hesitated. The chatter from outside the building had died down. From his position, he looked out the window. The quadrangle was empty except for a small blue-and-yellow truck far off in the distance. *It's now or never.*

His hand quivering, James turned the brass handle and opened the door. Ducking under the police tape, James surveyed the notoriously messy office of the late Manesh Warren. Loose typed pages had spilt over the back of his desk and lined the floor.

He sighed as a tear trickled down his cheek. This would be the last time he would find the office in such a state.

The floorboards protested as James tiptoed through the paperwork and to the front of the desk. James winced as the wheels of the leather desk chair scraped against the polished floorboards as he pushed it to the left. He assessed the damage. One piece of wood had moved back, revealing a gap in the floor. *Merde.*

James leaned over the desk and flicked his fingers through the top pile of pages. Then, after reaching underneath the mountain, James fumbled between the pages and the top of the desk. His fingers skimmed the leather mat that protected the mahogany desk from scratches. It was a long shot, but he suspected the police had found Manesh's laptop.

After releasing his hand from the piles of paperwork, James stepped back and slipped on the loose floorboard. As he crashed to the floor, his back struck the lip of the windowsill. A sharp pain shot through his lower back. While he was hunched over in pain, a sharp object dug into the back of his knees. He reached down and pulled out the piece of wood. The floorboard had come loose.

A mustard-coloured spine was nestled in the secret nook under the floor. James cocked his head and gazed at his discovery, taking his mind away from the ever-increasing pain in his lower back. It was a worn-out hardcover copy of Dan Brown's best-selling novel *The Da Vinci Code*. Not exactly reference material.

Sliding his fingers into the secret nook, James lifted the book out from under the floor. He gently brushed the dust off the jacket. As he grasped the spine and turned the book around, he found the pages were glued together. A faint blue glow shone from under the hardcover. He opened the novel to discover an old smartphone concealed in its pages. *Merde.*

This is the price you pay for snooping around—the discovery of secrets you wish you'd never known. Maybe it was his inner sceptic, but finding a secret phone was never good.

James lifted the device from its hiding place and stared at the screen. One message had come through. The details were hidden, but the number was not. A rock formed in the pit of his stomach as he gazed at the familiar sequence of numbers.

James tapped the screen to activate the phone. A set of nine dots appeared. Using his finger, he traced an L shape onto the glass.

After he gave it a few clicks, the screen burst to life and revealed nine applications. Exhaling deeply to calm his building anxiety, James tapped the messaging app and waited for the texts to load. His heart raced as he read the details of the only group of messages on the phone. After taking a deep breath, James struck the group of messages and scrolled through the contents. The last eleven words brought tears to his eyes: *I'm telling Liam about us, whether you like it or not!*

Manesh was having a long-running affair with Liam's girlfriend. Did Liam know about Manesh and Kate?

James surveyed the small office, pondering the events that had led him to enter a crime scene. The phone buzzed in his hand, and a small grey box popped up on the screen. He struck the notification. A fan forum materialised on the smartphone. At the top of the screen, a red dot hovered over an envelope.

James found a trail of messages between Manesh and another anonymous user by the name of "Da Vinci Rulz." Manesh discussed the *Commentary on Daniel* by St Jerome in considerable detail, from its value and discovery to the strange markings in the margins. *Merde.*

Hair lifted on the back of James's neck as he again experienced that feeling of being watched. He peered up and met the eyes of a familiar but unexpected guest. He was in trouble.

EIGHTEEN

THURSDAY: 8:30 A.M.

THE ELEGANT LADY Margaret Charlton sat poised in a leather armchair surrounded by a sea of mahogany furniture. James recalled his first summoning to that feared end of the research building. He was sure an expulsion was in the cards. He soon learned that the president of All Saints preferred to tear him a new one. It was a familiar pattern. That time, her large table was pushed up against the office's only window. Next to her massive desk was a classical French chaise longue, an antique. He was never too sure whether he should pay an entrance fee and observe her furniture from afar or sit. She nodded to the chaise. James strolled over to the couch and sat. He brushed his hands along the fabric. *Let the torture begin.*

Lady Margaret reached across her desk and past a trio of leather-bound books, picked up a teacup, and took a sip before returning the fine bone china to its saucer.

She gazed across the room at him. 'I remember the first time I heard your name. It was moments before I had to fire a seasonal lecturer.'

James blushed as he listened to her recollection of the events. Then he said, 'I was nineteen and flattered that this older, sophisticated woman was expressing an interest in me. It was an ego rub that I quite enjoyed.' James stared at the floor and cringed. 'Looking back, I would have accepted the love of anyone who offered it. But fast-forward ten years, and I see the inappropriate nature of the relationship and understand why you dismissed her.'

Lady Margaret took another sip of her tea. 'Why are you always in the midst of a scandal?'

James gaped in disbelief.

She held up her index finger. 'No, that's not up for debate.'

Shifting in his seat, James stuttered. 'I—'

'And I've also had to comfort my distraught daughters over you,' Lady Margaret said in a monotone voice, then she picked up her teacup and took another sip.

James grimaced. 'In my defence, I didn't realise your daughters were identical twins. I legitimately thought they were the same girl. They dressed the same. And Abbey was responding to Lizzie's name.'

Why does she insist on the trip down memory lane? It's worse than going to confession with my grandfather.

She frowned. 'And you're still peddling the same excuses.'

James leaned forward, rested his head in his hands, and stared at the pattern on the rug.

Lady Margaret straightened the pens lined up on the side of her desk. 'Do they still let you in the Turf Tavern?'

James sighed. 'Yes. All is forgiven.' He glanced up at Lady Margaret. 'I worked off the cost of repairs with a summer job.'

'Oh, so it wasn't a lifetime ban.'

Straightening, James took a deep breath and exhaled. 'I'll go out on a limb and assume I'm here because you found me snooping around Manesh's office.'

Lady Margaret pursed her lips and moved the teacup around on its saucer with her index finger.

James lifted his hand. 'I know you hate a scandal, but you have one coming your way. If what I've found comes out in the press.'

James hesitated as Lady Margaret stared at him with her cold grey eyes.

'Hear me out. I could investigate Manesh's death for you before the police and let you know what's coming your way. That way, you can be more prepared and orchestrate the damage control.'

Lady Margaret's expression softened. She picked up her teacup and took another sip. 'What's in this for you?'

A lump formed in James's throat as he nodded at Lady Margaret. 'The police put a block on my passport when they discovered I was planning on travelling to New York. So I have time on my hands.' James smiled at her. 'And I could sell a scaled-down version of the story with a brief reference to All Saints. It will have information the police aren't willing to share. You can read it first.'

Lady Margaret got up from her chair and walked to the door.

Merde. He'd gotten too cocky.

She opened the door and turned her head, avoiding his gaze. Taking the hint, James arose from the chaise longue and ambled to the door.

Lady Margaret glanced at James as he trekked past her. 'Oliver from IT is down the hall. He'll give you access to Manesh's computer and other work-related technology.'

James paused then raised his eyebrows at her.

'Amber can help you with your investigations.' Lady Margaret tilted her head down the hall.

He shook his head and laughed to himself. 'Amber Cooper?'

'Yes, she found the crime scene. Amber's experience was traumatic because she stumbled across the gorier elements of the crime. So be kind to her but not too kind.' Lady Margaret narrowed her eyes at him.

James grimaced. 'And she's coping well with her...' He shrugged. 'Condition.'

Lady Margaret sighed and strolled back to her desk.

'James, I hope I won't have any regrets,' she said over her shoulder.

NINETEEN

GREY CLOUDS BROKE OVERHEAD as a westerly breeze blew through his blue shirt and light-charcoal jumper. Summer was officially over. James gazed at the lush pale-garnet vine that crept out of the neighbour's garden across the red bricks of the terraced houses, thinking of the right words to ask.

That wasn't true. James knew the question he wanted to ask, but he wasn't writing a story. This situation was different, regardless of his promises. It was personal, almost delicate. Asking the most pertinent question straight off the bat was absurd. But he could imagine the response. James exhaled then breathed in the bucolic aroma of the vine. He knocked on the same door that he had fifteen hours earlier.

A dull grind followed by a rhythmic *click-clack* was the symphony that cried out from within the house. The door opened. A familiar pair of dark-brown eyes with long, thick eyelashes peered at him.

'James!' Kate sounded excited as she flung the door open.

She lunged and wrapped her arms around his neck then caressed his cheek. 'I'm so glad to see you. It's been such a long time.'

Grabbing James's hand, she led him into the house and sat in the nook inside the bay window. 'How have you been? You haven't changed at all.'

'Ah...' James hesitated, wondering how to explain the last few months and the lab break-in.

Kate squeezed James's thigh. 'I'll get us some tea.'

She brushed her hand along her green geometric-print dress then jumped off the bench and darted across the sitting room to the kitchen door. 'English rose?' Kate asked over her shoulder as she disappeared into the kitchen.

'Sure,' James replied.

Alone with his thoughts, James sat in the nook and stared at the back of the grey modular sofa. It had returned to its rightful position in the middle of the room, between the dark-stained coffee table and its matching entertainment unit. Since the awkward chat with Lady Margaret, president of All Saints, James had spent the morning searching for Liam, but there was no trace of him. The police had restricted access to the lab, and that narrowed down the possibilities. Liam wasn't in his office, the old college library, or any of the usual places. The police replied to all of James's enquiries with the standard answer featuring the rules for reporting a missing person. James reached into his pocket, pulled out his phone, and tapped the home button. He hadn't missed any calls, and no new messages had come through. Maybe he should call the hospital one more time.

Kate burst through the door, carrying the white wooden breakfast tray he had given them as a housewarming present when they first moved in. It held a transparent glass teapot and two light-blue cups with saucers. James smiled.

'You brought us this.' Kate grinned as if reading his mind.

James nodded. 'Yes, that was almost nine years ago.'

Kate flicked out the legs of the white breakfast tray and placed it on the light-blue cushion next to James, then she sat down on the nook at an angle. 'What's up? You seem a little preoccupied.' Kate wrinkled her brow.

He took a deep breath. 'Have you seen Liam recently?' he asked as Kate picked up the teapot and poured.

She paused. 'Is everything all right with Liam?' Kate placed the teapot on the breakfast tray. Her eyebrows drew together.

'Wow, you don't know,' James said in a shaky voice. 'An intruder murdered Manesh Warren to gain access to the research lab and stole the *Commentary on Daniel*,' James said as Kate's brown eyes widened. 'Liam and I were in the lab.' He stood and faced Kate. 'I haven't seen Liam since.'

'What?' Tears welled up in Kate's eyes. 'Were you or Liam hurt?' Kate stood and walked over to James and wrapped her arms around his waist.

'I'm sure Liam hid when the intruder entered. I was stabbed, but the wound was superficial.'

Kate gazed up at him. Her olive complexion turned white. 'Why aren't you in the hospital?'

'I was, but Liam wasn't there.'

She leaned back into his chest. 'He must be at the police station for questioning.'

'They're refusing to talk to me.'

'At least I know why Liam wasn't at the train station this morning.' Kate surveyed the sitting room. 'And the house was a mess.'

'I'm worried,' James said as his voice cracked.

Kate stepped back and rested her hand on his chest. 'Frenchy, you're so sweet, but I'm sure Liam is fine and is at the police station. He'll be back soon.'

'It's strange.' James stared out the bay window.

'What?' Kate followed his gaze.

A wrinkle formed in James's brow. 'He was wearing a gold Venetian theatre mask. The one without the bells.'

'Liam?' Kate held her breath.

'No, the intruder.'

Kate stepped back and struck the edge of the grey modular sofa. 'So the guy who killed Manesh and broke into the lab was a drama student?'

James grimaced. 'There's no drama course at All Saints.'

'Are you thinking of writing a story about this?' Kate's voice rose.

'Lady Margaret Charlton has asked me to investigate it for her. It's a PR-damage control thing.' James waved his hands at Kate then placed them on his hips.

'Wow, you saw her again, and she wanted to speak with you.' Kate smirked.

James smiled. 'Sorry. I shouldn't vent at you like this. It's not nice.'

'Tea?' Kate walked over to the bench, sat down, picked up the teapot, and poured. 'I think it might be strong. Sorry.'

Kate smiled briefly then bit her lower lip.

James sat in the nook. 'Where were you last night?'

'In London with work colleagues on a girls' trip.' Kate picked up the teacup and saucer and took a sip.

James picked up his teacup and cradled it in his hands. 'Where did you go? I'm planning on taking a trip to London soon.'

'The five of us went in and out of clubs in Soho. I wasn't keeping track.' Kate shifted in her seat. 'We were out all night, so I took the six o'clock train home.'

'You haven't slept?' James glanced out the window at the thick green shrubs in the front garden.

Kate raised her eyebrows. 'Planning on hitting a few bars?'

'What?' James leaned back. 'I'm a single guy.'

Kate's eyes widened. 'Oh—' She shook her head. 'You and Valentine broke up?'

Please don't make me talk about her. The break-up was too painful. With any luck, she wouldn't pry further.

They sat in silence and sipped their tea.

'I could search through the photos on my phone, view Google Maps, and try to create a list for you if you like.' Kate peered at him over the edge of her teacup. 'Are you sure it's Manesh?' She stared out the window at the empty street.

'Yes,' James said. 'The intruder removed his eye to get access to the lab.'

'None of this makes any sense,' Kate said, avoiding James's gaze. 'Why would anyone want to kill Manesh? He was such a kind and generous person.'

James rolled his eyes at Kate. 'Lady Margaret caught me snooping around Manesh's office.'

Kate swallowed something in her throat as she focused on him.

'I found Manesh's second phone.'

Her brown eyes glazed over, then she glanced away. 'You can't tell Liam.'

'I noticed a few disturbing things about his last text.' James cradled his teacup and tilted his head to the side. 'Did Manesh follow through with his threat?'

Kate placed her cup back on its saucer, lifted the teapot, and refilled her cup. 'One more?'

'Oui.' James held out his cup and watched the brown liquid swirl around the blue china. He grimaced as the teapot struck the white breakfast tray.

Kate took a deep breath. 'Yes. He was pressuring me to leave Liam. I've been with him for so long it's hard to walk away.'

James wrinkled his brow. 'Did he ever threaten you in person?'

'No way. He wasn't like that.' Kate's attention wandered to the floor.

He took a sip of his tea, considering his next few words. For once, he hoped to come across as nonjudgemental. 'You replied a few moments later. Do you remember what you wrote?'

'Yes.' Kate rested the teacup on her lap and sighed. 'You better keep quiet about this, or you'll ruin everything.'

'This doesn't look good for you. Especially if the police get hold of Manesh's second phone.'

Kate sobbed as she placed the teacup back on its saucer. 'He was going to ruin my life.'

'But didn't you do that when you started the affair?'

'It wasn't like that. It happened naturally.' Kate crossed her arms.

James rolled his eyes. *Well, that makes everything better.*

'You had a choice to put an end to it. This didn't just happen. It's a conscious choice.'

'I was angry, but I wouldn't have done anything. Besides, I think Liam knows or is at the very least suspicious.' Kate hung her head, avoiding eye contact with him. 'I don't need you giving Liam confirmation.'

James rolled his eyes. 'I won't do that to him. Besides, it's not my news to deliver.'

After placing his teacup on its saucer, James stood. He paced around the small sitting room. Then he stopped walking and faced Kate. 'What makes you believe Liam knows?'

Kate folded her trembling hands on her lap. 'Liam and I had an intense fight about Manesh one night in the Radcliffe library.'

'What was the fight about?' James leaned his left shoulder against the half wall near the stairs.

'I was working late the evening before I left for London. I was helping Manesh do some research. Liam came barging in, and he started yelling.' Kate slumped forward.

'Yes, I get that, but what did he say?' James asked, frustrated.

'Liam accused me of being more interested in Manesh than him.' Kate picked up her cup. 'This led Manesh to step in, but when it came down to it, he didn't have the guts, to be honest, like he threatened. Instead, he told Liam that it wasn't what it appeared and that he needed my help with research. After that, Liam yelled something about the conversation not being over.'

James ran his fingers through his hair. 'How do you think he came to this conclusion?'

A tear trickled down Kate's cheek. 'I'm not sure. We were super careful, and I deleted all of my texts. I guess he made a few assumptions.'

'Did you ever see them have a confrontation before this?' James pushed his glasses up the bridge of his nose.

'No, Liam and Manesh got along well. They were friends and enjoyed working together.' Kate stared across the room. 'I hope he didn't do anything stupid. But just between you and me, Liam has been butting heads with Manesh over the last few days.'

James walked over to the nook in the bay window, sat, and smiled at Kate. 'Liam didn't murder Manesh, because he died while we were in the lab together. Liam never left.'

Kate nodded and took a sip of her tea. Her posture stiffened. As her eyes wandered over to the door, Kate placed the cup on its saucer. 'I've got to go to work. If I don't leave for work now, I'll be late.'

After jumping up, Kate picked her bag off the step and dashed to the front door.

'Kate, I don't live here anymore,' James said as he stood up. 'Do you mind if I wait here for Liam?'

She froze. 'Ah—'

'I need to know if he's okay. I have no desire to involve myself in your relationship.'

With a shrug, Kate opened the door and hurried along the path, letting the door slam behind her. Still sitting in the room, James surveyed the empty house. He was growing restless. Suppressing the desire to snoop around the maisonette, James picked up the teacup and sipped the cold remnants of tea.

TWENTY

THURSDAY: 10:48 A.M.

JAMES STOOD at the bottom of the stairs and gazed at the first floor containing the three bedrooms. He glanced at the sitting room and recalled the first time he'd set foot in the maisonette—a happier time. Liam and Kate had just finished the first semester of their undergraduate degree and decided to rent their first home together. The same day, Liam asked James to move in with them. Together, all three of them shared the costs of the rent with their small student wages. His friends were in love, happy, and optimistic about their future together, a far cry from where they were today. James sighed and ascended the stairs to the upper level. *There's probably a special place in hell for people who rummage through their friends' belongings while looking for evidence of murder.*

At the top of the stairs, James turned left and walked down the short corridor and into the main bedroom. The door was wide open, and the room was neat, as undisturbed as if no one had lived in it for several days. A floral aroma with musky undertones floated past his nose as he ambled to the first bedside table.

Upon close inspection, he found that a layer of dust had crept in between the pleats of the vintage lamp's ivory-coloured shade and onto the white wooden letter *K*. Next to the letter was a small white candle in a glass jar. James clutched a tiny dark metal handle and listened to the dull hum of wheels spinning on tracks as he pulled out the drawer. It was deep, full of magazines and books. A small wooden tray rested on the grooves in the drawer. The usual items were present— lip balm, a packet of tissues, a hair tie, and a bookmark. James flicked through the pile. Nothing was hiding between the stacks of material. If Kate was as careful as she had claimed, then she wouldn't have left any evidence connecting her to Manesh in the house.

James closed the top drawer and opened the second. Crouching, he pulled out a pile of clothing that was neatly stacked inside. James sighed, dropped the clothes, shut the drawer, and stood. A slight shiver swept over his body as he walked around the bed, running his finger along the mattress, testing its level of support.

He stood in front of another bedside table, identical to the last one. That one had a wooden letter *L* shoved to the back of the table, hiding behind the lamp. A hardback copy of *The Last Templar* by Raymond Khoury rested on the table next to the lamp. James shook his head. *Obsessed much?*

James grabbed a tissue from the box next to the lamp and flipped open the cover to reveal an inscription handwritten by Kate. He slammed the book shut. A quiver built up in his stomach. Why had he promised to keep quiet about the affair? She would never tell Liam.

As James opened the drawer, an identical tray came into view. It contained a watch with a worn-out leather band, blue earplugs, and an eye mask from a Delta flight, evidence of their last trip to Miami. In the drawer lay a sealed packet of condoms, a pen, a pile of twisted cables, and a notepad. James grabbed the notepad and flicked through the pages—empty. He put the notebook down where he found it and closed the drawer. As he opened the second one, he noticed it was heavier than expected. It was full of hardback fiction books. James closed the drawer, sat on the bed, and surveyed the room. He sighed then reluctantly continued on his quest. Unlike the quests of Frodo and Samwise, his would most likely end in lost friendships.

James trekked to the small desk near Liam's bedside. It had no drawers, just a transparent magazine file, a plastic box file filled with paper, a silver computer connected to its power cable, and a small pot of pens. He flicked through the box file and pulled out pages of bank statements, HMRC tax statements, and bills. His fingers skimmed an unmarked brown paper envelope that blended in with the files.

After much deliberation, he pulled the envelope out of its hiding place and lifted the unsealed flap. James pulled out several pages of life insurance forms. He took a deep breath and placed the documents on the bed. According to the form, fifteen days ago, Liam had increased Kate's death and disability coverage by two hundred and fifty thousand pounds. *Merde.* What was he doing?

James returned to the desk and flipped through the files again. Blending into the brown cardboard of the suspended files was a mobile phone number written on a torn piece of paper. It read: *07530 457 690.*

He picked it up and put it beside the insurance documents. If he were honest, James had hoped to find incriminating evidence against Kate but not his best friend. Instead, he'd found a copy of a life insurance form and a mysterious phone number. *Is Liam considering an affair?*

James stared at the number on the page. Not knowing was getting under his skin. He pulled out his smartphone, then he remembered. He hit the home button and brought up a list of emergency contact numbers. Upon his second trip to Manesh's office, James had found the phone number of the mysterious Oliver from the IT department. It was a long shot but worth a try.

'Hello,' said someone with a thick Welsh accent.

'Is this Oliver Evans?'

'Yeah, it's me.'

James took a deep breath. 'I'm James Lalonde. Lady Margaret said you would help me with my investigations. I was wondering whether you can get me a little information about a mobile number.'

'Shoot,' Oliver replied.

'Wow, you can do that.' James raised his eyebrows.

'Yeah, I have a guy,' Oliver said with a cheery disposition.

James read him the numbers and grew tense as he listened to the rhythmic pounding of keys.

'Ah, Oliver, is everything all right?' James ran his fingers through his hair.

'Yeah,' Oliver said over the tapping sound. 'Do you want a name or everything I can find?'

'Yes. Name, occupation, stuff like that. I think it's linked to the lab or events leading up to the break-in.'

'Geez,' Oliver said. 'I'll see what I can do. I'll call you back.'

Oliver cut off the call, and dead air filled James's ear. He strolled to the tallboy between a pair of wardrobes on either side of the blocked-off fireplace. He opened the top drawer, ran his hand through the clothes, closed the drawer, and repeated the process for the second, third, and fourth drawers. Each time, James came up fruitless. Crouching, he pulled out the last drawer and rummaged through it. As he rifled through the clothing, his hand struck something hard and pulled it out from its hiding spot—a secret notebook.

In his hands was a limited-edition hardback Moleskine. James sauntered over to the bed, sat on the end, and flipped through the pages. It was Liam's journal, and it was almost complete. He skipped to the last entry. It was a recollection of that day's events, with no mention of the fight with Kate or seeing Manesh at the library. Perhaps the entry occurred after the fight. Maybe the fight didn't happen at all.

Fourteen pages later, he came across another entry. He stared at the page and read it several times, hoping he had somehow misunderstood. Liam had walked to the Radcliffe library to surprise Kate with a bottle of wine and a late-night picnic. Instead, he saw Kate and Manesh having sex in the reading rooms. In the journal, Liam recalled how he'd watched them through the ajar door. He described how shocked he felt and how he'd walked home in silence, feeling numb. By the time Liam was home, he felt differently. The last paragraph in that day's entry detailed how he'd smashed the bottle over the sink in a fit of rage. *Merde.*

James closed his finger in the book and rubbed the bridge of his nose. As a consequence of not wearing his glasses for several days, the strain in his eyes had become unbearable.

'Have you seen Liam?' a familiar female voice asked over James's shoulder, causing him to jump. 'I need his opinion on a piece of information for my thesis.'

James turned to find Amber standing at the bedroom door.

'How did you get in here?' James placed his hand on his chest and felt his racing heart.

Amber pointed over her shoulder. 'The door was unlocked. I just pushed it open.'

'Okay.' James stood.

Amber blushed. 'Sorry. I didn't mean to scare you.'

James raised his eyebrows. 'You're still working even though your colleague has passed away?'

She ran her fingers through her ponytail. 'Yes, I need to keep working on my thesis. I have a deadline,' she said in a high-pitched voice.

'I don't know where he is.' James sighed as Amber ran down the stairs, disappearing from view.

He shook his head and glanced around the room. Anxious

about Liam's whereabouts, James pulled out his smartphone and typed a text. *Is everything okay? Did you get hurt during the break-in?*

James stood and sauntered out of the room and along the landing. He paused outside the closed door of the bathroom and recalled the conversation he'd overheard the previous evening. Was it connected to Manesh's murder?

TWENTY-ONE

AFTER TWO HOURS of waiting at Liam and Kate's maisonette then wandering around town, James admitted defeat and stalked the quiet halls of All Saints, a quest he knew would be fruitless. He was about to leave for lunch when a savoury aroma of cooked ham and melted cheese drifted past James's nose as he drew closer to the English literature department's lunchroom. He stopped and listened to the chatter between the two female voices. Only one was identifiable—Amber. The tall, slender PhD student seemed to pop up everywhere. After he hesitated, the churning in James's stomach led him up the hall and into the staff kitchen. *Did she locate Liam?*

Leaning against the edge of the doorframe, James folded his arms and watched as Amber and a young woman held piles of thick textbooks, with toasted sandwiches wrapped in several layers of paper on the top. His stomach growled. He had eaten nothing since the night before. The two women dropped the books on the table.

'I'm starving,' the short, dark-haired woman said.

Amber pulled a chair out from under the table, sat, and unravelled the toasted sandwich.

Wow, she's calm. Is she on a new medication?

James uncrossed his arms and tapped on the frame of the door. Silence swept across the room.

'Hey, Amber.' James waved. 'Did you locate Liam?'

Amber blushed then swept a piece of her side fringe off her face and behind her left ear. 'I couldn't find him. I checked all the usual places including his not-so-secret spot in the Rad Cam.' Amber brushed her hand along the waxed paper.

James pointed at the sandwich. 'Queen's Lane?'

'Yes, it's still open. Same owners,' Amber said with a smile.

'I must pay a visit.' James strolled over to the table, pulled out a chair, and sat.

'Oh, sorry.' Amber placed her hand over her mouth. 'This is my research assistant, Matilda Grey. She's an undergraduate student working a summer job until the school year begins.'

Amber nudged Matilda. The tall, slender woman with elfin features tucked her short brunette bob behind her ears then shrugged. It was as if Amber had cast a massive spotlight on Matilda and the young woman wanted nothing more than for the floor to open up and swallow her whole. Amber seemed like more of an extrovert.

James smiled then nodded.

'How are you coping with the situation with Manesh?' He pointed at the upper level.

'Do you mean the assistant professor?' Matilda asked softly. 'If it's the same guy, he taught my Introduction to English Language and Literature class.'

'Yes, that's him.' James nodded.

'He was always rushing around, and I used to run into him all the time,' Matilda muttered as she teared up. 'It feels strange not seeing him walk up and down the staircase between the lab and his office.'

'It feels strange for me too. I used to visit him at his office when I was an undergrad. He was the same back then, always running.' James hung his head and tapped the table. 'The last time I was with him was at the reunion dinner.' James looked at Amber. 'You were there too.'

She nodded.

James's blue-green eyes glazed over. 'I wish I had spent more time with him.'

Amber smiled. 'That evening was intense, and a few people were arguing.'

'Manesh?' Matilda asked.

'Yeah, and others,' Amber said with a pained expression.

'I saw him on Wednesday morning,' Matilda said. 'Yes, yesterday. You remember.' She turned to Amber. 'Liam was yelling at him. Something about the library.'

'At first, they were yelling. Then they quietened as we walked past,' Amber said as she laid the toasted sandwich on the waxed paper. 'I think they knew we could hear them.'

Matilda finished a bite of her sandwich. 'It was about something more than an overdue library book.'

Amber grimaced and inched towards the kitchen wall.

James leaned forward and wrinkled his brow. 'Why do you say that?'

'Well, the last time I forgot to return a book, Kate sent Liam to chase me up. She's strict about that. Most libraries just give you a fine, but not Kate,' Matilda said. 'I guess that's only if Liam knows you.'

'To be honest, Manesh can be frustrating. He's messy and careless. It's enough to drive you up the wall.' Amber peered at her sandwich. 'I'll never have another moment where I get to tell him to tidy up.'

A clear film formed over Amber's eyes. James reached across and gave her hand a tight squeeze.

'Was this the first argument you witnessed between them?' James glanced at Matilda as he released Amber's hand.

Clonk. Matilda dropped the crust in her hand onto the waxed paper. 'Last week, I saw Manesh talking to someone, but he had his back turned and blocked my view of the other person.' Matilda tilted her head towards Amber as if she were in deep thought. 'It was from a distance. But his body language suggested that he was steamed.'

James murmured, 'So, the person he yelled at was shorter than him?'

'Yeah, I think so.' Matilda's pale-green eyes widened. 'As I walked away, they moved towards this building, and the fight continued.'

'I guess from what I saw last night, Manesh was probably having another fight with Liam about the book.' James leaned back in his chair and rested his arms on the table.

'No, Liam's taller. I would have seen him.' Matilda crushed the waxed paper and walked over to the bin.

James furrowed his brow. *I guess I could check the journal entries to eliminate Liam as the mystery person in this argument.*

'It could be Kate,' Amber said. 'She's shorter than Manesh and is the most likely person to pick a fight with him.'

'Although it could be anyone,' James said as Matilda walked out of the lunchroom, pointing at the upper level.

Amber leaned over the table and propped her head up with her fist. 'You seem worried. Do you not think the robbery and murder was an outside job?'

James frowned. 'No, I don't.'

Amber's eyes widened. 'Are you trying to tell me you think the murderer might walk the halls or grounds of this college?'

'Sorry. I don't mean to scare you,' James said with a sympathetic smile.

They sat in silence as James considered his next question. With Lady Margaret's words floating in his mind, he grabbed Amber's hand.

'How are you coping?' James sighed. 'Lady Margaret told me you discovered Manesh.'

Amber smiled. 'That's very sweet of you to ask. I'm on a more effective treatment plan that helps me cope with my

OCD. I'm in a much better place than when you last saw me.'

'That's great.' James nodded. 'Do you mind if I ask you a few questions sometime?'

Amber narrowed her eyes. 'Are you investigating Manesh's death? Lady Margaret wouldn't appreciate that.'

'Been there, done that, got the T-shirt.'

Amber laughed then blushed. 'If you like, I would love to help you. I want to know what happened to Manesh.' Then she shrugged. 'Maybe it will give me some closure.'

James smiled. 'I'll stop by at six p.m. or email you, depending on how my afternoon goes.'

TWENTY-TWO

THURSDAY: 2:31 P.M.

JAMES SAT on a black ergonomic chair and listened to the photocopier chug away in the background. Calendar printouts of the academic year were pinned on the soft-sided light-grey walls above him. A pile of bright-blue ethernet cables was stacked on Oliver Evans's in-tray. Oliver's light-grey hoodie, the official uniform of the IT engineer, was flung over the back of the empty chair. James shuffled in his seat. A sharp pain shot up his torso from his stab wound. He grimaced. The codeine was wearing off.

A familiar whistle floated down the hall. A lanky brown-haired man wearing a black *Space Invaders* T-shirt and skinny blue jeans sauntered towards James, holding a pastel-green cartoon alien mug.

'Are you sure I can't get you a cup of tea or coffee?' Oliver asked as he sat at his desk and sipped his tea.

Oliver jumped up from his seat as the photocopier protested with a series of sharp beeps. A few moments later, he came back with a pile of pages. Oliver placed the pages in front of his black keyboard and sat.

Facing James, Oliver grinned. 'You won't believe what I

found. I expected this number to belong to a girl. But it doesn't.'

James sighed. 'It's not good news. Is it?'

Oliver pursed his lips then exhaled. 'Good news for you, I guess. It's going to be a great story.'

Merde.

Oliver raised his eyebrows at James. 'The number belongs to a guy who operates under a few different pseudonyms. The most popular being Dr Teflon or Lloyd Waterhouse.'

James wrinkled his brow. *Why does that name sound familiar?* It was definitely a name that he had heard before his trip to Oxford. Or maybe Waterhouse was just a popular surname.

'He's a former pathologist who worked for MI6 who now operates as a killer for hire,' Oliver said as he stapled a pile of pages bearing the MI6 logo.

James's mouth hung open as Oliver slid the report across the desk.

'How were you able to get all of this information?' James asked as he flipped through the redacted document.

Oliver released the stapler's grip from another pile of pages.

'Lucy J. Knight was an investigative journalist who wrote a story on rogue MI6 agents for *The London Times*.' Oliver dropped the report onto his desk. 'Upon discovering information about Dr Teflon, the chief editor of The London Times killed the story. Several well-respected newspapers around the UK refused to print it.'

James shook his head. 'So she's a freelancer? Did she end up going to print?'

'She ended up leaking the files and the story online. Those redacted MI6 files were a part of the leak. Information about Lloyd Waterhouse, aka Dr Teflon, was among it.' Oliver pointed at the report in James's hands.

James grabbed his phone and created a new contact.

He glanced at Oliver. 'What are her contact details? I want to interview her.'

Oliver's face dropped.

James raised his eyebrows. 'What?'

'That leads us to the interesting part. Lucy went missing ten years ago.' Oliver slid over the next document.

Well, that's convenient.

'In your hands is a copy of the online forum where she shared the story. It has all the links and replies from the forum's members.' Oliver turned to his keyboard and typed his credentials on the lock screen.

James rubbed his fingers through his hair as he flipped through the reports. As damning as all of the recent information was, it wasn't proof that Liam had hired a rogue agent turned hit man. Since James was a journalist, it was his job to uncover the truth. The ethics of his next steps weighed on him. James's chest tightened as he stared at Oliver.

'Is everything okay?'

'None of this is proof that Liam hired Dr Teflon. Just that he had possession of this number.' James arose from the chair and paced the short corridor in front of Oliver's cubicle.

James faced Oliver. 'It's not evidence that he searched for the number. He could have got it from'—James lifted his arm in the air—'a stranger in a pub.'

Oliver stood and trekked to the door and closed it. Then, in silence, he ambled to his desk and stopped opposite James. 'I know a guy who can access phone records. No questions asked.'

James's shoulders tensed. 'Really?'

Oliver nodded. 'Yeah. I get it. You want to be sure before you throw your friend under the bus. Especially if you're going to throw Liam into Lady Charlton's den.'

What am I doing? Oliver was right. He was the worst friend in the world.

A rock formed in the pit of James's stomach. It would be so much easier if he weren't investigating Liam.

James shrugged. 'Who's your guy?'

Oliver smirked. 'Me'

James's mouth hung open.

'It's why Lady Margaret asked me to help you. She likes to know everything.' Oliver walked over to his desk and sat. 'I can see you're torn up over this, so I'll spare you the details and get back to you about whether Liam contacted the agent.'

James nodded. 'Can you give me a printout as proof? Just in case.'

Oliver nodded.

James sighed. 'This is going to seem like a strange question, but did you ever witness Manesh arguing with anyone in the weeks leading up to his murder?'

'Yes, but it wasn't an uncommon occurrence. Manesh could be, on occasion, quite divisive.' Oliver gazed off into the distance. 'He seemed to love confrontation. But over the years, I think he's gotten better at biting his tongue. At least, I thought so.'

James narrowed his eyes. 'So you saw him arguing with someone?'

Oliver grimaced and tilted his head in a rocking motion. 'I was in Lady Margaret's office for the millionth time, waiting for the computer to load. I was sipping my tea, and I heard incoherent shouting from below. When I peered out the window, I noticed that Manesh was having another row with someone. Based on the red mop of hair, I'm guessing it was Liam. They were too far away. But I recognised Manesh's jacket instantly.'

James took a deep breath. *Merde.*

Oliver smiled and pointed at his tabletop. 'Do you want to check Manesh's computer while you're here? I need to reset his password.'

James pursed his lips. 'Why do you have Manesh's laptop? I thought the police would have taken it as evidence. Did he put it in for a service or something?'

Oliver sighed. 'I got a frantic call from Lady Margaret asking me to get Manesh's computer before the police found it. Apparently, the caretaker called her the second the police showed up at the college.'

'And you snuck in and stole it. No questions asked?' James nodded as a tight expression swept across his face.

Oliver exhaled. 'It's better if you do what she wants. If you don't, she'll find a reason to fire you.'

Nice to see she hasn't changed.

Another thought came to James's mind. 'Is it okay if I try to guess the password? I have a theory based on how easy it was to access his hidden phone.'

'Sure.' Oliver leaned to his right, pulled the handle of the bottom drawer, and lifted out a silver laptop. He flipped open the lid and slid it across to James.

James typed in the word "Catherine," and the computer's welcome tune chimed as the apps materialised on the screen. *Merde, Manesh was obsessed with Kate.*

James opened the internet browser and waited as the All Saints email portal opened.

'His passwords are saved into the browser. He's not into web security,' James said over his shoulder as he pressed Enter.

'Nope,' Oliver replied as he hovered over James's shoulder.

'Wow, he sends Tom Noble regular emails.' James clicked on the sent items box on the screen. His eyes widened as he scrolled through the list of emails.

'Who is that?' Oliver leaned towards the screen.

James sighed as he closed his eyes. 'Another one of my friends from university.'

Oliver whistled as he stared at the screen. 'Is he still in Oxford?'

'Yes, he was in Oxford last night. He was attached to his phone and left early. He left his new girlfriend with us in the Turf Tavern,' James said as he recalled the previous evening.

Oliver pursed his lips and tapped his fingers on the table. 'Is Tom a bit of a workaholic?'

'Not since I've known him. He's always been a minimum-effort type of guy.' James clicked on the email and scanned the page.

'Wait.' Oliver grimaced. 'How did he get in? All Saints is more than just a minimum required effort.'

James hesitated. 'His father is Baron Andrew Noble. He's an alumnus.'

'Sorry, I don't know who that is.' Oliver leaned over James and stared at the screen.

James tapped the tabletop. 'He's a huge investor in this college. The Nobles have been attending All Saints since the school's founding.'

Oliver wrinkled his brow. 'Why does a rich kid owe an assistant professor twenty thousand pounds?'

'Good question.' James stared at the computer screen.

Oliver pointed at the screen. 'Manesh has been chasing him for months. Once a week.'

'But he doesn't always reply.' James hunched forward and tapped on the screen.

Oliver reached out and adjusted the angle of the laptop. 'Does he give excuses?'

'Just the usual ones. Waiting for money to come in from work. Then Tom said he lost his job, and a few days ago, Tom said he was waiting for a cheque.'

A digital sci-fi-inspired tone caused Oliver to jump. He patted his pockets. 'Sorry. I'd love to stay and chat, but I have a meeting about the installation of All Saints' new server.' Oliver patted his jeans, pulled out a set of keys, slipped off a tiny key, and handed it to James. 'This is the key to my desk drawers just in case you need the laptop. I'll keep the laptop in here. Let me know if you need more of my help.' Oliver gave James a thumbs-up then waltzed down the corridor, leaving James at his desk.

TWENTY-THREE

THURSDAY: 5:42 P.M.

MUCH TO HIS SURPRISE, it didn't take long for James to convince Amber to help with his investigation. Around three o'clock that afternoon, James found her staring off into the distance at her desk, surrounded by her usual pile of books. She had seemed to welcome the break, which was strange. Amber usually focused on studying. That was how he remembered her back in the day. Perhaps people changed after all.

They agreed to meet up after five in the foyer of the Macdonald Randolph Hotel. James did not, however, count on her intern, Matilda Grey, inviting herself along. After he mentioned the magic words "Lady Margaret Charlton" and the request she'd made in her office, Matilda backed off. Despite her sudden change of heart about inviting herself along, Matilda seemed annoyed, almost angry.

While waiting for Amber, James conducted three hours of research and called many antique dealers around Oxfordshire. It was a fruitless and disappointing three hours. James admitted defeat and decided he couldn't put off interviewing his friends any longer. Finding the manuscript at an antique dealer around Oxford was a long shot that would not pay off. Only an idiot would sell the *Commentary on Daniel* to a dealer, and the figure in black was not an idiot—his actions seemed well thought out. The break-in was planned. Or maybe his own traumatic memories gave the crime that appearance. James was too close to the story. He had to distance himself and remain objective.

A sharp pain shot through his side as he ambled to the wardrobe. He winced. In the reflection of the mirror on the wall, James watched Amber stand off to the side, glancing around the room, uncertainty in her eyes.

'Amber, take a seat,' James said over his shoulder as he crouched and struck the keys on the numerical pad.

The door to the safe in hotel room 223 opened, revealing the hollowed-out copy of *The Da Vinci Code*. James picked up a pile of documents, slipped them underneath the book, closed the door, struck the combination, and listened to it click. As he stood and closed the closet doors, Amber's slender, trembling frame caught his eye in the mirrored panels. *Merde, this isn't a good idea.*

James smiled at her.

Amber brushed her hand along her navy-checked shirt and dark-washed jeans. Her hands trembled. She was anxious. Why hadn't he considered that?

'Aren't we going to get in trouble with the police for this?' she asked as James ambled across the room and sat on the edge of her grey armchair.

He placed his arm around her. 'I've done this before. It's my job. Everything is going to be fine. We're just asking a few questions. That's all.'

James rubbed Amber's back as she stared at her clenched hands resting in her lap. James stood up, walked to the bed, sat opposite Amber, and smiled. She lifted her head and gazed at him with her widened hazel eyes.

'You don't have to come with me. I can tell you're

frightened, and that's okay,' James said. 'But if you come, know I won't put you in immediate danger.'

Amber swallowed, nodded, and straightened. Uncurling her clenched hands, she stood and pushed her black frames up the bridge of her nose.

'I want to do this,' she said.

Her curly brown ponytail bounced as she nodded. She placed her hands on her thin beige belt and stared into the distance. It was as if she was psyching herself up.

She's surprisingly attractive. Focus, idiot. No more distractions. Stick to the investigation, and keep things professional.

James raised his eyebrows. 'Let's do this.'

———

JAMES STOOD opposite the door of hotel room 322, with Amber by his side. Leaning in, he listened to a zipping sound and the rustling of plastic. Raising his finger to his lips, James leaned in a little closer. Amber stepped behind him as he inched towards the door. He turned his head over his shoulder and mouthed, "He's packing." He knocked on the door. The room fell silent. *Shuffle, shuffle.* A pair of feet ambled towards the door from within the room. A latch released, and the feet strolled away. James raised his eyebrows at Amber, who shrugged.

'It's open,' a voice said from inside the room.

James pushed the door open and strolled inside. The hotel room was tiny, holding just a double bed, two matching armchairs, and a bathroom. The room was a far cry from the luxury he had expected of Tom Noble. His friend hunched over a small matte-gold suitcase with a floral travel label bearing the words "Georgiana Burke." The suitcase lay open on the pin-striped white duvet. Fastened to the side handle was a brand-new JetBlue Airways label.

'Where are you going?' James watched as Tom overstuffed his suitcase.

Tom sprinted to the open closet. 'Georgiana was upset and left for London, and I need to pack and run after her.'

James grimaced. 'What is she upset about?'

Tom dashed to the bed with a small pile of clothes. 'Maybe the murder. She doesn't feel safe.'

'Lady Margaret has asked me to investigate Manesh's death,' James said as he hung his head, bracing for the inevitable kickback.

Tom gritted his teeth then exhaled. He turned to James. His cold, brown eyes glared at him. 'That's perfect for you. You always seem to enjoy sticking your nose in other people's business,' Tom said in a calm but aloof tone.

Merde.

James took a deep breath and straightened. 'I was in Manesh's office this morning and stumbled upon an email exchange between you and him. He was hounding you about your debt.'

Tom's expression went blank. He continued to pack. 'Your point?'

James rolled his eyes. 'I'm trying to eliminate you as a suspect. You know how this looks.'

Tom marched up to James and stopped an inch from his face. The onion flavour on his breath made James wince. Despite James's reaction, Tom continued to stare.

'Why should I talk to you? Leave it to the police.' Tom sauntered past James then paused. 'What are you doing here?' Tom asked Amber as he made his way to the closet.

James shook his head as he saw Amber's eyes glaze over. 'Leave her alone.'

Tom smirked. 'Ah, your next victim.'

He strutted to the bed and dropped a pair of pyjamas on top of the suitcase.

James sighed. 'What are you going to do when the police

like you for the murder? I assumed you would want me to figure it out before it came to that.'

'Fine,' Tom said through gritted teeth. 'I'm still going to pay back the money.'

Amber tilted her head. 'Tom, he's no longer with us.'

Tom exhaled. 'I realise that. I'm going to pay it back to his family.'

'So you have the money for him?' James asked. 'Why don't you just transfer it?'

'Because I want it to go to his family.' Tom's tone was sharp.

'I know you don't have the money to pay him back,' James said as Tom leaned over the suitcase and sighed.

'I have the money,' Tom said over his shoulder.

'Your luggage is in your girlfriend's name, and you're flying JetBlue. They're a discounted airline.' James walked up to Tom's bag and grabbed the airport tag.

Tom slammed the suitcase shut. 'Whatever.'

'Why did you borrow the money?' Amber asked. 'Manesh's worse than a high-interest loan. He's relentless and without remorse.'

'That's none of your business.' Tom pushed down on the suitcase to close it.

James sat on the armchair beside the small mahogany table. Tom's small room was almost identical to his.

'It's a business investment,' Tom snapped at James.

'An investment is returned over time. Manesh's father is an entrepreneur. He would know that.' James brushed the smooth fabric on the chair.

'You don't know Manesh as well as you think you do. Do you know what it's like to have him chase you?' Tom inched towards James.

The suitcase flipped open, and the top layer of clothes spilt out on the bed.

'What was the money for?' James asked in a harsh tone.

'I've got a gambling problem.' Tom stepped closer to James.

James took a step back as Tom crept closer and narrowed his brown eyes at him.

Upon reaching the chair, he picked James up by the collar of his navy-blue bomber jacket. 'Are you satisfied?'

Amber gasped then inched closer to James. 'Why didn't you ask your father for money?'

Tom glared at her. 'He cut me off.'

'You gambled away your entire inheritance?' James placed his hands on Tom's chest and pushed him away.

'Don't be stupid. The old goat froze my funds. The baron didn't want me to take the entire family down with me.' Tom stumbled backwards.

'What are you going to do now? Does Georgiana know?' James smoothed out the wrinkles in his bomber jacket.

'Of course not. I live with my sister and her boyfriend. She felt sorry for me, so she took me in.'

'How long have you been living with your sister?' Amber asked, stepping in between James and Tom.

'Two months.' Tom returned his attention to his suitcase.

James slipped his phone out of the pocket on the side of his jacket. 'What's her address?'

'What?' Tom turned around and glared at James.

'Her address,' James demanded.

Tom groaned. 'You're not going to let this go.'

That was the difficult part of every story he had ever written—trying to pry information out of people who didn't want to talk to the press. And he didn't blame them. No one wanted to be misquoted or doxed by crazy online trolls with time on their hands. But this time was different. If he didn't get the information Lady Margaret wanted, she would replace him with someone else. That someone else wouldn't care about family drama or reputations. Why couldn't Tom see that?

'Tom, if I don't do this, Lady Margaret will replace me with someone else. And that person won't care about your struggles or your difficult relationship with your father. You remember what she was like?'

Tom scowled. 'I've been staying at a rehab facility in Glasgow. No internet connection, nothing. My father made me go. And he said that if I get better and stop gambling, he'll consider reinstating my funds.' Tom returned to his suitcase, pushed the clothes in, and zipped it.

James narrowed his eyes. 'What made him change his mind? It's not something he often does.'

Tom's face softened. 'My mother.'

James smiled and hoped his next words wouldn't come across as insensitive. 'Look, I believe you. I just need the contact details, to double-check.'

Tom angled his ear towards James. 'Sorry?'

'We need to check this out so we can eliminate you as a suspect,' James said.

Tom's face flushed as he slipped a business card out of his back pocket. He handed it to James, and it listed the contact details of a therapist, Dr Archibald McKay. 'He's a resident. He works there all the time.'

'Where did you go after you left the pub early?' James asked.

'I tried to call Manesh, but he didn't pick up, so I went to his office. He wasn't there, so I went home.'

James opened the notepad app. 'What time was that?'

'Around eleven p.m.'

'What did you do for the rest of the evening?'

'Don't make me say it.'

'Tom, if you have an alibi for the time of Manesh's murder, just tell me. No one will tell the baron.' James shook his head.

Tom exhaled. 'Where do you think your findings will end

up?' Tom waved his arms in the air. 'The baron. He's the college's biggest investor.'

'I'll tell Lady Margaret to leave it out of her report.' James inched closer to Tom. 'Trust me. She doesn't want a scandal.'

'I'm a gambling addict who hasn't had internet access for two months. What do you think I did?'

Amber winced. 'You were gambling online?'

'Yes,' Tom said. 'All night. You can check with the front desk or check their service provider. It will show you the truth. That's how I got fired from work. I was gambling on work time and using a secure search browser. I was caught by IT and dismissed.'

James placed his arm around Tom. 'How long have things been like this for you?'

'Why don't you both leave and spare me further humiliation?' Tom pointed at the door. Tears welled up in his eyes and trickled down his cheeks.

'Tom, I do care about you,' James said with a sympathetic smile.

'I don't care.' Tom sighed.

James strolled to the door with Amber right behind. He grabbed the handle.

'Two years,' Tom said as he slid the suitcase off the bed.

TWENTY-FOUR

ALICE JUMPED as an icy hand rested on her shoulder, almost spilling her cup of cold coffee. She turned to see a set of perfect white teeth smiling back at her. 'You scared me.'

'Alice, he's been at the station for over four hours. You need to release him. It's not right.' The short dark-skinned man glanced through the one-way mirror at the ginger-haired man cuffed to the desk.

She stared straight ahead, considering her options. It was important to come across as authoritative and not use a nice-cop routine, especially after the events at the crime scene and her investigations into the backgrounds of everyone involved.

'Alice,' Joseph said in a smooth, soothing tone.

She turned the knob on the heavy silver door to the interrogation room at St Aldates Police Station and stepped into the room. Without uttering a word, Alice sat, slammed her police-logo coffee cup on the table, pressed Record, and then hit Stop. A robotic hissing played over the speaker in the room as Alice hit the replay button. She pressed Rewind then struck Record once more. As she sat, Alice pulled the manilla folder bearing the police logo out from under her arm and slammed it on the table.

'The interview with Liam Kennedy is starting at 5:47 p.m.' Alice gazed at the clock on the wall behind Liam. 'Thank you for agreeing to come down to the station.'

Liam grunted as his foot bounced under the table.

'Please start off by going through your evening in the lab until you came to be at the station,' Alice said as she read the open file.

'Okay, I was in the lab with James, and I had emailed Manesh. I asked him to meet us in the lab to discuss the *Commentary on Daniel* by St Jerome.' Liam stared at the table. 'Manesh is the leading expert on the *Commentary*. He's the best person to answer questions and explain its significance.' Liam lifted his head and gazed into the distance as if choosing his words. 'While we were waiting, James discovered a hidden message in the margin of a few of the pages. Considering the *Commentary's* age, whoever wrote it used lemon juice or something similar.'

Alice pursed her lips. 'Why did you take James to the lab? He doesn't work for All Saints. Did he express an interest in seeing it, for instance?'

Liam screwed up his face. 'No, I was excited to show him what I was working on. The manuscript is a rare find. I practically dragged him to the lab.'

Alice peeked at the red numbers on the recording timer. 'What happened next?'

'The lights went out. There's been a lighting problem, and we put in a request for it to be serviced. We kept examining the manuscript while we waited for Manesh. I heard a faint bang, but I assumed it was the generator.'

'And how did your guest react to all of this?'

'He panicked, but I reassured him it wasn't a big deal.'

'You could see well without the lights?' Alice peered at the glass panel separating the interrogation room from the observation room.

'No. There was a light from the exit sign, but it wasn't

helpful. James used a flashlight app on his phone. It was bright enough to see the page in front of us. That's when the intruder came in. James had turned off the flashlight. We both turned around, expecting to see Manesh,' Liam said. 'I'm finding it difficult to patch together the events. But I'm sure after noticing the black-hooded coat, I ducked down next to the table. Next, I heard some scrambling and a gasp. As I surveyed the lab, I saw James was stabbed, and he dropped the manuscript. While the intruder was distracted, I ran to the other side of the lab. After that, I remember little else.'

Alice narrowed her eyes. 'Could you see the intruder's face?'

Liam bit his lip. 'To be honest, I don't remember.'

'Okay.' Alice gazed across the table, picked up her coffee cup, and cradled it in her hands. 'What happened next?'

'I woke up in the hospital. The doctor explained that I had suffered a temporary loss of memory, maybe a few hours. I was told that I woke up several times in a row, asked the same thing, and had the same conversation with the nursing staff. They let me go around lunchtime,' Liam said. 'Once they discharged me, I went to the university because I remembered the book and wanted to check to see if it was still in one piece. That's when I ran into you.'

A droplet of sweat dripped down Liam's brow.

'Why did you want to check up on the *Commentary*?'

'It's delicate, and James dropped it on the floor. It's from the twelfth century,' Liam said. 'Do you know what happened to the manuscript?'

'The intruder stole it.'

Liam stared at her. 'What?'

Alice paused. He wasn't lying. None of the tell-tale signs were present. Sure, he was nervous, but he wasn't lying.

'I'm sorry, but I can't reveal more information than that. It's an ongoing investigation.' Alice placed her mug on the table as she considered her next question.

'According to your bank record, and later confirmed by the insurance company, you increased your girlfriend's life insurance by two hundred and fifty thousand pounds fifteen days ago.' Alice slid a stamped photocopy of the forms across the table.

Liam shuffled through the pages then put them down. The blood drained from his face, his skin whiter than a ream of copy paper.

'It's an update to Kate's life insurance policy,' he said.

'Why did you change Kate's insurance policy?'

'Several reasons. Kate received a significant pay rise, and we were planning on starting a family.'

'Do you recognise this text?' She slid a phone over to him.

Liam's eyes widened, and his face turned a paler shade of white.

'Yes, it's from me to Manesh.' Liam took a deep breath and gazed at Alice, who was scrolling through the messages.

'As per this text, you're threatening to kill Manesh if he doesn't end his affair with your girlfriend, Kate.' Alice raised her eyebrows. 'And you want to have children with a woman who thinks it's appropriate to sleep with your colleague?'

Liam exhaled. 'It's complicated.'

'You realise that you've increased your girlfriend's life insurance to two hundred and fifty thousand pounds the day after you caught her having an affair with the deceased. Do you get how this appears?'

'Yes.' Liam's lip quivered. 'I was hurt, but I still love her.'

Alice wrinkled her brow. 'Did you talk to her about this before you threatened Manesh?'

A tear trickled down Liam's cheek. 'No, I felt numb. It shocked me.'

'Later that day, you contacted a man known as Dr Teflon.' Alice pulled out a printout of Liam's phone records.

'Who?' Liam shook his head.

Alice sighed. 'You spoke on the phone with a killer for hire.'

Liam closed his eyes and took a deep breath. 'He told me his name was Lloyd Waterhouse.'

'That was the name he gave you?' Alice tilted her head and pursed her lips.

'Yes.'

Alice peeked at the glass panel. 'Where did you get his number?'

'An internet chat room.' Liam slumped in his chair.

Fascinating. He's talking and not asking for a lawyer. It's not a total surprise considering he has no record, not even an unpaid parking ticket. But most people ask for a lawyer. Should I remind him that he has a right to counsel?

Alice leaned towards him. 'You searched for a killer for hire?'

'Yeah.' Liam sighed as he stared at the table. 'After, I filled out the insurance form and faxed it off. I felt angry and cheated. I was emotional, and I made a crazy decision.'

'Why?' Alice pressed.

'I was angry. Haven't you ever made a rash decision in an emotional state?' Liam pointed at her.

Alice leaned back in her chair. 'Hiring a trained killer seems premeditated and planned, not rash.'

'I didn't hire anyone. I just enquired.' Liam straightened. 'I spoke in general terms. No names or locations were given. The second he answered, I knew it was a mistake. That's why I spoke broadly. I've done nothing wrong.'

'Yes, you have. I can charge you with soliciting for murder.' Alice picked up her coffee cup and took another sip.

'But I didn't hire anyone.' Liam sobbed. 'I'm happy to help you track this guy down and arrest him.'

'Really?' Alice slammed the mug onto the table. She was tempted to make a deal with the moron sitting in front of her.

It was both unorthodox and out of character. But it wasn't a terrible idea. She pushed it aside.

'I don't know how to track him down because he told me I'd never hear from him again.' Liam hung his head and continued to sob.

Alice eyed the file. 'According to our records, the conversation lasted for twenty minutes. What did you discuss during this call?'

'Lloyd was quite the salesman. He discussed price and promised things I didn't believe he could deliver.' Liam tapped his fingers on the desk.

Alice rested her head on her fist. 'Like what?'

'Clean and quick, easy death, no DNA or evidence left behind, no ties back to me, a clean money trail. He explained how to get the cash.' Liam gazed at Alice with tears in his eyes.

'What made you think he couldn't deliver on his promises?'

'Too sure of himself, and it sounded too far-fetched. I never gave him a name or location, and he was certain.' Liam rubbed the skin on the back of his neck. 'And no DNA left behind.'

'You mentioned he deals in cash. And what do you mean by "he explained how to get the cash"?' Alice's eyes darted to the recorder then back at Liam.

'Yes, Lloyd deals with cash only. He discussed the payment options and gave me two choices, part payments or something of value he could sell. Lloyd wanted thirty thousand pounds. He believed it was better to deal with cash. He said that he would be in Oxford for a week. After that, I would never hear from him again.' Liam hung his head as his cheeks turned crimson.

'Did he discuss how the exchange of cash would take place?'

'Yes, Lloyd said to meet in an alleyway. One payment

before, the second after, or he could steal something and sell it. He was pressing me on that subject.'

'Did you tell him about the *Commentary*?'

Liam shook his head. 'No way. But I think he must have known or heard about it.'

'What gave you that impression?'

'He mentioned antiques, art, valuable manuscripts, stuff like that.'

Alice furrowed her brow. 'You're claiming he knew.'

'I never came out and asked him.' Liam's palms sweated. 'Maybe he knew because Manesh has a big mouth. He talked about it all the time. It was driving us crazy. Because of the *Commentary's* value and Manesh's behaviour, the whole situation made us all nervous.' Liam shook his head.

'Who do you mean by "us"?'

'Myself and the part-time lab technicians.'

'There were just two payments. Is that correct?'

'No, there was a third to be delivered seven days later.'

'And you never mentioned who you were calling about, and Lloyd never asked?'

'That's correct. There was something about Lloyd that scared me. I didn't trust him. And I don't have the money or something of that value in my home,' Liam said, maintaining eye contact.

'What about the missing *Commentary on Daniel*?'

'It's insured for one and a half million pounds. The *Commentary on Daniel* shouldn't be in the hands of someone like Dr Teflon, as you refer to him,' Liam said.

Alice shrugged. 'If the job was complete, you would have money from Kate's insurance.'

'There's a cooling-off period. The insurance company would never pay me because my situation would seem suspicious. Lloyd was very clear about the cash up front or the item to steal. I'm sure he only gave me that option because I paused after he told me the price. The discussion on prices threw me.'

'Perhaps.' Alice stared at Liam. 'Did Lloyd Waterhouse say anything about what would happen after?'

'Yes, just one thing.'

'What was that?'

'Under no circumstances am I to share this with the police.'

'Did he give a reason?'

'Yes, he mentioned something about a short drop and a sudden stop.'

'He threatened to hang you?' Alice leaned across the table towards Liam and peered at the recording timer.

'Yes.'

'And he let you end the call just like that? You could change your mind?' A hint of suspicion lingered in her voice.

'Yes, that's why he made the threat. He arranged to meet at George and the Dragon on George Street if I changed my mind. The arrangement was to be there at 8:03 p.m. on Monday, and he would only wait five minutes, then Lloyd would leave.'

'And if you were late?'

'He would move on. No second chances,' Liam said as Alice glanced at the contents of the folder then focused on Liam.

'A few people saw you arguing with Manesh on several occasions. What were these discussions about?' Alice leaned back in her chair.

'The first time I spoke to Manesh was about a conversation I overheard him having in Pret-A-Manger.' Liam rested his arm on the table. 'He told the old guy behind the counter about the *Commentary on Daniel* and how All Saints insured it for a crazy price, how it was one of a kind, and how lucky he was to work on it.'

'And what about the second time?'

'The second time, it was about him screwing my girlfriend.' Liam stared at his lap then shook his head. 'Kate came home Monday evening smelling like his aftershave. The next day, I tried avoiding him because I was angry. No one ever makes brilliant decisions out of anger. But on Wednesday morning, I'd had enough. When I confronted him, Manesh said he tried to call it off, but Kate persuaded him to keep going. But he was probably lying. I'm sure of it. He's wrecked homes before.'

Alice narrowed her eyes. 'What do you mean, "wrecked homes"?'

Liam scoffed. 'You've never heard the term "home-wrecker"?'

'I need you to speak plainly for the record.' Alice pointed at the display on the tape recorder.

'A few years back, a friend of mine, Benjamin Brauer, was dating a girl by the name of Bianca Webb. They were in love, and he kept going on and on about how she was the one.' Liam struck the table with his index finger. 'These conversations happened while Manesh was present. A few weeks later, he was caught in the Rad Cam having an affair with Bianca, who was a student at the time. This was a couple of years ago.'

'Both Manesh and Ben were present at the reunion dinner?' Alice leaned back in her chair as she glared at Liam.

'Yes.'

'And how did they interact with each other?'

Liam sighed. 'There was tension, but there always is, especially between those two. Ben ignored Manesh, and he made it obvious. Manesh brought up Bianca, and Ben acted like Manesh didn't exist. He was cold. I think Manesh was used to Ben's demeanour.'

Alice spoke to the recorder. 'The interview is being paused at 6:07 p.m.'

She stood and left the room, leaving Liam alone and handcuffed to the desk. Would the captain let her use Liam to lure Lloyd out of hiding? Would it work?

TWENTY-FIVE

AGAINST HIS BETTER JUDGEMENT, James decided to visit DI Alice O'Donnell on a fishing endeavour. From the second she saw him enter the station, Alice was on to him. She was like a bloodhound tracking a scent. Perhaps as punishment, she made him wait.

James sat hunched over Alice's desk, waiting for her to return from the filing room. St Aldates Police Station was abuzz. The phone was ringing, and a dazed and confused homeless man argued with a petite female officer behind the counter. Her fingers, the nails polished in black, slowly crept towards the red button under the counter. A junior officer standing nearby was so focused on the photocopier that he obviously didn't notice the commotion around him. Another police officer sat at a nearby desk with his hat on his knee and his telephone in one hand. He appeared eager to get off the phone. The station manager's door behind him was ajar.

A familiar tall, dark, hooded figure wearing a golden Venetian mask appeared in the station's doorway. It made its way over to the gate that separated the reception area from the workstations. No one seemed to notice. Everyone was utterly unaware or perhaps disinterested that someone had just walked into the station off the street. It wasn't just someone but a prime suspect. James froze in his seat as the masked man surveyed the room then focused on him. As the figure stepped closer, a pair of large, bright-green eyes stared back. There was something familiar about the man, but he couldn't put his finger on it. James studied the room, but the entire station was busy and focused on their tasks.

A loud *bang* jolted James back to the present. He glanced up as his vision focused. Alice and a stack of paperwork came into view.

'Are you okay? You're very pale.' Alice gazed at him as he inspected the room, searching for the figure present only a second ago.

Was I seeing things? It seemed so real. Maybe I'm going crazy. Why am I having dreams like this now and not while I was in the hospital? He looked up at Alice.

'You were talking in your sleep. You kept saying "vert" over and over again.' Alice picked up her mug and took a sip.

She must think I'm crazy.

'It's French for green,' James said. 'I was having a crazy nightmare. There was something new about the hooded man that I hadn't noticed before. I honestly don't know if I should trust it.' James wrinkled his brow as he tried to recall his dream.

'What did you see?'

'A man with a hooded black coat, gold mask, and piercing green eyes staring back at me. The man was right here at the station. And there was something familiar about him.' James peered across the room at the unmanned photocopier.

'You're referring to the perpetrator who entered the lab?'

James nodded. 'Yes.'

'The perp had green eyes?' Alice leaned in towards James.

A look of recognition swept over James's face as he clapped his hand over his mouth. Then he slumped back in the chair and stared straight ahead.

Alice raised her eyebrows at him. 'James?'

He swallowed hard and shifted in his seat. 'I'm not sure if I should tell you. It's just speculation.'

'Tell me.' Alice narrowed her eyes.

James hung his head to avoid Alice's stern gaze. 'Owen was wearing a coat similar to the one the intruder wore.' James frowned. 'Why was he wearing a coat in summer? It's not even cold.'

Alice threw her notebook on the desk and shook her head. 'The description of the coat you and Liam gave me is generic. Many fashion houses could have made a coat like that. Unless Owen has green eyes, is the same height as the perp, and has no alibi, then you're jumping to conclusions.'

His right knee bobbed up and down. 'To be honest, I don't know the colour of Owen's eyes. I think he's a similar height to me, maybe a little taller.'

Merde, I just threw one of my friends under the bus. He was officially that guy.

Alice grimaced. 'This isn't my first murder investigation. My team and I will figure it out.'

James turned his head and gazed at the reception area as the old man shuffled out of the police station and let the door slam behind him.

'Are you remembering something else?' Alice leaned into his field of vision.

'No.' James sighed. 'I can't remember much about the events that unfolded. I feel like I've got missing pieces in my memory.'

Alice surveyed the room. 'I don't think you'll ever get it back, but maybe it will come out in your dreams. The sketch artist has finished speaking with Liam. It could be useful to get you to meet with him while your dream is still fresh.'

Alice stood then tilted her head towards the hall. James dashed after her as she strolled across the open-plan offices. She took a sharp turn and sauntered along a corridor.

'Are you good friends with Amber?' Alice asked over her shoulder.

James hesitated. 'More of an acquaintance.'

Alice stopped outside a wooden door with a silver nameplate reading "Charles Gilmore."

'And she's helping you with your investigation?' Alice smirked.

A droplet of sweat dripped down his brow. *She's got someone following me.*

Alice knocked on the door, turned the handle, and walked in without waiting for a response.

TWENTY-SIX

THE CRISP WHITE tabletop shone under the yellow lights. It was in stark contrast to the entire station. A polished silver screen with a matching white keyboard, trackpad, and penholder were the only things on the desk. Not a single page was in sight. A chemical fragrance lingered in the air. *How does this man function outside of his office?*

A tall man with pale skin and long, thin limbs swung around in his chair and stared at Alice. He wore thick black frames with equally thick lenses. His large blue eyes peered at her as if he was expecting an explanation for the intrusion.

'Charles, this is James Lalonde. He was in the lab with Liam Kennedy at All Saints.'

He groaned as he glanced at James then turned around, hunched over his computer, studied the screen, and clicked the trackpad.

'He has remembered something new about the perp, and I thought this would be a good time for you to create another sketch,' Alice said with a hint of uneasiness.

'I know how to do my job,' Charles said without taking his gaze off the computer. 'Take a seat, Mr Lalonde.'

Alice gave James a sympathetic smile as she strolled out of the office. *Merde. She's leaving me here with the sketch artist.*

'Mr Lalonde!' Charles snapped.

James took a seat next to Charles. 'Just call me James.'

'That would be highly inappropriate.' Charles stiffened. 'We're not friends. You're a victim of a crime, and as a professional, one should be careful not to blur the lines.'

James remained silent. Was Charles having a go at him, or was he always so matter-of-fact?

'What do you remember about the perpetrator? What significant facial features come to mind?' Charles turned to his left.

He opened the top drawer and pulled out a sketch pad and pencil. Charles tore off a page, placed it in the drawer, and slammed it shut. He lurched forward then looked up at James with his pencil poised.

James sighed. 'All I remember is a pair of bright-green eyes. They were vibrant.'

'What else?' A stern expression swept across Charles's face. 'Take your time.'

James leaned towards Charles, who was sketching on the giant pad. 'I couldn't see much because of the black-hooded coat and the gold Venetian joker mask. I think he had a small head because the hood draped over and partially covered his face.'

Charles glanced up at him from behind the sketchpad. 'I noticed you're referring to the perpetrator as a male. Do you know this for sure?'

James's gaze darted to the pristine tabletop over Charles's shoulder. 'I didn't exactly check because he was coming at me with a knife.'

'What about the eyes? What shape were they? Were the eyes big or small? I'll show you a few options on the screen to help you.' Charles clicked on the trackpad.

In the programme on the screen, a small tray popped open from the side toolbar.

'Here are a few options. I don't use them because I like to draw my own.' Charles stared at James.

'Those are too small. His irises were large.'

'This is hopeless.' Charles flipped the page and continued to sketch on the next one.

'There's no need for you to be so rude. This is all that I can recall.' James took a deep breath to calm down and resist his overwhelming desire to slap Charles. 'If you bothered to read the case file, then you would know I've been stabbed and have a concussion.'

'I'm not rude,' Charles said in a high-pitched tone as he kept the pencil poised on the page. 'How tall do you think they might be?' Charles said as he emphasised his choice of words.

'Definitely taller than me. So maybe about six foot two or three.'

'Not exactly accurate, but I can go with that.' Charles pursed his lips as he sketched. 'You mentioned a hooded coat. What did that look like?'

'It was oversized to the knee, a thick black material. He also had a thin frame. You could tell because it was baggy around the shoulders.' James closed his eyes and focused on the events of the previous day. 'The coat was something you would wear in winter. He also had his trousers tucked into heavy military boots.'

James opened his eyes and smiled at Charles, who gave him a glassy stare. He was getting under Charles's skin.

'What exactly do you remember about the perp leading up to when you blacked out?'

James wrinkled his brow. 'I was stabbed. I hit my head and got a concussion, but I don't remember that part. My last memory was when I saw my stab wound. After that, I guess I dropped the manuscript.'

'Fine.' Charles glared at James. 'What do you remember about the perp before you were stabbed?'

'All I remember is the knife coming towards me and a pair of green eyes, then the room spun.'

Charles fixed his eyes on the pad and sketched in the new details. Moments later, he held the sketch pad up for James to see. 'It's not exactly a work of art, but is this how the figured appeared to you?' Charles wore a stern expression as James leaned in and inspected the sketch. 'It doesn't have a face, but I can fill it in as you remember. Liam remembers a large pointed nose, and you remember a pair of large green eyes.'

James gazed off into the distance as he tried to recall the events that occurred in the lab. 'The mask had a nose with a rounded tip. It wasn't pointed unless he unmasked in front of Liam after I blacked out.'

Charles maintained eye contact for a few seconds then darted his eyes away. 'Possibly.'

'I guess that's the guy.' James nodded.

Charles took a deep breath. 'Has it ever occurred to you that the perp could be a woman?'

'No, a woman couldn't stab me with that amount of force. And he was my height.'

Charles exhaled. 'I thought you said the perp was taller.'

'A woman who's over six feet tall?' James raised his eyebrows.

'Actually, a woman of Nordic descent could be over six feet.' Charles tilted his head.

James rolled his eyes. 'His accent was British.'

Charles smirked. 'Maybe your ego can't handle it, but it's a possibility.'

'The perp was definitely a guy. I was there.' James spoke with forced restraint.

Could the man be any more annoying? Hopefully, James hadn't just jinxed himself.

'It's still a possibility,' Charles said with a hint of laughter in his voice.

'*J'en peux plus de cette merde,*' James said as he stood and marched to the door. *I can't take any more of this shit.*

'James, you were most helpful!' Charles yelled out as James flung the door open and let it shut behind him with a bang.

———

JAMES STOOD OPPOSITE ALICE, who leaned against the wall outside Charles's office. He took several deep breaths to calm himself.

'I can't believe you left me in there with that socially inept droid.' James pointed over his shoulder at the closed door. 'He picked a fight with me during the sketch.'

James walked down the hall and towards the workstation area, with Alice sprinting after him.

'So, you got the full treatment,' she replied. 'Charles doesn't like other officers present during sketches because he believes we'll intimidate the witnesses. And he's not picking fights on purpose.'

James rolled his eyes.

Alice stepped away from the wall and ambled down the corridor towards the workstations. 'Charles is on the high-functioning end of the autism spectrum. He's literal and doesn't understand that what he says is hurting your feelings,' she said over her shoulder.

TWENTY-SEVEN

THE COLD, polished wood of the chair sent shivers up my spine as I sat in the Christ Church Cathedral. My mind was fried. It was defeated by a riddle written in lemon juice on a sheet of vellum in a twelfth-century *Commentary on Daniel*. Sure, it was a little clichéd, but this was my new reality. My mind needed a break from my self-induced chaos and stress. Solitude was what I needed, and the cathedral was the only place where I could achieve that goal. I stared at the intricate vaulting of the nave ceiling, waiting for the anarchy to vacate my mind.

My smartphone rattled against the polished wooden chair, disturbing the silence. *Please, don't let it be him.* The last thing I needed was a follow-up call from that creepy octogenarian and his beguiling but dangerous American boss. My chest tightened as I gazed at the screen. I needed to get a grip. Panicking was futile.

After several deep breaths, I picked up the smartphone, hit the answer button, and brought the phone to my ear. True to their word, my informant got straight to the point.

'It's me again. Sorry to disturb you, but James Lalonde is still inside the police station with DI Alice O'Donnell.'

I sighed. 'Obviously, Mr Lalonde is adding to his statement.'

'No, DI Alice O'Donnell believes he's withholding information from the police. She's like a dog with a bone. She will not let this one go. And there's one last thing I need to tell you about.'

My stomach churned as my chest tightened. I took a few more deep breaths. 'What?'

'His female companion has disappeared. She's not at the station.'

I shook my head. 'Okay, thanks for letting me know.'

I smiled as I listened to my source hang up, then I placed the phone back on the polished wooden chair. The police were still no closer to solving the theft and murder. Interesting. But I highly doubted Lalonde was withholding information. I'd been trailing him since 3:15 a.m. that morning, and Lalonde was no closer to figuring it out than when he first started. Typical. I'd anticipated a challenging twenty-four hours. All the pieces were there. He just needed to put them in the right order. *What does he need? An assemble-by-numbers instruction booklet?* And to think I had been worried about getting caught. *Lalonde, should I give you a hint?* Better not tempt fate.

I glanced at my phone. *Shit. It's him.* I struck the home button, waiting for the phone to scan my fingerprint. A series of numbers materialised on the screen—map coordinates. Someone had been watching too much James Bond. It read:

51°45'30.4 "N 1°20'27.6 "W 20150828
1510. Delete after reading.

Great. I had less than twenty-four hours to solve the riddle, prove myself useful, or risk pushing up daisies.

TWENTY-EIGHT

SURROUNDED by an array of metal shelves laden with identical cream archive boxes, all bearing the Thames Valley Police logo and a barcode, the informant stood propped up against the metal frame of a shelving unit in the far corner of the evidence room. The lid of an archive box was cast to the side, and a clear, empty evidence bag lay open on top of it. A dull hum from the air-conditioning unit broke the silence of the room as the informant stared at the number of the last call made on the prepaid phone. Should she call her other contact?

A familiar shooting, stabbing sensation developed deep within the informant's chest as she slipped the phone into the clear evidence bag then placed it inside the archive box. While she was securing the lid on the crate, a dull creak caused the informant to almost jump out of her skin. Was someone listening in to her conversation? She'd promised Amber that she would keep her identity a secret.

Taking a deep breath, the informant listened to the stillness of the room. All she could hear was the hum of the air conditioner. The old CCTV camera was quiet—it was motion sensored. Usually, a metallic churning sounded as it moved around. Getting caught in the evidence room making secret phone calls was the least of her problems. James had killed a man, stolen a mediaeval manuscript, and was slipping away from the police's grasp. Despite what she'd said to Amber, she wasn't sure he would be arrested for his crimes. That was the origin of her anxiety—the secrecy of her source and the killer roaming around town.

Out of nowhere, shuffling footsteps echoed down the evidence room and in her direction. Tiny hairs stood on end at the back of her neck. The informant froze as the footsteps grew closer.

'Ellie?' a voice called out from behind her.

The informant whirled around to find Joseph standing four feet away, peering at her with a hint of curiosity in his deep-brown eyes. 'Looking into the old Rover Street case?'

She shrugged. 'Yeah, but it was nothing new. I got a little excited when I saw the tip come in a few days ago.'

Joseph pursed his lips.

Shit, he doesn't believe me.

'It's hard not to get attached to that case. The little girl has been missing for seven years, and the parents call Alice every few months, hoping for news.' Joseph hung his head and slipped his hands into his trouser pockets.

'Yeah.' Ellie nodded.

'Your grandfather is waiting for you outside the station.' Joseph glanced at Ellie then nodded in the door's direction.

Her grandfather?

Joseph narrowed his eyes. 'Did you forget?'

Ellie bit her lip then sighed. 'I'm never going to hear the end of this.'

With a polite smile, Ellie dashed through the maze of shelves towards the door, her head down to keep her face off the CCTV camera.

TWENTY-NINE

THURSDAY: 7:31 P.M.

WITH TREMBLING HANDS, James gripped the steering wheel. Amber was in the passenger seat. She hadn't uttered a word since he'd picked her up from her apartment. He hated silence. Part of him wanted to fill the stillness of the car with conversation. Should he tell Amber that the police were watching him and, by extension, her too? How would she react? And how would he bring it up?

James peered over at the tall, thin woman sitting in the passenger seat. She smiled at him as his eyes darted to the empty two-lane road ahead. He groaned on the inside as the hood of his bright-yellow Peugeot came into view. Perhaps there was some unwritten rule that all hire cars needed to be a hideous colour.

As the car veered along the winding Faringdon Road, James glanced in the rearview mirror for the tenth time in five minutes. It was empty. Not a car was in sight. Based on Alice's poignant remark, he'd expected to see an unmarked car with a plain-clothed police constable trailing it. It wasn't the remark that hurt but the knowing look Alice gave him. Deep down, she knew he had nothing but a handful of theories and no actual evidence. How had Alice known Amber was helping him with his investigations? Did she really come to that conclusion based purely on police surveillance?

One thing he knew for sure was that Tom was not the source. And Tom wasn't the thief or murderer. He had an alibi. James almost hoped the murderer had conspired between Liam and Dr Teflon.

Honk, honk. Amber reached across and gripped the steering wheel as a rusted pickup truck came into view, jolting James back to reality. With a turn of the steering wheel, the tiny yellow car swerved back to the left-hand lane. *Merde.*

As the pickup truck passed by in the right-hand lane, the elderly driver gave James a one-fingered salute.

Amber rubbed her hand along James's thigh. 'Are you okay?'

James fixed his eyes on the road ahead. 'Sorry. I have a lot on my mind.'

'Did something happen at the police station?' Amber squeezed his thigh.

James sighed as her grip intensified. Focus, idiot.

'DI Alice O'Donnell asked me the same old questions.' James shrugged. 'I guess she hoped I would provide extra information about the incident in the research lab.'

'So the police know nothing.' Amber released her grip.

James furrowed his brow. 'What makes you say that?'

'I guess because the police are questioning victims instead of suspects and corroborating alibis,' Amber said.

James raised his eyebrows. 'Maybe they're doing both.'

Amber sighed. 'I hope so.'

'So, what were you doing before you met me at the car hire company?' James turned his attention back to Faringdon Road.

'I walked to the Radcliffe Camera library and spent an hour conducting research for my PhD thesis.' She smiled. 'It's quite a pleasant ten-minute walk.'

'Did you see Kate?'

Amber shook her head. 'James, you never told me where we're going.'

Merde.

'Owen is staying at the Wizard and Ragged Staff B and B. According to Google Maps, it's a five-mile drive.'

Amber nodded. 'Is he the troublemaker from last night?'

He chuckled to himself. 'The one and only.'

James stared at Amber. She smiled. His eyes lingered on her black-and-white-checked shirt. For some strange reason, he had an urge to unfasten those small, clear buttons. Perhaps that was the actual source of his deliberations. Honestly, he enjoyed having Amber around. Based on her anxieties about interviewing Tom, Amber would probably take off at any mention of being followed by the police. Dishonest as it was, he decided not to say a word. Amber possessed insider knowledge about Manesh's last days, and that knowledge was valuable. But that didn't stop guilt from taking up residence within him.

THIRTY-THREE MINUTES LATER, James stood at the landing of the steep, winding staircase of the Wizard and Ragged Staff, clutching the handrail. The room spun as his heart raced. Sweat dripped from his brow. His fear of heights was showing.

Amber placed her hand on his lower back. 'It's okay. You won't fall.'

Merde. It's official. She must think I'm a wuss.

After several deep breaths, James ascended the wooden staircase to the top floor. Upon reaching the top, James clutched the newel post as he took several deep breaths and stared down the short hallway. Before him stood a lone wooden door bearing three golden numbers. James strolled across the landing with Amber following closely and knocked on the door.

Shuffle, shuffle. James listened to the sound coming from within room 201 of the luxury bed-and-breakfast run by Mrs Black and her husband, who had retired from the air force several decades ago. James and Amber had just spent the last twenty minutes listening to Mrs Black's life story as she gave them a tour of her property. But the impromptu tour felt like an hour. They were finally free of her and waiting on the other side of a door, listening to Owen amble across the room.

Sniff, sniff. James grimaced at the obvious signs of a cold coming from within the room. The door handle turned then opened to reveal Owen with a bright-red nose and a pair of matching red tartan pyjamas. James glanced over his shoulder to see Amber vigorously cleaning her hands. *Merde.*

Owen walked back to a double bed covered in tissues. 'You're more than welcome to come in, but be warned, I'm a petri dish hosting a viral plague.'

Fingers crossed that Owen wasn't in his usual mood and didn't stir the pot. Sure, he had a better chance of turning water into wine, but it didn't hurt to be optimistic.

James grabbed Amber's hand. 'Are you okay?' he whispered.

She paused then nodded. James released his grip on her hand and placed it on the open door, allowing her to enter first.

James rolled his eyes as he walked into Owen's room and closed the door. 'I realise you're sick, so I won't take up too much of your time. I just need to ask you a few questions.'

'Of course.' Owen sat down on the bed and peered over at Amber, who had put as much distance between them as possible.

She pulled out a tissue, squirted hand gel on it, and wiped the chair before sitting down.

Owen grabbed a tissue from the nightstand, blew his nose,

then discarded the tissue on the floor, missing the open plastic bag beside his bed. 'I assume this is about Manesh.'

James took a deep breath. 'Yes and no.'

'Now, I'm intrigued.' Owen picked up a nasal inhaler and breathed in its eucalyptus-infused fumes.

'I noticed last night you wore a thick black hooded coat. It stood out because it's summer. And I was wondering where you got it.'

Owen narrowed his eyes as he placed the inhaler on the bedside table. 'How does this relate to Manesh?'

'The person who killed Manesh wore a very similar coat,' James said with a sigh.

'So I'm a suspect because of a coat.' Owen sniffled and grabbed another tissue. 'Is this what you call investigating?'

James shook his head. 'I'm just trying to eliminate you as a suspect.'

'Really?' Owen tilted his head as he glared at James. 'Oh, you're chasing a page-one story.'

James sighed. 'No, Lady Margaret asked me to investigate the lab incident so she can do damage control when the press gets wind of the story.'

'Well, Hercule. You can take the coat and test it, but I'd prefer it if you didn't.'

Merde, not this again. James rolled his eyes.

'Why not?' Amber asked.

'I need it to keep warm, and it belongs to my grandfather. He wore it when he was living in Ireland,' Owen explained. 'I wore the coat because I was coming down with chills and a cold. And I left the pub early to get a good night's sleep. Not to knock off a ladies' man.'

'Ladies' man? Really?' James asked as he felt Amber's gaze linger on him.

Owen smirked. 'Oh, come on. You remember what Manesh was like. It hasn't been that long. He's worse than you. I'm sure Amber will fill you in on his current exploits.'

Owen wheezed as a slight smile formed on his face. James glanced over his shoulder at Amber, who shook her head.

James stared at Owen.

'Manesh always had a different girl. She was usually an undergraduate, in her early twenties, brunette, stunning. The man has changed little,' Owen said as his eyes widened. 'Maybe the father of his latest Miss Twentysomething decided he didn't like him sniffing around his daughter and hired a hit man.'

James shook his head. 'A hit man?'

'It's not that far-fetched. Some very wealthy families send their kids to university at All Saints,' Amber said.

James shook his head at her.

Owen held his finger in the air as he plucked another tissue out of the box and blew his nose. 'I just remembered.'

'What?' James and Amber blurted simultaneously.

'I caught Manesh checking out Kate quite a few times,' Owen whispered as he leaned forward.

Good news travels fast.

James was intrigued. 'How long ago was this?'

'The first time was in 2007 when he started working as an assistant professor.'

James narrowed his eyes. 'Wait. She was a student back then.'

'You were busy with a few extracurricular activities.' Owen lifted his fingers to create a pair of air quotes while James blushed.

'Did you ever point out to Liam how Manesh looked at Kate?'

'Never. I don't like to interfere with people's private lives. It's not up to me to judge,' Owen said with a sweet smile.

There's a first time for everything.

Owen threw the bunched-up tissue in his hand onto the pile on his bed then looked at James. 'Just out of curiosity, what did the killer look like? I heard you were in the lab.'

James cocked his head. 'I have a vague idea, but I'm doubting my memory.'

'Trauma has a way of skewing your memory.' Owen pulled a pillow out from behind him and patted it down.

'How do you know this?' Amber stepped closer to the bed.

'I'm studying to become a psychiatrist,' Owen replied arrogantly.

'What made you choose that career?' she asked.

Owen sighed. 'My grandfather was institutionalised back in the fifties. The treatment he received should be considered torture. They mistreated the mentally ill back then, and sometimes I wonder if it's any better now.'

'The doctors told me I had a concussion. And I feel like there's a gap in my memory. It's like putting a jigsaw together and realising you're missing pieces.'

'That's common, more than you think. You may never get these memories back. But to be honest, you probably don't want to.' Owen reached for the tissue box, pulled out a tissue, and blew his nose.

After discarding it on the bed, Owen smoothed out his pillow and placed it behind him. 'The brain has a way of forgetting the finer details of traumatic events, but they might seep into your dreams over the next few nights. It's not an exact science. You shouldn't take these dreams as facts because your brain may filter in new information like you would take an educated guess. So, it's more of a "this probably happened" as opposed to facts. Most people think you remember things like a film, but you remember bits and then piece them together, and your brain fills in the gaps. And your brain is susceptible to suggestions. So you can remember things that aren't actually your memories.'

Great. So my memory's useless.

'I had a dream a couple of hours ago, and I remember a feature I didn't recall earlier.'

Owen nodded. 'Yes, that's what I meant.'

'He was tall, over six feet, with bright-green eyes, a slim frame, and he wore a thick, hooded black coat.'

Owen rubbed the back of his hand against the tip of his bright-red nose. 'Ben fits that description, and he left the party early, but it could be anyone.'

'How well does Ben know Manesh?' Amber asked.

'Let's just say no one is ever going to accuse Ben and Manesh of being best friends,' Owen said.

James nodded with a tight expression on his tired face. 'They had a falling out seven years ago.'

Owen's eyes lit with a twinkle of mischief. 'The falling out was still in progress. When you mention Manesh around Ben, he gets quiet and acts agitated. Maybe they argued about something. Ben isn't exactly a good loser, and Manesh loved a good argument.'

James shook his head. 'So all you have is idle gossip and no facts.'

'Yes, I do.' Owen crossed his arms. 'I guess I know something you don't.'

'What?' James asked in a harsh tone.

Owen lifted his hands in mock surrender. 'Easy, Hercule.'

James shook his head and took a few deep breaths.

'Manesh hired Ben to take photographs of the manuscript,' Owen said with a sniff as he reached for another tissue.

'When?' James furrowed his brow.

'A month ago,' Amber said bitterly.

James turned around as Owen offered Amber a bemused smile.

She shrugged. 'I can't stand it when people hire family and friends as contractors. Nothing gets done to standard, and no questions are ever asked.'

'Sounds like there was more than one conflict in the lab,' Owen said.

James narrowed his eyes. 'What do you mean more than one conflict?'

Owen held his arm out towards Amber. 'Besides Amber's zero tolerance for subpar work, I'm talking about Manesh and Ben.'

'So Ben and Manesh had another fight?' James glanced at the wooden ceiling beams in Owen's room.

'Ben wasn't big on the details, but when he arrived last night before Manesh turned up, Ben told me he would never speak to Manesh ever again. He was done.'

'One more thing. I'm guessing the hotel staff can confirm you were here all night,' James said.

'Yes, I left the Turf Tavern at ten fifteen p.m.' Owen gave him a sarcastic grin. 'Hercule, am I still a suspect?'

THIRTY

THE SCENE before him was worse than the hotel staff at the Old Bank Hotel had led him to believe. Upon arriving there, James squabbled with the staff for ten minutes. The only thing the concierge admitted was that the evening before, Ben had seemed a little pale, so the concierge called a taxi to the John Radcliffe hospital. Afterwards, the grumpy old geezer muttered something about privacy then turned and marched away. So there James was, almost an hour later, feeling like an insensitive prick. *Merde.* He wondered whether he should leave before Ben woke up.

Drip, drip. James stood at the end of Ben's hospital bed with Amber by his side. Ben's skin was pale and lacked the usual rosiness in his cheeks that James had seen the previous evening. He looked like death warmed up.

Then Ben's thick brown eyelashes fluttered. His eyes crept open a millimetre at a time. James ambled along the side of the bed and placed his hand on Ben's shoulder as he tried to sit up.

Ben peered up at him. 'James? Amber?' He narrowed his eyes as he leaned against the pillows. 'What are you both doing here? Does everyone know?' Ben grimaced.

James sat on the edge of the bed. 'How are you feeling?'

Ben sighed. 'I've been better.'

Amber lifted the clipboard containing the patient file at the end of the bed and turned the pages.

James coughed. 'Amber.'

But Amber didn't respond. She fixed her eyes on the contents of the files.

'Feel free to read away. After all, it's only confidential patient information.'

With his mouth wide open, James gazed at Ben and grabbed his hand. 'You're not dying, right?'

Ben chuckled.

'Is this why you left the dinner early last night?' Amber glanced up from the file.

James bit his lips as she closed the file and hung it over the end of the bed.

Ben sighed. 'I felt a little unwell, so I returned to my hotel room. Then, around ten thirty p.m. or maybe a bit after, I started vomiting and went to the hospital. I was concerned I had food poisoning.'

James's eyes widened. 'Did the medical staff run tests?'

'When I first arrived, I sat in accident and emergency for a few minutes before they attended to me. It wasn't long until I got my stomach pumped, then I was put on a drip, and I've been here ever since. I'm also on an antibiotic. They're worried about the blood results because they check every couple of hours. But they won't tell me what's going on.' Ben pointed at the two bags of liquid attached to the tall steel drip stand beside his bed.

James narrowed his eyes. 'The medical staff aren't explaining the reasons for the tests or the results?'

'I think I might have blood poisoning, and that's based purely on how they're acting.'

James nodded. 'You've been admitted, so it's a sign they're taking your condition seriously.'

Ben pressed a button on the remote control resting near

his pillow and adjusted the bed so he could sit up. 'Have Liam and the others been asking about me?'

Merde, Ben hasn't heard. This is going to get interesting.

James sighed. 'Wow. I'm not sure how to tell you this...'

'What?' Ben leaned forward.

James let go of Ben's hand. 'Manesh was murdered last night. Unfortunately, it appears he was killed so someone could gain access to the research lab and steal the *Commentary on Daniel*.'

'Oh, shit.' Ben fell back onto his pillow.

'I was wondering if I could ask a few questions about what you remember leading up to the time of the murder. Is that okay?' James asked.

Ben rubbed his eye with his palm. 'Sure. Anything to help.'

'Can you remember the exact time you arrived at the hospital?'

James peered over at Amber, who had strolled to the side of the bed where he was sitting. 'Can anyone confirm the time you left for the hospital?'

Ben sat from the elevated position of the bed. 'Am I a suspect?'

James placed his hand on Ben's shoulder. 'We need to eliminate all the possibilities. It's just a standard set of questions.'

'My memory is quite vague. I'm not sure if I'm going to be helpful.' Ben wrinkled his brow and pursed his lips as if he was worrying.

'So you don't remember anyone helping you?' James asked. 'The concierge at the Old Bank Hotel mentioned they called you a cab.'

'But the lobby was empty. I don't remember that but I recall waiting for the taxi.' Ben hesitated. 'Actually, I saw Owen walking towards the Radcliffe Camera building with his coat over his arm. Maybe he knows.'

James glanced at Amber and raised his eyebrows. *Owen is a jerk. He sent me on a wild-goose chase.*

Amber lifted her chin. 'Did he see you?'

Ben's shoulders dropped. 'I'm sure he saw me while waiting for my cab. He sped up as he walked past the hotel. Owen was definitely not planning on stopping to chat.'

'And he wasn't wearing his coat?' James had a hint of suspicion in his voice.

Amber stepped closer to the bed. 'How far away was he?'

Ben shrugged. 'A few feet. He was on the other side of the road.'

James furrowed his brow. 'What time did the taxi arrive?'

Ben surveyed the room. 'My wallet might be in the top drawer. I got a receipt. The card machine gave me a printout.'

James opened the top drawer and pulled out a wallet bursting with pieces of paper. After rummaging through the contents, James found the receipt. The time was 10:59 p.m.

'What happened after that?' James stared at the small piece of paper.

Ben replied, 'The taxi arrived and took me to the hospital.'

James nodded.

'I'm sorry.' Ben clutched the steel pole of the drip then leapt off the bed and darted to the bathroom.

Bang. The door slammed shut behind him.

James sighed.

He shouldn't have come here. James felt like a jerk for asking Ben questions. And for once, he had someone else to blame for his insensitive actions.

James strolled around the bed to the set of drawers on the other side of the room. Upon opening the drawer, he placed the wallet inside, just as he'd found it. As he closed the drawer, his smartphone buzzed. It was a message from Lady Margaret:

Are you making any progress?

No text had come through from Liam. Ten hours had passed, so it was official. Liam was ignoring him.

Curiosity got the better of James. Reaching in, he grabbed the phone and struck the home button. Ben had no password. *What an idiot.*

Amber watched from across the room as James opened the email app and scrolled through its contents.

'You should see this,' he whispered, his eyes glued to the screen.

His eyes darted back and forth as he scrolled down to view the rest of the page. Amber strolled over to the other side of the room and stood behind him, reading over his shoulder. *Merde.*

James continued to read the text trail. What evidence could Ben have against Manesh? Then he realised something.

'But he has an alibi,' James whispered to Amber. 'He was getting his stomach pumped.'

'True. There's no way he could have left the hospital in his condition,' Amber said.

At least he was getting a clearer picture of the web Manesh had spun for himself.

James sighed. 'Any of these people might have killed him. And I still don't have any evidence.'

'Yes, but I think we already know where to find it.' Amber placed her hand on his lower back. 'Don't you think it's weird? Owen pointed his finger at Ben even though he had seen him that evening. Ben must have looked ill.'

James paused. 'I know he was deflecting. But what is his interest in the *Commentary on Daniel*?'

'I don't know.' Amber frowned. 'Maybe an interested party approached Owen about the manuscript, knowing he knew Manesh?'

James froze, and his eyes darted to the closed door as he considered Amber's theory.

'I'm not saying that's how it happened, but it's possible.

The *Commentary* is unique and well preserved. Maybe it appealed to Owen because he had a falling out with Manesh and wanted revenge.'

Merde.

James sighed. 'It sounds like Owen.'

Creak. The bathroom door opened. A foul odour wafted out of the small space. Ben emerged, gripping the steel pole of his drip, and made his way to the hospital bed. He glanced at James, who was holding his phone. Ben shook his head as he meandered over.

Amber darted around the bed and helped Ben get comfortable.

James rolled his eyes and placed his hands on his hips. 'You realise that what you were doing is blackmail, which is a criminal offence?'

'Only if you get caught.' Ben tilted his head and lifted his right shoulder.

'Ben...'

Ben shook his head. 'When you started working for the Student Press, I was the only one who wasn't surprised. You really have a thing for snooping around and discovering secrets.'

James ran his fingers through his hair. 'Why were you blackmailing him?'

'I've grown tired of watching him destroy lives. He did that to me once.'

James sighed. 'This is about a seven-year vendetta?'

'He had an affair with Bianca. That's why we broke up.' Ben crossed his arms and glared at James. 'I couldn't stand back and watch him do the same to Liam. He deserves better than that. He's a nice guy.' Ben stared at the light-blue crocheted blanket lying over the hospital's starchy sheets.

Amber watched the two men stare at each other in silence.

James narrowed his eyes. 'Why twenty thousand pounds?'

'I made a few poor business investments and needed to

recuperate the costs somehow. That's why I took Manesh up on his offer to photograph the *Commentary*. But he was so difficult to work for. He wouldn't let me use certain pieces of equipment. He kept calling me back to retake the photographs.' Ben sighed. 'And that's when I first caught them. I photographed the *Commentary on Daniel* at night after work. I came to the Radcliffe library earlier than usual, and there they were. Getting it on in the Lower Camera Reading Room, near the photocopiers. They used the same place every time.'

Amber screwed up her face.

Poor thing. She probably uses those copiers every day.

'I caught them several times, so I waited for the next time and filmed them, took a few incriminating photos on several occasions.'

James nodded slowly. 'Why?'

Ben shook his head. 'I needed several pieces of evidence from different sessions, just in case he pulled an "it was a one-time thing" excuse.'

'Is that what he did with Bianca?' Amber asked in a hushed tone.

'Yes, he explained his way out of it,' Ben said, 'but I knew deep down he was lying. You know, people rarely change.'

James grimaced. 'How often were they hooking up?'

'A few times a week.'

James gasped.

'What happened with the evidence? Did he pay you in cash?' James ran his fingers through his hair.

Ben sighed. 'He never paid me, and I still have the evidence.'

James narrowed his eyes. 'If you're in debt, how can you afford to live in the hotel you're staying at?'

'I had to move out of my home. My brother's company owns and manages the hotel. So I'm living there with his good grace.' Ben glared at James.

That had probably led Manesh to want to tell Liam about his affair. He had reached the end of the road. James couldn't ask any more questions without risking his friendship with Ben. A tactful retreat was his only option. Then he had a brilliant idea.

James bit the inside of his lower lip. 'Do you have any antique dealer contacts around Oxfordshire?'

'Are you hoping whoever stole the *Commentary* sold it off to an antique dealer?' Ben asked with a quizzical expression.

James nodded.

'Only an idiot would do that. But I can help you by calling around if you like. I've got nothing but time on my hands,' Ben said with a weary smile.

James nodded. 'Thanks, for your help. I'll let you rest. I hope you start feeling better.'

With a wave, James sauntered out of the room with Amber following closely.

THIRTY-ONE

WITH RELIEF, James handed the hideous monstrosity that he had driven around Oxford back to the hire company and boarded the bus to the city centre. Maybe next time, he would get a vehicle that didn't resemble a warning sign. As the stop approached, James jumped up and pressed the bell. Standing, he meandered to the back doors and waited for the bus to stop.

Five minutes later, the doors of the 400 to Oxford closed behind James as he followed Amber off the bus and onto the High Street footpath. Streets were deserted, and shops were closed.

James furrowed his brow. 'Do you think I'm making a mistake by not going back and confronting Owen?'

Amber slowed and waited for James to catch up. A wrinkle formed as she narrowed her eyes and stared into the distance for a few seconds.

'No, you're right.' Amber smiled. 'I guess I got caught up in the thrill of the investigation. And if he is Manesh's killer, he would probably kill again if he felt you were close to discovering the truth.'

James nodded. 'It's almost half past nine, and he is sick.

Owen won't leave town. He's in no state to travel. I need to talk to him again. I need to wait until he's in a position where he'll let his guard down.'

Amber bit her lip. 'Maybe you should talk to him in a public place. Just to err on the side of caution.'

A digital quack broke the silence of Oxford's streets. James pulled out his phone. A message had come through. It read:

> Meet me at the Rad Cam, first floor.
> Fascinating discovery.

'Ah...' James glanced up in time to see Amber avert her eyes onto the footpath below. 'Oliver just sent me a text. I need to meet him at the Radcliffe Camera library.'

A smile formed on Amber's lips. 'That's perfect because I've been looking for an excuse to get back to my research. I left my stuff at the Radcliffe, and I don't want it to get locked inside. It closes at nine, but Kate is staying late for a stock take and says she'll give me access.'

———

NINE MINUTES LATER, Amber pressed her Bodleian Library card on the scanner. The black door popped open as she gripped the handle and dragged it towards her. James followed her inside. Slap. Amber pressed her card against the second card reader and held the Perspex gates open for James. An alarm rang throughout the library, jolting Kate out of her trancelike state. She tore her eyes away from the computer screen at the enquiry desk and shook her head at them. *Kate took that better than expected.*

James waved and smiled at Kate as Amber sprinted towards the back staircase through the ground-floor level.

'I'm here to see Oliver. Unfortunately, I can't stay for a chat,' James said as he pointed at the ceiling.

Wandering through the sea of bookshelves and around the

circular computer desk in the centre of the floor, James inhaled the sweet, musty, bookish aroma. The yellow light of a study lamp flickered in the distance, highlighting the shiny varnished surface of the reading room's tables. It was rare to find the library empty, but a new academic year was about to begin, and that would soon change. A few seconds later, James ascended the back staircase to the Upper Camera Reading Room.

———

A BEAUTIFUL SEA of mahogany bookshelves glistened under the yellow ceiling lights and lined the walls of the circular building. It had been far too long since James had graced the reading rooms with his presence. Gasping for air, James paused at the top of the staircase and leaned against the stone walls. A sharp pain shot through his side. James surveyed the room while waiting for the not-so-subtle reminder of the previous night's events to subside. He needed to lie down.

Far off in the distance, hunched over a laptop under a yellow study light, was a familiar hoodie-clad man with a Playmobil-style haircut. As the pain diminished, James dragged his weary body along the dark-blue carpet and to the empty rows of study desks. Oliver nodded then looked back at the computer. After pulling a dark-stained wooden chair to him, James sat next to Oliver. Lowering his headphones, Oliver turned his laptop screen towards James.

With a beaming face, Oliver leaned in. 'I can't believe this is happening. It's almost as if I'm working for MI5, not a prestigious university.'

A rock formed in the pit of James's stomach. *Merde*. 'So, you didn't have any trouble accessing his phone records.'

Oliver leaned back in his chair. 'Considering Liam's history with passwords, this didn't come as a surprise. But this password-security thing is not a habit that's exclusive to Liam.

Most people don't have secure passwords.' Oliver shrugged. 'I accessed the phone records from the library because he does come here a lot, just in case he noticed the log-in and questioned it with the provider.'

Note to self: change all of my passwords.

James bounced his foot under the table as his eyes lingered on a familiar number. 'He contacted Dr Teflon.'

Oliver grimaced. 'Yes, but only once.' Oliver dragged the cursor over the phone bill entry. 'On Thursday, the fifteenth of August, at 7:13 p.m., Liam had a twenty-minute conversation. It was exactly twenty minutes, which is strange.'

James placed his hand over his mouth and stared into the distance. *Merde.*

'That's the day after he increased Kate's life insurance.' James sighed.

Oliver raised his eyebrows. 'Wowsers.'

Tiny hairs on the back of James's neck stood on end as his heart raced. James surveyed the room, but no one was there. Oliver glanced up then leaned back in his chair and scanned the Upper Camera Gallery. A digital *quack* disturbed the eerie silence of the reading room. James pulled out his phone from his front jeans pocket. A message had come through. It read:

Don't be alarmed, but I'm pretty sure someone is lurking in the shadows behind you. Be careful. xx

Oliver surveyed the circular reading room. 'It's just you and me on this level and Amber upstairs.'

James tilted his screen towards Oliver. *Click.* Oliver closed his laptop as James turned in his chair. The next quarter of the circular building was in darkness.

Oliver sighed. 'I didn't want to say anything, but Amber is a little paranoid and overcautious. You should ignore her.'

'Are you sure?' James gazed off into the distance. *One more reason I should start wearing my glasses.*

'Actually'—Oliver shifted in his seat as he opened the laptop—'Amber helped Manesh a lot during the early stages of the discovery of the Commentary before Manesh sold it to All Saints.'

James nodded. 'I recall her saying that she worked with him.'

Over Oliver's shoulder, James watched the window on the screen close as Oliver's long fingers glided across the silver keys of the laptop. 'She didn't just help Manesh. Amber practically did all the work for him. And there's no record of Amber being included or invited to join the research team.'

'Perhaps she declined him in person. After all, she is obsessed with her PhD thesis.' James rested his head on his clenched hand.

Oliver smirked. 'That's putting it mildly.'

'Do you think she would hold a grudge?'

Oliver chuckled. 'The other day, she tried to change the photocopier cartridge. There was a mini explosion, and she freaked out. I'm talking about a full meltdown. She insisted on going home to have a shower. Three hours later, she was back in the office, super calm.'

James narrowed his eyes and pursed his lips.

'I don't see her murdering anyone. Between her issues with mess and the medication, I don't think she could.' Oliver relaxed in his chair. 'But I'm no expert.'

As his eyes widened, James jolted upright. 'Manesh's chat-room friend.'

Oliver's mouth hung open. 'What friend?'

James took a deep breath. 'Moments before I got caught snooping around in Manesh's office, I found a secret phone hidden under the floorboards, nestled in a carved-out copy of *The Da Vinci Code*.'

'Of course you did.' Oliver laughed.

James placed his phone on the desk and leaned in, resting

his elbows on the polished wood. 'Do you think you could find their location or find out more information about them?'

'What an idiot.' Oliver shook his head. 'He told this person about the *Commentary*?'

James nodded.

Oliver closed the laptop. 'He spoke to a stranger on the internet.'

James ran his fingers through his hair. 'I know it's a lot to wrap your mind around, but do you think you could find this person's information?'

Oliver folded his arms and leaned back in his chair. 'Sure, I should be able to get the person's IP address, but that will pinpoint them to a general area, not a specific place. For instance, the Bodleian Library has purchased its own IP addresses, but they point to the official street address of the Bodleian, not the reading room where the person is located.'

James nodded. 'How—'

Thud, thump. James froze as he listened to a pile of books falling over in the background.

'Amber's right. Someone is hiding back there,' James whispered.

Nudging Oliver, James pointed at the marble staircase at the back of the building. *Time to make a run for it.* Without looking back, the two men grabbed their belongings and sprinted towards the staircase to the ground level, leaving Amber alone in the library with the intruder.

THIRTY-TWO

UNDER THE COVER OF DARKNESS, James ambled down the path towards the gate, with Oliver following closely. Looming ahead was the majestic bell tower of the University Church of St Mary the Virgin. The golden clock handles on its tower glistened in the moonlight. It was twelve minutes to ten.

At the gate, James and Oliver turned right and followed the cobblestone road around the Radcliffe Camera. As they reached the junction between Radcliffe Square and Brasenose Lane, a familiar black hooded coat flapped in the background behind them. James's heart raced as the dulcet nighttime melody of the square grew louder. Every rustling leaf or rolling stone set him on edge. At the last moment, James followed the cobblestone road to the right. A burst of pain shot through his side as he dashed into the partially closed Catte Street, hoping Oliver was following him. A heavy rock formed in the pit of his stomach as he sprinted up the street. He had left Amber in the library.

James glanced over his shoulder, hoping Oliver was following. A short distance behind, Oliver trembled as he struggled to run with a set of headphones around his neck and a laptop bag over one shoulder. James diverted his eyes to the left. Oliver nodded. Off in the distance, the hooded figure raced after them. The shimmer of the golden Venetian joker mask had come into view. Naturally, the police weren't following him when he needed them most. Typical.

Once James turned around, a familiar sight emerged. Looming behind them, a pair of bright-green eyes underneath a golden mask fixed on them as the figure stalked through the streets. *Merde.*

Turning right, James rushed down New College Lane with Oliver lagging. The waves of pain intensified as he made a sharp left turn into the dark, narrow St Helen's Passageway. As he followed the road, a familiar white facade bearing the words "Turf Tavern" materialised.

Oliver gestured towards the back door. 'Should we?'

James smirked. 'It would be rude not to.'

THIRTY-THREE

HIS CHEST TIGHTENED, and his breathing accelerated. Thoughts swirled in James's mind like restless waves of an ocean during a storm. Lying in the darkness, he stared at the ceiling. All he needed to do was sleep. It was a simple task yet so far out of reach, almost unattainable.

As predicted, the hooded figure had disappeared and never reemerged. After several drinks, Oliver and James braved the trip back to his hotel room, looking over their shoulders the entire time. The handover of Manesh's phone was uneventful. Was the stalking just a scare tactic? If it was, it worked.

The time flashed up on his phone—12:18 a.m. All he knew was that the hooded figure wasn't Ben. There was no way Ben could have stalked them through the streets in his condition. And whoever had killed Manesh had knowledge of the Commentary, its value, and maybe the inscriptions on the margins. Had Manesh told people about the riddle?

As James rolled over onto his side, a sharp pain tore through his body. He turned onto his back. There were four candidates who could be the hooded figure. First, there was the manuscript's original owner. The next suspect on the list was Liam's killer for hire, Dr Teflon. James wondered how long it would have taken a man like that to figure out the manuscript's value. Would he have been tempted to steal it for a profit? And then there was Manesh's chat-room friend. Why had Manesh talked to so many people about the *Commentary on Daniel*?

The last suspect on the list was Owen. He was too smug, almost like a cat who'd just caught a mouse. Even though Owen didn't perfectly fit the description, James got the impression that his friend knew something essential or had played a part in all of this. But he had no proof, just a niggling feeling. James's eyes widened as a lone thought drifted into his mind. He had forgotten another possibility—someone working at the university could have overheard something that piqued their interest.

James closed his eyes and sighed. He moved his hand around until he felt the cold metal of the pull switch. After tugging it, James sat then picked up a paperback copy of *The Martian* that was sitting under the yellow light of the lamp. As he opened the novel, a message lit up his smartphone's screen. Discarding the book on the soft-white duvet of the antique mahogany double bed, he picked up the phone. The message read:

> I'm being followed home by some guy in a gold mask. Please tell me you made it back to your hotel room?

An overwhelming dread swept over James's body as he tapped on the phone's screen and brought it to his ear. After jumping out of bed, James paced around the room as he listened to the dial tone. *Amber, pick up.*

'Hello,' Amber's out-of-breath voice muttered.

James ran his fingers through his hair. 'Where are you?'

'I'm walking along Brasenose Lane. And I'm taking my usual route to the N8 bus. I think he's going to follow me if I turn in to Turf Street.'

'Don't go on the bus. The streets are dark and secluded.' James paused at the foot of the bed. 'You need to go somewhere that's populated.' James rubbed the back of his neck as his gaze darted around the room. His eyes widened. 'Come to the Randolph hotel. You can stay with me. There are lots of staff here, and I know that whoever is following you doesn't want to be seen.'

James's hands trembled as he listened to the dial tone. He ambled over to the armchair and sat hunched over, staring at the screen. A rock formed in the pit of his stomach as he struck the redial button.

'The number you have called is switched off or unavailable. Please check the number and try again,' a robotic voice said.

The phone fell to the floor as James placed his hand over his mouth. *This is all my fault.*

TWENTY MINUTES LATER, a light knock at the door jolted James out of his panicked state. He picked his phone up off the floor, arose from the armchair, and ambled across the dimly lit room. James leaned towards the spy hole. Relief swept over him as he slid the gold security chain on its track then opened the door. Before him stood a tall, thin, trembling woman with reddened pale-green eyes. *Merde.*

James caressed her cheek. 'I'm so sorry. I shouldn't have left you behind in the Rad Cam.'

Amber exhaled. 'I really don't want to talk about it,' she said, then her voice broke.

James stepped aside, allowing Amber to enter. As she sauntered in, James felt her gaze linger on his pyjama pants. *Maybe I should wear a shirt.*

Letting the door close behind Amber, James turned and opened the glass-panelled doors to the wardrobe. He reached in, grabbed a navy-blue T-shirt, and put it on. Amber stood beside the armchair, brushing her hand along the arm of her gingham shirt.

James bobbed his head. 'Are you cold?'

Amber stopped brushing her sleeve. 'No. I thought I ripped the arm of my shirt.'

James nodded and stood beside her, staring at the bed in silence. Then he turned to Amber and smiled. 'I'm not sure what you want to do, but maybe we could go to bed.' James angled his head in that direction. 'Or we could chat first. I usually take the right.'

Inwardly, James cringed. *A comet tearing towards earth would be so welcome right now.*

Amber blushed.

James turned crimson. 'I wasn't suggesting that we...' He held his hands out. 'You know.'

Amber bit her lip. 'I don't mind talking for a bit.'

As James strolled to the other side of the bed, Amber sat on the armchair and removed her shoes. James picked up his novel, placed it on his bedside table, and slipped into bed. Across the room, Amber stood and unbuttoned her jeans then slid them off her toned, slender legs. Her thin beige belt was already curled up neatly on the side table. While folding her jeans, Amber caught James's longing gaze.

James glanced away in an attempt to conceal his smile. 'I'm so sorry,' James mumbled as he rolled over and faced the wall. He was really into her. And knowing his luck, she probably thought he was a creep. *Merde.*

Anxiety built up inside him as he stared at the wall. The thick white duvet tugged under his arm as the mattress floundered underneath him. Then Amber slipped into bed. When he faced her again, her expression was unreadable.

James sighed. 'I need to ask you about Manesh's last day before the reunion dinner.'

Amber smiled. 'To be honest, it was a typical day. I said hi to Manesh as he made his morning coffee, and then later that day, I saw him in the Rad Cam reading rooms. He seemed to spend a lot of time flipping through French history books. It's hard to say if it was for work or fun. But he left the Rad Cam around six thirty p.m.'

James narrowed his eyes. 'French history?'

'Yeah. He's been using the reading rooms over the last week.' Amber rolled onto her side and faced James. 'It's easy to get distracted while researching. It's hard to say whether it was Commentary related or just an obsession.'

James pursed his lips and stared off into the distance.

Amber moved into James's line of vision. 'What's up?'

'It's nothing.' James shrugged. 'I feel bad for getting you involved in this. I never meant for you to be in so much danger.' James leaned closer. 'I understand if you've changed your mind about helping me.'

'No, it's fine,' Amber said with a slight smile. 'Besides, I'd rather help you than wait for a masked villain to kill me.'

James sighed. 'Look, this is the reality of my job. People don't like me sticking my nose in their business. As a result, I receive death threats, and occasionally, as a fun bonus, I'll be stalked through the streets and threatened in person. But you don't have to put yourself in harm's way.'

Amber leaned in and gently kissed his lips. As she pulled away, James blushed.

'You know. Don't you?'

'Yeah, it's a little obvious.' Amber tossed her hair back. 'To me, at least.'

James's mouth fell open. 'How long have you known?'

'A while.' Amber gave him a coy smile.

James stared at Amber's rosy pink lips, longing to pull her closer. His gaze wandered up to her pale-green eyes. To his surprise, perhaps for the first time, he noticed the same longing staring back. After all the chaos he'd brought into her quiet, ordered life, she wanted him too. Should he go down this road with her? Was he just making it harder for himself to leave for New York if he got attached?

Inching closer, James firmly pulled Amber's slender frame to him. He tilted his head towards Amber and brushed his lips against hers. With a gentle tongue stroke, he deepened the kiss. Entwined, they fell back onto the Egyptian cotton sheet. Amber ran her fingers through James's hair as he kissed her again.

THIRTY-FOUR

FRIDAY: 6:33 A.M.

THE EARLY MORNING sun shone through the gap between the curtains and into James's eyes. Just five more minutes. That was all he wanted. Squeezing his eyes shut, James rolled over and drifted back to sleep.

A *whoosh* and *thud* jolted James out of his slumber and into the harsh reality of the early morning. A sharp pain shot through his left side. James grimaced as he dragged his weary, naked body out of bed. As the waves of pain intensified, James sat on the edge of the mattress. Turning to the right, James patted the covers. Amber was gone, and in her place was a ruffled duvet. *Interesting.*

After surveying the room, James located his pyjama trousers. While putting on his trousers, James shuffled to the mahogany desk near the wardrobe. Upon reaching the desk, James opened the small French designer wallet near the phone. He pulled out the key card for his hotel room. As the card slid out, a small photo of a young woman with ash-blond hair protruded from the wallet's canvas interior pocket. At the partial sighting of the picture, his heart sank. *Maman.*

As he dropped the key card onto the desk, James pulled out the photo with his left hand. A tiny chubby baby wearing dark-denim dungarees with a blue stripy shirt lay cradled in her arms. All the photographs James had of his mother were cropped off to the right. He smiled. With his right arm pinned to his stomach, James stood at the desk and stared at the photo.

He hadn't given her a second thought. And he'd made no progress in figuring out the truth about how she'd passed away. From age six, James had received many lectures about going through his grandfather's study and searching for information about his mother—after getting caught. Now, he had more evidence, another piece to the puzzle, but he couldn't pursue it. The investigation into Manesh's murder had proved more complicated than James had first thought. It wouldn't take only a few days. Instead, he needed to stay a little longer and dig deeper. Despite his many failings and bad choices, Manesh deserved justice. The truth needed to be exposed, not so Lady Margaret could do damage control but so the killer could be stopped and the *Commentary on Daniel* returned to All Saints. It was ambitious, but it was the right path to take.

James flipped open the small silver laptop in the centre of the desk, typed in the password, and waited. After clicking on the fourth browser tab, James scrolled through his emails, found the booking confirmation for his flight to New York, and read the cancellation policy.

———

ONE HOUR LATER, James sat at a small wooden table in the Queen's Lane Coffee House, sipping a cup of piping-hot green tea, waiting for his avocado-and-smoked-salmon bagel. Opposite him sat Kate Graham. She wore a white cherry-print dress. Or more precisely a tea dress as he discovered after receiving a polite reprimand for incorrectly referring to it as a summer frock. Amidst the chaos and drama of the night before, James had received a text from Kate asking him to meet her for breakfast the following day. The message was written with a hint of urgency and in stark contrast to the blissful aura of the woman sitting in front of him, sipping a green juice through a candy-cane-striped straw.

'I bet this brings back memories.' Kate leaned forward and smiled.

James frowned. 'The baguettes are okay here. I guess.'

Kate laughed. 'Frenchy, you're such a snob.'

As the kitchen door opened and slammed shut, a savoury aroma filled the tiny coffeehouse. A waiter holding two plates of food walked to their table and placed the food in front of them. Leaning across the table, James inspected Kate's plate. It was piled with toast, baked beans, a sausage, and half a tomato. British breakfasts were confusing for him, a far cry from his usual croissant and espresso.

'Yours looks good.' Kate smiled. She tilted her head and glanced at James's plate through the sea of cups and condiments scattered across the middle of the round table.

James wrinkled his brow and pursed his lips. 'Why is there always a tomato?' He pointed with his fork. 'And how do you know if that's a vegetarian sausage?'

'Hopefully, this is the vegetarian breakfast,' Kate whispered.

As he placed his fork on the table, James closed the bagel then picked it up and took a bite. He rolled his eyes as a slice of avocado slipped out of the sesame-seed bagel. Kate bit her lip as she pushed her baked beans around her plate. As he set the bagel on the plate, Kate peered up at James.

She brushed her hair behind her left ear. 'I need to ask a favour.'

Couldn't smell that one coming.

'It's Liam,' Kate said with a sigh. 'I'm worried about him. He's been acting strange of late.'

James narrowed his eyes. 'What do you mean by "strange"?'

'I can tell he's not sleeping well, which I'm assuming is why he's so irritable. He's been keeping me awake with his constant tossing and turning. And he never goes out anymore, not even to the corner store.' Kate placed her fork on the edge of her plate. 'He's shut himself up in the house like a recluse. When I leave, he bolts every lock on the door and slides the chain across.' Kate's hands trembled. 'Lately, I've been watching him before I leave in the morning, and he checks the locks more than once. I don't understand where his paranoia has come from.'

James gazed at his bagel. 'How long has he been like this?'

Kate's eyebrows furrowed. 'About a week.'

Merde, he must be feeling guilty.

'James, I was hoping you could keep an eye on him while you're here.' Kate leaned towards him. 'Maybe you could figure out what's on his mind.'

He sighed. 'Liam has been avoiding me too. So it's not just you.'

Kate's face dropped. 'Really? I was hoping he had turned a corner when Liam said he had the guys over for dinner.'

James picked up the sesame seed bagel from his plate and took a bite. As he chewed, he watched Kate reluctantly pick up a slice of toast. He couldn't bear to tell her the truth. What could he say except "Your boyfriend is feeling guilty about hiring a hit man to knock off your lover."

James swallowed. 'Obviously, he's having trouble sleeping. Memory loss is most likely a side effect. I'm sure it's nothing.' He squeezed Kate's hand and smiled at her sympathetically.

'How have you been since the lab break-in? Are you okay?' she asked in a soothing tone.

Ignoring the dull twinge of pain in his side, James waved her off. 'I'm fine.'

After picking up her phone, Kate tapped the screen and

slid the phone across the table. On the screen was a blog post from the ever-popular Web Doctor site. Or as he knew it, the bane of his grandfather's existence. His grandfather loathed the self-diagnosis trend thanks to the internet and sites like that one. After receiving texts from friends and relatives about potential aliments, he would go on the same rant about seeing a real doctor. The blog post listed the symptoms of posttraumatic stress disorder.

'Do you think Liam has PTSD? I think he's having nightmares,' Kate said as her eyes glazed over.

An uneasy sensation swept over James's body. Sure, some of Liam's symptoms could be a sign of PTSD. But Kate was missing a piece of the puzzle, a crucial component. Liam's erratic behaviour was most likely attributed to guilt. There was something in James that was desperate to cross Liam off his list of suspects, but every time he attempted to do so, a moment like that one cropped up. *This isn't good news.*

'Don't worry. I'll see if I can coax it out of Liam.'

THIRTY-FIVE

FAR OFF IN THE DISTANCE, a lone figure passed under the archway and strolled towards James. She wore a navy-blue military blazer with silver buttons that glistened in the morning sun. Her loose-fitted long-sleeve striped shirt rippled in the light morning breeze. James smiled.

As he drew closer, Amber hung her head then tugged at the hair around her loose bun as she continued to amble along. Together, they passed under the ever-expanding branches of the giant oak tree. James brushed his hand along hers. She flinched. Amber tilted her head as her cheeks flushed a rosy-pink hue.

'I'm off to the Queen's Lane Coffee House. Do you want a coffee?' Amber asked as she peered over James's shoulder and towards the college's blue gates.

The streets were empty and gates ajar. *Great, she's trying to leave.* He grabbed her hand as she walked past. Amber glanced at the beige gravel path.

He smiled. 'I missed you this morning,' James said in a hushed tone. 'You should have stayed a little longer.'

Amber turned a slight crimson. 'I had a meeting.' She

shuffled along the gravel. 'And I need to stick to my research schedule. I'm falling behind.'

She looked at him then redirected her eyes to the gate. *Merde.* He was making things worse.

James nodded as he slipped his hands into the pockets of his dark-rinsed jeans. 'I guess you're probably too busy to help me with the investigation.'

Amber took a step closer to the gates. 'I'm not s-sure,' she stuttered. 'Maybe.' Then she dashed to the gate and disappeared through the visitors' entrance.

Well done, idiot. You've scared her off.

With a heavy sigh, James sauntered towards the archway. It was time to get back to work. He had no time to stew over his tragic love life.

THIRTY-SIX

THE WARM RAYS of the morning sun shone in James's eyes as he ambled along the beige gravel path towards the archway. After his eventful morning, his best course of action was to search for Liam. Although he suspected Liam was at home, James checked his office at All Saints while he was in the area. As James approached the archway, far off in the distance, a lone figure dressed in black stood smoking, facing the L-shaped research building. A cool breeze whistled through the archway and straight through his white polo shirt, causing him to hunch over as he strolled along the path.

Standing in the Whittaker Quadrangle, James squinted at the figure. He looked familiar, another reason to wear his glasses. As James rolled his eyes and ambled along the path, an icy hand crept up behind him and covered his mouth, while a second hand gripped his bicep and dragged him through the large dark-stained wooden doors of the All Saints Chapel. His head was pulled back, straining the muscles in his neck as James resisted his captor. But his attempts were futile. Then he realised that no one knew he was there. Would Amber look for him if he went missing?

With the hand firmly over his mouth, James trembled as

he was dragged through the renovated chapel narthex. As James gazed up at the late-eighteenth-century stained glass windows, his heart raced. From behind, James's captor pulled him into the nave, where the college founders were buried. While attempting to resist, he was dragged along the black-and-white tiled floor and onto a pew. As James sat, his captor came into view. *Oh, la vache!*

Hovering over him was a frazzled, green-eyed, ginger-haired man. The dark circles and purple bruising around his eyes made them stand out. Liam held his finger up to his mouth. He was a mere shadow of the man James knew. Liam appeared battered, tormented, and crazy.

'You never saw me. We were never here,' Liam whispered as his eyes bulged.

James took a deep breath as Liam paced up and down the nave. Then, out of the blue, Liam paused and faced James. Hunched over, Liam slid his hands into the pockets of his brown corduroy trousers and sighed. As his racing pulse eased, James stood then ambled over to his tormented friend. The two stood in silence for a few seconds. What was going on with him?

James braced himself for whatever news Liam had for him. His friend had been secretive of late. Prior to that, Liam was always an open book. But James wondered whether he should trust anyone because they all had something to hide—not just the usual secrets but something dark. As a journalist, he despised secrets and felt it was his job to expose the truth and reveal what was hiding in the shadows. But his quest for the truth had alienated his friends, and that was something James wanted to avoid.

James hung his head then looked at Liam. 'What's up?'

Liam's hands trembled as a droplet of sweat dripped down his forehead. 'I know who killed Manesh.' He sighed as if an enormous weight had been lifted off his shoulders.

'Who?' James stepped closer to his friend.

'I'm not sure if I should say anything. I keep changing my mind and wondering if staying quiet is the best thing.' Liam's voice broke.

'It's okay. You can tell me.' James placed his left hand on Liam's shoulder, hoping the gesture would be reassuring. 'I won't rest until I figure this out.'

Liam's chin and lips trembled as he peered over James's shoulder. The Renaissance-era painting of Jesus's burial loomed above the baby grand piano in the chapel's narthex. It was not what James was expecting to see. Was Liam having visions?

'I can't say anything.' Liam bit his lip then stared at the floor's tiles.

'Why?' James asked.

'What if I tell you and that makes you a target? What if talking could get me killed?' Liam mumbled as he paced up and down the nave.

James stepped back to give Liam more room. 'Obviously, you're certain. Right?'

'Yes, I recognised the person immediately.'

'Why have you not told the police?' James stared into the narthex through the doorway in the vestibule screen. He couldn't believe his friend was holding back vital information.

'Simple. I keep my mouth shut, and I don't die.' A bitter tone lingered in Liam's voice.

James narrowed his eyes. 'Has something changed?'

Liam glanced at the chapel's stained glass windows. 'I keep dreaming about Manesh and the lab invasion. A part of me thinks that if I share what I know, the dreams will stop.' Liam sighed. 'But I'm terrified of talking. Coming here was a mistake.' Liam's shoulders dropped as he sauntered to the narthex.

James grabbed Liam's arm. 'Is the person still in Oxford?'

'I can't say. I shouldn't be here talking to you.'

James rolled his eyes. The gentle approach was no longer

working with Liam. After the most terrifying two minutes of James's life, Liam was going to waltz out of there and not say a word.

James pursed his lips and glared at Liam. 'Just knowing and being able to identify a killer would make you next on their list. Keeping quiet won't change anything. Isn't that a reason you need to tell me or the police? The police will protect you.' James leaned in and whispered, 'Tell me, and I will go to the police and deliver the information on your behalf. I'm sure Detective Alice O'Donnell will want to keep you out of harm's way.'

'I can't talk to you anymore. It's too much of a risk.' Liam grimaced as he headed to the vestibule screen that separated the nave from the narthex.

From outside the chapel, the sound of gravel crunching underfoot disrupted the silence of the nave. Liam froze, and a look of panic swept across his face. James maintained eye contact with Liam and mouthed, "It's tourist season." The crunching came to a halt. An eerie silence swept over the chapel. Inching closer to the vestibule screen, James angled his ear towards the wall. Was someone standing outside listening?

James grabbed Liam's arm and pulled him back into the nave. 'Go directly to the station and make a statement. Don't talk to anyone. Just run. I'll check outside first.'

On the balls of his feet, James crept through the nave, around the piano, and hid behind the closed wooden chapel door. In the reflection of the windows, James saw the Whittaker Quadrangle was empty. Whoever was eavesdropping had just left, possibly by the main archway.

James turned around to find Liam standing behind him.

'Why are you helping the police?' Liam had a hint of suspicion in his voice.

James sighed. 'Detective Alice O'Donnell put a hold on my passport. I can't leave until the police solve Manesh's murder.'

But he had other reasons—reasons he would rather not talk about. And then there was the Lady Margaret effect. The mere whisper of her name caused all conversation to cease, and joy immediately died. Liam didn't get along with her. How would he react if he knew James was working for her? James didn't want to find out.

'I don't know,' Liam said, breaking James's train of thought. 'Maybe I'll go to the police.'

'The best thing you can do is to talk. Detective Alice O'Donnell will protect you. Trust me, she will.' James placed his arm around Liam's shoulder. 'Take the gate along Parks Road. I'm sure whoever was listening headed off towards the visitors' entrance along Broad Street.'

Liam sheepishly walked out of the chapel. As James slumped against the wooden door, he wondered how Liam had come to his conclusions. At least he'd agreed to talk to the police.

THIRTY-SEVEN

FRIDAY: 8:36 A.M.

THE MORNING SUN shone from behind the bell tower of the University Church of St Mary and made Liam squint as he strolled down Catte Street. After taking a few deep breaths to avoid hyperventilating, Liam picked up his pace. All he had to do was tell the detective what he knew, and that was it. Then everything would be fine.

But deep down, Liam knew everything would not be fine. The second he crossed the road into Catte Street, Liam sensed a pair of eyes on him. Ever since he'd left the station early in the morning, Liam had felt as if he were being stalked. Considering that he'd spent the last twenty-four hours in police custody, thanks to his own stupidity, Liam assumed the police were following him. Since then, doubts had crept in, and he was no longer sure it was the police. The watchful gaze felt sinister. He felt like an innocent stag frolicking through the Scottish countryside.

In the early morning hours, Detective Alice O'Donnell had arrived at the station, looking a little dishevelled, then let him out and processed the forms for his release. Detective O'Donnell didn't say a word. She just let him go. And now

Liam wished he had begged her to stay. For a second, Liam peered over his shoulder, but all he could see was a blurry haze. His astigmatism had gotten worse. Like an idiot, he kept putting off a trip to the optometrist to collect his new contact lenses.

As Liam strolled past the Bodleian Library, he picked up his pace. Liam glanced over his shoulder then turned around. He'd suspected things would end this way. He should've told James the truth.

Liam increased his speed. He didn't want to make it easy for the familiar figure behind him. After pulling out his smartphone, Liam typed in the password and sprinted down Catte Street then Radcliffe Square. The patter of shoes hitting cobblestones echoed through the quiet, empty streets. Peeking over his shoulder, Liam met a familiar pair of bright-green eyes. Liam's heart raced as he refocused on the Rad Cam then turned in to the gate and sprinted along the path.

Liam wished he had gone to the station instead of returning to the Rad Cam. Regret built up within him. He should've confessed while he had the chance, but it was too late. As Liam sprinted up the path, the word "Closed" printed on a white sheet of paper came into view. *Shit.*

He took a sharp right-hand turn and dashed across the pristine green lawn. Liam stared at his smartphone, tapped the screen, then opened the email app and scrolled through the list. He opened a new screen as a sharp pain shot through his skull. As he dropped the phone, Liam clutched his head and raced across the lawn. His lungs strained in his rib cage as he dragged his weary body around the grass. The heavy breaths of the familiar figure grew louder.

A second blow to his head caused his world to spin. His legs gave way underneath him, and he fell to the ground. He twisted around to face his attacker. The world darkened as his back touched the soft grass. *This is the end.* A familiar face towered over Liam as darkness filled his vision. There was nothing more he could do. It was hopeless. All he could do was hope that James would notice his absence.

THIRTY-EIGHT

WHY HERE? James sauntered down the nave of All Saints Chapel. James paused and stared at the cherubim-and-vine detailing on the ornamental screen covering the wall behind the altar. To his left, encased in a carved wooden cabinet, lay the alabaster tombs of the founders, Sir Benedict Whittaker and his wife, Christiana. On the right side of the altar was the president's private pew.

It was such a strange place to discuss the lab break-in. Liam's choice of venue made no sense. Perhaps to a man suffering from trauma-related visions mixed with guilt, the venue made sense on some level. James sighed. He was being ridiculous. He was reading too much into things.

Frustrated by his overanalysis, James ambled along the nave towards the vestibule screen. Since Liam was on his way to the police station, next on James's to-do list was a talk with Oliver about the anonymous chat-room friend.

———

TEN MINUTES LATER, James followed Oliver through a sea of white doors with identical gold nameplates. As Oliver glanced over his shoulder, he angled his head towards a familiar closed door with police tape stretched across the doorframe.

'In here,' Oliver whispered as he opened the door while juggling a silver laptop in his other arm. Oliver ducked under the tape and disappeared into the room.

More secret discussions. There must be something in the water.

James rolled his eyes, ducked under the tape, and stepped into Manesh's office. In the centre of the room was a mahogany desk piled high with papers that spilt onto the floor —evidence from James's last visit. With his laptop nestled under his arm, Oliver strolled over to the door and closed it then whirled around. A smirk formed on his face then disappeared.

'The events surrounding the break-in keep getting stranger.' Oliver ambled towards James. 'Manesh first met his mysterious friend online in May. The IP address for the replies to the first conversation comes from a block of addresses purchased by the New York Public Library.'

James wiggled his nose to adjust the position of his spectacles. 'What?' James ran his fingers through his hair. 'I was expecting the address to point to the Bodleian Library or some other location in Oxford.'

Oliver nodded. 'What's fascinating is they disguised their location in all conversations after the initial chat.'

James narrowed his eyes. 'Whoever this is wanted to be seen as trustworthy by sharing his location.'

Oliver nodded. 'Yes. To someone like Manesh, who isn't an IT professional, a person sharing an IP address might be seen as more trustworthy. Whereas another person who shares very little about themselves online might seem suspicious.'

James peered out the window. 'The other thing I know about the chat-room friend is they want to be perceived as highly educated, as evident by the sea of big words.'

Oliver nodded. 'I'm not sure how far you've read into the discussion, but they knew a lot about the Spanish Forger. More than the average Joe.'

James turned around. 'So, they're a collector or at the very least want Manesh to believe they're an expert in some shape or form.'

Oliver blushed. 'Sorry, I've just made your investigations more complicated.'

James pursed his lips. 'I was hoping that finding the chat-room friend's location would narrow my list of suspects. But instead, it adds to it.'

Oliver grimaced. 'When do you meet with Lady Margaret Charlton?'

James sat on the windowsill. 'She's yet to summon me. But I suspect it will be any day now.'

'I have a meeting upstairs. I'll be free in a few hours if you need anything.' Oliver strolled to the door.

James lifted his chin as his glasses slipped down the bridge of his nose. 'What date did you say the person logged in to the internet at the New York Public Library?'

Oliver gazed over his shoulder. 'It was the same date as the chat-room app displays, 9:22 a.m. on the fourth of May.'

James's eyes widened as Oliver opened the door, ducked underneath the tape, and disappeared into the hallway. *Why does the date sound familiar?* James slipped his smartphone out of his pocket and tapped the screen. After searching through his calendar, which triggered a traumatising trip down memory lane, a string of texts appeared on the screen.

Not only was the fourth of May the day before he'd discovered Valentine was kidnapped, but it was also around that time that his friends Liam, Ben, and Owen had ventured on a guys-only trip to New York. As per usual, James couldn't attend because he was up to his eyeballs in work as editor of the *Northampton Tribune.* But from the third of May on, James had received texts containing photos from the trip.

In the text on the smartphone was a series of images of the interior of the New York Public Library, sent to him by Owen. All three friends were in the photos. He was so sure they were rubbing his face in it. But today, he was glad they did.

James strolled to the open door, lifted the police tape and stooped underneath, then closed the door behind him. An overwhelming dread swept over him. Was being at the exact location enough to warrant further questioning? What if he pointed his finger at the wrong person and they got tried for a crime they didn't commit? He needed more evidence. With frustration mounting, James sauntered down the hallway, plotting his next move.

———

JAMES DROVE FRANTICALLY along Appleton Road. With a screech of the brakes, he parked the hideous yellow Peugeot in the first available space in the street. The car was a bad penny. Apparently, it had been the only car available. So much for hoping to get a better vehicle. After slamming the car door behind him, James strolled towards the wooden door of the Wizard and Ragged Staff.

Anxious about the inevitable confrontation, James pulled out his phone and checked his messages. He sighed. Amber hadn't replied to his text. To avoid Owen's tendency for violence, James had hoped Amber would come along and thus give Owen a reason to keep his temper under control. It had worked the first time. After a fruitless search of the halls of All Saints, all James could find was Amber's phone and laptop sitting on her desk and her frazzled research assistant, Matilda. It was as if Amber had vanished or was avoiding being in the same room with the petri dish of germs that was Owen.

A sharp pain shot through James's side as he pushed open the heavy wooden door and strolled to the fourteenth-century bar-turned-reception-desk. Three minutes later, Mrs Black wandered out of the kitchen. Upon spotting James, her face lit up.

'I knew you would be back.' Her eyes darted around the room. 'Where's your friend?' Mrs Black leaned in and whispered.

James smiled. 'She's busy,' he said, hoping the thin grey-haired woman would drop the topic.

'Never mind, dear. You're quite handsome. You'll find a new girl in no time.' Mrs Black tapped James's hand.

After taking a deep breath, James leaned towards Mrs Black. 'My friend Owen, in room 201, has been quite sick recently. Do you know if he's feeling any better?'

Mrs Black furrowed her brow. 'No, he's still upstairs, ordering room service. And he's refusing to see a doctor.'

James nodded. 'Typical.'

'He seemed perfectly fine the night before when he was waiting for that taxi,' she said, staring off into the distance.

James glanced over her shoulder at the keys hanging on the rack. 'Was that on Wednesday, by any chance?'

She nodded. 'Yes, it was around eleven p.m.'

James narrowed his eyes. 'Are you sure he wasn't arriving?'

Mrs Black stepped back from the counter. 'I'll ask Herb. He was on the desk that night.'

The little old lady sauntered around the reception desk and walked across the bar to the staff-only zone.

———

A COUPLE OF MINUTES LATER, a tall elderly man strolled across the bar towards James with Mrs Black following closely.

Herb shook his hand with a surprising amount of force. 'On Wednesday night, the young man in room 201 arrived after eleven p.m. in a taxi and dashed upstairs.' Herb nodded.

'Yes, he had a thick coat, and it wasn't that cold out. It was draped over his arm.'

James nodded. 'So he arrived around eleven?'

The old man shook his finger at James. 'He went out fifteen minutes later and left in another taxi, dressed all in black, wearing gloves. Like he was going to a party.'

Mrs Black tapped James on the arm. 'We didn't recognise him at first because he seemed different. Almost taller.'

Herb grimaced. 'Maybe he wears lifts in his shoes, like that guy in that Impossible movie.'

James smiled. 'Thanks for letting me know. I'll go upstairs and check on Owen to see if he needs anything.'

———

OUT OF BREATH, James clutched the handrail as he stepped onto the top floor. The room spun. With a racing heart, James sauntered across the landing towards room 201. He had conquered the steep, narrow staircase of the Wizard and Ragged Staff. Anxiety built up within him as he knocked on the door. *Please be in a good mood.*

The door flung open. Before him stood Owen. His watery eyes widened as he dabbed his bright-red nose with a tissue.

'Hercule, you're back.' Owen raised his eyebrows.

James shrugged. 'The inhaler didn't help?'

Owen shook his head. 'Nope. Now the skin around my nose is peeling.'

'My *mamie* used to put Vaseline on my nose to stop it from peeling.' James smiled.

Owen smirked. 'God, you're still a mama's boy.'

James sighed. '*Mamie* is French for grandmother.'

Owen shook his head as he ambled to the sofa and sat. 'Grandmothers give you candy when your parents aren't looking. A mother makes you eat broccoli. Your *mamie* is more of a mum than a grandmother.'

James's heart sank. There was nothing he could say that would make Owen understand. It was a pointless conversation. Upon closing the door behind him, James sauntered across the room and sat on the edge of the desk.

James took a deep breath. 'On Wednesday night, when you left the Turf Tavern, did you see Ben during your travels?'

Owen pursed his lips and narrowed his eyes. 'Why would I see Ben?'

James closed his eyes and sighed. 'Ben saw you at ten fifty-nine p.m. a few streets away from the Rad Cam.'

As Owen tapped his fingers on the arm of the leather chair, he stared at James with a blank expression. *Merde.*

'After you returned to the hotel, what did you do for the rest of the night?' James clutched the desk underneath him with both hands.

'I recall'—Owen cleared his throat—'that I told you before when you arrived on my doorstep with Amber that I left the Turf Tavern at ten fifteen p.m. and went straight home. What I did the rest of that evening is none of your business.'

Owen rose from his chair, ambled across the room, then paused. He turned around and stared directly at James.

James's eyes darted around the room. 'Multiple people saw you in Oxford close to All Saints before the murder occurred.'

As Owen's face turned red, he lunged towards the desk, grabbed James by the throat, and pushed him into the wall. The wall shook, causing a picturesque scene of Oxfordshire to fall onto the carpet. Tiny fragments of glass scattered across the floor.

Gasping for air, James performed the only move he could, the one thing he'd never dreamed of doing to another man. But it had come down to kicking Owen in the balls or choking to death. As the room spun, James tried to thrust his knee up. A sharp pounding at the door caused Owen to freeze.

'Housekeeping,' a voice called out from behind the door.

With Owen's hands firmly around his throat, James thrust his knee into Owen's groin. A loud yelp disrupted the awkward silence of the room. Owen fell to the floor, curled up in the fetal position.

'Not today,' James rasped as he got off the desk and towered over Owen.

As James waited for the housekeeper to walk away, Owen sheepishly stood. His watery eyes glared at James as he walked to the door.

'Do you honestly think you're the first to threaten me?'

Owen snarled back, 'I can imagine you've pissed off more than your fair share of people.' Owen lunged and pushed James into the door. 'Keep your nose out of my business. Understand?' Owen pushed him again then stepped back.

As James opened the door, he looked over his shoulder. 'I also know you were in the New York Public Library on the same day and time as Manesh's chat-room friend logged in and spoke to him for the first time about the *Commentary on Daniel*.'

Owen grimaced as his face turned crimson. He clenched his fists as James stepped out of the room and closed the door behind him. 'It wasn't me!' Owen yelled.

THIRTY-NINE

ALICE STARED through the viewing room's glass panel at Zach, who was adjusting the transparent shield covering his face. She continued to look straight ahead as she felt the watchful gaze of Crown Prosecutor Ernest Lane. A bright white light suspended from the ceiling cast a round halo over Manesh's bloodstained white-collared shirt as he lay on the surgical bed. Zach's cream rubber boots squeaked as they rubbed against the green linoleum floor of the autopsy suite.

A short Congolese man stood by the door, grimacing. Alice smiled. After returning to work from six months of leave and passing his psychological evaluations, her colleague and friend Joseph had decided three months later to do fieldwork. He must have grown tired of desk duty.

Lane cleared his throat. Alice cringed then smiled in his direction, hoping a simple acknowledgement would suffice.

Lane smirked. 'Queasy stomach, Detective?'

'Seems to be a straightforward case.' Lane nodded as he looked through the two-way mirror.

Alice shook her head.

'Detective, you disapprove?' Lane mused. 'What are you expecting us to talk about while we're here?'

Alice took a deep breath. 'Any conversation between us would be rude and disrespectful to the victim.' Alice narrowed her eyes. 'At this stage in the investigation, it would be unprofessional of me to make rash judgements about the case being straightforward.'

Lane smirked.

A piercing squeal followed by a pop from the speaker overhead disrupted Alice's rant. Startled, Alice saw Zach sauntering around the surgical bed. He ran his finger along the barcode label on the edge of the table. With his back to the two-way mirror, Zach strolled around to the other side of the metal bed and halted as he reached Manesh's wrist. Zach lifted the wrist and squinted as he leaned over and read the number beneath the barcode on the white wristband. Cradling Manesh's fingers in his palm, Zach lowered his arm and rested it on the metal surface.

As he turned his head, Zach reached under his transparent shield and adjusted his paper face mask.

'There were no fingerprints that matched the victim in the database. So I enlisted the help of our forensic odontologist, Dr Li Mei Zhang, to do a complete dental reconstruction.' Zach pointed at Manesh's lips. 'As a result of the procedure, residue from the dental moulds is stuck on the victim's lips. Because he's been in the morgue refrigerators, his skin has become dry. Thus, removing the residue has become impossible without damaging his skin.'

Zach sighed.

After reaching into her jacket's inside pocket, Alice pulled out her smartphone, clicked the home button, and checked the audio recording that she had set earlier before tapping the screen and opening the notes app.

'I can confirm that the deceased is Dr Manesh Leigh Warren.' Zach held a finger up at Joseph. 'Before I let PC Abaagihab collect fingerprint and DNA evidence, I'd like to share a few initial findings with you.'

Lane rubbed the back of his neck.

Zach ambled around the metal trolley lined with surgical tools and headed to the silver countertop. Glancing across the room at Joseph, Zach picked up a pair of transparent bags containing the victim's dark-grey jacket and thick tortoiseshell-rimmed glasses. After placing the bags back on the counter, Zach shuffled to the surgical table.

'There is a partial fingerprint on the victim's glasses, which were discovered folded up inside the front pocket of his jacket. Perhaps the perpetrator removed them for obvious reasons.' Zach gazed at the countertop behind him. 'A few strands of long, curly, light-brown hair were found on the victim's jacket. I've placed the jacket in the plastic bag, careful not to disturb the evidence.'

Alice narrowed her eyes and pursed her lips. Amber.

Zach placed his gloved hands on his hips. 'And black fibres were sprinkled across the victim's white shirt and jacket. The fibres appear to be wool.'

Alice continued to type notes on her smartphone.

A squeak from Zach's rubber boots made Alice cringe as he strolled around the table. As he lifted Manesh's right hand, Zach turned towards the two-way mirror. 'While Freyja Andersson, the morgue technician, and I were removing the deceased from the fridge, I noticed a build-up of dead skin cells under the victim's nails on his right hand.' Zach placed Manesh's hand on the table, turned, and nodded at Joseph. 'Perhaps he scratched someone, possibly the perpetrator, but that's unlikely because there was no sign of a struggle at the crime scene.'

Lane raised his eyebrows at Alice.

'I can't comment. You need to wait for my report,' Alice snapped at Lane.

Zach murmured to himself.

Facing the two-way mirror, Zach paused then leaned over the victim. A tall, thin woman wearing blue surgical scrubs and a hair net hopped off the wheeled black leather stool and dashed to the metal trolley. Crouching, she rustled through the supplies on the second level of the trolley. She handed Zach a flat white sponge.

Five minutes later, Zach peered at Alice through the two-way mirror. 'He's wearing stage makeup to cover bruising under his left eye.' Zach scanned the body on the table then looked at the tall, thin woman. 'Freyja, I need another sponge.' He handed her the used one.

A mist formed on the outer rims of Zach's spectacles as he sprinted around the table and picked up the new sponge. Cradling Manesh's left hand, Zach dabbed the sponge on his skin. With wide eyes, Zach looked at Alice through the two-way mirror.

'The victim has bruising on his knuckles, which was also concealed by stage makeup. The foundation is quite thick. Based on the bruising available, both physical confrontations occurred within the forty-eight hours leading up to his death.'

Alice studied her screen and typed more notes as Lane tapped his fingers against the far wall of the observation room.

———

FORTY MINUTES LATER, Tchaikovsky hummed through the tin speakers in the autopsy suite and filtered through the intercom into the observation room. Zach placed the scalpel on the metal trolley and peeled back the flaps of skin. Alice walked to the back of the room with her arms folded, feeling queasy. The last thing she needed was for Lane to notice that he was right.

Lane strolled across the room and sat on the table's edge. He picked up the white mug of tea and took a sip. 'For a forensic pathologist, he shows a significant amount of care, considering at some point he's going to take a circular saw to the victim's skull and remove the skull cap.'

'To be honest, it's kind of refreshing. Sometimes pathologists can be a bit brutal when moving the body.'

Lane nodded as he took another sip.

A grinding sound from the circular saw echoed through the tiny tin speaker. Alice shuddered.

'I'm surprised to see Joseph here today. It's been almost nine months since the shooting.' Lane put the mug on the table and folded his arms. 'Has the bullet wound healed nicely?'

Alice stopped pacing. 'He doesn't like to talk about it. Despite my curiosity, I haven't asked. I'm almost too scared to bring it up. But he seems fine. He's been back at work for three months now. And I'm impressed that he decided to do fieldwork.'

'I'm impressed too.' Lane nodded.

Ten minutes later, Lane grimaced as he peered over Alice's shoulder. Scared of what she might find, Alice stared into the autopsy suite. Zach lifted Manesh's heart out of his chest and placed it on the scales. A few seconds later, the arrow on the capacity dial stopped moving. Zach picked up the heart from the scale pan and cradled it in his hands. He watched the heart as he moved it around. Still clutching the organ, Zach leaned forward and gazed into the chest cavity.

'The bullet entered the chest and grazed a rib. After that, it entered the right ventricle and went straight through. It's lodged between the T8 and T9 vertebrae. Any injury to the heart is fatal. There's no way the victim would have survived this. The eye was removed after the victim's death, made evident by the sprinkle of blood on the jacket, trousers, and shoes,' Zach said as he hunched over the body.

Alice turned away as Zach stood upright and walked past the metal trolley and yellow disposal bin towards the countertop, where a tray was lined with organs.

Zach cleared his throat and looked at Alice through the two-way mirror. 'From what I can see, there's no evidence of poisoning, but I'm going to send a few samples off to Toxicology just to be certain. Those results may take a while.'

———

TWENTY-TWO MINUTES LATER, Zach stepped away from the surgical bed and rubbed his bloodied gloves down the sides of his blue surgical scrubs. Alice's eyes widened as she stared at the red smears on Zach's trousers.

'He's almost religious about it,' Lane said as he glanced into his third mug of tea.

Alice nodded as she watched Zach remove his latex gloves and throw them into the yellow disposal bin.

'The manner of death is homicide, the cause of death is a gunshot wound, and the mechanism of death is exsanguination. I'll know more once I get results from the extra tests I've requested from Toxicology.' Zach walked across the room and stood in front of the two-way mirror. 'Hopefully, I will send you both my report soon.'

Lane jumped up from the desk, walked over to the wall, and hit the intercom button. 'Dr Dalgleish, just a question about the bruising. Could that confrontation have been between the victim and the perpetrator?'

Zach stared at the body. 'Based on the position of the bruise and the angle at which someone would have hit the victim, I would say whoever hit Manesh was shorter than the person responsible for his death.'

FORTY

HUNCHED OVER, James squinted at the laptop screen as the morning sun shone through the double window in Manesh's office. James sighed then stood, pushing the wheeled chair back. He closed the mocha-brown pencil-pleat curtains. A digital quack called out from behind him. A message had come through on his smartphone. It could be from only one person—Lady Margaret.

A familiar sharp pain shot through his side. Closing his eyes, James took a deep breath then released his grip on the curtains. Grimacing, he dragged his weary body to the desk and sat. He rolled his eyes as the message came into view. It read:

> You have until 9:00 p.m. to get some
> answers before I find someone else who is
> more suited to the task.

Lady Margaret was straight to the point and merciless. Yet despite her faults, she possessed one reassuring trait—she was predictable.

Manesh's inbox was a sea of organised chaos. He had kept every email he'd ever received. There was no filing system, just never-ending emails. James had scrolled down to the ones received over the last few weeks. Reading them was a tedious task. James ran his fingers through his hair as he stared at the screen. Then it dawned on him. Frightened that he was going to forget the idea, James picked up a pen, jotted a note, and flipped through the pages of his pad. Why hadn't he thought of that before?

It was the most logical thing to do in that situation. Scrolling back through the emails, James reached the date that Manesh had signed up for the chat room. Creating a timeline of Manesh's life events, starting from the chat-room sign-up to his death, was James's biggest priority. Optimistically, James hoped it would provide him with a clear understanding of a potential motive and narrow down the list of suspects. *Fingers crossed.*

Farther down the page, a subject line stood out like a lone neon sign along a dark, deserted road. The email was received one hundred and twenty-six days before Manesh was murdered. It was from Stanley Whittaker. James wondered why the last name Whittaker rang a bell. He didn't know anyone with that last name.

In the email, Stanley suggested that Manesh arrange a courier to transport the *Commentary on Daniel* if he didn't wish to make the trek to his house. James furrowed his brow as he read the archaic sentences a second time. Perhaps Stanley was a retired expert on religious manuscripts. Still clutching the pen, James jotted another note then refocused on the screen.

———

FIFTEEN MINUTES LATER, James gave up. He couldn't find any more correspondence between Stanley and Manesh. As he scrolled through the emails, another subject line jumped out at him. The email sent from a nearby printer contained a scanned PDF with a subject that read "contract of sale."

James double-clicked on the PDF. It was a simple contract of sale, stating that All Saints College had purchased the *Commentary on Daniel* for twenty thousand pounds. Attached to the back of the agreement was a series of emails where Manesh told Lady Margaret that while he was on holiday in Bilboa, he'd stumbled across the *Commentary* from an antique dealer and paid twenty-two thousand euros for the manuscript. Believing it to be the work of the Spanish Forger, Manesh suggested studying the manuscript along with the other forgeries. The study could help identify the Forger and the life he lived. It was an ambitious project. The responding email from Lady Margaret highlighted her interest and an agreement to purchase the *Commentary* and financially support Manesh during his research.

Merde.

James jumped up from the chair and paced the room. Then he paused, closed his eyes, and sighed. All Saints had purchased the manuscript around the same time Manesh had hired Ben, which led to the photographs and the extortion attempts. *Coincidence?*

James rolled his eyes as he returned to the desk and sat. As he scrolled through the emails, James discovered Manesh had wasted no time in assembling a team of lab technicians. Manesh fired away a series of emails to a few other PhD research students employed by the college. It wasn't long before he hit a massive roadblock in his research. On the morning of July 8, Manesh reached out to Amber, enquiring about an expert in mediaeval literature written in ecclesiastical Latin.

From then until the day Manesh was murdered, Amber had replied with great enthusiasm. On August 1, Manesh received an email from Lady Margaret pressuring him to provide a final list of his research team members to

Accounting. Amber's name was absent from that list. Two days after finalising his team, Manesh received an email from Amber, who had arranged a meeting between Manesh and Professor Xavier Watson.

James smiled as he read the old professor's name on the screen. Watson had been his favourite professor during his undergraduate course. To leave no stone unturned, James scrolled the cursor across the screen, clicked on the calendar icon, and waited for it to load. James discovered that Manesh had met with Professor Watson three times before he died, not including their initial meeting organised by Amber. The last meeting was four days before Manesh was murdered. *Interesting.*

James moved the cursor then clicked the inbox icon and scrolled through the list of emails. A fax sent by the All Saints College administration office caught James's attention. It was received on Saturday, August 22, the same day as their final meeting. Did Professor Xavier Watson send Manesh a fax?

After hesitating, James double-clicked on the attached PDF and waited for it to load. James scrolled through the document, some insurance papers.

The manuscript was not a forgery created by the Spanish Forger. It was the real thing. Manesh had increased the insurance for the *Commentary on Daniel* to one and a half million pounds several hours after he met up with Professor Xavier Watson. That news would've derailed his research proposal and grant. The killer must have known that. James's eyes widened as he stared at the screen and leaned back in his chair. Could his favourite university professor be behind the murder? Why would he orchestrate something like that? Was there no one he could trust?

FORTY-ONE

NESTLED in a Victorian-style armchair in Clovervale Hall's library, a grey-haired man ambled across the room while carrying two teacups. In his early seventies, Professor Xavier Watson was a tall, thin man with a bald, shiny head and a thick layer of fluffy grey hair on the sides. James smiled. Xavier hadn't changed much since that fateful day of the launch of Clovervale Hall's bed-and-breakfast in April of the previous year. Since his retirement almost three years prior, Xavier had spent his days supervising the renovations of the manor house then running it with his wife, Flora. Technically, Flora ran the bed-and-breakfast. She was a force to be reckoned with. She had a sweet, polite exterior, but the second someone crossed her, they would live to regret it. Amid some grim circumstances, James and Xavier had worked together to solve the murder of a close friend and colleague who was one of the bed-and-breakfast's first guests.

On the side, Xavier collected rare books, mainly first editions and a few mediaeval manuscripts. The results of his newfound hobby were as expected. A sea of stained mahogany bookshelves surrounded them, all lined with books on two topics: ecclesiastical Latin and mediaeval literature. As a result, the room had a museum-like atmosphere. Any moment, a security guard was bound to jump out and scold him for sitting on a piece from the collection.

Xavier placed the two teacups on the round table between their armchairs and smiled. The professor's infamous polite smile often preceded him tearing someone a new one.

'It's been a while.' Xavier pointed his chin down and peered over his thin-framed spectacles.

James picked up the teacup and stared at the floating slice of lemon. 'Yeah, I miss our monthly tea sessions.'

Xavier smirked. 'That's not my fault.'

I knew that one was coming.

Glancing up, James tilted his head. After taking several deep breaths, he relaxed into the chair. 'Did you ever meet up with Manesh or get to see the manuscript he was researching?'

'Yes, I met up with Manesh a few times.' Xavier picked up the teacup and took a sip. 'I heard you witnessed the break-in. Are you okay? Did you get to see the manuscript for yourself?'

'I'm fine.' James nodded. 'The *Commentary* was breathtaking, and the dragons were unique. What did you think of the initiums?'

Xavier smiled as he cradled the fine bone china cup in his hands. 'Yes, the initiums were quite spectacular and on the theme.'

James tapped the side of his teacup. 'Did Manesh ever give you the impression that he thought the *Commentary* might be stolen? Or that people were after him?'

'No, it never occurred to him to even ask that question. He was way out of his depth. At first, I believed he didn't know that the Commentary wasn't a forgery. Then, as our meetings went on, I was certain he was waiting for me to recognise something in the manuscript. Like there was a secret that only he had discovered.' Xavier shook his head. 'His behaviour was bizarre, almost erratic.'

James took a sip of tea. 'What do you mean by "bizarre"?'

Xavier narrowed his eyes and stared across the room over James's shoulder. 'It was as if our meetings were a performance, an abysmal performance, like a new actor in his first play. Everything seemed set up. Manesh obsessed over the pages with me. The same pages every time.'

James wondered whether they were the same pages he'd examined in the lab. 'And you noticed nothing unusual about the pages?'

A blank expression swept across Xavier's face as he glanced at the empty teacup in his hands. 'No, I carefully studied the script and the initiums. There was nothing of consequence in the manuscript. However, there was a lot of evidence for the manuscript being dated to the late twelfth century, around the time when Glastonbury Abbey was believed to be burned to the ground and the contents of their library lost forever.'

He knows something. Why isn't Xavier sharing it with me?

James placed his cup on its saucer. 'Did Manesh say where he discovered the *Commentary*? Or hint at how long he'd had the manuscript?'

Xavier raised his eyebrows. 'Manesh purchased it for an absolute bargain from the late Doris Whittaker's estate at the end of April. But I first saw the text sometime at the beginning of August. I met him once in the lab at All Saints. I told him it was most likely an original. Either that or the Spanish Forger had reached a new level of genius, but that's highly unlikely.'

James wrinkled his brow. 'How do you know?'

The old man leaned back in his chair. 'That level of genius wouldn't be left in an estate like Doris Whittaker's. That *Commentary* was handed down between the generations and its value forgotten.'

James picked up the teacup, clutched it, and peered at a familiar stain on the carpet under the round table. 'So he knew it was real when he sold it to the university?'

As he sipped his tea, Xavier furrowed his brow as if deep in thought. Glancing up, James watched a look of recognition sweep across Xavier's face, but it lasted only a second.

'Manesh changed the insurance to one and a half million pounds four days before he died.' James took another sip of his tea.

Xavier's grey eyes widened. 'Four days before, you say?'

'Yes.'

'That was the week he met up with me almost every day. It was rather peculiar. Amber arranged the meetings, and he picked my brain about everything from the paper to the Latin. And he was obsessed with the dragons in the initiums. Manesh was certain they were of great significance. It was strange he kept meeting up with me. Then he stopped. Now I know why.' Xavier looked out the window. 'Imagine how Doris Whittaker's family would have felt if they had known about all of this,' Xavier mumbled. 'Doris's great-granddaughter is working at All Saints. What was her name?' Xavier furrowed his brow as he stared through James.

The man had an exhaustive knowledge of mediaeval literature and Latin but couldn't remember a name. James rolled his eyes.

Xavier shook his finger. 'I saw that. You're going to be my age one day, and some little punk will sit in front of you and roll their eyes because you can't remember some insignificant fact.'

Second scolding of the day. Check.

James bit the inside of his lip and braced for another scolding. 'Aren't you a little jealous that he was researching something that was really in your field of expertise? I would be.'

Xavier waved his left hand at James as he cradled the teacup in his right. 'No, research is a young man's game. I'm too old to play Indiana Jones with an ancient text. But Manesh was happy to have me on board and to give me credit.'

'Really?'

'Yes, Manesh had flaws, but deep down, he was a good man.' Xavier narrowed his eyes and dropped his chin. 'Why are you so interested in Manesh?'

'So much about the murder and theft makes little sense. I still can't figure out the motive other than theft. I feel like there's more to it than that. It's too simple.'

Xavier smirked. 'The Dragon Lady has you under her thumb.'

'Yes, my interest in the manuscript is not entirely my natural curiosity. I was given an incentive.' James sighed. 'And Detective Alice O'Donnell has put a hold on my passport. I can't leave until the case is resolved.'

'Where are you planning on going?'

James shrugged. 'New York.'

'Why New York?' Xavier sounded suspicious.

James slowly exhaled. 'It's a long story.'

'I have time.'

James sighed and gazed at the slice of lemon resting at the bottom of his teacup. The rose-flavoured green tea had become cold and sour.

'A doctor from accident and emergency told me I reminded him of someone. Turns out that he knew my mother. He said she was sick and died in New York.' James slumped in the chair and hung his head. 'My grandparents told me she died in Paris. I feel like I've been lied to my entire life. I need to figure this out. Not knowing the truth is killing me. I don't understand where I'm from and who my parents are.' James glanced up at Xavier. 'All I have is lies and secondhand information. I can no longer tell the difference between the truth and the lies.'

Xavier shook his head. 'You must drop this thing with your mother and focus on your career. I don't see how travelling to New York will help you figure out who you are.'

James argued, 'I need to figure this out.'

'It will only end in heartache.'

'I don't care,' James snapped. 'I need to know the truth. I need to understand who I am. One day, I'll have a family of my own, and my kids will ask me these things, and I'll have no answers, just lies told to me by people I should've been able to trust.'

'Once you open Pandora's box, it can't be closed.' Xavier got up and strolled to the other side of the room.

'I need to know the truth. That's why I'm helping Lady Margaret and, by default, the police. The quicker I figure this out, the quicker I can get to New York.' James watched Xavier trek to the desk.

'If you must go to New York, I obviously can't stop you. But if you do, I have a contact in New York at the *Daily Voice* newspaper. I can land you an interview for a position. A friend of mine is always searching for fresh talent.' Xavier opened his top desk drawer and pulled out a business card. 'You've clearly made your mind up. You've changed, James.'

'Please don't be mad at me.'

Xavier walked across the room and handed James the business card. 'His name is Patrick Evans. I can give you an introduction if you'd prefer.'

James shook his head. 'Sorry, I have to go. I have appointments to keep.'

'You're always so busy. You're going to burn yourself out if you aren't careful,' Xavier scolded.

James stood and hugged Xavier then walked out of the library. He knew exactly where he was going next. The path before him was becoming very clear and had drifted away from Liam.

FORTY-TWO

FRIDAY: 11:30 A.M.

A WAVE of regret swept over James as he peered at the early-nineteenth-century portraits of Stanley Whittaker's ancestors that lined the walls of the family's estate. Those manor houses were the same, nothing but gloomy halls lined with images of long-gone relatives from a by-gone era. The paintings made James nervous. It was all in the eyes. James often felt they were watching him. Stanley looked over his shoulder. James's eyes darted away from the portrait. Hopefully, he hadn't just extended the tour from hell.

It had been nineteen minutes since James had first arrived. The tall, wiry man with a thick head of snow-white hair answered the door with a groan. He'd stepped aside to let James in, and the customary small talk began soon after. Stanley assumed James worked for All Saints because of his connection to Professor Xavier Watson. Instead, like an idiot, James told Stanley he was a journalist. As usual, James's mouth landed him in a spot of trouble. At least that time, it wasn't of the life-threatening variety.

James jumped as Stanley cleared his throat, jolting him back to reality.

Stanley pointed down the hall. 'This is where the proper

bed-and-breakfast begins. With help from my wife, Victoria, daughter Jane, and my granddaughter Tilly, I've arranged for the rooms to be renovated. But I still have to stick to certain limitations because the manor house is Heritage listed.' Stanley smiled as he pointed down the hall. 'The rooms in this west wing are out of bounds due to said renovations.'

James nodded as Stanley dropped his arm, whirled around, and strolled to the east wing.

'Currently, I have three guests, and their rooms are all in this wing. But it's not all hotel-style rooms. I have the facilities to host functions, parties, weddings.' Stanley looked at James's hands.

Trying to book me for a wedding?

James shrugged. 'The renovations must be expensive.'

Stanley narrowed his eyes. 'We're managing. Obviously, three guests won't cover it, but we also need good reviews to attract more customers. So let me know if you want to stay and get the full experience.'

James hadn't seen that one coming.

With determination, Stanley strolled across the landing towards the east-wing rooms. The entire floor was dark and quiet with not a single guest in sight. Was that on purpose?

James smirked. 'I guess you were hoping the *Commentary on Daniel* would contribute a great deal of revenue to your new venture.'

Stanley froze then sighed.

James raised his eyebrows. 'Don't tell me you thought I wouldn't bring it up?'

'I felt obliged to say yes to the interview with you.' Stanley leaned against the bannister for support. 'Xavier told me the Commentary was real and not a forgery, as Dr Manesh Warren insisted.'

James folded his arms and nodded.

Stanley clenched his left hand then released it as a look of annoyance swept across his face then disappeared. Concerned about a potential confrontation, James stepped back and glanced over his shoulder. *Merde.*

He sighed then faced Stanley. 'It's okay to admit you were counting on the money from the Commentary to fund these renovations.' James placed his hand on his chest. 'I certainly would have been counting on it. Of course, anyone in your position would have done the same thing.'

Stanley narrowed his eyes. 'How very understanding of you, Mr Lalonde.'

James's heart raced as he observed Stanley's calm reaction.

'Yes, I was pissed that I didn't get to auction the *Commentary* off at Christie's.' Stanley shook his head. 'However, the money I received from Dr Warren helped fix a section of the estate's roof. We had a leak, so the money came at the right time.'

James slowly nodded. 'Twenty grand for a roof leak?'

Stanley leaned his tall frame against the bannister. 'It was a lot more than that, but we didn't quite have enough money.'

James nodded. 'You must have been furious when you learned of Manesh's deceit. Did you ever confront him?'

Stanley jerked his head back. 'What are you suggesting?'

'The evening Manesh died, I was at a dinner with him,' James said. 'I saw a message from you flash on the screen, saying you needed to talk to him. Did you get a chance to have that conversation?'

'That's none of your business,' Stanley snapped. His face flushed crimson, and a small vein bulged on his forehead.

'Where were you on Wednesday, the twenty-sixth of August, around eleven fifty p.m.?' James straightened.

Stanley smirked. 'I have a cast-iron alibi for the time of Manesh's death.'

'Really?' James pursed his lips.

Stanley paused, then a wave of recognition swept across his face.

'On Wednesday, we had three guests booked in the B and

B that night.' Stanley's eyes gleamed. 'One guest had a bath overflow, and I had to call a plumber. The plumber arrived at eleven nineteen p.m. He can place me here until midnight.'

'Which plumber did you call?' James asked.

Stanley gazed over the bannister at the ground-floor foyer. 'Why? Do you have plumbing issues, Mr Lalonde?'

James wrinkled his nose. 'I'm sure you're aware of the break-in at All Saints and the theft of the *Commentary*—'

'Xavier told me,' Stanley said in a sharp tone.

'Well, you know that Lady Margaret has asked me to investigate the incident, and I'm sure she'll be relieved to rule you out as a suspect.' James watched Stanley tighten his shoulders. *He's afraid of her.*

With a trembling hand, Stanley reached into his pocket and pulled out his wallet. After flipping open the smooth black leather, he paused for a second and removed a business card. Stanley glared at James then surrendered the card.

'That night, I called Bill Wallace from Plumb Force out to the estate. He arrived at eleven nineteen p.m.,' he said, peering over James's shoulder.

'And the guest?'

Stanley flushed. 'Room 203. Tim Porter.'

James glanced at the first numberless door in the east wing as Stanley straightened then stormed across the landing and down the main staircase.

———

TWENTY MINUTES LATER, James stood opposite a third identical white numberless door. He looked down the pristine white corridor, and an intense glow from the morning sun shone in through the lace curtain draped across the window at the end of the hall. The interior architecture was beautiful. Each archway on the upper-level hallway was adorned with delicately carved mouldings, and fluted flat pillars supported the arcs. They reminded him of the pillars that supported the porticoes of temples he had seen in Rome while on a trip there with his grandparents. Identical glass-lantern chandeliers hung from the ceiling.

Tim Porter, a short, balding man in his fifties, opened the door. With a smile, James enquired about the events that had unfolded late Wednesday evening. The man brushed his hand along his polished head as he recalled the events.

Tim dipped his head. 'It was around ten forty-five p.m., I think. I fell asleep while running my bath and woke to a knock on the door. The water dripped down through the floor, and the carpet was drenched. To be honest, I'm glad Mr Whittaker isn't charging me the full cost of repairs.'

'Do you remember when the plumber arrived?' James asked.

Tim pursed his lips. 'The gentleman arrived quickly. Maybe around eleven? I can't remember. I didn't see Mr Whittaker again until after midnight. He seemed swamped.'

James smiled. 'Thanks. That's all I need for my report. I hope you enjoy the rest of your stay.'

As Tim closed the door, James sighed. *Interesting. Someone has a shaky alibi.*

FORTY-THREE

AN ORCHESTRA of honking car horns was the background accompaniment as James paced his hotel room in a panicked state. Strolling across the room, James threw his sunglasses on the freshly made bed, followed by his unlocked smartphone. Open on the screen was a text message to Amber that he'd sent four hours ago. Now he had two people ignoring his texts.

Thanks to traffic, it had taken almost fifty minutes to drive back from the Whittaker estate. He was exhausted. James sat down at the small desk. After pulling his charcoal-grey backpack off the armchair and onto the table, James tugged at the zipper then took out a pile of index cards and a pen. So many pieces of information about the case were piling up, and there was no way he could simply think them through. He needed to see it all from a visual perspective. Mind mapping the case then stepping back would give him clarity. As a journalist, James had done that many times. The technique always came in handy when he had a tight deadline and no idea how to write a story. Mind mapping would help him discover which of his friends had murdered Manesh and, in turn, point to the location of the *Commentary on Daniel*.

After dropping the backpack on the floor next to the table, James spread three rows of index cards across the desk.

A heavy, persistent knocking on the door broke his train of thought. *Returning to this hotel room was a stupid idea.*

James dragged his aching body off the chair and ambled to the door. As he opened it, a pair of hands pushed back with surprising force. Staggering, James struck the foot of the bed as Alice burst into the room with an intense look in her eyes.

'Since you discharged yourself from the hospital, I've sent many PCs to follow you. And it occurred to me you went to Manesh's office yesterday morning searching for something.' Alice placed her hands on her hips and stared at James. She wasn't in her police uniform but in plainclothes. 'I suspect you wanted to erase the evidence of the chat-room conversation. That's your first mistake because we already knew about Manesh's conversation with the user "Da Vinci Rulz" before you set foot in the building. I got suspicious when the officer on duty captured you on a camera, leaving All Saints holding a worn-out copy of *The Da Vinci Code*. At first, I thought nothing of it. Upon closer inspection of the photographs, I noticed the pages were stuck together and the book had been hollowed out.' Without taking her eyes off James, Alice reached into the folder tucked under her arm, pulled out a photograph, and handed it to him.

Clutching the photograph, James gazed at the short, intimidating woman before him.

'Judging by the size of the novel, I'm guessing you found a second phone that the victim had hidden, which, I might add, you have not surrendered to the police. Thanks to the search history supplied by the All Saints IT department, I know this phone exists because Manesh doesn't access the chat room from his personal laptop found at his apartment or the smartphone found on his body at the crime scene. And we both know why you kept that to yourself.' Alice stepped closer and glared at him. 'You're an intelligent guy. You know better than to incriminate yourself.'

James smirked. *Really, Detective? Is she trying to intimidate me into a confession?*

Alice took a deep breath. 'Instead, you stopped by the police station to see if I had come up with something. To encourage me to trust you, you shared a little more information about the case under the pretext that you suffer from various PTSD symptoms. You also shared information about a conversation overheard between Manesh and your friend Tom, who were arguing about debt repayment. You sent me down a rabbit hole that has no bearing on the case. But I suspect "Da Vinci Rulz" is your username. Any old fool can reroute an IP address. After all, you have friends who know how to do things. One of them came to see me this morning.' Alice took another deep breath.

James stared at her trench coat. The pockets appeared to be empty, with not even a phone or handcuffs inside. That meant she'd come on a whim, an irrational last-minute decision. The police didn't seem to have any more information than him.

'So, while you were engineering my trip down the rabbit hole, you collected the manuscript from wherever you were concealing it and sold it to this man.' After reaching into the file under her arm, Alice handed James a grainy black-and-white photo. 'And one of your friends staged the break-in.'

Merde.

His heart raced as he peered at the second photograph. Alice was building a conspiracy theory, hoping he would somehow incriminate himself. While trying to conceal his panic, James handed the photos back.

Alice pursed her lips. 'Yes, I know about your relationship with him. He has a rather unique private collection of rare items. Two items have gone missing since this man has travelled in and out of Europe over the last four months. This manuscript and a sword, Excalibur. On Monday, he arrived in Oxford via his private jet. Did you know he always bypasses customs?' Alice handed James another surveillance photo.

It was the image he expected to see. He glanced at the picture and gave it back.

'Would you like to know how I discovered your connection to the buyer?'

James sighed. 'Go ahead. Dazzle me.'

'I did a routine background check, called your work, and discovered you had resigned after the unfortunate incident with the Arthurian sword, and then, by chance, I discovered your actual name. It wasn't a tremendous leap. After that, I discovered your place of birth, the ambiguous nature surrounding your parentage, the chat room, the meeting.'

'So, you're trying to say that you've joined a few dots and come up with a conspiracy.' James folded his arms.

Alice narrowed her eyes and furrowed her brow. 'It's not a conspiracy.'

It was his turn to do what he did best—call people out on their crap. 'Despite the lack of physical evidence, you have decided I'm suspect number one.'

Alice threw the folder onto the bed and stared at James. 'I'm collecting evidence.'

'There's none to collect. I didn't do it, and you know it. But that doesn't matter because you've made up your mind. You've rearranged the facts to suit your theory. And I've noticed you haven't read me my rights.' James held his finger up as Alice opened her mouth. 'You can't read someone their rights unless you're arresting them, and you can't arrest me based on this evidence.' James pointed at the photos spilling out of the folder and across the white duvet cover.

'You're involved in this. I know it.' Alice's gaze hardened. 'Somehow, you're involved.'

'While you were spinning your web of conspiracy, I was "down the rabbit hole," as you describe it. And I discovered

Manesh purchased the manuscript and held on to it for almost three months before selling it to All Saints as a forgery created by the infamous Spanish Forger. And Manesh sold it for a measly twenty-two thousand euros, claiming he found it in an antique dealership in Bilboa. After the sale, he met up with Professor Xavier Watson, who told me it was real and not a forgery. And he suspected Manesh knew this the entire time. Four days before his death, Manesh increased the insurance to one and a half million pounds.'

Alice raised her eyebrows. He had piqued her interest. Hopefully, that was enough to distract her from her newfound hobby of framing him.

'Does the initial purchase price sound familiar, Detective? Converted from euros into pounds, it's almost twenty thousand.'

'What? He sold it to the university as a forgery, knowing it was real,' Alice said with suspicion in her voice.

James froze and stared into the distance, remembering a significant piece of news. Perhaps the most crucial of all.

Alice narrowed her eyes. 'What's going on?'

A rock formed in the pit of his stomach. How could he have forgotten?

'Liam.' James leaned over the foot of the bed. He picked up his sunglasses, turned, and sprinted to the door. As he inched closer to it, Alice grabbed him by the arm. Another wave of pain swept through his body as she pulled back.

'What about Liam?'

'Liam said that he recognised the intruder in the lab. He kept quiet out of fear of repercussions.' James's eyes glazed over. 'He was going to the police station to tell you. I promised him you would keep him safe. And he clearly hasn't turned up.'

'Where and when did Liam meet you?'

'Four hours ago, he pulled me into the All Saints Chapel.' James wiggled his arm free from Alice's grip. 'Liam was super paranoid about someone overhearing. And I've seen the man in black again. But in reality, he followed me and Oliver, the IT engineer from All Saints, after we left the Rad Cam last night. Then he circled back and attempted to follow Amber home. We need to find Liam.'

'You're not coming with me because you're still a suspect,' Alice snapped.

'Let it go.' James rolled his eyes. 'I'm not involved. Everything you have on me is a coincidence, except for my name. That's deliberate.'

Alice glared at him. 'Why?'

'The name I use is the name my grandparents gave me. They chose my mother's maiden name.'

'Why?'

'They're old, crazy, and probably believe they were protecting me. Or maybe they genuinely don't know my father's identity.' James placed his hand on his chest.

'What about brunch?' Alice reached across the bed, picked up the grainy photos, and shoved them in front of James.

'I have to meet with him. It's the terms and conditions of a sum of money I received upon graduation. And it's his favourite meal.' James rubbed the back of his neck.

Alice folded her arms. 'You're forced to have brunch with him.'

'Not exactly. Mr Harper Thompson manages my mother's estate and has continued to manage her assets now that I've inherited them. He came to my graduation and introduced himself as my mother's friend, whom she met in Paris during Fashion Week. A part of the arrangement is we meet up for brunch and chat, and he charges me a smaller fee. I suspect he misses my mother, and perhaps I remind him of her. Occasionally, he shares an anecdote about her.' James swallowed a hard lump in his throat. 'That's why I put up with all of this. I'm practically orphaned. You'll never understand what it's like to grow up and not know anything about your family, parents, or who you are.'

Alice shook her head. 'Do you have any idea how crazy this sounds? Do you expect me to believe this?'

'Yes, because this is my life. This is my truth. I don't have answers. I only know fragments of information about who I am. And I get this information from a group of people who have been lying to me since birth.' James took a deep breath to calm his racing heart. 'So, I searched Manesh's office. At first, I didn't care about solving the crime to bring a killer to justice. All I wanted was to leave and go to New York, but you put a block on my passport. Now, I can't go to the one place in the world where I need to search for answers and figure out who I am, and my past. I'm stuck in Oxford with you and this case.' James pointed at the photo. 'And if he's involved, I know nothing about it. He would never tell me. He's very secretive. If you don't believe me, ask around.'

TWENTY MINUTES LATER, James stood in the centre of Liam and Kate's sitting room. As James took a deep breath, he glanced around. Everything was in its place. Well, almost everything. Paperbacks and hardback fiction lined the dark-stained corner bookshelves. Three remote controls were lined up on the coffee table, next to the *TV Guide*. A thick duck-egg blanket was folded and draped over the arm of the grey modular sofa. A bowl of dried-up cereal lay on the edge of the dark-stained coffee table. The afternoon sunlight shone through the bay window, highlighting a trail of dust. Upon James's closer inspection, a crusty layer of milk circled the bottom of the bowl. He grimaced.

The two-bedroom maisonette received a lot of sun through the front window in the summer. That was about seven days a year. Gloomy grey clouds and chilly winds were the year-round forecasts. Paris wasn't much better.

Most people would dismiss such a sight, but it was a bad sign in that house. For as long as James could remember, his friend had been a creature of habit and a perfectionist. Leaving a bowl of cereal on the coffee table would have gnawed at his mind all morning.

A loud, persistent knock disturbed the eerie silence of the maisonette. With his stomach churning, James ambled between the coffee table and the sofa and to the door as the knocking intensified. He braced for the inevitable.

'Police, open up!' a familiar voice yelled through the door.

Merde. Twice in the same hour. Should he start the countdown to his arrest?

Frightened by what was lurking on the other side, James released the latches with a trembling hand and opened the door.

With a quizzical expression on her face, Alice stood on the doormat and silently stared at him.

A hard lump formed at the back of James's throat as he clutched the door. *She's on a fishing endeavour.* That sceptical mind of hers was hoping he would incriminate himself. He could sense it.

She narrowed her eyes. 'Do you know how most criminals get caught?' Alice strolled into the house, pushing James and the half-open door to the side. 'They turn up at the scene of the crime.' As she reached the staircase, Alice turned and looked at James.

'Only a sociopath would do that.' James furrowed his brow. 'I'm going to go out on a limb and guess that you already know I don't have the correct profile for that.'

Alice shook her head. 'What are you doing here? You've shown up at another potential crime scene.'

'He's not at the station?' James asked as his voice broke.

Alice exhaled. 'No. I've asked my team to call a few other stations in Oxfordshire.'

James ran his fingers through his hair. 'I've only been here for five minutes.'

Alice reached into her pocket and pulled out an evidence bag. 'Sorry, but you need to surrender your keys to this house.'

James shrugged. 'The door was ajar when I arrived. So all I did was push it open. It wasn't obvious from the street, but as

I stepped onto the doormat, I saw it was open. I swear, I've only been here for five minutes, and I've tried not to touch anything other than the door.'

James rubbed the back of his neck as he paced. He looked at Alice. 'The front door wasn't locked. Liam is not that kind of guy.'

'You've mentioned that twice.' Alice tucked the evidence bag into her pocket then reached inside her jacket and pulled out a notepad and pen.

'Something must have distracted Liam from his usual routine.' James gazed out the window and, through the thick shrubs lining the front of the property, studied the bus station across the street.

Alice raised her eyebrows as she followed James's gaze.

'Maybe I'm making a big deal about this, but hear me out.' James walked around the sofa then ambled along the narrow gap between the couch and the coffee table. James stared through the window. 'I've lived with Liam for four years, and he had the same routine. Liam didn't stray from it, not even once. And he hasn't changed. Every morning before Liam left for the university, he would wash up his bowl. Then Liam would pick up his bag, which was always left on the bench in the nook, leave, and lock up. And he would always double-check the door. Even if he was running late. This scene doesn't fit with the man I know.' James held up his finger as he glanced at Alice. 'Plus, he never ate breakfast in here. Breakfast was always eaten at the kitchen table.' James pointed at the bowl.

'Yes, the room gives off a certain vibe.' Alice slipped her notepad inside her jacket then sauntered around the room. 'Okay, so I'll go with your theory. Something distracted him from his usual routine. How was he behaving when you met up with him?' It was as if she enjoyed asking questions she knew the answers to.

'He was anxious and panicked.' James walked around the

sofa then stood and gazed out of the large bay window. 'When Liam was anxious, he used to pace a lot. More than me.' James glanced over his shoulder. 'One morning before exam week, I found him walking around the downstairs area, clutching a cereal bowl, staring. He barely passed an English literature exam the next week. Perhaps he saw someone watching him, which made him leave in a hurry.' James pointed at the bus stop across the road. 'And on the way, he decided that talking to me was his best move, but by the time Liam found me, he had changed his mind.'

'Are you suggesting that someone was watching and following him?' Alice strolled across the room, stood next to James, and stared out of the window. 'Did he say something to you?'

'No, but he acted like whoever was in the lab with us would know if he told anyone. It was implied.'

'Okay. How do you think the scene would've played out?' Alice looked up at James. 'Where would this person stand?'

'The bus stop across the road. Liam was sitting on the couch. Maybe he noticed he was being watched. That could explain why he left the bowl here.' James pointed over his shoulder at the coffee table. 'Whatever happened started here.'

'But isn't that too obvious?'

'That's the point.' James locked eyes with Alice. 'Perhaps the person wanted Liam to notice him standing outside. An attempt to scare him into staying silent, just like my experience the night before. It makes sense that if the man in black was following me, Oliver, and Amber, he would also monitor Liam.'

Alice pursed her lips. 'Stay here. I'm going to check the rest of the house.' She headed to the kitchen door and disappeared. Minutes later, the slamming of a door against the staircase caused James to jump. As Alice ascended the stairs to the upper level, James looked over his shoulder. A wave of

panic swept over James as a single thought lingered in his mind
—no.

———

TEN MINUTES LATER, heavy footsteps descended the
staircase, interrupting James's train of thought. Alice traipsed
across the sitting room, clutching her smartphone.

'Nothing seems missing from the bedrooms since I was
last here.' Alice surveyed the room. 'No one slept here last
night. Everything is too neat.' Alice frowned.

He grimaced.

'The perp followed him to the university. When he
observed Liam talking to you, the perp made an impulsive
decision.' Alice placed her hand on her hip as she scrolled
through her smartphone.

James whirled around. 'Do you think Liam is dead?'

'I can't say. I shouldn't be discussing this case with you.
You're a victim and a suspect.'

James rolled his eyes. 'You expect to find a body
somewhere between here and the university?'

'Obviously, if someone was following Liam, they saw him
talk to you.' Alice took a deep breath. 'Usually, stalking is done
out of desperation, leading to a decision made by rash
judgement. I can't think of a reason the perp would keep him
alive. I'm sorry.'

'I think we should do a reenactment of the scene.'

Alice shook her head. 'It won't tell us anything we don't
already suspect.'

'Perchance you could stand at the bus stop. Together, we
can figure out whether we can see each other.'

'Fine.' Alice headed to the front door.

James winced as she slammed the door. She waltzed along
the footpath across the street and stood next to the bus stop.
Then James walked to the kitchen door, reenacting Liam's

possible moves. He paced the sitting room then paused. At some point, Liam had sat on the sofa.

Deep in thought, James sauntered to the couch and sat opposite the bowl. With his face screwed up, James reached into his back pocket and pulled out his smartphone. A tingling sensation swept through his body as he placed it on the table. James glanced out the window. Across the road, Alice leaned against the bus stop. The waist-high brick fence and the out-of-control shrubbery partially obstructed James's view, but he could still see her. Liam must have been terrified.

James picked up his smartphone and dialled Alice's number. 'I can feel you watching. If this is how it played out, it would explain his decision to talk and his last-minute change of heart.'

'Yes, this is a plausible option.' Alice peered down the street. 'I'm going to call for backup and retrace his steps.'

'I'm coming with you.' James headed to the front door.

Alice sighed into her phone. 'This is a police investigation. You're not coming.'

James rubbed the back of his neck. 'You need me to show you where I met Liam and how the conversation played out.'

Alice groaned. 'Fine.'

A wave of nausea swept over James's body as he struck the red button on the screen. *I've let Liam down. I should've escorted him to the station.* Anxious about his return to All Saints, James slipped the phone into his pocket. It buzzed immediately. *What does she want now?*

James yanked the smartphone out of his jeans pocket and stared at the number on the screen. As he struck the home button and brought the phone to his ear, he looked over his shoulder at Alice, who was standing by the bus station.

'James, I'm Bill Wallace from Plumb Force. I got your message about the Whittaker Estate.' The thick Scottish accent echoed out of the phone's tiny speaker.

'Yes, this is James.'

'Stanley might have been a bit confused about what happened Wednesday night. I turned up at ten minutes till eleven. At every call out, I log the mileage and the time I arrived in my van's log, which says ten fifty p.m. After I made the initial assessment, I sent Stanley out to purchase a spare part from one of my suppliers while I turned off the water. He couldn't figure out how to do it. I have a guy who has a twenty-four-hour shop. That was around eleven oh five p.m.'

James nodded. 'Do you remember what time Stanley returned?'

'It was after midnight. Stanley got lost, apparently. And couldn't find the part.'

'Thanks for getting back to me,' James said, then Bill hung up.

A stony expression swept across Alice's face. She had snuck back into the house and was listening to his conversation. He hadn't heard a thing. Was she proving a point? Or maybe she was plotting his demise as per usual. All he knew for sure was that it wouldn't be too hard to convince her to go to All Saints Chapel with him.

FORTY-FIVE

FRIDAY: 1:03 P.M.

STANDING IN THE WHITTAKER QUADRANGLE, James peered up at the large stained glass windows of the chapel. Then he whirled around and gazed down the length of the quadrangle through the archway. Behind him stood Alice, notepad out and pen poised.

She had said nothing for the entire car trip between Liam and Kate's house and All Saints. To top it off, she made him sit in the back seat of the police car like a common criminal. A brief gleam in her eyes told James that she enjoyed seeing him behind the barrier. That glimmer had vanished, and her usual icy stare was back.

James looked over his shoulder. 'Detective, I'm pretty sure I was standing there, looking in this direction, when Liam grabbed me from behind and pulled me through the chapel's narthex and into the nave.'

Alice raised her eyebrows. 'At what point did you realise it was Liam who pulled you into the chapel?'

'Hmm.' James tilted his head. 'It wasn't until he dragged me across the black-and-white floor and pushed me onto a pew that I realised it was Liam. The entire process took maybe less than a minute.'

Alice frowned as she scribbled notes. 'Not long, then.'

James jerked his head back. 'I know this isn't a big deal to you, but I was terrified.'

'Last time I checked, I wasn't your therapist.' Alice glanced up then strolled towards the large dark-stained wooden doors of All Saints Chapel.

James shook his head as he ambled to the chapel doors.

'What did he say to you?' Alice asked, disappearing into the narthex.

James grimaced. 'He dived straight into a paranoid rant about us never being in the chapel or having this conversation. Liam appeared to be delusional or suffering from stress related to the break-in.'

As James walked through the narthex and into the nave, his fingers floated along the polished black baby grand piano. In front of him, standing in the vestibule's archway, Alice surveyed the ornamental screen covering the wall behind the altar.

Placing his hand on her back, James squeezed past Alice, sauntered to the pew, and sat. 'I sat here. Liam was hovering over me.'

Alice nodded, slipped her notepad and pen inside her jacket, and wandered around the chapel, inspecting the artwork.

James exhaled. 'Liam came out and said he knew who killed Manesh.'

Alice paused and nodded as she reached the altar rail. Hunched over, she stared at the cherubim-and-vine detailing on the ornamental screen.

Feel free to enjoy the scenery, Detective.

James shook his head. 'Then, he became all indecisive and claimed that telling me would put my life in some kind of danger.'

Gripping the gate, Alice gave the altar rail a shake. She

leaned over the railing with a groan and squinted at the founder's tomb.

Merde.

'We heard footsteps on the gravel outside. Liam panicked. I dismissed it because it's tourist season, and visitors can pay a fee to visit the grounds.' James ambled to the altar.

Alice inched forward towards the founders' tomb. Grabbing her arm, James pulled her back into the nave. She narrowed her eyes at him then turned and stared at the tomb.

'Is that an effigy?' Alice had eyes fixed straight ahead.

A bead of sweat dripped down James's brow, and his heart raced. *Any second now, she's going to make the connection between the chapel and the Whittakers.*

'James.' Alice glared up at him. 'Is this an effigy or a memorial?'

James sighed. 'No, it's the tomb of the college's founders.'

Alice pursed her lips and placed her hands on her hips. 'You're sweating.' Her eyes lingered on the droplet of sweat gliding down his face.

Please don't ask.

Alice ambled along the pews on the left-hand side of the altar. 'Was Liam religious at all?' She continued to stroll the length of the nave.

James grimaced. 'Not really. I think his interests were purely academic.'

Alice froze. 'Why here?'

Forcing a smile, James shrugged as he looked down the nave at the biblical portrait in the narthex. She was clearly going to figure out that he was investigating the Whittakers.

Alice headed towards him with her notepad and pen. Frightened that he was going to be interrogated, James stepped back.

She grimaced. 'Are you suffering from some type of trauma?'

'No.' Maybe he should just tell her.

Tilting her head, Alice glanced at the restored ceiling. 'Was Liam involved in the renovations at all?'

James shook his head.

Alice tapped the end of her pen against her notepad. 'Is there any connection between Liam and this chapel that you know of?'

Glancing over his shoulder, James looked up at the cherubim on the ornamental screen. Alice knew. He could feel it. She must have read the emails and was wondering whether he knew too.

'James, is there something you're not telling me?'

James rolled his eyes. 'There's no direct connection between Liam and the location. I don't know whether he was trying to give me a hint or was just taking shelter in here because he heard a noise outside.'

'Really?' Alice's furrowed brow hinted at her suspicion. She walked to the vestibule screen. 'I forgot to ask, who are the college founders?'

A rock formed in the pit of his stomach. 'Sir Benedict Whittaker and his wife, Christiana.'

Alice froze then whirled around. 'Do you know a Stanley Whittaker? Manesh had a few emails from him.'

———

IT WASN'T A FLAT-OUT LIE, but it wasn't the whole truth, either. No one told the entire truth—it was too complex. His ability to withhold the truth wasn't the only thing that surprised James. Perhaps for the first time, a certain detective was agreeable to his suggestion to walk the most plausible route to the station from the All Saints Chapel— almost too agreeable.

Hoping to find his friend hiding in the Rad Cam with his girlfriend, James ambled along the cobblestone street surrounding the infamous circular library. With Alice by his side, James nodded towards the library.

'Kate is an assistant librarian at the Rad Cam. We should check that he's not hiding out with her.'

Alice stopped. 'You think he's hiding out in the library? A moment ago, you acted like Liam might be hurt or dead.'

James winced. He hoped Liam was hiding or even on the run. But deep down, he knew that wasn't the case. That cynical part of him thought Liam was already dead, and James was on the hunt for a body. Perchance out of desperation, James fought back the tsunami of pessimistic thoughts and tried to be optimistic. *How do people live like this?*

A series of digital hoots cried out amongst the sea of chattering tourists with selfie sticks and digital SLRs. Alice pulled out her smartphone. Like magic, the tourists parted as she strolled towards the gates of the Rad Cam with James following closely. That was why she wore the uniform.

As James opened the black iron gate, Alice held up her forefinger and answered her smartphone.

Standing in the middle of the path, James watched Alice talk. She wasn't within earshot. That was on purpose, no doubt. It was a work call, or maybe she ordered everyone about at work and in her personal life.

Alice hung up her phone, took a few steps, then stopped in the middle of the open gate. 'That was Joseph.'

James's heart raced.

'Joseph has located a signal from Liam's phone. Technically, the signal comes from the tower closest to the city centre. Perhaps he's hiding somewhere on campus, or he left his phone behind. No one at the station has heard from him.' Alice slipped her smartphone into her pocket.

James thought he was going to be sick. 'I'm sure he had his phone with him.'

Alice remained silent.

'And the signal. Can you tell if it's moving?'

'The technology isn't there yet,' Alice said with a sympathetic smile.

'When I saw Liam this morning, he said he would walk to the station,' James said as he followed Alice's gaze.

She stared at the building then turned her attention back to him. Alice pursed her lips. 'Did Liam have any places he would go if he wanted to be alone?'

James shrugged. 'I'm not sure. He went missing between classes a few times, especially during the weeks leading up to exams and assignment deadlines, but he wouldn't tell me where he was.'

'Do you think anyone else would know?'

'Maybe Kate?'

'I don't trust her.'

James sighed. 'You're getting no arguments from me.'

Alice jerked her head back.

'Just for laughs, let's see what Kate says.' James strolled up the path as the heat from the midday sun barbecued his skin.

He inspected the thick lawn surrounding the footpath and slid his hands into his pockets. Alice was a few steps behind him. Even though there were other suspects, James couldn't help feeling he was on trial. The jury was out, deliberating his fate. That was why he preferred to work alone. No suspicions or feelings got in the way, and no one asked questions about his complicated past and why he knew so little about his parents. It was better that way.

Across the lawn at the watchful sea of tourists surrounding the Rad Cam, a bright light shone from the long blades of grass. James stepped off the path and onto the forbidden lawn.

Shielding his eyes from the glare, James stepped closer to the bright light. As he drew nearer, a familiar smartphone lay faceup. His heart raced as he crouched and peered at the fingerprints on the touch screen. A trail of blood droplets was scattered from the phone and along the blades between his shoes. The first droplet was on the corner of the phone. Merde.

A lump formed at the back of his throat. He stared at the crimson droplets and tried to fight the tears.

'There's blood.' James's voice broke.

'Don't move. I have to call the forensics team.'

James stood.

'What did I say about moving?' Alice snapped.

James glared at Alice. 'I just stood. That's all.'

'Do you think it might be Liam's?'

James nodded. 'It's his make and model. I know the passcode.'

'Fine.' Alice pulled a pair of gloves from a Ziploc bag and tiptoed across the lawn. 'You need to be wearing these.'

James slipped on the gloves then picked up the phone and struck the home key, careful not to disturb the blood. 'It's numerical. I've got a pretty good idea what the password will be.'

'I thought you said you knew?'

'Just a hunch.' James typed the combination on the screen and watched as the previous screen loaded in silence. 'It was Kate's birthday.' James looked at Alice.

'Can people be this stupid with passwords? All you need is a bit of information about someone, and suddenly, you've cracked their passwords and PIN numbers.' Alice stared at the grass.

James watched as her expression changed from frustration to panic.

'Don't move.'

'I haven't disturbed the blood on the ground or on the phone.'

Alice's mouth fell open. 'You never told me you were right on top of the blood or that it was on the phone.'

'Ah—' James showed Alice the screen. 'Liam was reading a work email from Amber about the *Commentary* before he was attacked. Why was he thinking about work? Does this mean Liam changed his mind about going to the station? He told me he knew who killed Manesh. How is a work email more important than that?'

Alice folded her arms. 'Don't move. This is a crime scene. I'll need your clothes and shoes for testing.'

'What am I going to wear? I'm pretty sure you have strict laws about nudity.' James glanced at the phone, took a screenshot, sent it to himself, and handed it to Alice.

Alice cradled the phone in her gloved hands as she scowled at him. 'You're not walking around in those shoes. They're evidence. You could have stepped on evidence as you walked across the lawn. You're contaminating the crime scene.'

James glared at her. 'Just me?'

'No, you fool, me too. That's why I'm so mad.' Alice pulled out her phone and called for backup.

Glancing at the droplets of blood on the grass, James realised he had made a colossal mistake. He needed to bite the bullet and tell Alice about the Whittaker's, the Commentary, Manesh, and Stanley's shaky alibi. *She's going to be furious.*

———

WEARING A BRIGHT-YELLOW POLICE VEST, Ellie sauntered across the well-manicured lush green grass then roped off the area with standard-issue yellow crime scene tape. A short, stocky police constable dragged a second yellow tape across the other side of the lawn, creating a barrier at the gate leading to the black iron fence surrounding the Radcliffe Camera library. A crowd of tourists formed around the perimeter of the famous landmark.

For the last thirteen minutes, he'd tried to reason with Alice, but he had admitted defeat. There was no point arguing. It was a battle he was never going to win. James watched as she sealed an evidence bag containing his shoes.

She might be beautiful, but that didn't make up for the fact that she was infuriating. Something about her drove him crazy and not in a good way. He was furious. The lack of sleep from the night before, which was entirely his fault, was taking its toll. He couldn't understand why she wouldn't let him bag up the bottom of his shoes then collect them later. Instead, Alice insisted on bagging them up, leaving him to stroll barefoot in Oxford at the height of tourist season. What were the odds that he'd stepped on a crucial piece of evidence as he walked across the lawn? And what about her shoes? *There better be some damning evidence on my soles that points to Liam's whereabouts, or there will be another serial killer on the loose.*

James marched towards the library.

'Where are you going?' Alice demanded.

James stopped, rolled his eyes, and took a deep breath before slowly facing her. 'Isn't it obvious?' He scowled.

Alice stared at him as if expecting another response.

He rolled his eyes again. That was his new thing. All he ever seemed to do was argue and roll his eyes. Working alone seemed like a dream that was permanently out of reach.

'I have a sudden desire to read.' He continued to walk towards the library. James loved the library. It represented something he desperately craved—silence. There was no talking, no questioning, no one taking away his shoes, just silence and books.

'You're contaminating the crime scene!' she yelled as James stormed off.

'Yes, I confess. I killed my best friend.' James whirled around. 'Also, I found the time to commit a murder amongst everything else I did this morning. In fact, I'm so productive that instead of being behind bars, I should give a TED Talk on my productivity hacks.'

For what seemed like the longest two minutes of his life, Alice stood in an eerie silence, studying him. Clearly, she was trying to figure out whether she could use that as an actual confession. She peered at the blood splatter on the footpath then glanced up at him.

Alice placed her hands on her hips. 'And where will you be?'

'Upper Camera Reading Room, searching for evidence. The damning variety.' James stomped to the closed entry and bashed his fist on the door.

FORTY-SIX

THE CHILL from the air conditioner blew straight through James's white polo shirt and sent shivers racing through his body. For some reason, Kate loved setting the thermostat to levels that rivalled a morgue refrigerator. Standing at the closed exit gate, James pleaded with Kate as she dashed around the counter. The library was in a stock take, and she was about to banish him and Alice from the crime scene. As the creased skirt of her cherry-print tea dress disappeared, he sighed. She was seconds away from pressing the button that would unlock the front door.

He needed to tell Kate the truth. Alice would be pissed, but that was almost inevitable.

'Kate, I was in the Upper Camera Reading Room with Oliver last night. I just want to go back and inspect the area. Someone followed me to my hotel, and now Liam is missing.' James took a deep breath. 'I know I'm grasping at straws, but I swear the intruder was in the library with us.'

A wide-eyed Kate popped up from behind the counter. 'Did you say Liam?' Her voice broke. 'I sent Liam a text this morning after our chat, and he hasn't replied. I thought he was angry at me.'

James forced a smile. 'The police will not be impressed that I told you already. But you need to know. They may want to check out the library. I promise I won't interfere with the stock take, and I'll leave a tag on the shelves if I take something back to a workstation.'

'And you think this will help you find Liam?' she asked through a sea of tears. 'I'm sorry. I just feel so guilty. And now he's missing. I should have known something wasn't right.'

<hr>

AFTER JUMPING THE EXIT BARRIER, James sauntered around the circular maze of the entrance and lower reading rooms, past the computer bay, and ascended the stairs to the first level. A familiar sharp pain shot through his side. He lifted his polo shirt, and a small patch of blood had formed under the bandage. He was pushing his weary body too far. Leaning against the stone wall, James surveyed the mahogany bookshelves. The afternoon sun shone through the windows of the dome-shaped ceiling.

James dragged his aching frame along the blue carpet, past the rows of mahogany tables with identical study lights and towards the bookcases that lined the perimeter of the building. As he sauntered along the bookshelves, he paused at the location where he'd heard the books fall over the evening before.

Near the spiral staircase leading to the Upper Camera Gallery, a collection of history books called out to him. One stood out like a prime rib in a vegan restaurant. The book had been returned to the wrong section of the library. James dragged the four-hundred-page book on *The Archaeology and History of Glastonbury Abbey* off the shelf. Coincidence? Or was he building a conspiracy theory?

As he trekked to the nearest study desk, he spotted a few pages of white paper folded into three portions and wedged behind the books on the shelf. Against his better judgement, James lunged towards the bookshelves and wriggled the pages free. Once he opened the pages, a phrase printed in all caps jumped out at him.

It was the last will and testament of Doris Anne Whittaker. But that wasn't the only thing hiding there. A familiar riddle and symbols were typed on the following pages. References, notes, and a reading list appeared farther down the page. Someone was trying to figure out the riddle, and he knew who.

Then something dawned on him. Amber had slept with him the night before as a ruse to distract him from making the obvious connection. *Merde.*

Ambling back to the study desks, James turned his attention to Doris's will. According to its terms, the *Commentary on Daniel* was bequeathed to Amber. So, Stanley must be Amber's grandfather. James ran his fingers through his hair as another realisation dawned.

FORTY-SEVEN

'WHERE IS HE?' A stern voice echoed through the stillness of the Radcliffe Camera library.

Any second, Alice would appear at the top of the stairs. He had a choice to make. James felt uneasy as a lone thought drifted into his mind, but he would go through with it anyway. With an eye on the empty entrance of the main staircase at the other end of the first-floor reading room, James folded up the notes nestled behind Doris's will and slipped them into the pockets of his jeans. There was something alluring about the riddle found on the pages of the manuscript. Perhaps Lady Margaret would be less cheesed with that information if the manuscript was not returned. *Fingers crossed.*

Leaning forward, James unfolded the will and reread it. He paused. It meant that upon Doris's death, Stanley had sold off the *Commentary* in haste, hoping to secure funds for his bed-and-breakfast venture while knowing Amber wanted to keep it. She must have been furious to discover Manesh had purchased it at a bargain-basement price. *But the murderer couldn't have been her. Amber has OCD and issues with messy situations. How would she have coped with killing Manesh and gouging out an eye?* It made little sense. He was obviously missing something. There must be someone else.

Earlier that evening, Professor Xavier Watson had had trouble recalling the name of Doris's great-granddaughter, who was working at All Saints. However, based on his ability to remember Amber's name earlier in the conversation, it wasn't her but another person. James gasped as he stared off into the distance. During his interview with Stanley, the older man had mentioned his daughter, Jane, and his granddaughter Tilly. After reaching into the pocket of his trousers, James pulled out a smartphone and typed a message to Lady Margaret.

> Just out of curiosity, what's the surname of Stanley's daughter Jane?

A second later, a reply came.

> Why?

James placed the smartphone on the polished wooden tabletop. He wondered why she couldn't just answer the question.

The phone buzzed. Another message had come through.

> Never mind. I see why you're asking. Stanley has multiple family members working for the college at many levels, including an intern, Matilda Grey. She's Jane's daughter.

'Who's Matilda Grey?' A familiar voice boomed overhead, causing James to jump in his chair. 'And where did you find that?'

Jolting upright in his chair, James met Alice's icy gaze. 'It's the last will and testament of the late Doris Whittaker, the original owner of the *Commentary on Daniel*. And Matilda Grey is Stanley's granddaughter. She works as an intern with Amber at All Saints.'

Alice narrowed her eyes. 'Where did you find it? Did you have this the whole time, or did you just happen to find it lying around?'

James leaned back as Alice inched forward. 'I found it over there behind that book on the history of Glastonbury Abbey.'

'Anything else?'

James pursed his lips then shook his head. 'Not that I recall.'

'Shit. Another crime scene.' Alice stormed off. 'I haven't even had lunch.'

———

NINE MINUTES LATER, James stood outside a fourteenth-century tavern called George and the Dragon. Predictably, a wooden sign bearing a fire-breathing dragon tossed about in the afternoon breeze. Alice cleared her throat as he peered through the stained glass windows.

'Charles eats here all the time. And he's super picky with food,' Alice said with a smile.

James groaned inwardly then stepped back. There was something unnerving about her cheery disposition. Or maybe she was just a monster on an empty stomach.

'What?' Alice asked. 'Charles isn't joining us.'

'There's something I need to tell you. At first, I thought it was a coincidence. But now, I'm thinking differently.'

'Okay.' Alice sounded cautious.

James took a deep breath. 'Before Manesh was murdered, he was chatting with someone who went by the name of Da Vinci Rulz. The IP address for this individual points to the New York Public Library. A group of my friends were in New

York around this time, and a certain someone you have on your radar lives there too.'

Alice gripped James's arm and pulled him closer. 'How do you know this?' she whispered.

'Oliver Evans from the All Saints IT department helped me track the location.'

Alice glared up at James. 'Is your so-called brunch friend involved in this? Tell me now.'

An uneasy feeling swept through James's body. 'I don't know. He has a thing for mediaeval swords, not manuscripts. If it was a sword, then I'd say yes without hesitation. I'm more concerned that one of my friends is involved somehow. I have a bad feeling about it.'

Alice shook her head.

'I'm serious. Don't go after him on your own.'

'So you're concerned about me?' Alice glanced up at him inquisitively.

'During my brunch, he let it slip that he's been in and out of the country, and I wonder if he has something to do with the disappearance of Excalibur. A young woman was murdered in pursuit of that sword.' James paused. 'Yes, I'm worried, but maybe I'm being paranoid and he isn't here for the manuscript and this is a family squabble.'

Alice tipped her head. 'You think this is orchestrated by the Whittaker family?'

James exhaled. 'It's the option with the least number of assumptions. Honestly, I don't see him using the New York Public Library to talk to someone in a chat room. He's far too secretive for that.'

Alice groaned as she opened the door and stepped inside the tavern. With a sigh, James followed her. As he strolled through the open door and surveyed the sea of polished wood, he spotted a tall man with pale skin and long, thin limbs. The man was hunched over a bowl of orange soup. Not him?

'I must confess I've been curious to check out this tavern,'

Alice whispered in James's ear before ambling past the tables and to Charles.

Why did he feel like she was luring him there for another fishing expedition?

As Alice approached the table, she pivoted and made a beeline for the bar. Curious, James sauntered after her. Standing within eavesdropping distance, he listened in on the conversation.

Alice reached into the left pocket of her police vest and pulled out her smartphone, tapped the screen a few times, then thrust it towards the short, thin barman. He ran his hand across his buzz-cut hair.

Alice cleared her throat. 'Do you recognise this man? He was supposed to be in your bar on Monday, the twenty-fourth of August, at eight p.m.'

'Love, my name's Iain,' he said with a thick Irish accent. 'And if ya order a drink, I'll gladly talk to ya about all the men I've seen in this bar until ya wee heart is content.'

A stony expression swept across Alice's face. For the first time, the infamous look wasn't directed at him. Iain stepped back from the bar and glanced at James as if the guy was hoping he'd throw out a life raft and save him. James shook his head. Time to bury a body.

With one hand on the pepper spray attached to her belt, Alice leaned towards Iain. 'I'm Detective Inspector Alice O'Donnell. If you don't answer my questions, I'll haul your arse down to the St Aldate's Police Station and charge you with harassing a police officer.'

Iain laughed and shook his head. 'Love, he's an old geezer who drank alone all night. He's completely harmless.'

Alice groaned. 'This harmless old geezer is wanted by the FBI, the French police, and MI6. He's a very dangerous man.'

The bartender stepped back, picked up a glass, then polished it. 'He seemed harmless and drank alone. He left alone around midnight.'

'How do you know?'

'He sat right over there in front of me all night.' Iain pointed over Alice's shoulder. 'The only peculiar thing about him was that he was dressed in a black hooded coat. The material seemed quite thick. But he was an old geezer, so maybe he's sensitive to the evening breeze.'

She released her grip from the pepper spray then tapped the screen on her phone, turned it around, and showed Iain. 'What about him? Was he in your bar on Monday night, same time?'

'Na, love. I'd remember him. I have a soft spot for redheads.' Iain winked at Alice.

'My hair is auburn.' Alice marched off to Charles's table as James stood opposite the bar, stifling a laugh.

————

FIVE MINUTES LATER, after an awkward conversation that started with Charles voicing his preference for eating alone, Alice and James sat at the round table in the corner of the room. Charles clicked his fingers in the barman's direction. Seconds later, Iain waltzed across the room with a pen and notepad in hand.

'Your usual?' Iain gazed up from his notepad. 'Chicken salad with avocado and beetroot with balsamic vinegar on the side. No iceberg lettuce and no breadsticks.'

'Yes.' Charles gave Iain a polite smile then turned and stared at Alice.

No bread? How barbaric.

While Alice studied the chalkboard menu above the bar, James's phone buzzed. As he slipped the phone out of his pocket, a notification flashed on the screen. James rolled his eyes. The message read:

I suppose the invitation to Manesh's funeral
and wake is your doing. Keep your nose out
of my business.

'I know Owen,' Charles announced as he peered across the small round table at James's phone.

The room fell silent.

James looked up from his screen. 'How?'

A familiar stony expression swept across Alice's face.

Perfect. She's in RoboCop mode again.

'Last weekend, I was on a hunting trip in the Cotswolds with my brother, Morgan. Owen was with us.' Charles picked up the frosty glass of water and took a sip. 'He was super handy for repairing the hunting rifles. Mine got jammed a few times.'

James furrowed his brow. 'I didn't realise Owen was into hunting.'

Charles nodded. 'That girl who called in the crime scene also comes with us, but she's more of a beater and looks after my family's beagles. I think she comes along for the dogs. The dogs love her.'

Alice leaned back in her chair. 'Do you mean Amber?'

'Yes, that's her name. Owen invited her.'

James cleared his throat. 'How often do you go hunting with them?'

Charles furrowed his brow. 'Every few months. Are you interested in joining us?'

That was what Alice meant about Charles taking things literally. *He thinks that my questions are because I'm interested in hunting and not purely because of the murder case.* So his harsh behaviour in the sketch session was just Charles trying to be professional.

Clang. Charles dropped his spoon in the empty soup bowl and pulled out his smartphone. 'What's your number? I'll text you and let you know about our next trip. Sometimes, we shoot clay pigeons too.'

That sounds like a great idea. Go hunting with Owen while he's in possession of a weapon. What could possibly go wrong?

Charles stared at him.

James sighed inwardly as he pulled out his phone and exchanged numbers with Charles. And the best part was the look of shock that swept across Alice's face. Yes, it was petty of him. But enjoying the simple things along the way wasn't a crime.

FORTY-EIGHT

TURNING in to New College Lane, James followed the narrow laneway towards Hertford Bridge. The bright afternoon sun lit the road ahead, causing him to squint. A bicycle bell chimed several times before a cyclist whizzed past. After jumping to the side, James crashed into the tall brick walls of the colleges on either side of the lane. With a minor scrape on his elbow, he ambled to the next bend in the road, shielding his eyes from the sun.

The earthy aroma from the foliage in the college gardens beyond the walls made James daydream about summers in France when he was a boy. He wished he was anywhere but there, on the way to an impromptu appointment with Lady Margaret at All Saints. Concerned about her reaction to the news he was about to deliver and his request to search Amber's office, James dragged his feet.

After casting his mind away from the meeting, he found another niggling notion popping up. Ever since Charles had innocently revealed the connection between Owen and Amber, a heavy feeling weighed on James's chest. Was he jealous? James pushed the idea out of his head. Then a more sinister thought took its place. Would Owen help Amber get the Commentary back? What lengths would he go to in order to help her?

Before the next bend in the street, James paused as a family of five posed for a photo. James shook his head and finally admitted the truth. He was jealous and overlooking a simple fact. By nature, Owen was self-absorbed. He wouldn't help someone unless there was something in it for him.

As the family disappeared down the lane towards the Bodleian Library, James sauntered along College Lane. Clouds floated above, shielding his eyes from the bright sun. Crimson droplets were scattered along the narrow edge of the road, near a bush with yellow flowers.

With curiosity growing, James ambled across the lane, crouched opposite the thick overgrown bush, and peeped through the black iron fence. A sprinkle of crimson droplets littered the leaves on the lower part of the bush. Careful not to disturb the evidence, James carefully pushed aside a lower branch. To his surprise, the droplets on the leaves didn't move. They had already dried. As he stared at the garden bed, James froze. Lying in the earth was a black revolver.

A sense of dread rushed through James as he realised he had to make another call to the police. Alice was going to be suspicious. Things were not looking good for him between that, discovering Liam was missing, and his late mother's connections to an eccentric billionaire with a love of mediaeval swords. He closed his eyes and sighed. The chatter in the laneway subsided as another group of tourists moved towards the next landmark. Maybe the gun had nothing to do with the *Commentary* and Liam's disappearance. It could be part of another crime.

James slipped his smartphone from the front pocket of his jeans and took a picture of the blood. As he stared at the image on his screen, a pair of footsteps broke the silence of the empty laneway. *Merde.*

'Mr Lalonde.' An unfamiliar commanding voice echoed down the lane. 'I didn't realise you were a keen gardener.'

A short, dark-brown-skinned police constable stood a few metres away from Hertford Bridge with the bright glow of the afternoon sun radiating behind him. It was the police constable from the crime scene at All Saints. The man had hovered over him as he was lifted into the ambulance in the early hours of Thursday morning. He was also present at the crime scene at the Rad Cam. James rolled his eyes.

'Don't tell me you were naïve enough to think that Alice would let her favourite amateur sleuth and potential suspect roam the streets of Oxford unattended?'

'I'm not surprised.' James stood. 'And I suspect you won't be shocked to learn that I found blood droplets on the side of the road and a gun discarded in a garden bed. I didn't touch the gun. Only the branches.'

'Yes, I saw you didn't reach through the fence.' Joseph crouched and peered into the bushes.

James stepped away from the scene. 'I have a meeting with Lady Margaret at All Saints College.'

Joseph groaned as he stared into the bushes. 'You better not keep the aristocracy waiting.'

AFTER A SHORT BUT nonetheless awkward meeting with Lady Margaret, James stalked down the halls of the research building in All Saints, hoping not to run into Amber or Matilda. Within a few metres of the closed door to Amber's office, James paused. He listened to the stillness of the upper level. It was an invasion of privacy, but James needed more concrete evidence to push aside his doubts or confirm them. Everything he had at that point was circumstantial. Sure, he'd found Doris's will in the Rad Cam, which provided motive but no facts to suggest that Amber had hidden the pages behind the book.

On his toes, James inched down the hall. Upon reaching the closed door of Amber's office, he placed his ear to the door and listened. All he could hear was the humming of the air-conditioning system. He turned the door handle, pushed the door open, then slipped inside.

The scene before him was shrouded in chaos. It reminded him of his grandfather's study at home. As a child, he'd found the study laden with pages, a microscope, glass slides randomly tossed to the side, and a necktie resting around the neck of a human skeleton. But the current scene was on another level.

On Amber's desk was a stack of metal basket-style trays, each with paper waiting to be sorted or filed. A large calendar-style notepad filled with notes, sketches, and random numbers sat perfectly centred on the tabletop, still open to January 2015. In the top tray was a stack of envelopes from the day's mail run. Three piles of periodicals were slapped down on the left side of the desk. A small wicker bin was on its side, its contents scattered across the floor. Discarded in a metal pen holder was a ballpoint pen with bite marks on the end. How was she coping with such a mess? Was it a treatment for her OCD?

With his heart pounding, James ambled through the obstacle course to Amber's desk, leaving the door ajar. Resting on the second tray was a mobile phone bill with lines highlighted in yellow. He froze as a familiar dial code caught his eye. James tugged on the top desk drawer. To his surprise, it opened. Lying inside was a mobile phone. Could she still be in the building?

As he stared at the smartphone, it buzzed. He picked it up, and a series of dots appeared on the screen. He made an L shape on the screen with his finger, and the phone unlocked. Why choose such an obvious passcode? A sharp pain shot through his chest as he stared at the open screen. He shouldn't be snooping.

Pushing his anxiety to the side, James clicked on the messaging app. The first group of messages was from him. The second was from Owen. He couldn't resist. A few seconds later, the message trail appeared on the screen. Scrolling through the messages, James discovered Owen had indeed invited her to the hunting trip in the Cotswolds, and she'd confided in him about Stanley's sale of the Commentary. In a series of back-and-forth messages, Owen recommended taking legal action. After she admitted that she didn't have the funds to cover the cost of hiring a lawyer, Owen sent another message. It read:

James's chest tightened as he reread the text over and over again. At first, Amber appeared to dismiss the notion. But a few months ago, she'd sent a simple message to Owen. It read:

Discarding the phone to the side, James tugged at the bottom drawer, desperate to see what other secrets he could find in Amber's office. The drawer wriggled free. Inside lay a second mobile phone, a repeat prescription, and two boxes of bright-green colour contacts. *Merde.*

After slamming the second drawer shut, James picked up the first smartphone, scrolled through the messages, and clicked on the email icon. Halfway down the screen, an email from Stanley jumped out at him. Unsurprisingly, the email exchange was a series of harsh words about the sale of the Commentary being in poor taste and against the wishes of the late Doris Whittaker. Farther down the screen was an email from Doris sent one month before she died. Without hesitation, he clicked on the email. It read:

To: Amber Cooper
From: Doris Whittaker
Date: 21 March 2015, 09:15:31 GMT

My dear Amber,

I just wanted you to know that I've set aside the Commentary on Daniel for you. But be warned that my despicable son has his eye on it and will probably sell it off the second I die to cover the cost of his deplorable bed-and-breakfast dream.

Just think, strangers sleeping in my ancestral home.

God Bless,
Doris

But none of that was the most disturbing thing he found in the office. The New York phone number displayed on the mobile phone bill on the second tray haunted him. With a racing heart, he slipped Amber's phone into his empty jeans pocket then took out his phone and typed the number into the search engine. Sure enough, it was the number for the main switchboard for Harper ThompsonX. As his mind spun out of control, a *creak* from the floorboards in the hallway outside Amber's office caused James to jump. He needed to hide. He inched across the office and hid behind the door and listened. All he could hear was the hum of the air conditioner, a refrigerator, and a second creak of the floorboards.

FIFTY

———

FRIDAY: 3:37 P.M.

A SLOW, gentle drip and a lingering damp smell filled a once-empty warehouse on the outskirts of Oxfordshire. The windowless warehouse was made of iron sheeting, its insides completely shut off from the world. The only way in or out was through a lone door cut from a similar iron sheeting. It was more like a giant shed than a warehouse.

Its isolation made the warehouse an ideal location for what I had to do next. Or what I had been putting off doing next. Any minute, I would get a call from the American or his octogenarian assistant, reminding me why I was there. In truth, I had made a mistake, but there was no turning back. It was too late.

A small yellow light bulb with a lampshade and a long dangling cord hung in the centre of the room. Underneath the light, a ginger-haired man with pale skin was tied to an old dining chair. Hours earlier, I had tied Liam's arms around the back of the chair then placed linen around his mouth as a gag. Sitting on the edge of a metal table in the shadows, I waited.

Liam's eyelashes flickered as his head bobbed forward. Finally, he woke. Slowly lifting his head, Liam surveyed his new surroundings. Then he paused and stared straight ahead at me. Squinting, Liam turned his head and studied the door on the far side of the room. Was he planning an escape?

The second prepaid phone I'd purchased that week buzzed on the table. Unlike the other one, the new one had no GPS tracking other than from the nearest cell tower. Liam froze. I picked up the mobile phone, flipped it open, and listened to the only possible caller.

'Amber, tie up any loose ends and proceed as planned,' said the voice on the other end of the line.

Before I had time to reply, the line went dead. A beep then another tap filled the room. The place was silent except for a slow drip. Looking up, I watched Liam lean forward, straining against his bonds. I didn't want to be doing this, but it was too late for me. There was no going back.

Although Liam seemed confused about his location, he didn't appear scared. A part of me was impressed. I had underestimated his courage. All of that was about to change. The two men I worked for expected perfection from their contractors, which meant Liam was one of two or possibly three people I needed to silence before I left the country.

I took a few steps forward and watched recognition sweep across his face. As I strolled across the room, Liam's eyes widened. I pulled down his gag and took out a revolver. It was the second one I'd sourced from Owen after I foolishly discarded the other one along New College Lane after the drop-off. I was an idiot. With any luck, I would receive a call from Owen letting me know the weapon's location. *Fingers crossed.*

'Listen'—I thrust the gun forward—'I followed you to the All Saints Chapel. I realise this isn't news for you. However, you don't know that I watched you speaking with Lalonde.'

A blank expression swept across Liam's face. *Wow, I've definitely underestimated you. You're quite the actor.*

'Your charming French friend,' I added to jog his memory. 'Tall, dark-blond hair, sleeps with anything with two x chromosomes. A giant pain in the arse.' A hint of irritation lingered in my voice.

I positioned the gun towards Liam's head, hoping that a little incentive would improve the man's ability to cooperate. *Please don't make me do this.* I was weary from lack of sleep over the last forty-eight hours, and my temper was showing. Over the years, I'd struggled to tolerate stupid people, but I'd always kept my cool. Not that day. I didn't want to kill more people, but the demands of my job were changing. As hard as it was to admit, I was desperate. Then came the surprising realisation that once you killed that first person, the rest became a little easier. It was almost as if I'd become detached from reality. That was how I felt. It was a shock since I hadn't known I had it in me. I had to finish the job, or the men I worked for would come find me and clean up the drama themselves. Without a doubt, I would end up in a plot next to Manesh, Liam, Owen, and probably Lalonde. That wasn't how I'd imagined spending my twenties.

'I was supposed to kill you in the lab, but I thought that knocking you out would give you a concussion and, as a result, cause a disturbance in your memory, making you doubt whatever you remembered, but it didn't work out like that. And now that we're here, I guess I need to kill you.' With my arm extended, I pointed the gun at Liam's head. 'What did you say to Lalonde?' I cocked the hammer of the revolver.

Stepping closer, I briefly lowered the gun.

'What do you have against him? Did he reject you or something?' Liam snapped as he watched me inch closer.

'Do you really think being a smart-arse will get you out of this predicament?' I pointed at the revolver.

Taking a couple of deep breaths, I tried to keep my composure. Nothing good could come from letting Liam get inside my head. Sure, being with Lalonde had been a fantasy from my undergraduate days. Turned out fantasy was better than reality.

'He knows nothing.' Liam strained against the bonds. 'I said nothing. I was going to talk, then I decided that was a stupid idea. The police think I killed Manesh. No one knows you're involved. If you kept your cool, you could have just gone overseas or slipped under their radar.' Liam stared at the revolver.

'Yes, I have money to burn, just like you, James, and your other band of misfits,' I said, peering down at Liam.

Even though Liam was tied to a chair, he still had no clue. He didn't know what it was like for everyone else in the real world. In the real world, people didn't have trust funds, parents as alumni or retired professors.

'I might come from an aristocratic family, but they cut my mother off when she chose a supposedly unsuitable partner. As a result, they cut her out of her grandfather's will, and she lost her inheritance.' I watched Liam's mouth open. 'In my great-grandmother's later years, after the death of my parents and my great-grandfather, they accepted me back into the family. But I can't just skip out of the country because I still don't have the money.' My voice rose. 'I stole the Commentary because it was bequeathed to me in my great-grandmother's will, and my stupid grandfather sold it at bargain-basement prices to a con man. But you and Lalonde were in the lab. You both ruined everything. It was supposed to be an in-and-out job, but Manesh wouldn't grant me access to the lab, no matter how often I slept with him.'

'You slept with Manesh too?'

'So, you know about Kate and Manesh?' I narrowed my eyes at Liam.

Liam sighed. 'Yes, I'm just surprised he had the time to sleep with you and work on the *Commentary*.'

I shook my head. 'I'm not proud of it, but yes. It was a last resort. For a few months, I gave that man so much help and support, but he didn't select me as part of the research team. I practically told him what to do. I gave him step-by-step instructions. An idiot's guide, if you will.' I could feel my face flushing. 'So I worked on the manuscript while Manesh was preoccupied with extracurricular activities. Then later, you took over the workload with that ridiculous team of amateurs. So he left me with no choice. First, I had to follow him and use his DNA to get access. Then I carefully removed his eye. It needed to be intact so I could access the lab via the iris scanner. This is where you and Lalonde royally screwed things up. You hid, which was smart, but Lalonde played the part of the action hero and protected the *Commentary*.' I clenched the revolver.

A bead of sweat dripped down Liam's brow as he stared into the barrel of the gun.

'On the eleventh of July, an American billionaire that Manesh had blabbed to online approached me. He wanted the *Commentary* for a higher price, an offer of employment, and an American visa. Naturally, I took the higher price.' I lowered the revolver. 'And as a silver lining, I could finally get one back on that despicable girlfriend of yours. For years, she'd teased and humiliated me. She made my life miserable. I couldn't wait to see the expression on Kate's face when Manesh ended up dead.' A look of horror swept across Liam's face. 'Let's just say it wasn't as great as I'd imagined. It was better.' I pointed the revolver at his temple then leaned in as Liam pulled away.

'I'll do anything. I'll even help you escape. Just don't shoot.' Liam sobbed.

'I'll ask you one more time. What did you say to Lalonde?'

A tear trickled down Liam's face. 'Nothing, I swear.'

I sighed. 'You spent an awfully long time discussing nothing.'

Liam hung his head. 'I tried to give him a hint, but he didn't get it. James knows nothing.'

I pulled the gag up over his mouth. I couldn't handle any more tears or chats. A part of me was changing my mind, but that wasn't an option. To stay alive, I had to kill Liam. And I had to murder my one-time lover. That was going to be difficult.

Glancing at the revolver, I froze. Paralysed with fear, I stared into Liam's watery green eyes. It was too much for me to handle. I lowered the pistol then strolled back into the darkness. I needed to clear my head.

Peering at my watch, I exhaled. *It's almost time.* The deadline was fast approaching. In less than thirty minutes, I had to kill two people, possibly three, then be at the agreed-upon location. I stood in the shadows opposite Liam. I lifted my trembling hand, aimed the gun, and pulled the trigger. Blood slowly poured out of Liam's stomach. *Shit, I missed.* But help was too far away, so he would die eventually, and I was running out of time. That was just an excuse, I was ashamed to admit, but I couldn't bear to pull the trigger again. I was so weak. I sauntered to the door, leaving Liam hunched over, tied to a chair in the middle of the warehouse. Two more to go.

FIFTY-ONE

———

FRIDAY: 4:27 P.M.

SITTING on the edge of Alice's desk, James tapped the tabletop as she watched her phone. It had been over an hour since she'd asked for a warrant to search Amber's residence. According to Alice, the small station was usually quiet at that time in the afternoon, and that day, it was quite peaceful. The ticking of the clock on the station wall was driving James mad. Taking a deep breath, he decided he needed to tell Alice about his illegal search of Amber's office. He braced for the storm to come.

James cleared his throat. 'After I met with Lady Margaret, I decided to—' He hesitated. 'Perhaps misguidedly, I got a little curious and took a peek into Amber's office.'

'You what?' Alice gave him an icy stare.

'Hear me out.' James jumped off the edge of her desk and inched away. 'I found what appears to be a prepaid smartphone in her top drawer. It's the number I've been texting her on, and I now realise that you may not know about it. Because she has a work phone paid for by All Saints.'

Alice sighed. 'You touched it. Didn't you?'

James clenched his jaw as the words echoed in his mind. 'Yes, I took it with me.'

As he slid the phone across the desk, Alice pursed her lips. 'You realise I can't use this as evidence because it wasn't removed from the crime scene according to the correct procedure? Ernest Lane is the crown prosecutor for this case, and he will love this.'

With a sense of dread, James recounted the texts and emails he'd found on the prepaid phone. 'There's one last thing. In Amber's bottom drawer, I found two boxes of colour contact lenses.'

Alice's stony gaze softened. 'What colour?'

'Bright green.'

She nodded. 'That's everything.'

James sighed. He had to tell her. 'On her most recent mobile phone bill, she was preparing for accounts. I noticed a phone number with a New York City dial code.'

Alice's eyes widened.

James shrugged. 'I researched the number, and it's the main switchboard for Harper Thompson X.'

Alice pursed her lips then looked over at her silent phone. 'Is that one of your estate manager's businesses?'

James groaned as he walked across the room and sat on the edge of her desk. 'Yes. He has an experimental science and technology business that he keeps separate. There's no known address, just a number. It's super secret.'

'Really.' A smirk swept across Alice's face.

'Why are you so suspicious?'

Alice's brow wrinkled. 'Let's see. Is it because you're withholding the truth?'

James sighed.

'We've received information from a source that you organised the theft of the Commentary and the murder of Dr Manesh Warren.'

James took a deep breath and held it for a few seconds. He exhaled. 'And you got this from an anonymous source?'

Alice narrowed her eyes. 'I must consider all possibilities and treat the tips seriously until proven otherwise.'

'I'm not involved with Alexander's companies. All he does is manage my late mother's estate. The quarterly meeting is all the involvement I have with him.' James shook his head. 'Anyone in the science division could use this number. I doubt whether he's involved in Harper ThompsonX anymore.'

'How do you know him? The truth.' Alice's voice was harsh.

James exhaled. 'When I was sixteen, I was in my grandfather's study one day. He'd been marking papers, and among them, I found a handwritten letter to him from Alexander. It was one of my many attempts over the years to figure out who my parents were. So, I contacted Alexander, and he told me he was a close friend of my mother. We kept in contact. I hid this from my grandfather. To this day, my grandfather does not know about my meetings and dealings with him. But he avoided talking about her. He said he couldn't talk about her passing. It was too painful. And he refused to talk about my father. He said that he couldn't talk about him, either. So it was a fruitless search. Now and then, he lets some anecdote about her slip. That's the real reason I keep attending these meetings.' James's eyes watered. 'It's all for the anecdotes for me. Then out of the blue, he turned up at my graduation ceremony at All Saints. My grandparents were annoyed. We met up, and he presented me with a cheque. That's when I learned about my mother's estate.'

'So Alexander Harper Thompson turned up at your graduation with a cheque?'

'Something like that. I had always written to Alexander. He didn't tell me he was coming. We met up at the same café that's in the social media image you found.'

'And your recent meeting?'

'The same old same old. We discussed the performance of

stocks, property, etcetera.' James hung his head, then he glanced up. 'This time, he brought his assistant.'

'What was his assistant like?'

'The creepy type who stands silently in the background.' James bit the inside of his lip. 'A while back, I thought someone was following me. They were driving a black car with tinted windows. So I asked a contact I met while working at the Northampton Tribune to investigate him. But it was a fruitless search. He's a ghost. When I turned up to the Queen's Lane Coffee House meeting, I recognised him from the black car.'

Alice whirled around in her chair and frantically bashed the keys on her keyboard.

Looking over Alice's shoulder, James shook his head as he read the search results on the screen. She was going after Alexander like a bull in a china shop. The man had deep pockets, and with that probably came friends in high places. She wasn't going to listen to him, but he had to warn her.

'Promise me you'll let go of your plans to chase down Harper Thompson Corp. I have a bad feeling about them. Instead, pass it on to Interpol or someone with more clout and resources.'

'What aren't you telling me?'

James jumped off the desk. 'Nothing. It's just a feeling I get. His assistant is trouble.'

'Detective O'Donnell.' A familiar voice called out from behind them.

Joseph stood in the doorframe. His uniform was free of creases, and the bottom of his tie lightly skimmed his belt.

'This is Joseph,' Alice said as she turned around and greeted him with a smile. 'This is James Lalonde.'

'Ah, we've met.'

Alice narrowed her eyes at James then softened her gaze. 'Oh, that's right. At the Radcliffe Camera library.'

James bit his lip. 'No, I discovered the revolver in the

bushes along New College Lane. Then, miraculously, Joseph turned up at the right time.'

Joseph tugged at the collar of his shirt.

Alice raised her eyebrows at James.

'He's taking credit for my work,' James said as he waved his arm in Joseph's direction.

'Excuse me for interrupting.' Joseph peered briefly at James then faced Alice. 'I have something you need to see.' A few seconds later, Joseph strolled out of the office and down the hall.

'Follow me.' Alice dashed down the corridor after Joseph.

He stopped halfway down the hall then turned and looked at Alice and James. His eyes darted between the two of them.

I definitely don't feel like a third wheel.

'He can't come with us,' Joseph said as he peered over his shoulder at Alice.

Alice groaned. 'I don't trust him to be left alone in my office or in the station and not snoop around or discover confidential information.'

'This is extremely unorthodox,' Joseph muttered, a sense of uneasiness in his tone.

———

JOSEPH TREKKED down the hall and stopped outside a door next to Charles's office. Then he turned the door handle, stepped inside the office, and took a seat at his desk, with Alice and James following closely. The office was white and minimalist. Standing next to Alice, Joseph hunched over his keyboard and typed his password while covering his movements with his left hand, an attempt to disguise his password from his unwanted guest. For the first time, James would have rather been next door, reliving the sketch from hell with Charles. Joseph opened a screen on the computer.

'Funnily enough, I got an email back from the lab. They

ran the revolver's serial number through the database, and it came back with a match.' Joseph turned around in his dark-blue swivel chair and gazed up at James. 'It's registered to a Leonard Swift. Evidence of blood splatter was found inside the barrel, which means it was fired at close range and might have been jammed at some point. So it was repaired between the time the crime occurred and when it was discarded. There are also fingerprints. But we don't know anything for certain.'

James groaned. 'Leonard Swift is Owen's father.'

Joseph sighed. 'It hasn't been listed on the Gun Loss Register.'

Alice nudged James. 'So either your friend Owen is supplying her with weapons, or she stole it while on the hunting trip and they haven't noticed. And he might have fixed the gun for her.'

Merde.

'She might have gotten her hands on another weapon.' Joseph pointed at the screen. 'Leonard Swift has quite the collection. You'll have to question Owen.'

James tugged at the white collar of his polo shirt. 'Owen is staying at the Wizard and Ragged Staff bed-and-breakfast. I'll send you the address.'

With her eyes fixed on the screen, Alice strolled over to the desk and sat on the edge. 'It's been three hours since we discovered the blood and Liam's phone outside the Radcliffe Camera library. What's taking them so long to approve the search warrant?'

James paced the length of the office as a realisation came to mind. 'Once Liam tells Amber what he told me in All Saints Chapel, he's of no further use to her.'

A hard lump formed at the back of James's throat, and his eyes watered.

Alice sighed. 'That's been weighing on my mind since you discovered Doris's will in the Radcliffe Camera.'

James dashed to the door. 'We need to find Liam before it's too late.'

'You have to wait for the magistrate to approve the warrant. Without that, you can't go anywhere.' Joseph stood then strolled across the room.

'I can.' James reached for the door handle. 'You and Alice can't.'

Joseph placed his hand on the door, preventing James from opening it. 'If you do something stupid, like finding Liam or, for argument's sake, let's say that Amber finds you and shoots you, we can't intervene until the warrant is approved, which means you could bleed to death by the time we can help.'

'That's not entirely true.' James stepped back from the closed door. 'You can enter a premises without a warrant if you suspect someone has been injured. I think the truth here is you don't want to.'

'Police procedure exists for a reason,' Joseph said as James rolled his eyes in frustration.

We're going to arrive when it's too late.

'It's easy for you to wait.' James's voice broke. 'Your best friend hasn't been kidnapped or potentially murdered.'

LEANING against my 2001 white Toyota Corolla at the agreed-upon meet-up point along Eynsham Road, I hunched over, pulling my black trench coat across my chest. The late-afternoon breeze had an icy bite for that time of year. As I pushed the sleeve of my jacket back and glanced at my watch, my stomach churned. I took a deep breath then slipped my dry, cracked hands into the pockets of my trench coat as an overwhelming urge to wash my hands swept over me.

I hated being outdoors. The sight of the open fields, tall trees, and the sign advertising the camping grounds triggered my OCD. That and I hadn't quite tied up all the loose ends. Lalonde was conveniently hanging around the police after he'd snooped around my office and stolen my phone. That was only a minor setback but a nonetheless startling discovery after I returned to my office to retrieve my phone. A few moments later, my informant called and let me know of Lalonde's whereabouts. The issue could be rectified if he stepped away from the police's shadows.

I peered down the road, but there was no traffic except for the occasional vehicle driving towards the university. Inside my pocket, my chafed hand brushed across the smooth surface of the archaic flip phone. After pulling it out, I opened the phone and reread the instructions again—another compulsive habit that I needed to break. I was in the right place. Once I arrived in New York, I needed to find another therapist. My medication wouldn't last very long.

They were fifty-one minutes late. Had the police caught up with them? I dismissed the thought. If that had happened, I would already be in a holding cell. Lalonde clearly had no concrete evidence. I wondered if he'd found my contact lenses.

A small black hatchback sailed by towards the next town. The city centre was a nineteen-minute drive in the opposite direction. Waiting was taking a toll on my nerves, possibly a deliberate move on their part. I sighed with relief as I heard rubber rolling across tar. Glancing up, I observed a black Bentley with dark-tinted windows approaching. It stopped on the other side of the road.

Clutching the gun in my left pocket, I watched the American climb out of the vehicle, followed by the tall older gentleman. My heart sank as they walked across the road.

'Amber, I'm incredibly sorry for our late arrival. We were held up by an unexpected turn of events,' the American said smoothly. 'I trust that you've tied up those loose ends.'

'Of course,' I lied as my hand trembled.

The American turned then waved his forefinger at the older gentleman standing a few steps behind.

'Miles, hand over the visa and instructions,' he said, walking to the car. He grabbed the handle, opened the door, and slid inside.

I could feel the watchful gaze of the older gentleman as he walked towards me. It was sinister, but that was nothing new.

'Here is your passport, visa, and your flight details.'

I sighed inwardly as Miles reached inside his black suit jacket and pulled out a white envelope.

'You will receive further instructions upon your arrival.

Someone will wait for you at the airport.' Miles stared at me with wary green eyes.

'How will I know who's waiting for me?' I asked as my voice broke.

Miles pursed his lips. 'They will hold a sign. It will most likely be someone from HR.' Miles strolled to the opposite side of the car and opened the door.

'What about the money?' I asked before he slid inside.

'Just one moment,' Miles said calmly as he reached down into the car.

I inched along the side of my white hatchback as the events unfolded in slow motion. The older gentleman pulled out an automatic with a silencer and aimed it at my head. Seconds before he pulled the trigger, I dived behind the car. There was no way I would stick around and see how great his aim was. I somehow knew he wouldn't miss. Despite his old age, he was agile, intelligent, and devious. I would've hired him too.

With a racing heart, I crawled through the bushes and across the field as I heard the gentleman take a few steps towards the Bentley. Then I turned and noticed no one had followed me. That was suspicious. I commando crawled to the road at my front but stayed hidden in the bushes. Upon getting closer, I heard the two men talking.

'Miles, don't bother. She's got no money and nowhere to go but home. So we'll ambush her at her house then finish things off,' the American said from within the safety of the car. *You double-crossing prick.*

FIFTY-THREE

A BLACK BENTLEY with dark-tinted windows turned the corner into Station Street. Alexander peered out the window at the maisonettes as the car rolled past. Miles sat next to him with his ear glued to his phone, staring out the window in the other direction. Hanging up, Miles took a loud, deep breath.

'What's wrong?' Alexander observed his friend and long-time assistant.

'I'm afraid we must skip our delightful reunion with Amber and leave immediately for New York.'

'What a shame. You know I hate leaving loose ends behind. I like everything to come full circle.'

'Ideally, I share your sentiments. But my contact overheard James Lalonde and Detective Alice O'Donnell talking about obtaining a warrant to search Amber's premises.' Miles gazed at the smartphone in his hands. 'He's trouble.'

'He's just a boy looking into the death of his friends. He's a giblet. Completely harmless.' Alexander waved his hand at Miles as he turned and glanced out the window.

'You need to leave, sir, unless you want to spend time in a police station calling your lawyer.' Miles tapped the screen of his smartphone. 'I, for one, do not want to get caught.'

'Okay, let's get out of here.' Alexander groaned. 'Is there something you can do about Amber?'

'Yes, I'm so glad you asked. I have a contact who will have no issue cleaning up.'

'Perfect, make arrangements. I want nothing pointing back at me.'

Miles dialled a number then drew his phone to his ear. When the person on the other end of the line picked up, he said, 'I'm sending you the cash and the instructions. Be discreet. I know you don't like that, but this is sensitive.'

'Fine,' a refined English accent said through the tiny speaker. 'I'll start the job the second I get the money.'

The line went dead. Miles slipped the phone into his pocket and peered out the window as the driver turned the vehicle around.

FIFTY-FOUR

FRIDAY: 5:08 P.M.

WITH MY HEART POUNDING, I ascended the three flights of stairs towards my flat. Hugging the wall of the internal cement stairwell, clutching the revolver tucked inside the sleeve of my trench coat, I inched closer to the top, one step at a time. On the way home, I hadn't spotted the American's black Bentley parked outside, driving along Station Street, or on any of the side streets. Despite all that, I wasn't taking any chances.

Inside the envelope was a new passport with a visa and an airline ticket. They had planned on framing me from the start. I guess after killing me, they'd planned to drop my body off at my flat or leave me where I lay with my new passport, new identity, and plane tickets, with a bullet to the head. It was a neat finish for them. I was the fall guy and too stupid to see it. I wondered if they'd cancelled the flight. Why did they get me a new identity and visa if they'd planned to shoot me on the spot? Did they change their minds?

I had only one choice left other than spending time in jail —I had to skip the country and never come back. At least I had a new identity known only to two slick criminals who would most likely be out of the United Kingdom before the end of the day.

A tear trickled down my cheek as I reached the third level. I strolled along the corridor towards my flat. As I arrived at my front door, I leaned against the wall and listened. No sound came from within my home other than the clock ticking in the living room. I reached into my pocket and pulled out the keys while grasping the revolver in my other hand.

With extreme caution, I slid the front door key into the lock and pushed it open. Anxious about what might be waiting for me, I slipped the gun out of the sleeve of my trench coat and ambled around my flat.

I tiptoed down the hall then paused at the first closed door. Scared of what might be inside, I pushed the door open. I pointed my gun into the room as I squinted into the darkness. Fumbling around, I located the light switch and turned on the light. My bedroom was empty. Next, I meandered around the room, opened my wardrobe, and closed the doors. No one was in the room.

Moving on to the next room, a little farther down the hall, I repeated the same procedure, sweeping every inch of my home. All the rooms were empty. I must be going mad. Slipping the gun into my pocket, I strolled down the hall to my living room then sat down and pulled out the white envelope. After taking several deep breaths to ease my racing heart, I got up from the couch, waltzed over to the double doors that led to my small balcony, opened them, and let the afternoon summer breeze into my flat.

I need to get out of here.

Eager to leave, I dashed to the entry door. Turning to the left, I opened my coat closet and pulled out a small wheeled suitcase. As I grasped the black handle, the skin on my fingers cracked and bled, then I marched to my bedroom. I threw the bag onto my bed and opened the flap. Frantically, I sprinted to the closet and opened the door. Grabbing the clothes before me, I tugged them free from the hangers. Jolting upwards, the hangers spilt out of the wardrobe and onto the floor. I trekked to the suitcase and shoved the garments inside. There was no time for folding.

I glanced at my watch. The longer I stayed, the greater my chance of getting caught. Five more minutes, then I needed to get out of there. Racing to the closet, I pulled out several pairs of trousers and flung them across the room at my suitcase. Next, I sprinted to my chest of drawers, pulled out more clothes, and hurled them into the suitcase. Time was up. After cramming the clothing inside the case, I leaned on the bag and zipped it.

Dashing down the hall to the kitchen area, I wheeled the suitcase behind me. Once I reached the kitchen, I opened the fridge, pulled out my medication, unclipped a repeat prescription from the magnetic clip on the door, and shoved it all into my coat pocket. Leaving the suitcase leaning against the counter, I walked to the sofa and sat. Out of curiosity, I pulled out my phone, dialled the airline, and waited for someone to pick up.

'Hello, Big Sky Airlines.'

'Hi, I'm calling to check when I need to be at the airport. I'm worried I might miss my flight if I turn up late. My flight number is BSA2164. I'm flying to New York.'

'The gates close at 7:28 p.m. Ideally, you must have your luggage checked an hour before that time. If you check in over the phone, it will save you time at the airport.'

'Okay.'

'Your name, miss?'

'Melissa Rose Carroll. There's a seat number on my ticket.'

'Just one moment,' the voice said on the other end of the line. 'Ah, Miss Carroll, your personal assistant just called to cancel your ticket. Would you like to reactivate the booking?

According to the company policy at Harper Thompson X, you'll need a new purchase order number.'

'Um, no, I'll call work and find out what's going on,' I lied.

'Okay, have a great evening.'

Tears streamed down my cheeks. I felt trapped. I had only one option: run without an itinerary. It wouldn't be long before the two men caught up with me. There was no way they would leave without cleaning up their mess, but I couldn't work out why they hadn't arrived at the apartment before me. It was strange. My best option was to board a train to London then catch the Eurostar to Paris. It would be easy to get lost in the crowd in a big city.

A loud, forceful knock at the front door caused me to freeze. Moments later, as the knocking persisted, I jumped up, pulled out my gun, and stepped towards the open double doors leading to my balcony. As the knock became louder, the door shook. Someone was trying to burst through the door. *They've finally come for me.*

I peered at the gun shaking in my hand. I had no options.

FIFTY-FIVE

LEANING against the door to Amber's apartment with his ear pressed against it, James listened to Amber's movements as he tugged at his police-issue stab-proof vest. By his side and wearing the same vests, Alice and Joseph leaned against the wall. After thirty minutes of debating, Alice and Joseph had finally agreed it was plausible for them to do a welfare check out of concern for Amber's well-being. Deep down, James knew they were present to babysit him on his idiotic venture, as Joseph had so eloquently and tactfully described it.

'She's talking to Big Sky Airlines,' James whispered as he listened to the one-sided conversation within the apartment.

Out of the corner of his eye, James watched Alice make a hand signal in Joseph's direction as she crept towards the door. With brute force, Alice slammed her fist against the polished wood as James stepped out of her warpath. Without pausing, Alice continued to knock. That icy stare swept over her face as the door rattled in response.

Waving Alice back from the door, James threw his right shoulder into the wood. After each strike, a sharp pain ran from his left side to his shoulder blade. Squeezing his eyes shut, James pushed through the pain as he fought against the front door. With one final attempt, James rammed his shoulder into the wood, and it buckled. She hasn't secured the dead bolt.

After taking a couple of steps back, James kicked the door open with his left leg. Those years of playing rugby hadn't gone to waste.

'I can do that for myself,' Alice whispered behind him as he strolled into the apartment.

Sorry for helping.

At the far end of the living room, Amber aimed a gun in his direction. On the inside of her right wrist were two tiny scratches that were one or two days old at the most. She shook her head at him. As Alice pushed past him, Amber adjusted her aim towards the detective.

'Don't move, or I'll shoot.' Amber's voice quivered.

Alice lifted her hands. Standing behind her, Joseph gripped the radio on his shoulder. After tapping Joseph on his shoulder, James shook his head.

'Amber, I'm just here to talk. I'm quite confident we can work something out between us,' Alice replied as she inched closer to Amber.

Fear filled Amber's eyes. With a trembling hand, she stepped back into the open double doors. James froze. She was acting like a wild, cornered animal.

'Amber, put the gun down on the floor and slide it over to me. Then we can start negotiating.'

Amber took another step back. 'It's too late for that.'

'If you lower the gun, everyone will be less on edge, and we'll be able to talk,' James said as he felt Joseph's watchful gaze. James inched closer to Amber.

'Stay back,' she said. 'I told you to stay back.'

James bit the inside of his lip. 'It's just me. I'm not going to hurt you. And I'm not here as a part of the police team. I'm like a go-between. Please trust me. I'm on your side.'

Amber scowled at James. 'I don't need your help.'

'Really?' James replied. 'Look around. I'm the only one here without an intent to arrest you.' James looked at Alice, who was turning red. 'We know you're not doing all of this on your own. The police are after Alexander and his associates, not you.'

'Thanks for the mansplaining.' Amber narrowed her eyes at James.

'You realise you're next on their cleanup list? Right now, your best option is to let these two police officers arrest you. That way, you'll be safe and alive. And you'll be able to negotiate a lighter sentence for information leading to an arrest.'

'You can't protect me from them.' A tear trickled down Amber's cheek.

'The police can protect you,' James said. 'Why don't you tell me what actually happened? Then we'll go from there.'

'I can't.' Amber stepped back.

'I'll get you a good lawyer.' James placed his hand on his chest. 'I promise.'

She surveyed the room as she gripped the gun. 'The *Commentary* was bequeathed to me in my great-grandmother's will, but my stupid grandfather sold it to a con man.' Amber's eyes darted to Alice as James inched forward. 'After discovering Manesh had purchased the *Commentary on Daniel* for a measly twenty grand, I helped him with his research, hoping he would invite me to join his team. For a few months, I gave that man so much help and support.' Tears streamed down her cheeks. 'I practically gave him step-by-step instructions—an idiot's guide. He knew diddly-squat about the *Commentary*. It was all my work. But Manesh wouldn't grant me access to the lab. So I changed tactics. Turns out, no matter how often I slept with him, he refused to give me access.'

Alice crept forward. 'How does Alexander Harper Thompson play into all of this?'

'On the eleventh of July, the American that Manesh had blabbed to online approached me in a pub, asking questions about the manuscript. He wanted the *Commentary* and was willing to pay its value, offered employment at his company and a visa. So I stole the *Commentary*. I had no choice.' Still pointing her gun at Alice, Amber stared at James. 'It was supposed to be an in-and-out job, but you and Liam were in the lab. You both ruined everything. And then you played action hero. Why did you have to be there so late at night?'

'Did you choose to murder Manesh, or did something go wrong?' James tilted his head.

'It was the only way in.' Amber sobbed. 'The lab is protected by biotechnology. The only way in is with someone who has the bio credentials. But that wasn't possible. The American kept phoning me for updates about the *Commentary* and pressured me with an excessively tight deadline. He kept saying to do what was necessary and to leave no loose ends.' Amber cried.

'I had to gouge his eye out because Manesh was never going to cooperate, even at gunpoint. You remember what he was like. But I couldn't do it while he was still alive. That would have been inhuman.'

Alice narrowed her eyes. 'That's when you returned to the scene and called the police.'

Amber shook her head. 'I shouldn't have returned to the crime scene, but I panicked. I thought I had left something behind and wanted to clean up any evidence. That's when I slipped in his blood. And that's when I realised I had to phone it in to the police.' Amber sobbed as James strolled across the living room and sat on the edge of her TV bench.

Alice glared at him.

'I just need to sit down. I'm in pain.' James rested his right hand on the white polished wood then leaned over. As he looked at the view from the balcony, he noticed a tiny red dot on Amber's back.

Merde. The cleanup crew has arrived.

With a wave of pain shooting through his side, James lunged, hoping to grab Amber and pull her out of range of the sniper rifle.

For a second, he peeked at his thin stab-proof vest. Fingers crossed.

'Stay away,' Amber warned him as she fixed her gun on Alice.

Joseph tilted his head towards Alice. James nodded in response.

'Amber, James is right. We know you're not doing all of this alone. If you help us bring in the people you're working for, we can give you a reduced sentence. And we can keep you hidden and safe. We've done things like that before.' Alice inched forward.

With a wild look in her eyes, Amber shook her head, stepped back, and stumbled over the doorframe. Joseph and Alice froze as the red dot navigated the room and fixed itself at the centre of Alice's chest.

The sniper was going to sweep the room and pick everyone off, one by one.

'Alice, get down!' James yelled as Amber regained her balance.

Amber squeezed the trigger, and a loud bang echoed through the outside courtyard and into the small apartment. Amber released her grip on the revolver. A darkened patch formed on Alice's police-issue vest. A look of horror swept across her face as she fell to the ground.

'I didn't mean to,' Amber sobbed as she stepped back onto the small balcony.

Joseph dropped to the floor and crawled over to Alice. James bit the inside of his cheek as Joseph placed his hand under Alice's neck and caressed her forehead. Then, glancing over at James, Joseph shook his head.

James cast eyes on the balcony as Amber climbed onto the brick ledge. *Merde.*

'Amber, get down off the ledge. It's going to be okay.' James inched to her and held out his hand.

'This whole thing was a disaster from beginning to end. I just want it to be over.' Amber stared at James's hand. A second loud bang filled the courtyard as a tiny blood spot appeared on the front of Amber's trench coat. She clutched her chest as she fell backwards to the courtyard below.

After diving to the floor, James crawled into the apartment, towards Alice and Joseph.

Joseph peered over at James with his watery brown eyes. 'She's gone.'

'What is the point of these vests?' James asked as a tear dripped down his cheek.

'Nothing is ever truly bulletproof,' Joseph said as he struggled to compose himself. 'She was the only one who would work with me since I returned to fieldwork.'

'Really?'

'Yeah.' Joseph bobbed his head. 'I've radioed in for backup. They should be here in five minutes.'

'I don't mean to be insensitive, but we still don't know where Liam is being held or, at the very least, what happened to his body. We need to find him.' James surveyed the room.

The red dot had disappeared.

'We need to let the police handle the search. We're too emotionally involved in the case.' Joseph stared at the pool of blood under Alice's body.

'Screw the rules, Joseph.'

FIFTY-SIX

FRIDAY: 6:42 P.M.

DONNING a white crime scene jumpsuit and matching boot covers, James sat on Amber's sofa beside Joseph and watched the forensics team sweep the room for evidence. They both resembled a pair of benched players during a cricket match—all in white, looking bored while the other players continued on with the game. A sea of yellow cards was scattered across the floor. Ellie was hunched over, attempting to remove a bullet from the wall. A hard lump formed in his throat as he replayed Amber's last moments. How had he not seen that she was involved in everything? The signs were all present.

He had to concentrate on finding Liam, but an obstacle course of red tape lay before him. There was no way he was leaving without going through the proper formalities, and Joseph wouldn't bend the rules. After being trapped in Amber's open-plan living area for over an hour, James needed a change of scenery. Nudging Joseph's side, James stood. Without hesitation, Joseph pulled James to the couch and glared at him.

'I can't sit and watch them bag and tag everything. So I'm going to search Amber's bedroom. Just in case you forgot, there's another victim out there waiting for us to rescue him.'

James dashed around the yellow evidence tags and down the hall, Joseph following.

As the open bedroom door came into view, James slowed. Then, stepping into the doorframe, he surveyed the chaos. Closet doors and drawers were flung open, and clothing spilled onto the timber floorboards. A duck-egg duvet had slipped off the double bed and onto the floor.

'Joseph, we've already checked the bedroom. You'll find nothing in there,' a voice called out from behind.

'I know,' Joseph said with an exasperated sigh. 'He just wants to help. We'll be a second.'

James peered out of the window. The bright summer sun seemed out of place after the events that had unfolded. After he trekked across the room, James sat on the chair tucked under the small white desk on the left-hand side of the bed. The tabletop was bare apart from a few pens and a black analogue clock.

'James, you don't have much time. The crime scene officers will be back any second now.' Joseph strolled across the room and patted him on the shoulder.

'I don't care. I've called every antique dealer in Oxford. Not a single one has seen or has possession of the manuscript. On the other hand, Amber never mentioned whether she gave Alexander the *Commentary*, so maybe she still has it. We need to check if Amber was intelligent enough to not hand over the book and see if anything here will lead us to Liam. Hopefully, Liam will still be alive.'

'That's highly unlikely,' Joseph scoffed.

'No, Liam could still be alive. I'm not giving up on looking for him,' James snapped as he opened the first small drawer in the two-drawer white unit on the tabletop.

'I mean the book. I'm not that much of an arse.' Joseph sauntered to the bed then sat and shook his head as James closed the drawer. Then he opened the second one. Inside lay a brass-bound script for Much Ado About Nothing. After closing it, James stood and stared at the notice board propped against the wall. For a moment, he smiled at the photos on her pinboard, images taken in happier times. She seemed not to have a care in the world.

With a sigh, James ambled around the bed and rummaged through the top drawer of her bedside table. He closed it then pulled the next drawer open.

Joseph sighed. 'Do you even know what you're searching for?'

'Anything that leads me to Liam or a clue where she might have hidden him. It has to be somewhere familiar but out of the way, somewhere that means something to her.'

'And you think you're going to find it in here?'

'I don't know. Maybe.' James glared at Joseph.

'You loved Amber. Didn't you?'

'I think love is a strong word. It was just a brief fling.' James blushed and continued to rummage through the drawer.

Joseph raised his eyebrows. 'It's obvious that you feel more than that.'

'Obvious to whom?' James asked as a lump formed in his throat.

'It's okay to admit you loved or were at least falling for her. It's normal to develop an attachment like that.' Joseph brushed his hand along the smooth surface of the small white desk.

'Fine.' James's gaze dropped to the floor. 'There was a part of me that hoped things would work out with her. But I wasn't thinking clearly. I hate feeling like this. I was developing feelings for a woman who meddled in my friendship circle and kidnapped my best friend. And I overlooked her obvious ulterior motive. On top of that, it wasn't real.' James faced the drawers. *I've said too much.*

Joseph tapped his fingertips on the desk. 'Why do you think you quickly made an attachment to her?'

James rubbed the back of his neck. 'I just told you. It was her plan.'

'There must be another reason.'

'What?'

'Your mother died when you were young. I saw that in your primary school records.'

'You speak French?'

'Yes, I'm from Congo. French is one language I learned as a child,' Joseph said soothingly. 'Do you know much about her?'

'No,' James whispered.

Joseph nodded. 'Were you aware that Amber lost her mother when she was thirteen and spent the last few years living between foster homes before ageing out of the system? A shared experience can be pretty powerful.'

A look of realisation swept across James's face. 'Yes, I had a long chat with her in the dining room one evening during the final year of my undergraduate degree. But that was seven years ago.'

Joseph slipped his hands into the pockets of his jumpsuit. 'Still, a shared experience can form quite a bond. Perhaps, on some level, you felt connected to her, even after all these years.'

'Wait. You researched my mother as a part of this investigation?' James clenched his jaw.

'Yes, Alice was determined to check your claims, and we were hoping to find a connection between you and Alexander or at least your family.'

James rolled his eyes and slammed the drawer shut.

'I can give you what I know.' Joseph stood, strolled around the bed, and placed his hand on James's shoulder.

'Why?' James narrowed his eyes.

'I escaped the Congo as a child with my grandmother. I spent years living in refugee camps before settling in the United Kingdom. Until this day, I do not know what happened to my parents or my brothers. I have no way of knowing. I recognise this in you because I've had a similar experience.' Joseph glanced at the floor.

'You should be a therapist. You'll make a fortune.' James opened the third drawer and rummaged through its contents.

'So, Amber kidnapped Liam? Is that correct?' Joseph peered at the drawer.

Where is he going with this? Why state the obvious?

James sighed. 'Yes, he went missing after he told me he knew the intruder's identity.'

'I think you might be onto something when you mentioned earlier that Amber might hold Liam in a part of Oxford with sentimental value.'

'The problem I'm having is that Amber always kept to herself. She was always studying. I only spoke to her a few times, apart from our recent fling. But there was one time at All Saints between classes.'

'What happened?'

James closed his eyes and sighed. 'She asked me if I wanted to go for a drink at a nearby pub, but I couldn't. I was banned from the pub for some time.'

Joseph jerked his head back. 'You were banned from a pub?'

'I was twenty-one and accidentally started a fight with a drunk Belgium tourist. I ran into him and knocked his beer flying. He was super mad. It's a side issue. The pub is still open.'

'What else did she do during her spare time?'

'Apparently, she took part in an amateur drama society. In one photo on the board, they're holding a newspaper article from the *Oxford Chronicle*.'

'That paper closed its doors two years ago.'

'I remember she slipped out of classes early to attend. This one time, I caught her using an old ticket as a bookmark.'

'I thought you said you barely spoke to Amber when you were at university?'

'I went to All Saints for three years, and I spoke to her maybe five times at the most.' James shrugged. 'I think she said they held the rehearsals—' James's eyes widened.

After unzipping his white jumpsuit and pulling his smartphone out of his jeans pocket, he tapped the screen and opened an internet browser. 'I think I know where he is. It's all making sense.'

Joseph frowned.

'The gold Venetian theatre mask. The drama society. I remember way back in 2008, she was in a production of *Much Ado About Nothing*. And it was located here.' James pointed at the screen. 'I don't think she planned on hiding him here, but the location means so much to her. And it's somewhat remote. No one would witness her coming and going.' James waved his arm around.

Joseph scanned the room. 'I see your point. But it could be a long shot. Amber might be keeping Liam somewhere remote. That's plausible too.'

James rolled his eyes. 'True. But you forget she's not a career criminal. This is not something she has done before. Therefore, I believe she would use a familiar place because familiar is comfortable.'

Joseph placed his hands on his hips. 'You're planning on going to that rehearsal space? That's insane not to mention dangerous.'

'This isn't my first time doing something dangerous, as you described it. Worst-case scenario, I'll find an empty, abandoned building.' James tugged at the hood of his jumpsuit. 'But what if I find Liam before it's too late because I wasn't afraid to take a minor risk?'

When Joseph opened his mouth, a digital quack called out from the tiny speaker on his smartphone. James stared at the notification on his screen. An email had come through. With a few short clicks, James opened the email. It was from Dr Archibald McKay. As James clicked out of the screen, a second email from the Macdonald Randolph Hotel, sent three hours earlier, caught his eye.

James sighed. 'I just received two emails confirming Tom's alibi. One from Dr Archibald McKay confirming his addiction. The doctor is also asking me to support Tom through his rehabilitation. And the other is from Tom's hotel confirming his internet usage, which started at thirty minutes past ten in the evening through to a little after three in the morning.' A solemn expression swept across James's face. 'He has a serious problem, and his father has practically abandoned him.' James tapped the button on the side of his smartphone then slipped it inside the white jumpsuit.

Joseph nodded. 'Forward those emails to me, and I'll chase it up with the hotel.'

The summer sun shone through the sheer curtain in the bedroom and burned the back of James's neck. He strolled to the window. As James reached out to close the second set of thicker curtains, a small, clear hook lay bare on the wall. He gasped at the gold Venetian theatre mask on the floor, propped up against the chest of drawers. The mask had once been hidden by the thick curtains.

'It's here.' A look of horror swept across James's face.

From the hall outside the room, a familiar voice cleared its throat. 'Sorry I'm late. I was in the middle of an autopsy.' Zach tapped his index finger on the doorframe. He sighed. 'I don't know how to tell you this, but Alice is still alive. She has a faint pulse. I've called an ambulance. She's lost a lot of blood.'

'What—' Joseph stared straight through Zach.

Sensing that Joseph was too distracted by the news, James slipped out of the bedroom and meandered down the hall and into the living area.

'Where are you going?' Joseph bellowed.

James froze.

'You know where I'm going,' James said over his shoulder.

Joseph sighed. 'Not without me, you're not.'

FIFTY-SEVEN

FRIDAY: 7:09 P.M.

TWENTY-SEVEN MINUTES LATER, Joseph steered the unmarked police car up the unsealed dirt road to Applewood Farm, the home of Amber's former rehearsal space. While he'd waited for Joseph to negotiate their departure from the crime scene, James called the owner of the property. The former owner's granddaughter was happy to let them visit. She must be desperate to rent out the space.

'We're almost here,' Joseph announced as he entered the farm's driveway then drove down the trail to the abandoned warehouse.

After he parked the car, Joseph leaned over the steering wheel and stared at the building. 'This is a warehouse? It's more like a shed. And you're sure this is where Amber attended the rehearsals for the amateur drama society?' He glanced at James.

James shook his head. 'No, I didn't bother checking. I thought I'd just wing it.'

Joseph leaned back in the driver's seat. 'I don't like to make assumptions.'

'So, are you going back to the station?' James asked with a shrug.

Joseph clicked the button on his seat belt then opened the car door. 'No, I'm going in with you.'

'I thought you said this was dangerous.' James had a hint of a smile.

'I'm going to ignore that comment because you're not in a great place, emotionally speaking,' Joseph said as James rolled his eyes. 'And according to my research, you've been stabbed twice in four months. So you're hardly an action hero who runs from town to town, saving the day.'

'Geez, you're very judgy, Joseph.' James opened the car door and strolled towards the warehouse.

'This doesn't seem like a safe rehearsal space. It's clearly violating a few health and safety codes.' Joseph slammed the car door and slid the keys into his pocket.

'Apparently, the old man who used to run Applewood Farm was a huge theatre fan and used to direct all the plays. But he died in 2013, shortly after the closure of the *Oxford Chronicle*, and the club stopped running. That's what his daughter said on the phone.' James squinted as he gazed up at the corrugated iron shed. 'She was under the impression that Amber would restart the club.'

'I know. I was eavesdropping.'

James nodded. 'And that's why you get along with Alice so well.'

Joseph groaned. 'The building's unsafe.'

'I'll let you call a building inspector when we return to the station.' James peered at the police constable. 'Please tell me you've completed more fieldwork than just traffic control.'

'What's wrong with traffic control?'

'You seem a little scared. That's all.'

'I've been shot in the line of duty. And I'm about to enter a premises with an amateur who has a habit of getting stabbed.' Joseph tensed. 'Also, we don't have a plan.'

'The plan is, we open the door and check if Liam is inside.

If Liam is alive, then we call for an ambulance.' James walked to the warehouse.

'What if someone is in there?'

'The two men who paid Amber to steal the manuscript are most likely on a private jet to New York.'

'I realise that, but what about the sniper who shot Alice? He could be waiting.'

'If he wanted us dead, we wouldn't be alive right now.' James took a deep breath.

'I want to know what you plan on doing if he's in there.'

'We're making so much noise that if there was someone inside, we would know about it by now.' James pointed at the empty fields of overgrown grass surrounding the warehouse. 'The worst-case scenario is that the building is empty and we must continue the search for Liam. I get that you're scared, but I'm not waiting for news about a dead body and finding out that if we'd found him earlier, we could have saved him. You're welcome to stay in the car, but I'm going in.' James strolled towards the closed door of the iron warehouse, hoping for no surprises. Hoping that his friend was alive and well.

Joseph had made some excellent points, none of which had crossed James's mind until then. So why did the sniper shoot Alice and Amber but not everyone else? Then he realised the answer.

James whirled around and stared at Joseph. 'They have an informant at the police station. That's why Alice was shot. She was meant to die because she knew too much and discovered the truth. Ergo, she was considered a liability.'

A look of recognition swept across Joseph's face.

'What?'

Joseph peered at the dirt path. 'Nothing, just an unsubstantiated theory.'

James stepped back. 'It's not me.'

With a slight tremor in his hand, James turned the handle. To his dismay, the door was locked. It shook violently as James jiggled the handle. The small clumps of dirt in the path crunched underfoot as Joseph sauntered up behind him. Glancing over his shoulder, James watched Joseph slip his hand into his police-issued stab-proof vest.

'Do you have a tool kit in the car?' James continued to jiggle the doorknob.

Joseph shook his head, pulled out two paperclips, then held them in the air. 'I have something better.'

Within seconds, Joseph straightened the paper clips then nudged James to the side as he inserted them into the lock and shimmied them around. 'Stand back. You're casting a shadow, and I can't see.'

'We need a torch.' James reached inside Joseph's pocket, pulled out the keys, then ambled to the car and opened the boot.

Only three things were in the trunk—a blanket, a first aid kit, and a flashlight. James picked up the flashlight, closed the boot, and strolled back to Joseph, who slipped the lock off the door.

'It's open.' Joseph flashed a couple of rows of perfectly straight white teeth. The most perfect teeth James had ever seen.

———

JAMES TURNED the handle then pushed open the door. With anxiety building, he scanned the room as the torch in his hand flicked. In the middle of the warehouse was the very sight he'd hoped to see: His ginger-haired friend was strapped to a chair. Liam's head and shoulders were slumped forward. From where James was standing, his friend appeared to be napping. But something else caught his eye. James's heart pounded as he fixed the flickering torchlight on Liam. A dark crimson stain covered Liam's abdomen. James was too late.

A droplet of blood dripped from Liam's side and added to

the pool between his feet. James wept. It was not the reunion James had imagined. He'd expected to spend a weekend in the pub, drinking with Liam and whoever else joined them. For months, James had been looking forward to the evening. Even as the events of the last few days had unfolded, he still held on to the possibility that his friends would be back in the pub, just like they had always been. His uncharacteristic optimism had proven futile.

All that was left was regret. James regretted all those invitations he'd knocked back because he was working late, slaving away editing copy for a newspaper that was most likely never read but used to wrap broken glass or fish bones after a day at the beach.

A familiar warm hand rested on James's shoulder. 'We should take a closer look. I realise it seems quite bad, but we still need to check for a pulse,' Joseph said in a hushed tone.

James clenched the torch as he dashed towards Liam, with Joseph following.

James's stomach dropped as he gazed at Liam's paper-white skin, which had a hint of grey. Joseph politely smiled at James as he placed two shaking fingers against Liam's neck.

'He's cold.' Joseph stepped back and frowned.

James pressed his fingers against Liam's cold neck then glanced at Joseph. 'He has a pulse.' James grasped Liam by the shoulders and gently shook him. 'Liam, wake up.'

James grabbed the chair and shook it. Liam briefly opened his eyes then closed them.

'Whatever you do, don't untie him.' Joseph grabbed the radio on his vest and called for backup.

FIFTY-EIGHT

TO JOSEPH'S SURPRISE, James didn't insist on travelling in the ambulance with Liam to the John Radcliffe Hospital. Instead, James followed him to the car then sat in silence as Joseph drove to St Aldates Police Station. Thirty minutes later, James sat in the vacant chair next to the PC's desk and listened to the forensic ballistics report, which didn't disappoint. According to the assistant at the crime laboratory, three sets of fingerprints were on the gun. As Joseph hung up the phone, James leaned forward.

There was no shaking the man. Despite his shortcomings, James was proving useful.

Joseph nodded. 'There were three fingerprints on the weapon you found earlier. One belongs to Leonard Swift. The other two belong to Amber Cooper and Owen Swift.'

James nodded. 'You have his prints on file?'

Joseph sighed. 'I shouldn't be discussing this with you, but yes. Because he has a firearm licence, we have his prints, and then there are his priors.'

'Priors?'

'We aren't a knitting club, Mr Lalonde,' Joseph snapped.

James nodded. 'So, he got in a few fights and was taken into the police station.'

'Owen told you?' Joseph sounded sceptical.

James shrugged. 'Just a lucky guess.'

Like a fool, he had fallen right into James's trap.

Leaning back in the chair, James crossed his arms and gazed at Ellie, who was standing at the photocopier, staring at the reflection in the metal plate of the commemorative plaque hanging on the wall. Joseph followed James's gaze. When Ellie shifted her eyes to the copier, his heart raced. He was jumping to conclusions. Joseph peered at his screen. With a few clicks of the mouse, he brought up the time sheet that listed the comings and goings of every police officer in the station.

'She's your informant,' James said in a hushed tone. 'I remember her from both crime scenes. And she's obviously watching us, or me.'

Closing his eyes, Joseph took a deep breath. James was right. But there was no way he would agree with James out loud. *Stick to the facts.*

'Not that you'll listen, but I can't spitball theories with you. I have to stick to the facts.' Joseph glared at James.

James smirked. 'Well, if you want to stick to the facts, I know where Owen will be at half past ten tomorrow morning.'

Grinding his teeth, Joseph leaned back in his chair as he pretended to consider James's words. Glancing at James, Joseph observed his confident demeanour. Maybe he knew something, but what would that cost him? There was only one way to find out.

Resting his elbow on the arm of his chair, Joseph leaned to the side. 'I'm assuming this information will not come free?'

James's cold blue-green eyes stared back at Joseph. There was something calculating about his gaze. Not that Joseph knew the man well, but it was the first time he had witnessed such a drastic change in behaviour. It was eerie. But pulling Owen into the station for questioning was more important than a sudden personality change. Until then, James had displayed a great deal of restraint. Joseph hoped he would maintain control. Maybe he should keep following James, just in case.

'Someone in this station is framing me for a series of crimes I did not commit or is helping someone achieve this. I want to know who and why.' James's eyes flicked over to Ellie.

Joseph took a deep breath. 'Place and time?'

'Half past eleven tomorrow morning at Rose Hill Cemetery. It's where the funeral for Manesh is being held.'

'How do you know he'll be there?'

James hung his head. 'I went to All Saints with this guy. Trust me when I say he will be there. I know Owen. Manesh got on his nerves, but on some level, Owen enjoyed the arguments. He loves causing trouble. He'll be there.'

'I know he's staying at the Wizard and Ragged Staff Bed and Breakfast.'

James nodded. 'Yes, that's true, but if you wait for a little while, he'll think he's got away with his part in this mess. And you'll lure him into a false sense of security. Then, when you approach him after the burial, he'll be caught by surprise. Owen won't be prepared, so he'll make mistakes. The worst thing you can do is give him time to prepare.'

'Okay, you raise an interesting point.' Joseph rested his chin on his fist. 'How do I know you won't help him escape questioning?'

James leaned forward. 'I've read the texts between Owen and Amber. First, he gave her the idea to steal the manuscript back. Then he supplied her with the weapons. When she was approached by Alexander, she was already open to the idea. He didn't have to convince her. I will not help Owen get away with this. I want to see justice served.'

Joseph nodded, then reality set in. Letting a layman watch an interview through the two-way glass was unprofessional.

What would the super think? He surveyed the room. They were short-staffed. Maybe he could have James around for security.

'Fine.'

THE PETITE ELLIE sat across from Joseph in the interrogation room as he pressed the start button and began with the usual interview formalities. Sweat trickled down her brow as she stared at her hands. He sighed.

'I have done nothing wrong, I swear.' Ellie's voice broke.

Joseph politely smiled. 'I know you're a new recruit and have broken no rules on purpose. But I guess you had the best intentions and took your job seriously. You wanted to ensure the bad guys got what was coming to them.'

Ellie nodded and sniffled.

Joseph leaned forward. 'The best thing you can do is tell me who your sources are, how you came into contact with them, and if you said anything about the investigation. If you tell the truth, I'll be able to help you.'

Ellie nodded. 'It was close to three in the morning, and I was at the station alone working on a few things after the crime scene at All Saints when Detective Alice O'Donnell's phone rang. A young female voice was at the end of the line. At first, I didn't realise it was Amber. She said that she turned up at the crime scene to witness James turning off the generator, murdering Manesh, removing his eye to access the lab, and then leaving with the manuscript. It seemed plausible. After all, he had time to return to the crime scene and stab himself. Towards the end of the call, I realised it was Amber. Then she told me she was too scared to say something to Detective Alice O'Donnell. She wanted to remain anonymous. I kept calling Amber to talk her into going on the record. But she refused.'

'And you believed her?'

'Yes, it seemed to fit. When I left at six in the morning, as the morning staff came in, an older gentleman was outside near the bus stop. The gentleman said he was an investor at All Saints and funded the research on the *Commentary on Daniel*. He, too, was worried about the crimes that had taken place. Then, he let it slip that a journalist, James Lalonde, had enquired about the manuscript. At the end of the conversation, he gave me his business card and wanted to be kept up to date with the investigation.'

'Please tell me his name wasn't Lloyd Waterhouse?'

Ellie screwed up her face. 'Don't you mean Miles Waterhouse?'

Joseph narrowed his eyes. 'Alexander Harper Thompson's personal assistant.'

'Yes!' Ellie cried. 'He kept waiting for me outside the police station, wanting to talk to me, taking me to expensive dinners. That's why I believed his story about being an investor. I didn't tell him anything other than Alice had suspicions about James. That's what he wanted to hear. I promise I said nothing confidential.'

Joseph sighed. 'Ellie, the fact that James was a suspect was technically confidential. Alice believed he was working for Alexander.'

Joseph hit the pause button on the recording then left the room.

———

AFTER CLOSING the door behind him, Joseph strolled across the waiting room then peered into the two-way mirror as Ellie slumped over the metal table and sobbed. *I wonder if Lloyd and Miles are related or if it's just a coincidence. Maybe they could both be living under aliases.*

'Ellie seems pretty gullible,' James said, breaking Joseph's concentration.

'I have to tell my boss about this, and Ellie will probably get suspended, or maybe he'll make her do more training. She didn't do this on purpose. Ellie wasn't good at spotting the manipulation. Ideally, she should have been given more supervision. But we're short-staffed. And we had to fast-track her crime scene training.' Joseph sighed.

'While you were in the room, a police constable announced that Alice was in the critical care unit at the John Radcliffe and is now stable.' James nodded. 'That's good news.'

'No news about Liam?'

James shook his head. It was too late to visit Liam. The hospital wouldn't allow it. He needed to know if his friend would be all right. Maybe he could stop by tomorrow morning before Manesh's memorial service.

FIFTY-NINE

THE BRIGHT LIGHTS of the city of Gloucester twinkled overhead as Alexander stared out of the small window of his private jet as it flew from the Oxford international airport to New York. Even though things hadn't gone as planned, he had secured another one-of-a-kind item for his growing collection.

Alexander sighed as he recalled the unfortunate loss of funds spent excavating the Tintagel Castle ruins only to lose his grasp on the legendary sword, Excalibur. But he had to wait. Eventually, it would return to him. After all, Maximilian Nicholls had the perfect incentive—his mother, comatose in a private wing at his medical facility in Massachusetts. And Alexander's other contact had royally screwed up.

By nature, he was a pessimist. It was the key to his success —plan for the worst and trust no one. In fact, he didn't allow himself to trust Miles, not even for a second. He studied his friend and longtime personal assistant, who was reading the latest edition of the *Daily Voice*. The forty-eight-point banner headline read 'Renowned Scientist Sabotaged New Drug.'

Alexander rolled his eyes. That was another disaster that waited for him the second he stepped onto the tarmac. Another mess to clean up.

The newspaper crinkled. Miles's green eyes gazed over the top of the page. He closed the paper, folded it in half, then cast it onto the polished wooden table.

'Penny for your thoughts, sir?'

Alexander glanced at him. 'Nothing, just weighing up my wins and losses.'

Miles narrowed his small green eyes. 'Still annoyed about Excalibur. It's not over yet. Besides, you now have the *Commentary on Daniel* to add to your collection. Who knows where that will lead you?'

A buzz from under the newspaper broke the silence of the cabin. Miles pulled out his smartphone then pursed his lips as he peered at the screen.

'I know that look.' Alexander rested his elbow on the arm of his chair and propped his chin up.

Miles frowned. 'You've had worse news.'

Alexander sighed. Miles loved to play games. It was his greatest flaw. Everyone had one, and it was the bane of Alexander's existence, a punishment from the gods for all his misdeeds.

'I've just been informed that you've been added to an MI6 watch list. So for now, you cannot enter the country. Even under the radar like we've been doing for the last few years.' Miles placed his smartphone, screen down, on top of the *Daily Voice*. 'Welcome to the club.'

Alexander straightened. 'Surely, we can take one more trip.'

'It's a shame because I've got word of an early-fifteenth-century illuminated edition of *Divina Commedia* with a commentary in Latin, believed to be created in the workshop of the Mezzaratta in Bologna.' Miles gazed over Alexander's shoulder. 'But there is one person who might retrieve it for you.'

Alexander waved his hand. 'Maximilian is a wild card. And Alistair is in jail.'

Miles gave Alexander a knowing look. 'Not Mr Nicholls, my contact.'

SIXTY

SATURDAY: 9:55 A.M.

STROLLING UP THE CORRIDOR, James grimaced as his polished black dress shoes squeaked against the grey linoleum. His heart raced as he approached the ward where Liam was staying. Nervous about the state in which he might find his friend, James took several deep breaths. While he put off seeing his friend, James listened to an anxious voice in the ward.

'You're making a huge mistake.'

The grinding of metal rings along a track brought the conversation to an abrupt end. He needed to stop eavesdropping. With guilt growing within him, James continued his trek to the partially open door of the ward. As he stepped into the doorframe, James ran into a short middle-aged woman with a bob.

A look of frustration swept across her face. 'And who are you here to see?'

James swallowed a hard lump in his throat. 'Liam Kennedy.'

The stare in her hazel eyes intensified. 'Good. You can start by talking some sense into that ignoramus.'

Stifling a laugh, James stepped to the side and let her pass.

As he regained his composure, James ran his hand down the front of his dark-grey suit jacket and fastened the button. James surveyed the empty ward. There were three empty beds and a closed blue curtain to his left.

James tilted his head as he listened to the ruffling of fabric from behind the curtain. 'Liam?'

A familiar mop of ginger hair popped out from behind the fabric. Large bags had formed under Liam's eyes, and his skin was more pale than usual, but it had lost that greyish hue from the last time James had seen him. As Liam drew the thick blue curtain along the rail, relief washed over James. To his surprise, Liam wore a black shirt, trousers, a tie, and black shoes.

Merde. Now the ignoramus comment made sense.

James sighed.

'Save it.' Liam groaned. 'I'm not listening.'

James rolled his eyes. 'Wouldn't dream of it.'

Liam gestured to the window at the end of the four-bay ward. 'I'm coming back. I just want to check out and attend Manesh's funeral.' Liam crossed his arms.

'Sorry.' James hung his head. 'I was concerned. That's all.'

'I'm sorry too,' Liam grumbled. 'I should've told you it was Amber who killed Manesh and stole the manuscript. But you were getting quite close to her, and I was worried that I would put you at risk if I said something. I should've gone to the police station but had to go past the Rad Cam to see Kate.' Liam lowered his head.

'You did what you thought was right at the moment. That's all anyone can expect of you.' James strolled across the room and hugged his friend.

Liam stepped back and pushed James away. 'It's not that. I'm so ashamed of what I did.'

James nodded.

'I considered hiring a hit man to kill a colleague because he was having a slice of my girlfriend. I was so angry. Who does that?' Liam asked through a sea of tears. 'I feel so guilty. No woman is worth that much drama. Why didn't I just end things earlier?'

James sighed. 'Letting go is hard. When you've been in a relationship for so long, it becomes familiar, even comfortable. Comfort is addictive.'

Liam rested his arm on the drawers next to his hospital bed then tapped the top as he stared at his feet. 'Am I going to be arrested?'

James shrugged. 'Honestly, if Detective O'Donnell was going to arrest you, then she would have done it after your interview.'

Liam glanced at James with reddened eyes. 'Do you think I'm an idiot for wanting to go to Manesh's funeral?'

James ambled to the bed and sat. 'There's nothing wrong with wanting to say goodbye. He was a friend, after all.'

'How's your stab wound?'

James grimaced. 'It's healing, and the pain is intense. But I've got used to it. It's not my first knife-related injury.'

Liam's green eyes widened.

'Long story,' James said as he stared off into the distance.

———

SOMEWHERE ON THE other side of the John Radcliffe Hospital, in a private room, Alice lay in a bed with crisp white sheets and a light-blue crocheted blanket. Next to her, Joseph sat in a light-blue chair. Pulling down her oxygen mask, Alice smiled at him. Joseph placed her hand in his and gently squeezed it.

He smiled. 'I have a confession to make.'

Alice smiled back. Joseph had a look in his eye that she'd seen before. The glance said he had prepared something and needed to get it off his chest, but Joseph had remained silent so far. For whatever reason, he had kept the knowledge to himself.

He shrugged. 'You're the only reason I returned to work after they shot me all those months ago.' Joseph rubbed his brow. 'Yesterday, I genuinely thought that I had lost you.'

'I know,' she whispered. 'Things weren't the same without you. I'm glad you came back.'

Joseph stroked her hand. 'It's more than just missing you at work. I love you.'

'Me too.' Alice smiled. 'You're not so bad.'

He caressed Alice's hand.

Closing her eyes, she took a deep breath. *Joseph won't like this.* A couple of seconds later, she opened her eyes. There was no use putting it off. She had to tell him.

'There's a file in my top drawer at the station.' Alice took another deep breath. 'You need to give it to James. He needs to know what he's getting himself into. I must warn him about Miles and what might await him in New York. Now that our investigation is ending and MI6 takes over, I need you to do this before he leaves.'

Joseph hung his head. 'I will. First, I have to arrest Owen and Stanley. I have a long day ahead, but I promise to warn James.' He squeezed her hand once more. 'You get he won't listen, right?'

Alice brought the oxygen mask up to her mouth. 'Yes, he's stubborn.'

Joseph smiled. 'And you're able to recognise that trait in others?'

Alice stifled a laugh as she lay back in her hospital bed and stared at the ceiling.

SIXTY-ONE

SATURDAY: 12:00 P.M.

A THICK LAYER of grey clouds hung overhead as Manesh's elderly parents, Amina and Nathan Warren, walked to the polished wooden casket, holding a spray of white roses. After placing the flowers in the centre of it, Amina stared at the polished wood as tears ran down her face. Nathan wrapped his arm around her then kissed the top of her head. A cool breeze drifted through the Rose Hill Cemetery, causing the tall green trees to sway. The Warrens had done the one thing every parent assumed they would never have to endure.

Gazing across the burial plot, James observed Owen staring at the casket. The man seemed calm like he didn't have a care in the world. How did Owen reconcile his meddling with Manesh's death? Did he feel any sense of remorse? Perhaps he didn't see himself as having any involvement.

As the hours had ticked by since events unfolded in Amber's apartment, James became more sure that if Owen hadn't supplied the weapons, Alexander and Miles would have stepped into that role.

Liam nudged James's side as Owen locked eyes with him. His brown eyes glared at James from the other side of the burial plot.

Leaning to the side, Ben whispered in James's ear, 'Could Owen be any pettier? Once you think he's reached an all-time low, he defies the odds.'

James sighed as the casket was lowered into the burial plot. His stomach twisted as he mulled over the events of the last few days. Justice was not quite served. Despite Manesh's shortcomings, he deserved recompense. The scales were still uneven. Even if Owen and Stanley were arrested, two leading players were most likely in New York by then, far from the reach of the Thames Valley Police. Perhaps that was the real reason James needed to go to New York, to ensure Miles and Alexander would be held accountable. It was time for him to move on. Too much had taken place, too many lies uttered and too many secrets revealed. Things would never be the same for his friends.

As the screeching of the spools on the lowering device halted, a familiar voice gasped. James glanced to the left and spotted Kate, standing on the other side of Ben, wearing a simple black dress with her hand over her mouth. Liam nudged James for a second time.

'I shouldn't have come,' Liam whispered. 'It's too soon for me to see her.'

As he refocused on Manesh's grieving family, Lady Margaret, who stood behind Amina and Nathan, nodded at him. Next to her was Oliver. He was like a duck out of water, in smart casual attire, free of his usual hoodie. That was a meeting that James was not looking forward to.

———

FIFTEEN MINUTES LATER, after the crowds had dispersed and the grieving family were walking through the cemetery and to their cars, James and his four friends stared into the grave. As Owen opened his mouth, the loud crunching of grass underfoot interrupted his train of thought.

He turned around to find Joseph strolling towards him. James bit the inside of his lip as Owen wiped a bead of sweat off his brow.

Ambling around the perimeter of the group of friends, Joseph held a file under his arm. He paused then nodded at James. Curious about what was going to unfold, James walked towards Joseph. As he drew closer, Joseph pulled out the file and handed it to James.

'Here's everything I have on your mother,' Joseph said in a hushed tone. 'Don't get too excited. It's not much, just a few photos.'

James's heart sank as he grabbed the folder. Scared of what might lie inside, he stared at the folder, unsure whether he should open it.

Joseph cleared his throat. 'Inside is a document from Alice. She woke up this morning and insisted that you should have it. Of course, it's completely unorthodox, and we could get in serious trouble for giving it to you. But under the circumstances, it feels like it's the right thing to do.'

'What?'

'It's a printout of Miles Waterhouse's MI6 file with parts redacted. They took all the good stuff out before we saw it. After reading it, you should get a sense of what he can do, even at his grand age.'

The hairs on the back of James's neck stood on end as he peered down at the file.

Without uttering a word, Joseph dashed after Owen, who had begun the trek to his car. In seconds, the short Congolese man had grabbed Owen, wrestled him to the ground, then secured cuffs around his wrists.

Liam patted James on the shoulder. 'What's going on?'

'Three guesses where Amber got the gun she used to shoot Manesh.' James nodded toward Owen.

'I didn't notice Owen creeping away from the burial site.' Ben stared into the distance as Joseph pulled Owen off the ground and walked to the car, clutching Owen's bicep. 'I can't believe it.'

Liam slipped his hands into his pockets and gazed at the ground. 'Turf Tavern?'

Ben nodded. 'Yeah. We should have a drink for Manesh.'

———

FIFTEEN MINUTES LATER, after Liam entered the Turf Tavern, James stood outside the late-thirteenth-century pub. Next to him were Lady Margaret and Oliver. He sighed. Oliver strolled towards the door then turned back and gazed at Lady Margaret.

Oliver nodded. 'I'll go inside.'

James smiled at Lady Margaret. Before he had time to speak, she held up her index finger to silence him.

'This was not the outcome I had hoped for, but you kept me up to date and let me know about the insurance increase, its value, and the drama with the Whittaker family.' She nodded.

James shrugged. 'A friend of mine, who is in the tavern, assisted me in searching the antique dealerships in the area. Unfortunately, we couldn't locate the *Commentary*. I'm pretty sure it's on its way to New York. Getting it back will not be difficult.'

Lady Margaret raised her eyebrows. 'You're going after the manuscript?'

James sighed. 'That and other things. It will take a while. Technically, the manuscript was never supposed to be sold to All Saints.'

'I know,' Lady Margaret said in a hushed tone. 'If it ever makes its way back to me, I'll return it to Matilda. She's Amber's cousin.'

The two stood quietly as James contemplated his next words. A digital quack broke the silence. James pulled his smartphone from the inside pocket of his grey suit jacket. After tapping the screen, James brought up the message. He stifled a laugh.

'What's going on?' Lady Margaret peered over the top of the screen.

James smiled. 'I've received a text from Charles. He's a sketch artist for the Thames Valley Police. The message is super long, but I'll paraphrase it for you. Apparently, after arresting Owen, Joseph brought Stanley in for questioning. Charles hopes they will charge Stanley with selling off part of Doris's estate, but he's not holding his breath. MI6 are taking over the case because of the involvement of a couple of individuals, and they found fingerprints belonging to Amber on Manesh's spectacles.'

Lady Margaret sighed. 'It's a pity she was shot before she could name her associates.'

James nodded.

'I'll leave you to your thoughts. You were too quiet on the way here. I could tell you have something pressing on your mind.' Lady Margaret placed an air kiss on either side of his cheeks then strolled towards the door. '*À bientôt.*' She disappeared into the tavern, closing the door behind her.

After turning around, James stared through the glass windows at his friends inside. He had made up his mind. It was time for a change. Much to the dismay of Professor Xavier Watson, James had decided to take him up on his offer to secure an interview at the *Daily Voice* in New York.

After a couple of clicks, James typed a message to Xavier and pressed Send.

THE PAIN in his right side intensified as James lifted his suitcase into the luggage rack in carriage L. It was the last railcar on the train. Lifting that suitcase was a huge mistake. With a grimace, he sighed at the medium-sized suitcase on its back on the lower level of the luggage rack. The only other occupant in first class had scored prime real estate. *Typical.*

James hobbled down the short, dimly lit aisle to seat number twenty-five and sat. It was his favourite seat, single, with a table by the window. He hated the four-seat dining table arrangement. Nothing was more awkward than avoiding eye contact with a complete stranger for an entire seventy-five-minute journey. First class wasn't extravagant, like on an airline or the Eurostar. It was a simple higher-priced ticket with a larger seat, a table, and a free coffee. Nothing to write home about. Standard was perfectly fine, but that day, he pushed his penny-pinching ways aside and bought the higher-priced ticket. His weary, injured body needed extra space, and so did his legs.

The owner of the medium-sized suitcase smiled at him from seat forty-one, situated towards the end of the carriage. *With arms like those, he couldn't put his bag on a higher level?*

James forced a smile. He glanced out the window as the train pulled out of the station. For once, he was on time and hadn't missed the train. Not that anyone would believe him.

A few minutes later, a woman in a Great Western Railway uniform wheeled the snack cart up the aisle.

'Coffee, tea, juice, snacks?' she asked with a polite smile.

Caffeine after five in the evening—he was turning out to be quite the risk taker. 'A black coffee, please. No sugar.'

'That's an interesting accent. Where are you from?' she asked as she poured the coffee into a takeaway cup.

James watched the woman fasten a plastic lid on the cup as the carriage bobbed along on the tracks, causing the trolley to sway in the narrow aisle. 'Central western France, Poitiers. It's a small university town.'

'Like Oxford?'

'Yes,' James said as a robotic *quack* screamed out from the inside pocket of his grey suit jacket. 'Do you have a copy of the *Daily Voice*? The New York edition. I know it's a bit of a stretch to ask for an international paper, but I thought I'd ask.'

She held up her index finger as she crouched and rummaged through the bottom of the cart. Moments later, she sprang up holding a newspaper and handed it to James.

'I know this is super unprofessional, but this is my last trip for the day,' she said in a hushed tone as she blushed and swept a lock of auburn hair behind her ear. 'And I was wondering if you wanted to go for a drink later once we reach Paddington Station.'

James smiled. 'Okay.' He shrugged, opened his wallet, pulled out a business card, and handed it to her. 'I'm going to New York in a few days, but I'd still like to go out for drinks.'

'I'm Charlotte, by the way.' She clutched his business card and wheeled the cart down the aisle towards the next train car.

James reached into his pocket and pulled out his smartphone. A message had come through from an unknown number. It read:

Curiosity grew within him as he stared at the blunt message. *Coincidence?* It must be. *Or is it a prank from Liam?* He dismissed the thought. Liam wasn't in a joking mood. He was sombre and terrified that he was going to be arrested.

Amid his sea of thoughts, the phone in his hands rang. Someone who didn't want to disclose their number was calling him. Is it the same person? He struck the red button on the screen as he pulled the phone to his ear.

'Hello,' James said cautiously.

'Hyde Park. Nine p.m. Come alone. It's about Lucy J. Knight,' a digitally disguised voice said.

Silence filled James's ear as he opened his mouth. The unidentified caller had just hung up with no further details or clarifications given.

After leaving a question about the articles Lucy J. Knight was trying to peddle to newspaper editors in London on Reddit, someone had gotten hold of his number. Had Oliver given it out? James fired off a message to Oliver, placed the phone on the table in front of him, and gazed at the scenery that zoomed by as the train hurdled towards London.

A massive part of him was considering turning up at the meeting point.

But that would be insane. Right?

ALSO BY A. D. HAY

James Lalonde Amateur Sleuth Mysteries

James Lalonde thought his days of stumbling into murder cases ended with his rookie reporter years. Five years later, as a seasoned editor, he's wrong. From stolen legendary swords to missing manuscripts, James discovers that trouble follows him everywhere, and someone has to solve these crimes.

The Locked Room (Prequel)

It's the opening of Clovervale Hall, an exquisite bed-and-breakfast in England. James Lalonde has an all-expenses-paid trip. But there's one thing he didn't count on—a killer roaming the halls. Soon, James discovers everyone has secrets worth killing for. Can he uncover the truth before the killer strikes again?

The Last Exhibit (Prequel)

When Will Thatcher doesn't show up for work, James Lalonde must attend afternoon tea at the Carmichael Estate. The pleasant gathering ends abruptly when a body is discovered on the front lawn with strange markings on its neck, and a priceless Van Gogh is missing from the wall.

Suspicion (Book 1)

When James Lalonde's girlfriend leaves him, he's forced to cover her story about the local museum's latest acquisition—the legendary sword Excalibur. But when he arrives, Excalibur is missing and there's a dead body at the crime scene. Can James clear his name and find the real killer?

Duplicity (Book 2)

James Lalonde's university reunion takes a deadly turn when a hooded figure murders a professor and steals a priceless mediaeval manuscript, moments after James discovers a secret code within its pages. With his passport confiscated and everyone hiding secrets, can James find the killer before they strike again?

———

Rookie Reporter Series

Five years before James Lalonde discovered that the legendary sword, Excalibur, was stolen from Elizabeth's flat, he was a gofer dreaming of writing his first byline. The Rookie Reporter mystery series follows James's first year as a journalist, starting with his first-ever case.

The Reporter at the Gate (Book 1)

Rookie reporter James Lalonde finally gets his first story - a simple interview with soon-to-be magistrate Albert Harrington. But when he arrives, he finds blood, an empty safe, and no body. With Detective Khan suspecting him of murder, James must clear his name and solve the case before losing his story.

The Woman in the Lake
(Book 2) - Coming Soon

James Lalonde thought being a groomsman at his ex-girlfriend's wedding would be the most awkward part of his weekend. He was wrong. After the bride's body is found floating in the château's lake, he becomes the prime suspect, and awkward becomes deadly. Can James clear his name before the killer strikes again?

GET A FREE COPY OF THE LAST EXHIBIT

A Body is on the Front Lawn. A Priceless Painting is Missing. A Killer is on the Loose.

When Will Thatcher doesn't show up for work, James Lalonde is forced to attend an afternoon tea with Alistair Carmichael in Will's place. The lovely autumn afternoon tea comes to an abrupt end when a body is discovered on the front lawn of the Carmichael Estate with strange markings on its neck.

But something is missing, a priceless painting is off the wall. However, it's no ordinary painting, it's a Van Gogh purchased in an auction a few months prior.

But, trouble has its watchful eye on James.

———

Get a free copy of The Last Exhibit at:
authoradhay.com/read-free/

AUTHOR'S NOTE

Originally, Duplicity was called "Silence" and was supposed to be a novella—a story that's under forty thousand words. When I finished the first draft it was over, fifty thousand. Oops!

There's something about me and word counts—I'm a unique blend of exceeding the target and then going back and adding more content. It's something I've come to accept about myself but chuckle at as I share this with you. To be honest, this story was the second James Lalonde novel I wrote. The first is yet to be published; the third was Suspicion. I wrote out of order without realising it.

Years after I wrote the first draft of Duplicity, I decided to eliminate a significant storyline—a romance between James and DI Alice O'Donnell. The storyline seemed unprofessional and out of character for Alice, so I changed it, created distance between Alice and James, and then made his investigation independent of the police. Along with a plethora of other writing decisions, I added an extra thirty thousand words to the original fifty-thousand-word first draft.

About Story Idea

Way back during National Novel Writing Month in November of 2015, this novel started as an idea about an unknown person gouging out the eye of a professor to gain access to a secret lab in a college at Oxford University. After that, the idea for the rest of the story came to me quite quickly. It wasn't until halfway through the first draft that I realised the stolen artefact should be a mediaeval manuscript. During revisions, I decided that the manuscript would be a one-of-a-kind edition of a Commentary on Daniel by St Jerome. While the commentary is real, the special edition with the dragons in the initiums is not.

During the long revision phase, I read an article about bad password and online security habits, and I was shocked at the number of bad habits I had adopted over the years. And I consider myself a relatively tech-savvy individual. So, naturally, this made its way into Duplicity.

About the Prologue

In the spirit of research, I turned to The Name of Rose, a mini-series created in 2019, directed by Giacomo Battiato, to describe the scriptorium in the prologue. While we're on the topic of the prologue, Glastonbury Abbey was, in fact, burned down. And the contents of its magnificent library, along with the tombs of many saints, were lost forever. As a result, some of the characters in the scene are based on people alive at the time, especially Abbott Peter de Marcy. In contrast, Brother Piers of Damerham and Brother Guiscard are inspired by real people but fictionalised for the scene.

After the death of Abbot Robert on the 29th of April 1184, King Henry II transferred the custody of Glastonbury Abbey to Peter de Marcy, a Cluniac monk and brother to the Bishop of Albenga, who had great influence in Rome. Sixteen days later, on the 15th of May, 1184, the abbey was burned to the ground. All the monastic buildings, except the bell tower, were reduced to ashes.[1] Unfortunately, as I did my research, there was not a lot of detail about how any monks survived the great fire, which is incredibly sad.

Also, you would've noticed that in the prologue, the commentary's author is referred to as Jerome of Stridon. But after chapter one, he is referred to as St Jerome. This is because Jerome of Stridon was canonised by Pope Clement XIII in 1767, years after his death in 419 AD. Because the prologue scene is set in 1184 AD, minutes before the great fire, I'm assuming the author would've been referred to as "Jerome of Stridon," just like everyone else at the time.

Riddles and Codes

Moments before the lab break-in, as seen in chapter five, James and Liam discover riddles and codes in the margins of the Commentary on Daniel. If you've reached this point in the novel, you would've noticed that I don't reveal these codes or resolve them as a plot thread. However, these riddles and codes will feature in an upcoming book within the James Lalonde Amateur Sleuth Mystery series. It will either be in book five or six, but most likely in book five. A few things need to happen to James before he uncovers the secret behind the riddles.

All Saints College

For those of you who are anglophiles or live in the area, you would've noticed that All Saints is not a real college within the university city of Oxford. All Saints is inspired by All Souls College and Trinity College. In fact, the grounds and gardens of the school are heavily inspired by Trinity College. After a visit to Trinity College, Oxford, I decided to use its grounds as inspiration. You can see a few photos from my trip on my Instagram account or my blog.

———

Got a burning question about James Lalonde? If so, then check out my FAQ page on my blog.

———————————

1. Source: The British Library, https://www.british-history.ac.uk/vch/som/vol2/pp82-99#anchorn65

THANK YOU!

Behind every author is a mother who enthusiastically reads every word they ever write and believes wholeheartedly that their books are page-turners—my mother is no exception. Thank you for letting me torture you with my early drafts, finding all the mistakes, and enjoying my books.

And to my husband, thank you for encouraging me to write and put my stories out there for people to enjoy.

A huge thank you goes to my alpha reader, Eric, whom I stumbled across on Fiverr of all places, for your knowledge of guns and witty comments on my revised draft. I'm unsure if you meant to make me laugh, but you did. And you helped me to create a more realistic story. Your input was invaluable.

Naturally, a story is nothing without an editor—thank you to Angela for helping me craft every line in this story. I couldn't have done it without your guidance. And thanks to my proofreader Kim for finding all of those last-minute errors.

Lastly, I would like to thank the numerous individuals who will remain nameless, who sneakily took photos and videos of the interior of the stunning Radcliffe Camera Library. For those who are not aware, it's not open to the public. There are scene descriptions in this novel that exist because of your tenacious appetite for rule-breaking. In the spirit of fairness, I once took photos of a certain interior room featuring famous jewels in an English royal fortress in the heart of London. Accidentally, of course!

ABOUT THE AUTHOR

A. D. Hay is a passionate bibliophile and can usually be found reading a book, and that book will most likely be a murder mystery. She is the author of the *James Lalonde Amateur Sleuth Mystery* and the *Rookie Reporter Amateur Sleuth Mystery* series.

When not absorbed in a gripping page-turner or writing her James Lalonde series, she is a board game addict, loves to travel around Europe, drink tea and rosé, and eat pizza. She is obsessed with journalism, art history and is a closet religious thriller fan.

Born in Brisbane, Australia, she has spent more than a decade in London, where she lives with her husband.

———

You can sign up for a free mystery, The Last Exhibit, behind-the-scenes updates, and bookish research at:
authoradhay.com/read-free/

amazon.com/author/adhay

bsky.app/profile/writeradhay.bsky.social

bookbub.com/authors/a-d-hay

facebook.com/AuthorADHay

goodreads.com/authoradhay

instagram.com/writeradhay

threads.com/@writeradhay

tiktok.com/@authoradhay

x.com/WriterADHay

youtube.com/@AuthorADHay

www.ingramcontent.com/pod-product-compliance
Lightning Source LLC
Chambersburg PA
CBHW050744190726
48285CB00005B/1516